Tent *of* Blue

RACHAEL PRESTON

Tent
of Blue

GOOSE LANE

Edited by Laurel Boone.
Cover illustration after photography by Helen Burke.
Cover and interior design by Julie Scriver.
Printed in Canada by Transcontinental Printing.
10 9 8 7 6 5 4 3 2 1

National Library of Canada Cataloguing in Publication Data

Preston, Rachael, 1962-
   Tent of blue / Rachael Preston.

ISBN 0-86492-342-2

I. Title.

PS8581.R449T46 2002   C813'.6   C2002-903029-3
PR9199.4.P74T46 2002

Published with the financial support of the Canada Council for the Arts, the Government of Canada through the Book Publishing Industry Development Program, and the New Brunswick Culture and Sports Secretariat.

Goose Lane Editions
469 King Street
Fredericton, New Brunswick
CANADA E3B 1E5
www.gooselane.com

To the memory of my grandfather, Ernest Naylor,
who loved to read, and of his favourite author,
J.B. Priestley, who loved the music halls.
But most of all to Ian, for believing.

I never saw a man who looked
With such a wistful eye
Upon that little tent of blue
Which prisoners call the sky,
And at every drifting cloud that went
With sails of silver by.

— Oscar Wilde, *The Ballad of Reading Gaol*

Part One

I

Vancouver: May 1952

The piano arrives twenty minutes before the first students. Anton stands to one side while the delivery men, thick gloves on their hands, heavy boots on their feet, carry the second-hand upright through the apartment door. When they set it down on its casters, it wobbles like a drunkard, hammers crash against the strings in discord. Anton stiffens, a lump in his throat. He glares at the piano, then at his mother, but she won't meet his eyes. The men ignore him. He's too old to be cute, too young to be in charge, he doesn't look strong enough to help them. Anton is accustomed to dissolving before people's eyes. The men mean nothing. What concerns him is where his mother found the money for a piano.

"In through here." Yvonne smiles, extending her arm towards an open door. The red-haired man walks backwards, pulling his freight, trusting the taller, thinner man to guide him. Across the living room and into the first bedroom off the hall. The piano brings with it the smell of another world, stale smoke and beer. Or perhaps it is coming from the men. Harold often smelled this way.

Anton follows, then stops by the doorway. The men startle at their reflection in the mirror that runs the length of the far wall, the practice barre that bisects it and them. They grin. The taller one mugs and prances, pointing shod feet, mitt-shaped hands. The men's boots sound menacing in the empty room, grit grinding into the perfect floor, its smooth, wide oak boards polished to a fine dull sheen. No splinters here to tear silky ballet slippers, turn slender ankles, break delicate feet.

With neat, quick steps Yvonne leads the piano men to the corner by the window. A long, thin patch of morning sun marks the floor. It will grow larger as the sun climbs in the sky. Yvonne beckons and the men turn the instrument to face the room. Satisfied, she bends to pick the record player up from the floor. After only three weeks of lessons her records sound tortured: scratched and nicked where she has repeatedly lifted the arm and set the needle back down, hoping to catch the beginning of a movement, a steady tempo, adagio or largo, occasionally allegro, though her students are young and lack the dexterity and experience for shimmery bourrées, the rapid beats of entrechat. Now the records skip and repeat, run along the lateral ruts the diamond has carved, jolted by impatience or sometimes a stray foot, an off-balance rond de jambe.

The red-haired man stoops to assist, takes the record player from Yvonne's small hands. Perhaps he has noticed her massaging the fingers of her right with the fingers of her left. Nerves, she always tells Anton. She smiles at the man. She is wearing pale pink lipstick. A string of pearls adorns the bodice of her pale pink dress. Anton has never seen this dress before. The skirt, cinched neatly across her tiny waist, falls in a fashionable flare over her slim hips and ends just below her knees. Her stockings have thin, straight seams that run down the back of her shapely calves. Or up, depending on how you look at them. Anton watches the taller, thinner delivery man's eyes running up along those seams, he's no doubt wondering exactly how and where they end. His eyes seem like razors, ripping through his mother's clothes, tearing a hole in Anton's thin chest. The backs of his knees feel watery, insubstantial. How could he ever protect her if she needed protecting?

The record player is tucked away in the room's small closet, the men leave, and Anton heads back to his room.

Disappointment rankles. She'll see it in his face and there'll be a scene. She'll plead poverty, show him her slim, pretty feet and, her anger held in check but cracking the edges of her voice, complain about her ankles and point out how she stands, day and night, working to support him. Anton's bicycle recedes further from his grasp. He is trapped utterly, condemned by his gammy foot and his mother's stubborn purse strings. Last month she began setting the seal on his fate, selling Harold's Packard, claiming it was useless to her because she didn't have her driving licence. Anton could scarcely bring himself to speak to her that day. Had it slipped her mind that he was turning sixteen this summer? That he could learn to drive it? Or did she not trust his misshapen foot on the pedals? Asking for bus fare is tantamount to treason. The mirror, the barre, moving expenses. If Anton wants to visit English Bay or Stanley Park, he must walk there. But suddenly there is money for a piano. And a rehearsal pianist. Someone has to play the thing.

His mother catches him by the elbow before he can close his door, her grip firm, and leads him to the lesson room. Anton is at first too surprised to resist. He has avoided this room, the largest bedroom in their apartment, since they moved here three weeks ago. Ballet leaves a pool of acid in his stomach. He screws up his nose as they step through the door. Dust and sweat edge out the smell of wax. Every dance room smells the same. Anton sneaks a glance at himself in the mirror: a thin boy-man with wild eyes, silver-blue, and thin, sunken cheeks, hair coal-black like his mother's. He is, he notes with alarm, now a head taller than she is, despite his stiff posture, his rounded shoulders. He moves woodenly across the floor, even more uncomfortable with his reflection than he is with his body. *Poor old Anton Crouch.* He looks away, then spots the long cane pointer leaning against the wall in the corner. *Point two three, flex two three.* The urge to flee is strong. His mother's hand on his arm burns.

She leads him to the stool in front of the piano. Up close the piano is a sad-looking specimen. The faux-inlay roses are scratched and faded, chips and splinters mar the scrollwork across the upper panel. A large stain the colour of dried blood spills down the fall board. The white keys are yellow and crazed, the black ones dull and pitted. The piano must have belonged to a liquor-swilling horse, Anton thinks. Or a large dog.

"Sit," she commands.

Anton lowers himself onto the stool. The sun warms his back. Surely she doesn't expect him to play?

She leans over his shoulder to strike the keys. Her pearls tickle his neck, and Anton catches the sweet scent of Lily of the Valley, so sweet it momentarily fogs his mind. He closes his eyes, pulls the flowers deep into his lungs. "All you have to do is follow this." His mother grasps the forefinger of his right hand, pushes it down on one key and then another, up and down. "La la dee dee, rum pom pom."

The piano sounds more pitiful than it looks. Even to Anton's untrained ear the notes sound flat, lack resonance. She repeats the sequence, then moves his hand further down the keyboard and begins a similar set of notes again. Anton winces. One of the keys in the middle is completely dead.

"La," his mother sings, striking the mute key. Anton's nail, pressed beneath his mother's finger, turns white. "La. Just sing la." She smiles, rubs his head. "It couldn't be easier. And when you finish two sets like so, just go back to the beginning."

Anton stares at her in horror. When did she dream up this torture? He runs his gaze up and down the keys. There are dozens of them. He places his hands over their cool surface, splays his fingers. Which one did she start with?

His mother points and taps a white key to the right of the silent one. "This one," she says, reading his mind. It looks no different from the rest, no obvious blemishes or scars. He runs his finger over the ivory, feeling for chips or ridges. Nothing. She presses her thumbnail into the fall board directly above and wiggles it, gouging the surface. A tiny pale crescent moon now points to the beginning. Anton strikes this first note. It starts out strong but fades quickly, muffled by age or embarrassment or both. His fingers hover above other keys, unsure where to go next. His mother's students will be here any minute now. He strikes the first note again. A bead of sweat trickles down his temple. Already the sun has crept up his back to the tender flesh on the nape of his neck. He wipes his brow. What next?

His mother turns and opens the window, and instantly he wishes it closed again. Air still crisp rushes into the room, trailing lilac and apple blossom and children's laughter, the distant bop of a wooden bat as it hits a ball, the tinkle of bicycle bells, the hum of a Saturday morning in spring. A large ache grows in Anton's chest. His mother leaves the room, her heels click-clicking across the floor in quick, staccato steps. Saturday is her busiest teaching day. Anton is trapped inside until dinnertime.

The doorbell rings, and the first of the students arrive. Shapeless, tittering twins. Karen and Sharon. The girls' hair, pulled tightly off their faces, makes their eyes seem too large for their heads; they look like baby birds. Anton hunches down, hidden by the piano, but watches their reflection as they shuffle in front of the mirror, pull their leotards out of the cracks of their flat, skinny bottoms, fuss with the elastic on their soft ballet slippers. They glance frequently in the direction of the piano, elbow each other. Giggle.

"Stretching and warm-up, ladies. Starting on the floor. Legs first, tummies, back and arms."

The girls drop, bellies to the floor, then slide their knees up and out, toes together. Their legs must be made of rubber. Like snakes, they raise their torsos and rest on their elbows. They stare at Anton in the mirror and smile. Twin frogs, he thinks. Bug-eyed, ready to catch flies. He should have brought a net.

His mother is walking towards him. She has pens and paper with her, scissors, tape.

"You can use the barre to stretch those hamstrings, ladies," she calls to the twins as she approaches the piano. Her hands work quickly as she cuts a sheet of paper into tiny oblongs and then tapes them to various keys — some of the black, but mostly the white. Anton can only sit mutely, his face growing hot with humiliation as his mother hums and counts notes aloud, pausing to scribble numbers and dots. Number one below the crescent moon. Two keys up is number two, a near-by black key number three. La, she writes on the dead key, a little cross beneath it. A kiss?

"The dots indicate how many times you hit the note. All right?" Her voice is much too loud. She must realize this. Anton needs no mirror to know his face is now scarlet. Even his eyes feel hot.

"Standing at the barre, ladies. Second position." The twins straighten and assume their stances with a serious grace of which Anton would never, five minutes earlier, have thought them capable: left hands on the barre, chins held high, legs apart, feet turned out. His mother nods at him to begin, then taps the floor with her stick. Pliés.

"Arms up and out. Ready. Down, two, three. Up, two, three. Find your centre of balance, ladies. And down, two, three. Up, two, three. Bend, two, three. Straighten, two, three."

Anton struggles to keep up, his fingers tripping over each

other. Only his mother's counting keeps him in time. Already his wrist is throbbing. "Da," he says every time he hits the dead key, his mouth dry, his lips sticking together. He cannot believe how many times this note is needed. Out of the corner of his eye he monitors the twins in the mirror. With every "Da" their arms drop a shade lower. Eventually they turn their heads in unison to stare at him.

"Down, two, three. Up, two, three. Come on, ladies." Anton's mother tries to coax the twins back to attention, but the distraction is too much. They bend their knees again, then one nudges the other from behind. Instantly both sisters' bodies buckle with laughter.

"Da," says Karen. Or Sharon. He can't tell them apart. The other sister loses control, squats on the floor.

"Da," she splutters. And the two of them stagger and reel with laughter, tears in their lashes.

Anton feels himself floating away. He floats up to the ceiling and looks down on the boy seated at the piano with his hands in his lap. He is no longer a part of the scene unfolding below him. He grows large, godlike, unfurling across the ceiling, a dark, roiling cloud. Up here he is big and powerful, so big and powerful he could, if he wished, zoom down on top of his mother and squish her like an insect.

II

West Yorkshire: November, 1935

The air in the room felt damp and cold. Her mother must have been out all afternoon. Yvonne was still sweating from dance practice — three sweet stolen hours today — and could easily catch a chill. She knelt by the red brick hearth to light the fire, balled up some sheets of old newspaper, stacked a few pieces of wood on top. Took one off again. Should she use the coal? Her mother might balk at the waste. It's Saturday night, Yvonne would say. I was heating the curling iron for your hair. Give the crowd a jolly send-off.

A sharp rap at the door. Had someone been waiting for her? She opened it to a pair of glittery eyes crested with thick, shaggy eyebrows. Face creased like a linen rag. It was one of the comedians, someone she couldn't recollect her mother having billed with before. A sour, foul-tempered man whom she'd done her best so far to avoid. A neckerchief was tucked around the top of his shirt, thick makeup caked his skin, but only the right side of his features had so far been painted.

"Kindly collect your mother," he spat, and turned on his heel. Yvonne watched him retreat down the hall, suspenders swinging across the backs of his legs. He stopped at the bathroom at the end of the hall and pushed open the door. Yvonne felt cold and hot at the same time. Several of the other performers had poked their heads into the corridor at the sound of the comedian's voice. He stepped to one side.

Yvonne's mother lay in the bathtub, head lolled back, mouth agape. She looked dead.

Silent in her tattered ballet slippers, Yvonne tiptoed down the hall towards the bathroom. Though she could see the others glancing back and forth between the comedian and herself, she kept her eyes front and her back ramrod straight, her chin tilted ever so slightly upwards. It was how she imagined prima ballerinas held themselves in times of great duress. As she drew closer to her mother's body, a trickle of sick down the side of the bathtub confirmed what the flip-flopping in her stomach had already told her.

She stood rooted at the door to the bathroom. Gin fumes. Gin and bile. The stench made her eyes water. There was no hiding her mother's addiction anymore. Not that Frances Hoyfield had bothered hiding her boozing for a long time. Nor had she tried to sanitize it, tone it down with a glass, a slice of lime, a splash of tonic or orange. She drank the bitter, flowery liquid neat from the bottle. But always after the curtains, never before. This much was new. Yvonne bit down hard on the insides of her cheeks. The pain drove away her own desire to vomit, pushed her tears behind her eyes. Everyone was watching. And some of the people on this Leeds bill had known her since she was an infant, her mother even longer. It was important that she appear strong and capable. She took a deep breath to ready herself. She had less than two hours to clean up her mother and get her dressed and backstage at the City Varieties Pavilion, ready to go on as the carefree, salt-of-the-earth, reasonably sober Nell Rose.

Gently, Yvonne cleared her throat. Her mother stirred, her pendulous breasts lifted and bobbed in the water. Yvonne fought back an urge to throw a towel over her mother's private parts, her dark tangle of hair, submerged, distorted.

The comedian was still standing behind her. She turned and saw the disdain on his half-face. Something Brooks. Her dislike for him hardened into hate. She stepped inside the bathroom and closed the door. Her mother snorted, went back to whatever horrors seeped through the layers of gin to make her eyes and face twitch.

Yvonne rolled up her sleeves. Sometimes her mother could be out for hours, sometimes Yvonne could disturb her simply by blinking or swallowing. Frances had had a skinful this time. In the snug all afternoon. Pulling her mother from the bath and dragging her down the hallway was out of the question. Yvonne had to wake her up without provoking her foul temper, always fouler after she'd passed out. Yvonne leaned over the bath, plunged her hand into the water, now barely lukewarm, and pulled out the plug. She sniffed the air, aware of another smell besides the gin and bile. Yvonne's face began to burn, her throat swell closed. She looked around the bathroom for the source. A pile of red in the corner. Her mother's stage costume? Please God, no. Yvonne picked it up by the shoulder. The smell made her gag. She turned it around. The flounce, the frilled pink underskirts, brushed her legs. There it was: a large wet patch across the back, and in the middle, the darker stain of excrement.

Yvonne steadied herself against the lip of the bath. How easy it would have been if she alone had found Frances, how easy to push her mother under, hold her head down. She swallowed, her anger a hard lump moving from the base of her throat to settle behind her breastbone. Now she was trembling. This would be her fault. Reason didn't even enter the equation. The water was leaving the bath in rapid gurgles, her mother would soon wake up. Had she been planning to go on stage in that dress tonight? Had she been trying to clean herself up? The red dress was a crowd favourite. People who lined up outside the music hall to listen to Nell Rose belt out "There's a Stile by the Meadow" and "Down Honeysuckle Lane" and other, raunchier tunes and kick up her legs on stage expected to see this long red dress with its pink Edwardian flounces, its black trim — after all, that's what Nell's billboard pictures showed her wearing. People, her mother brayed, came to the music halls because of nostalgia. As far as Yvonne could make out, people came for a cheap drunk and a lark, or to jeer and catcall. After all, where was the fun in yelling at the silver screen? But music halls had been on the decline for more than twenty years, and the venues were all as worn and grubby as the turns themselves. Even revue, which aped the music halls with a nod and a wink, a sharp jab in the ribs, was tired and, to the younger generation at least, vaguely embarrassing. People now flocked to the cinemas to see Mary Pickford and Douglas Fairbanks light up the screen. Only watery-eyed old men with ageing floozies on their arms bothered with the music halls anymore.

Mentally Yvonne ran through the gowns in her mother's wardrobe. The green and the lilac dresses both needed seam repairs under the arms. Despite her liquid diet, Nell Rose was bursting out of her costumes. There were several on the rack she'd never squeeze into again. Yvonne should have been sewing this afternoon but had put it off. She had wanted to dance, not sit in a poorly lit room plying needle and thread, her body craving the giddy sensation of flight, the exhilaration of movement and creation, the pounding of blood in her young veins. The yellow dress, Yvonne remembered, was clean but needed ironing.

Should she wake her mother or rush back to the room and start ironing? How long would the Brooks fellow wait? And how many others would be needing the bathroom before showtime? If she finished quickly enough, her mother might not even remember the red dress, the shit stains. The gurgling grew louder, the bath was almost two-thirds empty. Quickly Yvonne pushed the plug back in, scooped up the red dress before anyone else discovered it and ran back to the room.

Throwing the dress in a corner — she'd deal with it later — Yvonne set the iron to heat up and stoked the fire. She stacked a couple of pieces of coal on top and placed the curling irons over the flames. Sitting down on the edge of her cot, Yvonne pulled off her dance slippers, ran her hands over her feet, thick with calluses. Her toes were becoming hammered, box-like. This was good. They were growing stronger every day, as was her dancing. Her turnout was almost perfect as far as she could tell, though she'd only pictures in a book and Kitty's word to go by. Yvonne was grateful for the older woman's guidance, her encouragement, the way she corrected her posture, the angle of her arms, the turnout of her legs. And Kitty wasn't afraid to stand up to Nell. But Yvonne yearned for something more expressive, more heartfelt. As soon as Kitty was gone, she was all loose limbs and angles, shaking her head and twisting her arms, more Isadora than Pavlova, dancing that sprang from something primeval inside, her head and heart together. Depending on her mother's moods, Yvonne would sometimes put off her practice, wait until the performers were on the stage or in their dressing rooms. Then she would go back to the little rehearsal room and stand at the barre Kitty's husband set up for her wherever they found themselves, and dance by the spill from the street light outside. She wouldn't dare turn on the lights in case any of the stage hands found her. She couldn't abide their teasing. And if they were pretty sure her mother wasn't suddenly going to appear from nowhere and box their ears or crack their backsides, their jokes were smuttier, more menacing, and left her feeling dirty and ashamed. Daring ones now reached out to slap her bottom or pinch it.

Yvonne stretched her legs, then set up the ironing board, filled a cup with water, soaked and wrung out a linen rag and, the iron now ready, began pressing all the layers of the yellow dress. She prayed that no one else would want the bathroom before she finished and that her mother, now lying in a few inches of rapidly cooling water, wouldn't wake up.

But God wasn't listening, or he was off on other, more urgent business. Yvonne heard the banging first. Then her name.

"Yvi!"

Two short, sharp syllables. Her mother was hammering on the bathroom door.

"Yvi!"

She'd left her mother with nothing to wear. How could she have been so short-sighted, so stupid? Feeling weak and colourless, she grabbed her mother's dressing gown and rushed to the bathroom. Frances snatched the garment from her but had trouble negotiating the sleeves. Yvonne fumbled to help, tied the sash. The iron. Had she forgotten the iron?

The smell of scorched fabric filled the room. The iron was sitting dead centre on the front skirts. Yvonne picked it up and started to cry. She glanced towards the crumpled dress in the corner, a blur of red. Was there time to wash out the stains? The door swung open and there stood her mother, swaying on her feet, a murderous look in her eye.

"You useless little trollop," she said, then lurched towards her. Yvonne threw down the iron and tried to dodge out of the way, but Frances lunged for her daughter's head. Wrapping her soft, shiny-skinned drunkard's hand around Yvonne's hair, she pulled her towards the fire.

"I'll dry those eyes of yours in one stroke. You hear me? Burn them out of your head." She held her in place, head bent at an awkward angle. With the towel she grabbed the curling tongs from the fire and waved them in Yvonne's face.

A strangled sob escaped Yvonne's throat, a wild animal loosed and running for cover. The curling iron came down towards her face. Yvonne threw herself backwards, felt the hair rip from her scalp and heat sear through her chest. As her mother let her go she crashed to the floor, banging her head on the edge of the hearth. Everything went dark.

III

Vancouver: May 1952

There's a shadowy face in the bay window. Anton startles, checks his descent from the top step of the porch, almost topples. The empty pop bottles in the string bag he's carrying clatter against his leg. Anton holds his breath, looks back at the front door, expecting to see his mother appear, eyebrows raised, hands on hips. He could be halfway to the store by now. He turns back to the face in the window. It's Clarice Hart's window. Her living room window, if Anton isn't mistaken, or her bedroom window, depending upon the layout of her apartment. He's never seen the inside of Clarice Hart's apartment, nor does he want to. Clarice Hart is utterly mad. She howls at the moon, she bristles at the sun. Night or day, sudden, vicious, blue-throated rages thunder through her apartment walls; growls send tremors through the floorboards. Anton has not lived here nearly long enough to be able to shrug these episodes off. At night he buries his head in his pillow; in the day he turns the radio up high — Harold's radio, the only object of Harold's he can bear to have around him — or sings loudly. His mother stops whatever it is she's doing, her jaw stiffens, her back hunches.

But who does the face belong to? Clarice Hart went out almost an hour ago. Anton heard her; the air inside the house, a once-grand Shaughnessy mansion carved into apartments, two downstairs, three up, expanded as she left, tension dissolved, it was easier to breathe. A visitor, then?

Anton waits for a sign of life, a clue as to the face's identity. The string bag is heavy. Carefully he shuffles it from his right hand to his left, trying to stop the bottles from chinking against each other. The handles have cut an angry groove across his palm. In all this time the face hasn't moved. A small, sad face, Anton thinks, an impression he takes from the way the head seems sunk into the shoulders, and still, like the faces of people who are very sad, people who can hold themselves for hours, days even, without moving, as though movement might shatter the mask they have prepared and presented to the world.

Anton takes the steps slowly, one at a time. He wants to keep an eye on the face in the window to be sure it doesn't move while he isn't looking. But Anton must watch where he places his feet. The wooden steps are worn and sagging, in need of repair. A lot about this house is in need of repair, but the rent, Anton's mother has told him a hundred times already, is affordable, the rooms large enough for her to start her own little enterprise. Anton had been surprised to learn his mother ever had time for dreams. It seemed to him she expended all her energy dodging Harold's fists. Even after Harold was gone she appeared worn out and flat, her edges as raw as her bitten cuticles. It seems overnight she has grown stronger, prettier.

The dark circles have disappeared from under her eyes, the line of her mouth has softened.

Anton steps onto the flagstone path that runs to the garden gate at the front and snakes around the landlady's side of the house, then turns and looks back at the window. He smiles. The face doesn't move, but the waves of sadness emanating from under the propped-open sash seem stronger, palpable. He raises his hand in salute. Nothing. The face remains as impassive as ever. Anton has seen this before, felt it even: people who look yet see nothing before them, faces that stare, not outwards at a view or people passing by, but inwards, watching their past on a loop in their minds, living, not in this time, but in some other, possibly kinder time. The longer Anton stands and stares at the face, the more the waves seem to build into a kind of wall. The wall holds him back. From where he stands Anton is unable to determine whether the shadowy features are male or female, young or old.

He takes a deep breath and expels it in a short, high laugh. Perhaps if he looks as though he is having fun the owner of the face will come out and join him. They could chat for a while, and then they could walk to Stanley Park, though he knows it's a long walk from here, too long, really, and feed the ducks in the pond, stroll around the seawall, watch the ocean and the boats bobbing about on its waves. Anton also knows, technically speaking, that the sea that laps up against the shores of the park, the salty spray that in rougher weather catches pedestrians on the seawall unawares, doesn't quite belong to the ocean here, but rather to Burrard Inlet. And, of course, Anton must first take the bottles to the store and buy his mother ten Black Cats with the deposit money. He wishes he had the courage to come home with ten black cats, real ones. He smiles, imagining forty furry black paws step-stepping behind him in a feline formation.

A squirrel chatters from the plane tree in the yard. Anton tips his face to say hello. The sky, an intense shade of blue, appears to stretch into forever. Anton stares heavenward till his eyes water. A hawk hovers high above him, hungry, watching. Anton imagines himself as the hawk, flying far and away above the city, then diving earthward towards his prey, the rush of cool blue air past his ears. Or better still, a pilot in a Spitfire, snug in the cockpit, the sleek plane an extension of his body. His eyes narrow, his skin tightens. Enemy aircraft on his wing, he banks left, thumb poised at the ready over the firing button. Three short bursts from the four Browning 303s on each wing take out the port engine on the Heinkel 111 in front of him. A couple more bursts cripple the plane to his right. He banks again, making a sharp inside turn to shake the ME 109s on his tail, then executes a half roll and a dive to stop his engine flooding from the G-force.

Anton turns back to the face, pulse jumping, skin twitching. Nothing. The face remains stubbornly put, stiller even than the air around it. Now he's irritated. He begins to wonder whether the face belongs to a person at all or whether it isn't some mannequin Clarice Hart has dressed and placed in the window to scare the birds or the tenants. Or — he chews his lip, a space opening in his chest — perhaps the face has taken note of his limp, his clumsy shoe, and is now playing possum so it doesn't have to befriend a boy who cannot walk properly, doesn't have to pretend to be nice to a cripple.

Down the garden path he walks. Four and a half minutes to the store, four and a half minutes back. Can he complete the circuit without passing someone from the school? Without passing anyone at all? He has yet to make it all the way. Some pretty child stops in her tracks, points. Her blue eyes widen, then twinkle in the beginning of a laugh or a cry. Some lout calls to him across the road, "Hey, Hopalong." Or worse.

Cripple. Misfit. Reject. The names run round in his head, jarring his brain, making his eyes hurt. These are the names kids whisper loudly in the corridors at school, names teachers write in notes home to his mother, names on letters and forms that get secreted away in the filing cabinet in the office, in the filing cabinet in hospital, names brandished like weapons in that other dark place, the place where people screamed through the night. Anton squeezes his eyes shut and turns his head aside before opening them again. It's another trick he's learned. This way the picture is never fully formed in his mind. He doesn't have to hear again the anguished howling or smell the stench that came from the walls and the floor, from the creatures there with him, and he can almost pretend that it didn't happen, that such memories aren't part of his life.

If he had a bicycle, the trip would take a mere minute and a half each way. Of course, first Anton would have to learn how to ride a bicycle. It can't be so difficult. It has to be easier than getting his mother to fork over the money for one. But a bicycle, he knows, would solve all his problems. On a bicycle he would look no different than any other teenager. Gone would be the horrific limp, the lurch in his hips, and the pain in his heel cords that he tells no one about, least of all his mother. But having a bicycle, he also knows, is next to impossible. His mother stands on her feet, day and night, till her ankles swell, and still she can barely make ends meet. A bicycle is beyond their means. Anton wishes he could take a part-time job like other boys so he could save the money to buy a bicycle. But who would hire him?

He leaves the safety of the garden and makes his way down Cedar Crescent, past the wedding-cake houses with sagging porches and additions that spoil their symmetry, make them look as if they have kicked out sideways in anger. Anton walks on the left side of the street, hugging the wall. It's a habit he's acquired walking to school. School is now only three blocks away, but he leaves early, hellishly early, and stays late, hiding behind books in the library; he doesn't emerge until the sports teams are safely on the playing fields or in the gym and the stick lads that hang around outside have gone home.

There's a small throng congregated at the corner of Granville and Sixteenth, jostling each other, hands in the pockets of their dungarees, white throats showing in the open necks of their shirts. He would like to approach these stick lads, lean against the railings next to them, pull out his lucky piece of shrapnel. Piece of a buzz bomb. I found this lodged in the front door of the house when I came home from the fish and chip shop, he would tell them, his voice cool and detached, his eyes beneath his heavy fringe of hair taking in their astonishment. Pass us it here. Let's have a look, then. In the middle of your front door, eh? Smack bang in the middle. Should've seen the house next door, though. Door blown off, windows out, roof gone. They'd whistle then at his lucky escape, shake their heads in awe at this survivor from the home front. He'd shrug. You got used to it. Sometimes thirty, forty, even more flying bombs would pass overhead in a day. Got so we didn't hardly bother looking up — here he'd raise a careless eyebrow. Though that wasn't exactly true. After the Ashcrofts' house was demolished, Anton had listened harder than ever for the bomb's telltale roar, like an out-of-tune motorbike heard from several streets away. Abigail Ashcroft had been killed in a blast that hit his street. Anton had liked Abigail. She had called for him to walk to the temporary school every morning and never once asked about his limp.

One of the boys makes loud kissing noises as Anton approaches. He has a thick neck, wears a leather jacket, is probably the leader. Stick lads, Anton thinks, his gut clenched, though none of them actually wield sticks. Stick lads is what Harold called all boys who hung around buildings and street corners with nothing to do. He said they started off as lads who ran sticks across railings and fences, lopped off the heads of flowers, took potshots at cats and small dogs. They grew into thugs and thieves. Anton believes Harold was a stick lad once.

Anton throws his shoulders back, walks as straight and true as he can past them, their curled lips and cold, cruel eyes. The bottles rattle. Anton thinks he recognizes the boys' faces, steels himself for their taunts. *Sticks and stones may break my bones*, he chants in his head. *But names will never . . .* A foot slides out suddenly from the pack. Anton hears their laughter as he hits the sidewalk with a thud, pain in his knees, burning in his wrists, his scraped palms. The bottles, briefly airborne, land and pulverize one another with a sickening crash.

Snip. Snip. Pruning shears. Mr. Cunningham must be outside, sleeves rolled up, his shabby grey pants hanging from faded brown braces, feet in rubber boots. Wellingtons, his mother calls them, though Anton has seen pictures of the duke in school history books, and he was wearing nothing of the sort on his feet.

Mr. Cunningham is bent over a rose bush, snipping off the dead flowers. Hearing Anton open the garden gate, he straightens and turns.

"Afternoon, son." He lifts his battered hat from his head and replaces it. His gardening hat makes him look peculiar and old. Anton likes much better the dark grey trilby Mr. Cunningham wears to work. Mr. Cunningham, he thinks, would look good in a uniform. Someday, when they've known each other a little longer, Anton will ask him about the war. Infantryman or pilot, tank battalion or navy. Anton can almost see the double vee of stripes on Mr. Cunningham's right arm. A corporal at the very least. He stares at the shrivelled petals in Mr. Cunningham's hand.

"How's your garden today?" he asks him. It isn't, strictly speaking, Mr. Cunningham's garden, it's the landlady's garden, mad Clarice Hart's, but they both know what he means.

"Fine, son. Just fine." He smiles. Mr. Cunningham smiles a lot when he's in the garden. Anton respects the flowers, they look nice and everything, but he doesn't understand a man's taking such an interest in them. Mr. Cunningham runs his eyes quickly over Anton's ashen face, his dusty pants, his bloody hands. "I have some blooms here you can take in for your mother." He stoops over a patch of top-heavy lupines. Snip. Snip.

"Thank you." Anton steps towards him, takes the flowers, some purple, some pink, that Mr. Cunningham holds out. Anton glances at his front window, then back at the flowers. His mother is waiting for cigarettes, her eyes dark with impatience. Anton smiles gratefully. Flowers are a poor substitute, but they may soften his mother's ire, distract her briefly. They came from Mr. Cunningham.

"Give her my regards."

"Sure. Thanks."

Heels click-clicking down the pathway. Anton turns around. His heart leaves his chest to drum painfully at the back of his throat. The girl of his dreams is walking towards him. The edges of his vision blur. All he sees is blond hair twisted into a French roll, a heart-shaped face, red lips, creamy skin, eyes that belong on a movie poster. She must be an actress. His eyes travel downward. A white and red cravat at her neck, a navy blue suit that hugs her fine figure, navy blue high-heeled shoes that flatter her ankles. She's carrying a tidy matching navy blue suitcase. Anton and Mr. Cunningham step aside to let her pass. As she walks past she gives Anton the fullest, most beautiful smile he has ever known: red lips pulled wide, revealing perfectly shaped small white teeth. Her eyes grow smoky. Anton feels his face flush, sweat break out in the hollows beneath his eyes; he is light-headed with love. For surely this is what love is, this tizzying fall from a great height, this rush of blood down his legs and through his toes. The dreamgirl sweeps by and climbs the rickety steps, leaving a trail of achingly sweet scent, sweeter than even his mother's perfume. Anton watches her until she disappears inside. Mr. Cunningham is smiling at him.

"That's young Miss Daniels," he says. Mr. Cunningham is not so old he cannot remember the intensity of a teenage boy's ardour. "Jasmine Daniels."

Jasmine. A flower, a perfume, a spice.

"She lives upstairs in the apartment across from me."

Which explains the four doorbells. One of the other reasons his mother had been keen to move into this house was the suite of empty rooms over them. Never having been converted, they would never house upstairs tenants. No one to bother us, she'd said. Though it seems to Anton it is his mother's classes that would have been doing the bothering.

"She's away a lot." Mr. Cunningham is being kind. Anton is still too flustered to form the questions to such answers. "Works as a stewardess for some airline."

Jasmine Daniels works as a stewardess. Instantly the pain in Anton's knees and palms vanishes. She travels to places hot and exotic, sunbathes on black sand beaches, drinks bright-coloured mineral waters from coconut shells. Anton imagines the beautiful Jasmine walking up and down the aisles, smiling at people, fluffing their pillows, kissing children goodnight.

Mr. Cunningham clucks his tongue, squeezes Anton's shoulder and turns back to his gardening. Anton stares at the flowers in his hand. Black Cats or no Black Cats, he'd rather give them to Jasmine Daniels, who lives upstairs in the apartment across from Mr. Cunningham. Lucky Mr. Cunningham.

Leaving Mr. Cunningham clucking and shaking his head, Anton heads across the lawn towards the other side of the house, the side where Clarice Hart lives. Anton has not ventured down here before, though as the house sits on a corner lot it's obvious to anyone that there's nothing treacherous about either the garden or the lawn. It's simply the idea of walking beneath Clarice Hart's windows that has never appealed to him. But things have changed.

Anton shades his eyes and stares up at the window he now knows belongs to Jasmine Daniels. A path of ivy winds up the wall. He steps across the flowerbed and tugs at a vine. Is it strong enough to take his weight? He wishes he could climb to her window, it is, he believes, her bedroom window, and thrust Mr. Cunningham's flowers under her nose. You are the girl of my dreams, he would tell her.

He steps backwards, hears the crunch of greenery beneath his feet. He looks down at the trampled stalks, the crushed flower heads. If Clarice Hart catches him . . . Anton freezes. If Clarice Hart thinks Anton is wilfully destroying her garden, she'll lock him in the basement, cut his hands off, boil them up and feed them to the neighbourhood dogs.

A sharp voice behind him. "Your mother's looking for you, young man."

Anton leaps from his skin, drops the flowers. He turns around, finds himself staring at a mottled face, patches of red creeping around the crepey neck. It's mad Clarice Hart, hands on her wide hips. The red patches on her face are still moving, worms beneath her skin, snakes in her blood.

"I wasn't doing anything wrong."

"You were snooping."

Anton glances quickly back up at Jasmine Daniel's window. "I wasn't, honest."

"Oughtn't to be staring in windows not your own, young man."

"I wasn't staring." Her logic baffles him. Adults are always so imprecise. Though his knees are shaking and his voice is cracked, he feels compelled to argue. "How can I be staring in a window fifteen feet above my head?"

"You were staring in my window, young man."

Blood drains through his feet, sucked up by the grass. The face. That was no guest. It was mad Clarice Hart sitting by the window, staring at ghosts. Anton feels hollow inside. The face was no one he could make friends with after all. He stoops to pick up the flowers and, giving mad Clarice Hart a wide berth, heads back to the front door. As he turns the handle, he glances towards the landlady's window one last time, just to be certain. The face is gone.

IV

Leeds and London: November 1935

Yvonne hammered at the side-stage door. Shivering, she stood unprotected in the rain for several minutes before the door opened and a stagehand leaned out.

"You look like a drowned rat."

She stepped inside past the gangly boy, pulled back the hood of her oversized cape, a cast-off of her mother's, and took a few deep breaths. The corridor spun, the floor heaved.

"You all right, miss? You look a bit peaky."

"I just need a minute." She wasn't sure which hurt more, the bruise on her head, the patch of bloodied scalp or the burn on her chest. All three throbbed in time with her heart, still thumping madly from the long half-walk, half-run in the rain. She'd rested only briefly along the way when the nausea had become too much, acid rising in the back of her throat. Having wakened alone in a room once again cold and now dark, Yvonne had panicked and simply taken her cloak and fled. She hadn't even a few coppers for the tram. While she'd walked, the rain lashing her gloveless hands as they held the edges of her cloak together, she'd worried whether her mother was actually at the theatre or was getting sozzled in one of the dozen or so pubs she passed along the way.

"Has Nell Rose gone on yet?" She prayed her wristwatch, a gift from a one-time suitor of her mother's, was running fast.

"Singing as we speak. But making a right cock-up of it, if you ask me."

Yvonne shivered. Who was handling her mother's props? Whatever had she dressed herself in? Yvonne was truly in for it now.

"I didn't," she said, narrowing her eyes and peering down her nose at the boy. He had spots on his chin and a lock of greasy red hair that he repeatedly brushed from his eyes. He looked about fourteen but, Yvonne decided with a sniff, a very young fourteen.

"There's some folk about to start giving the bird out there, they are," the boy said and laughed. "She shouldn't last long at this rate, I wouldn't reckon." He threw the bolts on the top and bottom of the door and leaned closer to Yvonne than she cared for. "If you ask me, I think she's had a swig or two at the old gin bottle."

More booze? Or was this the same drunk she'd been on this afternoon? Yvonne tried to make her voice as imperious as possible. "As I said before, I didn't ask. You must be either a very deaf or a very stupid boy."

A wave of nausea made her dizzy. She leaned back against the door, her stomach turned inside out. She'd had nothing to eat since noon.

"You want some more fresh air? I can open the door back up again if you like."

"No," Yvonne snapped. "Now just leave me alone." She began making her way into the belly of the theatre, wincing as she pulled the bodice of her dress gingerly from the sticky wound on her chest. She felt around it, cooling the hot, tight skin there with her nearly frozen fingers. The burn needed washing and dressing; it could easily turn septic.

Yvonne heard the stomping of feet and the catcalls before she got to the wings. It was a restless, edgy crowd. Saturday night could go either way.

"Damned Northerners," Neil Parsons said.

"Hardest fuckers to please." His brother Gavin, voice bitter. A grumpy face atop a fancy costume. He spat on the floor beside him. Yvonne took a step back.

Kitty's husband Karl walked up behind the brothers, slapped them on their glittery blue backs.

"London on Monday, lads," he said in his blunt Northern accent. "And everything's sweet again." He winked at Yvonne. Karl's parents ran a fish and chip shop in Shipley. Karl was as broad as the Yorkshire moors.

Yvonne tiptoed closer to the stage. Panic edged out the pain from her burn. Her mother was singing a Jenny Hill number,

"The Boy I Love Is Up in the Gallery," and trailing the flounces on her lilac and lavender skirts behind her. Had she sewn the burst seams herself? How could she even thread a needle in her state? For it was clear to Yvonne that the stagehand was right. Her mother had been at the sauce again. She teetered, left to right, as she strolled. Yvonne barely had time to wonder if the crowd could tell when Nell went over on her ankle. "Whoops," she called out, righting herself, then hiccupped loudly. Someone in the crowd whistled. Embarrassed laughter floated up from the front rows. Humiliation wedged itself like a sharp stone between Yvonne's heart and her ribcage. Dizzy and disoriented, she reached out to grab Karl's arm.

"Hey there, lass," he said. "You not feeling well? Go see Kitty, she's about somewhere. She'll fix you up." Gently he tried to push her back. But Yvonne, eyes riveted on her mother, would not be deterred. "Yer mam'll be all right, lass. You'll see."

Side-stepping Karl, she slipped around the Parsons brothers to stand by the curtain. If only her mother would turn and see her standing there, rooting for her, she would pull herself together. But Nell was planted at centre stage. She swatted at an imaginary foe. Sing, Yvonne chanted under her breath. Sing. Please. Just pull yourself together and start singing again. When she was younger she'd seen her mother on countless occasions turn a hostile crowd, lead them into a rollicking singsong with a Marie Lloyd or Vesta Tilley special, or a rousing "Tipperary" or "Ta-ra-ra-boom-de-ay." Now she was stoking their ire. Gin. Mother's ruin, they called it. She took a deep breath to steady herself. *Mother's ruin.* Just as she thought she might pass out, Nell began to hum. Within a couple of bars she'd found her place and resumed singing.

"Got anything new, love?" A heckler from the gallery, ale in his belly and some girl to impress. The stomping grew louder.

"'My Old Man,'" she shouted back, cueing the conductor.

"I said, have you got anything *new?*" It was the same heckler, only the voice had turned nasty. Restlessness spread from the wooden benches in the pit and gallery to the plush seats in the stalls and dress circle, an anxious breeze rustling through the theatre. People coughed, shuffled in their seats.

"This is revue, you stupid Northern bastard," Gavin Parsons hissed. "It isn't meant to be new."

But Nell wasn't to be deterred.

"My old man said follow the van," she sang, and cupped her ear to the audience for the rejoinder.

"And don't dilly dally on the way." The response was lame, dying out until only a handful of people sang the last words. Yvonne wanted to curl up in shame.

"And don't get run over," hollered another, younger voice, again from the gallery. This time the crowd cackled. Yvonne drew back into the shadows behind her eyes and imagined floating onto the stage in a gauzy dress. She twirled and stretched, leaping through the air, the audience so stilled she could hear their surprised intake of breath. Around and around she spun, bringing them to their feet in adoration. They lobbed flowers at her feet, thronged around the backstage door for a glimpse of her before she stepped inside a long black brougham waiting at the curbside. The rustling and murmuring grew louder. Now she wanted only for her mother to leave the stage, to pull together what little dignity she had left and walk off. Why stay out there for more baiting?

Hands fastened around her arm, drew Yvonne gently but firmly back from the spill of stage light, pushed her between the stacks of sets and dusty old props. Kitty. She put her finger to Yvonne's lips. Heavy footsteps drew closer, then a man's voice.

"She won't sing another night in this theatre." It was the

City Varieties manager. "I've got the Odeon to contend with just down the road, the place is chock full of folk near every night." Through an opening in a canvas screen Yvonne watched him mop his glistening head and brow with a huge spotted handkerchief. Nervous giggles bubbled inside her. Kitty glared.

"We're not booked another night in this theatre." Gavin again, his voice flat with disdain.

"If that's your attitude, I'll have none of you back, ever." He tucked his handkerchief into his top pocket, pulled it out again, wiped his face as he walked, footsteps receding quicker than they had approached. Yvonne slipped out from her dusty hiding place.

"Thanks," she mouthed at Kitty, and stepped back up to the wings.

"Show us a bit of leg, love." One of the gallery hecklers again. A wolf-whistle. Nell hiked her dress to her knees, kicked up her legs.

"Show us your daughters," called another voice. Several rows in the back burst into laughter. Yvonne smiled, then clamped her hand over her mouth. Louder whistles, more stomping. Nell ignored them, carried on with her song. Everyone backstage shuffled about nervously.

"Bloody woman," Yvonne heard Gavin hiss. She hung her head. This could be the end. The manager would almost certainly wire her mother's agent in London.

Abruptly, the music changed: undulating scales, a trill, a ker-ker-boom from the timpani — the opening bars of the Parsons' act. The manager was probably down in the orchestra pit, swearing under his breath and threatening to fire everyone. The brothers, a moment ago muttering and whispering behind Yvonne, seemed suddenly to fill with air and brightness as they brushed by her in their sparkling blue costumes.

Nell Rose marched off stage as if she were the wounded

one. "Why I bother giving my all for the likes of a crowd like that I'll never know."

Yvonne caught Kitty's eye and turned away, shamefaced. Nell Rose hadn't given the show her all in years, and knowing that Kitty knew this too, Kitty with her regal good looks, her wide amber eyes, chafed at Yvonne's pride.

"Now, Nell," said Karl. "Can't have them getting to you, girl. Gotta show 'em we're made of stronger stuff than that. A few tatty trouble-causers in tenpenny seats, that's all. They carry on any longer we'll get Marty and his lads to stand in the gallery with 'em."

Yvonne giggled at the image of the five strapping tumblers standing with folded arms at intervals across the gallery. It'd be enough to put a hush through any crowd. Her mother grabbed her arm and yanked at her. The neckline of her dress scraped across the weeping sore on her chest. Yvonne gasped loudly, tears in her eyes.

"I don't know what you think's so funny, my girl. I slave away, night after night, wasting my talents on yobs and hooligans just to put clothes on your back and food in your mouth, and you repay me by standing there laughing."

Yvonne turned her head to avoid her mother's bloodshot eyes, her breath rank with gin fumes. She glanced at Kitty, then at the floor.

"Give the girl a chance, Nell," said Karl. "The audience is not her fault."

The grip on Yvonne's arm tightened. "And I'll thank you to keep your nose out of what has never been your business." Frances was back in charge. Her words never slipped when she was reaming someone out. "You see to your tunes and your wife's fancy footsteps. Leave the raising of my girl to me."

Yvonne followed her mother back to her dressing room. At times her mother separated before her eyes, became two

Frances Hoyfields, then one again. Black motes danced into and out of her vision. Her mother muttered to herself along the length of the corridor. For once Yvonne paid no attention, her smarting wound blocking out everything else. All she had to do was endure the taxicab ride back to their quarters, and then she could lay down her pounding head and sleep.

Nell's London agent, Ned Metcalf, was not amused. He kept them waiting for close to an hour. The door to the street opened and closed with irritating frequency. A steady stream of people came and went, and still Yvonne and her mother sat there. The door hinges needed oiling. Yvonne imagined the skin inside her ears sloughing off in tiny bloody whorls. Her fingers strayed repeatedly to the patch of gauze on her chest. Her mother had dressed the wound with precious ointment she kept for her own unspecified ailments. Though the ointment had no smell Yvonne could recognize, it had taken the smart out of the burn. Tired from the long train ride, Yvonne tried to close her eyes, but every time the door squealed she couldn't resist peeking. Though she loved London for its bustling, humming streets, its ragtag crowds as well as its ladies and gents, its variety and its opulence, the city was vast, and travelling to and from their rooms to anywhere was wearying. A mean-looking dwarf with a pointy red beard waddled in and sat on the chair across from Yvonne, leering at her. When Ned Metcalf called the little man into his office, he stuck his tongue out at Yvonne and wiggled it, then winked.

"You couldn't fuck a gnat if you tried, you pint-sized freak," Frances snarled.

Yvonne tried to disappear into the folds of her cloak. Being made to wait while lesser-known acts and two-bit sidekicks were being shown into the office first was obviously fraying her mother's nerves.

Nell Rose was dropped from the bill. Two weeks pay was all they had to live on.

"I might be able to find you a spot at the Kings, in Hammersmith, or the Embassy, on Eaton Avenue, Frances." Ned Metcalf always called his acts by their real and not their stage names. Yvonne wondered how he kept all the names straight in his head. "But you crossed a line with that little number you pulled up in Leeds. Legless, so I 'eard. You can say good-bye to the Hippodrome or the Coliseum. And the Palladium, Victoria Palace. They all have strict rules. No, no decent theatre'll look at you now, not once word gets out. And, mark my words, Frances, it will." He paused to stub out a Woodbine. The ends of his fore and middle fingers were dark yellow with nicotine.

"I'd be putting my neck right on the line if I was to send you out again and pretend I didn't know nothing about you falling about on your arse on that stage. Blotto." Ned Metcalf had a habit of looking at you with his eyelids almost closed, like a mole, and this made his face difficult to read. He pulled a contract from one of his drawers, pushed it over the desk at her. "It'll be less money, of course." He smiled, briefly revealing a bottom row of crooked, badly stained teeth.

The ticking of the clock on a shelf behind them grew louder. Yvonne stared around the room. Papers spilled from every shelf, lay piled on every surface. An assortment of props appeared to be in use as paperweights, a couple of walking canes, one broken, a black silk hat with a grubby pair of white gloves laid across it, a stuffed pheasant (what would someone do with that?) and — she startled when it first caught her eye — a ventriloquist's doll. Would the owners ever be coming back to claim these items? Or, like her mother, had they suddenly found themselves discarded, no longer funny or beautiful or able to reach the necessary notes? Yvonne fidgeted, waiting for her mother to sign the contract.

"How much less?" she asked eventually.

"Oh" — Ned Metcalf's eyes were closed again — "about two pounds a week."

Her mother scraped her chair back and stood up to leave. She made a performance out of tucking her pay packet into her handbag, drawing on her gloves.

"How about putting the girl on instead?" he called out as she reached the door. Yvonne's heart imploded. She could feel stars pricking all over her scalp and her face. Dancing? Did he mean dancing? She could go on as a dancer? Or a vaudeville singer in the vein of her mother? Frances never flinched. She pulled the door open and strode out without so much as a backward glance.

Yvonne was frantic, torn between loyalty to her mother and her own desperation to go on stage. This was pride at its most ridiculous and dangerous. What would they live on? Her mother could soon drink a hole in that money. Yvonne tucked Ned Metcalf's words away in the back of her mind. He'd seen her on stage with her mother when she was a little girl. Nell had dressed them in identical clothes and had Yvonne sing and dance with her to some of the less bawdy tunes. By the age of eleven, Yvonne, with her long, pretty dark hair, was attracting more attention than her mother. Frances's steady alcohol diet was beginning to show. She had gained weight and looked slack-jawed; her face had begun to sport a web of fine red veins. Nothing that makeup and corsets couldn't hide, but Frances had pulled her daughter from the stage nonetheless.

Yvonne had to literally skip to keep behind her mother. She caught up to her as she reached the corner.

Frances never broke her stride, and her words came pinched

and imperious between her huffs and wheezes. "I was doing this years before you came along, and I'll be doing it years after you're gone." She was red in the face and breathing hard. "I'm the one who brings in the money. I'm the indispensable half of this arrangement. And it might benefit you to remember as much."

Yvonne grasped at her mother's arm. "Mama, I would never . . . not if you didn't want."

The transformation was instant. Nell allowed herself to be halted, caught her breath, then leaned over her daughter in a dramatic gesture and kissed her wetly on both cheeks. There were tears in her eyes. "Of course you wouldn't, my child. You're a good girl, the way I raised you to be. You wouldn't turn your back on your mama, would you?"

"No." Yvonne sobbed into her mother's fur collar. They embraced, then Nell took her daughter's slender hand and threaded it through her arm.

"Well, I've got money burning a hole in me pocketbook. Let's go have a slap-up meal someplace posh, shall we?"

Yvonne kept stealing sideways glances at Kitty. With the fur collar on her coat turned up around her ears and a white fur hat on her head, she looked like a Russian princess. Yvonne had no intention of removing her coat, even though she would feel the cold more when she left, because her stockings were held together with too many large and ugly darns. But she wondered if Kitty was ever going to take the hat off. People behind them would never be able to see, and, as this was a ballet, being able to see the stage was important.

She was restless, trying to keep still and appear adult, yet wanting badly to stare at the people coming in and taking their seats, at the theatre itself. Though she'd rarely been to the front of the houses where her mother played, had never watched a performance from there, Yvonne was acutely aware of how much grander the Sadler's Wells theatre was, how much finer the decor, the carpet, the chandeliers. The deep pile on the plush seats seemed to coddle her. She sighed and leaned back, hoping to steep herself in atmosphere.

"How's your mother, Yvi?"

Yvonne tensed, locked her gaze on the rich blue of the stage curtain. "Not so good." She could feel Kitty turn towards her.

"Drinking a lot?"

"Uh-huh." Yvonne stared now at the rows of people's heads in front, the fur-edged collars, the hats, the tight, tidy curls of permanent waves. She didn't like betraying her mother in this way, gossiping behind her back, revealing sordid details. She turned the question back out to her friend. "How's Karl?"

She felt Kitty's warm hand on her cold one. "Karl's well."

"And the others?"

"Relieved to be back in the big city, you know how the crowd is." Now Kitty was rubbing her hand. "But we're on a different bill this season, we'll be staying on in London the rest of the winter." She paused. "Any more work on the horizon?"

Kitty meant for her mother, and the answer was no, and the next answer was never, but surely even Kitty wouldn't ask. There was Ned Metcalf's offer, but Yvonne wasn't so sure she should mention it, knowing Kitty wouldn't approve, would think she was too young, too unprotected to have her own turn. She was forming the words in her head when the orchestra began its warming strains and saved her. She snatched back her hand. "You should take off your hat," she whispered loudly, then leaned forward in her seat to signal her wish to end the conversation.

As the lights dimmed and the orchestra hushed, Yvonne felt a thrill rush through her. The blue curtains parted, swept silently to the wings, floodlights bathed the stage in pink, and a single oboe began, a brief flurry of violins, and then a clarinet. Another set of curtains parted, the music burst into life, and in an instant the stage was transformed: a painted castle in the background, a village in the fore, and dancers in peasant costume revelling in celebration.

Life on the Sadler's Wells stage was a fairytale. From the tinkle and bluster of spine-thrilling music to the sets, the costumes, the lights and the whisper of dozens of satin-slippered feet across the stage, Yvonne was enthralled. The atmosphere, elegant and refined, lifted her completely out of herself. For a girl who had lived her whole life within earshot of the fierce, almost vindictive laughter of vaudeville and revue crowds, the rapt appreciation of the Sadler's Wells audience was sublime. Here at last was dance untainted by carnival.

When the set changed and the prince's hunting party began their pursuit of the swans, Kitty leaned towards her charge and whispered, "You see the strong pointe work and all those fast turns?"

Yvonne nodded.

"See how she extends her leg so very high, and then balances on pointe for a long time? How high they jump?"

Again Yvonne nodded eagerly, never taking her eyes from the aerial creature on stage.

"This is the classical style, not my favourite."

"Shh," someone hissed behind them.

Kitty leaned closer and kept on talking. "I prefer the romantic style, the balances are more fleeting, the lines of the dancer are softer, and the leg extends down and out instead of up. It doesn't look so stiff and formal." For a moment she placed her hand over Yvonne's and squeezed. "It's more like your precious Isadora Duncan."

In the interval the house lights came up, but Yvonne and Kitty remained in their seats.

"The third act of *Le Lac des Cygnes* is famous for Odile's — the Black Swan's — fouettés. She looks like a human top, thirty-two whipping turns on one leg." Yvonne could hardly believe such a feat was possible. "Sometimes," Kitty said, "the story in this ballet gets a little lost. You remember the sections with the corps de ballet?"

"You mean when everyone is on stage dancing?"

"The whole company, yes. Those scenes are called *divertissements*, something to divert the audience's attention from the main story for a while."

"Why?"

Kitty smiled and shrugged. "Usually because there isn't too much to the story in the first place, so they need to stretch it out."

Amazing. Her friend was so clever. Yvonne soaked up all the new words. *Divertissement*, she whispered over and over, mimicking Kitty's French pronunciation. Fouettés. Pas de deux, adagio, petit battement, she repeated, committing the new words to memory. Entrechat, grand jeté.

At the end of the show Yvonne was surprised to find her face was wet with tears.

"That was magnificent," she said, hugging her friend.

"Care to come backstage with me? One of the dancers is a dear friend of mine. We trained together."

Yvonne was surprised. If Kitty had once been such a good dancer, then why wasn't she on stage too? Why did her friend get to dance with the Vic-Wells Ballet company in this exquisite theatre, while Kitty had to settle for making fun of her talents, her dancing style, in revue and variety?

Kitty burst into laughter. "I can read your mind." Yvonne flushed and looked down at her feet. "Call it a lack of faith if you like. I lacked something, the bravado, the iron will perhaps, the determination to succeed at any cost. Remember, Yvi, all greatness carries a great price." She grasped one of Yvonne's cold hands and kissed it affectionately. "You could warm your hands on your red cheeks. Now come with me." And she led Yvonne down the aisle to the exit sign near the stage.

Kitty was all tears and hugs for her friend. They clucked and fussed over each other, and Yvonne was quickly forgotten. Dancers slipped by her, pulling on long woollen stockings over their legs, layers of cardigans and jumpers over their bodies. Yvonne was so busy trying to stay out of the way that she failed to notice she had caught someone's attention. But then she felt male eyes upon her, she felt exposed, she felt someone peeling back the thinnest layer of her skin, a sensation overwhelming but not entirely uncomfortable. As she looked up into a pair of pale blue eyes, Yvonne held her breath. He was tall and broad, so much taller and broader than the other male dancers that on stage — she remembered him as one of the peasants — he had seemed out of place. But, standing now in the doorway to the changing room corridor, with the naked light bulb shining down on him, his own crude spotlight, he seemed the perfect dancer, the perfect male. He took a step towards her, one beautiful, poised and gracious step.

"My name is Alexander," he said, and parted his lips in a smile. "Alexander Nikolayevich Kavanov. A long Russian name, no?" And he laughed, a deep, warm, throaty sound that Yvonne felt in every hair on her skin. He took her hand and held it to his lips. "I am delighted to make your acquaintance."

Yvonne felt her feet lifting off the floor, the air rushing back through her body. She hoped she would never land.

V

Vancouver: June 1954

Anton squeezes past the rhododendron bush and slips down the east side of the house. Chopin, floating from the open window in the middle, grows louder. His Opus 17. Snarled and scratched, the record skips in a dozen or so places. It's one of his mother's favourite pieces. Difficult music, the type of music Anton has no desire to play properly or well. Just hearing it makes his fingers ache. Of course she rarely asks him to produce anything more sophisticated than "Twinkle, Twinkle, Little Star." Still, if his mother's students could dance to, say, some Frankie Laine numbers, then Anton probably wouldn't be sneaking around the way he is right now, pretending he's still at school on library duty or practising with the debate team or any of the other plausible non-sport-related activities he's suddenly developed an interest in. Because the modern music he has on occasion slipped into the practice room to play comes easily to him. He's merely plink-plonking out the melodies, of course, hasn't the first clue how to execute a chord. But Anton is surprised by how deftly his long fingers — he has, so he's been told over and again, his father's graceful hands — slide up and down the keys, all eighty-eight of them, the forty-eight yellowed ivory ones, the forty stunted black ones; how the notes seem to be already there in his head.

He flattens his body against the wall, moves crab-like beneath the window of his mother's studio. The rhododendrons, in heavy, fragrant bloom, fill his head, make his eyes swim.

"Hold your arms like so, Arabella." Yvonne's voice drifts out with the music. A scratch and a click as she lifts the needle. "Look, look in the mirror. You are a willow tree. You must think like a willow tree. Your hands are like bunches of bananas."

Anton's right heel spasms. The lines are familiar. They are the lines she used with him, back when she believed dancing would cure him, magically reshape his arches, lengthen his Achilles tendons. He wriggles the cramp from his foot, looks down, checks his passage. He must be careful not to wear a path between the flowers. One giant step over the geraniums on the corner and he's home free. He throws down his satchel and spreads himself out on the lawn, palms down, touching the earth, face to the sun, drinking in its warmth. He likes the solitude of the back garden, with its wraparound laurel hedge, its twisted monkey puzzle tree, its yards of soft green grass.

Spring this year is unusually warm and dry, and Anton draws out his school days later and later. Homework and piano can wait. But not too long. He doesn't wish to arouse suspicion, have his mother asking where he's been and what he's been doing. Just long enough so that he can enjoy his daydreaming unfettered, without guilt.

Movement. Anton turns his head, blinks. Nothing. He tips his face back to the sky and his daydreams. Most of his daydreams these days revolve around Jasmine Daniels. Anton sees himself in the corner of a Parisian café, there's a red and white checkered tablecloth, and the glow from a flickering candle casts intriguing shadows upon his face. He is smoking, the cigarette in his right hand, his left playing with a heavy gold lighter. Jasmine sashays in, turning all heads, and stands by his table. Her lips are a bright vermilion, the rest of her face in smoky shadow. Anton is plagued by the lover's curse: no matter how he tries, he cannot conjure up the face of his beloved. The lips are probably Dietrich's or Monroe's. Jasmine sits down — why can't he call up her face? — and they hold hands across the gingham tablecloth. They don't talk; words aren't necessary or desirable. Even in his daydreams, words remain beyond Anton's grasp. There's a treachery to speech. People so rarely mean what they say: It's for your own good, or This will make you feel better, or You'll be home again in no time, as if they have any real concept of time, ignoring the cold, plain fact that time has no sense of fairness, forgetting, or perhaps — lucky for them — unaware that time expands with pain and horror.

The light pattern flickers and blurs again. Another migraine? Anton brings his hands to his eyes before opening them, squinting through his lashes at the sun. Or are the people from that dark place back again, slipping silently in and out of the shadows, hovering on the edge of his vision? He raises himself on his right elbow and stares as a clutch of pellets? stones? sails in an arc through the air and lands silently in the grass. He waits, baffled. Another sprinkling. What on earth? The missiles are coming from Clarice Hart's window. What is the mad bat up to now?

Then he sees them. First one, then three, then five. Eventually there must be seven or eight of them, though it is difficult to keep count because they all race around so much. Squirrels. Fat ones. Thin ones. Black ones. Grey ones. Squirrels with bushy tails, squirrels with scrawny tails. They scamper across the lawn, scuttle up the monkey puzzle tree and back down again. They're picking up whatever it is the old bat's throwing out the window. Peanuts. Some begin scratching at the lawn, burying a hoard for later, others, less prudent, chew the shells to get at the peanuts inside, their paws as dextrous as hands — from this angle he realizes how ludicrously large these are in relation to their rodent bodies, it's as if they're wearing mitts. The old bat can't possibly be feeding them out of kindness. Most likely she's poisoning them or fattening them up for squirrel pie.

One squirrel, a fat grey one with a luxuriantly bushy tail, sits like a begging dog in front of the Hart window, watching for more. It almost catches the next nut in its mouth, strips the husk quickly — mitts or no, their hands work efficiently — munches on the seed and waits again.

"She'll give you the evil eye, fatso," Anton whispers. The squirrel turns its head and chatters at Anton, switching its tail, then turns back to the window.

"Hey you, sitting there." A man's voice. Old and raspy. Though the man sounds far away, Anton snaps obediently to attention, his spine ramrod straight. "You're a cheeky young fellow, aren't you?"

Me? thinks Anton, his heart thumping at the base of his throat.

"Look at you, you young monkey, just sitting there taking it all in. Having a good old gander at everything." So there was someone sitting in the front window the other day. A man. Is he angry with Anton for staring? The man's tone is half-serious. Or is he teasing? Teasing confounds Anton, flusters him. He frowns. I'm only teasing, people say, and they laugh and slap him on the back. I'm only joking. But the joke is so rarely funny, and the words imply he's stupid for not under-standing the nuance. The squirrel picks up another nut and begins nibbling at the husk.

"Come here, little fella."

"Me?" Anton manages to mumble, his tongue thick inside his mouth.

"I won't bite you."

Bite me?

The squirrel looks from Anton to the face Anton cannot see. Anton scrambles to his feet, picks up his satchel and walks slowly towards the window. He plans on hanging back a little. It could be a trap. Clarice Hart behind the drapes, ready to pounce.

"Come on, come on," the voice wheedles. "Where are you going?" Puzzled, Anton hurries the last few steps. The squirrels scamper off at his approach. Anton stoops to pick up a peanut. As he straightens he turns to stare in the direction the voice came from. But the sun is so bright he can see only a rectangle of dark that is the open window and, in the pane above, a crooked reflection of the monkey puzzle tree behind him.

"Sir?" Anton calls towards the dark space.

Silence. The face has lost its tongue.

Anton takes a step closer. "Sir?" A little louder this time. "You called me." The silence from the open window, like a small dark mouth in a wall of pale grey siding, seems cavernous. The sun on the back of his head is burning. Crows caw loudly above him. Anton is growing annoyed again. First a face that stares without acknowledging him, and now a voice that calls out but won't speak.

"Are you there?"

Nothing.

Anton shakes his head. "Is this some kind of a joke, sir?" He flinches at the peevish quality of his voice. He sounds so young, babyish. Suddenly he feels ridiculous. Shame prickles his face, even the roots of his hair tingle. The fat grey squirrel. The man, whoever he is, was obviously talking to the stupid squirrel.

"I'm sorry," Anton begins, moving a couple of steps closer. Any nearer and he'd have to crane his neck too far, the sills of the first-floor windows all sit close to eight feet off the ground. "I didn't mean to scare them away. I just thought . . ."

A long, thin hand reaches out from the darkness, a hand so frail-looking that Anton believes if he shook it he could crush it in his own, feel its bird-like bones snap and crack, see the dried-up flesh crumble to dust. The hand trembles as it grasps the wooden stick that jams the window open, rattles it. Anton is both repulsed and fascinated. He imagines the heavy pane and its wooden sash rushing suddenly downwards and smashing the hand, its long, withered fingers dropping to the grass below, Mr. Cunningham finding them later, jammed in the blades of his lawnmower.

The stick won't budge. The hand appears to grow frantic, jiggling the stick and hitting at it, but all in vain. The window, Anton knows from struggling with a sister frame in his bedroom, is too heavy.

"You don't have to be scared of me," Anton calls into the dark space, surprised by his own boldness. "I won't hurt you." His heart has dropped into his belly where he can feel it pounding behind his navel. The hand stops its struggle. "I . . . I just wondered if" — Anton has started a sentence he has no idea how to finish. He looks around madly, casting for ideas — "if, um, if you wanted me to . . ."

Wanted him to what? His mind is a blank. The hand withdraws. Anton can think of nothing to bring it back. A shadowy face, a faraway voice, a fragile hand. To whom do they belong? A rapid series of sharp cracks and a blind slams down in the window. Anton stands awhile, expecting to see fingers push a crack between the slats, a pair of eyes peek through it. But the blind remains obstinately still. Eventually he shrugs, swings his satchel to the other shoulder.

"I couldn't see you anyway," he mumbles, retracing his steps around his mother's side of the house. He has no desire to lie back down on the grass again, to be watched by some dried-up old man hiding behind blinds.

VI

London: November 1935

Yvonne was early. She walked briskly around the outside of
Covent Garden, cobbled streets jammed with lorries, carts
harnessed to blinkered horses, feedbags hooked around their
ears. Because her fingers were beginning to burn from the
damp cold, she told herself that if he wasn't there by the time
she arrived back at the church, she would wait inside the
market. But on her last turn around the piazza, there he was,
pacing under the portico. She stood still, her skin buzzing,
every pore, every hair alert. He moved as if he owned the
space around him, as if he were still on stage, everyone watching, spellbound. *Look over there*, she wanted to cry out to the
people hurrying about their tasks, the pasty-skinned, the pot-
bellied, the scrawny-limbed. His shoulders were so broad and
square that with each stride the folds of his overcoat floated
out around him so he seemed to glide in slow motion. The
buzzing spread to her head. She slipped her hands inside her
cape and held herself tightly, freezing fingers sending goose-
pimples across her skin, hardening her nipples.

"Out of the way, girl," a voice cried, and Yvonne stepped
quickly to one side as the cart and horse and driver that were
almost upon her passed. Hoping he hadn't witnessed her
foolishness, she held back, catching her breath, watching from
behind a stack of crated Brussels sprouts. He turned on his
heel, strode to the farthest eave and turned again. Now he
took papers and a pouch of tobacco from his pocket, rolled

a cigarette and lit it. Though her legs were still trembling, Yvonne hurried over.

"Alexander Nikolayevich Kavanov." She'd been practising for days. He turned at the sound of her voice, and she saw relief wash over his features, softening them.

"How charming these Russian names sound on your lips."

Yvonne bowed her head, unable for the moment to say anything else.

He smiled. "My friends usually call me Alexei."

"Alexei," she repeated. In the flat grey light of this late November afternoon Alexei's eyes, uncommonly pale and flecked with white, appeared at odds with his smile and the warmth in his voice.

"I was beginning to think I was waiting at the wrong St. Paul's."

"Oh. Am I late?" She should have stayed put instead of wandering about.

"No. I am perhaps too eager to see you." He was so serious, so solemn in his forwardness that Yvonne could only stare at the cobbles, the arc of ash hanging from the end of his cigarette.

"It is the poorer cousin, no?" She looked up and he gestured toward the doorway under the porch.

What did he mean? "The entrance is around the other side. This door is bigger, but it isn't real." She giggled, then clapped her hand over her mouth.

"A sham?"

"Yes. A sham."

"I think that this church is nothing like the cathedral. It is not so interesting to look at."

Yvonne glanced around at the columns and the ceiling of the deep porch as if seeing them for the first time. "No." She'd planned on showing him around, had rehearsed the whole scene in her head a dozen times. *It is the actors' church*, she would have said, *they call it the handsomest barn in England,* and waited for him to nod before continuing. *Many famous people of the stage are buried here.* At this point she would take his hand and lead him to the church's humbler west-end doors and point out the plaques on the wall. *See. Vesta Tilley and Vesta Victoria, and look* — here she would glance back at him, tuck a tendril of hair behind her ear — *the beautiful Marie Lloyd. My mother billed with her once, many years ago. And here is Albert Chevalier.* But remembering the richness of the blue velvet curtains in the Sadler's Wells theatre and the braying laughter of her mother's audiences, Yvonne flushed with shame. It would be like hawking the Victoria and Albert to someone lined up outside the British Museum. She slipped her hands inside her cape again, tips of ice through the cotton of her dress.

"You are shivering. You would like to go inside?"

She shook her head. "You're right. As churches go, it is boring." She glanced across at the market entrance.

"Fruit and vegetables are more to your liking?" And though his eyes remained cool, this time Yvonne was able to return his smile. At the market entrance he held the door for her, and she took his arm, feeling wiry sinew and muscle through the fabric of his sleeve. Men's bodies were so much more powerful than women's. Closing her eyes for a moment, she imagined them on stage together, he lifting her effortlessly high into the air, she dancing in space, the belle of the hushed crowd at their feet.

The market was busy, and as they threaded their way between people and the stalls, dodging barrow-boys and pushcarts piled high with empty boxes, the stone floor treacherous in places with wilted and bruised produce, Yvonne grew bolder. Now she dared to lay her other hand atop his arm and draw herself closer, breathe in the tobacco and clove scent of him. And it felt like the easiest thing in the world not to speak but simply to stroll the aisles and gaze at ribbons of colour, mound after pyramid of carrots and turnips and cabbages, sprouts and onions, to allow the competing calls of the hawkers and the clang and rumble of handcarts to filter through her, and at every turn to take in the press of smells: the smoke-and-wet-leaves aroma of roasted chestnuts, the citrus tang of oranges, the earthy perfume of apples.

Yvonne could have wandered away the entire afternoon on the arm of her handsome suitor, circling the glass-roofed gardens of Michaelmas daisies, chrysanthemums and aspidistras, but after a while she felt a shift in his gait, a restlessness beginning to unsettle him. He stopped in front of a tea shop.

"Would you like to take some tea with me?"

Yvonne hesitated. If she walked back to the rooms, she could spend her tram fare.

"My treat."

And so they stepped inside and ordered tea for two and sticky buns.

Facing Alexei across the table Yvonne grew shy again, thinking of how closely she had held herself to him as they'd walked, the imprint of his shoulder and arm, the press of his thigh still on her skin.

Alexei unfolded himself in the chair. "So, Yvonne Hoyfield, you like to watch ballet."

"Yes. I like to watch." But I want more than anything to dance as you do, to have what you have, she wanted to tell him. But held back. Yvonne had watched her mother and too many beaux, sharks and operators over the years not to have learned something about the needs of men. And men needed, above all else, room to talk about themselves. Besides, she figured there had to be five or six years between them, and she didn't want him getting around to the awkward question of her age.

"How long have you been dancing?"

Alexei leaned back, one long leg stretched out at a careless angle. Yvonne noticed how the waitress and customers stepped sideways to accommodate him rather than ask him to move. "Many years," he said. "Ever since I was a child. I entered the Choreographic Technikum, the ballet school in Leningrad, when I was only nine years old. And I trained under the great Vaganova. She brought about many reforms for the Soviet ballet. And I was a favoured pupil." His story had a flat, re-hearsed sound that she recognized from listening to turns long since bored with their lines and their lives. It was almost as if he no longer believed what he was saying.

"But you dance because you love it, the sensation of dance, right? The way it makes you want to fly out of yourself." She could feel her eyes glistening as she spoke, the excited catch in her voice.

He smiled. "Of course. I have danced for the Ballets Russe both in Paris and in Monte Carlo."

"To dance in Paris and Monte Carlo," Yvonne whispered.

"Yes. So always I am learning and changing styles and look-ing to be a better dancer, so that one day I may be a principal in some company."

"Oh, I'm sure you will." Yvonne's hands fluttered over her sticky bun. She was hungry, but she had so much to say, so many feelings churning inside her that she had no room for food.

When he smiled this time it was with his whole body, ten-sion unknotting from his face, shoulders, arms and down through his legs. "You say kind things. You make me feel so . . . how can I say it in English . . . ?

Yvonne swallowed, aware that people were staring over at

them. How could they not? Alexei had draped himself with such artful carelessness that the energy he was sending around the room was palpable. He felt wide open and dangerous, and Yvonne's heart began to trip a little faster.

"Invincible."

"But you will, I know you will. I can see your name in lights."

"What? All of it? It will take up too much room, no?"

She laughed as though he'd said the funniest thing she'd heard in her whole life. "You know what I mean."

"Perhaps. Perhaps not. Perhaps I am too Russian."

"Oh?" Yvonne sneaked a glance down the length of his torso, his long lean legs. What could possibly be wrong? Was he too tall? But Alexei had seen her looking and could not quite hide a different kind of smile. Yvonne pulled at her sticky bun until she felt her face cool down.

"It must be so wonderfully exciting to dance on a stage in front of all those people." A proper stage, with an orchestra, not a band, and a sober audience who clapped in the right places and didn't sing along or catcall.

"Yes, but the director is not fond of the Russian dancing style. I think that she will make sure I am only ever a character dancer."

"Could you go somewhere else? Another company perhaps?"

"Perhaps." Smoothly he leaned forward in his chair. Yvonne felt the air shrink between them. She wanted to stroke his arm where it lay on the table. "With someone like you by my side, perhaps I could do almost anything."

Yvonne pinched herself.

He waved a hand. "But not in this country. Ballet is in its infancy here. Alicia Markova and Anton Dolin, two principal dancers with the Vic-Wells, formed their own company this autumn. But I was not invited to join them."

"Maybe when they get bigger they'll ask you?" She moved her hand to the other side of her plate so that her fingers now rested against the edge of his sleeve. He covered her hand with his, thumb rubbing up and down her forefinger.

"They asked more than forty dancers from around London. For now I will have to content myself with the temperament of Ninette de Valois." He looked directly into her eyes, holding her with his gaze. Yvonne now saw how the flecks of white almost formed a circle around his pupils. He had the eyes of a wolf. "So, Yvonne — may I call you Yvi?"

She nodded.

"You live with your mother?"

She nodded again.

"And I in a dormitory. What a pity." Yvonne thought she might pass right through the table and into his arms.

"Your parents are not here?"

"My parents did not survive the fighting between the Red and the White armies."

"I see." The buzzing was back in her head. "In Russia?"

He nodded, his eyes still holding hers.

"So you're an orphan?" If she leaned over to kiss him, the cups and saucers, the sideplates, the teapot would all crash to the floor.

But Alexei, it seemed, could pluck grace from the air. Taking her hand, he brought it to his lips and kissed it. Such long, thick eyelashes he had. Without looking up he said, "My mother rode with me on the train from Omsk, in Siberia, all the way to Leningrad. I was to live with her second cousin there while attending the school. I never saw her again."

Yvonne's eyes filled with tears. Alexei crooked his forefinger to catch them as they spilled, took the finger to his lips, then to hers. He pulled her to her feet, paid the bill and then, arms wrapped around each other, the young couple walked out into Russell Street.

At the corner of Bow Street, Alexei pulled her to him so that her face was nestled against his chest. "It is getting late." He kissed the top of her head. "And I must be getting back."

Church bells began to ring for evensong, and Yvonne knew, though there were no longer any stage calls to get her mother ready for, that she too should make her way home. When Nell emerged from her gin-induced stupors, she was often low and weepy, would lie for hours in her daughter's arms, whimper like a puppy if Yvonne, her hands cold and cramped, stopped stroking her hair or rubbing her neck. There would be hell to pay if she stayed away much longer.

"Until tomorrow, then." Bending to kiss her, Alexei grasped Yvonne's hands and brought them inside his coat and around his back. And though she could count his ribs, beneath the harsh wool of his jumper she felt also the anvil shape of him, the supple lines of his back. It was like clinging to sun-warmed wood.

When Yvonne floated home from her third meeting with Alexei in as many days, her mother was waiting for her.

"Well, don't you look like the cat that swallowed the cream."

Yvonne planted her feet, clenched her fists. She would not be goaded.

"Come on then. What have you got to be smiling about? Got some fancy bloke tailing your tushie?"

Yvonne scowled at her mother, then looked away.

"That's it, isn't it?" Frances burst into life, sitting up sud-

denly on the sofa where she had lolled all day. Sometimes she
lolled all night too. Without work, she hardly bothered getting
up and rarely changed out of her dressing gown. "You've got
yourself a fancy man." Yvonne felt lightheaded.

"Well, you won't be whoring around under my roof, young
lady. Don't be coming back to me with any babies in your
belly." She grabbed the edge of Yvonne's cape, dragged her
around the sofa to face her, and pulled Yvonne down till their
faces were only inches apart. "He hasn't bed you yet, has he?"

"No. He loves me."

Her mother let go, leaned back into her sofa, kicked her
legs over the arm. "They all love you. That's their style. That's
what they want you to believe." She moved a few objects
around on the occasional table, opened her cigarette case,
took out a cigarette and lit it with a match from a box of Swan
Vestas. "So, you're still a virgin, then."

"Of course."

Nell placed her cigarette in the ashtray and opened her
arms wide, Yvonne's cue to go to her. "Good girl," she said,
delivering a smacking wet kiss on Yvi's forehead and hugging
her. "You're a good girl for your mama."

Yvonne waited a few moments, then gently pulled herself
from her mother's embrace.

"Who is he, then?" her mother asked, taking another pull
from her cigarette. "Let me guess. Some tatty newspaper seller,
or have you hooked yourself a delivery boy? A baker's helper?
A printer's devil?"

"He's a dancer."

"A dancer, eh?" Her mother's badly drawn eyebrows shot
up. "What kind of a dancer?"

"He dances with the Vic-Wells company."

"Who?" Frances picked up her gin bottle from the floor
and held it to the light.

"Ballet," Yvonne said. "I don't expect you'd know about it."

Quick as a flash Frances dropped the empty bottle, pulled her daughter around by her shoulder and slapped her hard across her face.

"Hold your tongue, child. Don't presume to know what I do and don't know." She pushed her away. "Now get out of my sight. Go on, walk the streets awhile, see if that doesn't help you remember that your mother knows best."

Hunger drove Yvonne back home later, as Nell knew it would. When her daughter walked back in the door, she asked, "Care to come down to dinner with me?" She crooked her arm for Yvonne to take, and together they stepped from the room and down the wide, canted stairs, a loving mother and daughter out for a stroll.

Nell seemed so composed and reasonable throughout the meal, sipping slowly at her wine, dabbing her mouth with her serviette after each forkful, that Yvonne relaxed. She mentioned Kitty's telegram and the ballet, and explained how she had met Alexei. She loved pronouncing his name, it made her feel exotic and foreign. She was building to mentioning dancing with him, a little speech she'd rehearsed while wandering the streets in the cold.

"Have you given any more thought to Mr. Metcalf's offer, Mama?"

"I have."

"And?" Yvonne set down her fork, flushed food from her teeth with her tongue.

Nell continued eating as she spoke. "You're fourteen years old now, of an age where many youngsters are already out working, helping to support their families."

My God. Mama was going to let her on stage again. In her own role? Doing something of her own choosing? Yvonne didn't even mind if she had to sing. She had a passable voice, fairly sweet, so she'd been told, as long as she got to do some kind of dancing as well. She could build up a name for herself first, see her mother settled, looked after, while Alexei worked his way through the ranks in his ballet company, and they would not have to embark on their tour together as two unknowns. Yvonne pushed her plate away, too excited to eat any more. Everything she had ever wanted seemed suddenly within her grasp. She would show her mother one of the routines she'd been working on when they got back to their lodgings.

Nell opened the door to the room without unlocking it, the first indication that all was not right. Yvonne knew she'd seen her mother turn the key and pocket it before they left, she could even recall the thunk as the deadbolt had slid home. The second was the gentleman in a frock coat standing by the fire, his back to the room.

"This is Mortimer Jackson, Yvi." Her mother held out her arm towards the gentleman's broad back. On cue the portly man turned. "Of Jackson's Biscuits."

Yvonne stared at the man's round, red face and the absurd monocle perched between his left eyebrow and cheekbone. He was as overdressed as the most eccentric of the turns Yvonne had seen on stage over the years, a caricature of the Edwardian age. Wherever had he found such a coat to cover so large a body? Yvonne looked to her mother, then checked her balance as the floor shifted beneath her feet. Frances never introduced her daughter to her male acquaintances.

"Pleased to make your aquain . . .," she began, watching her mother walk towards the bedroom door and open it.

"Now, you be nice to Mr. Jackson." Nell patted her daughter

gingerly on her shoulder, an unnatural, rehearsed movement. Yvonne flinched, stared at her mother in terror. In her peripheral vision she saw Mortimer Jackson leave his post at the fire and step inside the bedroom. She felt at once cold and hot, and then heavy, heavy enough to sink through the floor to the rooms below. A force more potent than gravity had fastened her feet to the worn oak floorboards; she could not lift them if she tried.

"Go on," her mother urged, gesturing with her eyes towards the open bedroom door.

Yvonne's lips were stuck together. She opened her mouth to protest, tasting blood as the thin skin near the corners of her mouth ripped. "But — "

"Shh, shh, now." Her mother placed her finger over Yvonne's lips. Yvonne pushed her lips against her mother's skin, wanting to mark it. This is my blood. "You be a good girl, now." Nell smiled sweetly, and Yvonne felt something break inside her. "And no tears, lovey. Mr. Jackson don't want to see your tears, right?" She pushed her daughter gently by the shoulders, but just as she was about to shut the door, Nell pulled her back, whispered fiercely into her ear, "Your mama's sorry for this, gel. She's so sorry." And the door closed.

Yvonne stood at the door, her back to the room, for what seemed a lifetime. She sensed her mother standing just on the other side. When Mortimer Jackson cleared his throat, she turned slowly. He was sitting on the edge of the bed, already half-undressed. Her ears must have been dammed up, for she'd heard nothing of his preparations, his moving about. His jacket was hung on a hanger Yvonne's mother had obviously left out for him. His cravat was loosened, and he was removing his collar. She sought his eyes, a silent plea, but it was his turn to look down and away. He stood up to unhook his braces and release his trousers, which he hung with deliberate care over the arm of the same hanger. He did not remove his shirt. He did not remove his socks and garters. Yvonne could not take her eyes from the stretched vee shape of them. Jackson stood up and walked over to her. Seeing her fear, he moved his mouth into a smile, a flush spreading over his large, wide face. Absurdly, he patted her shoulder. Then he took her arm and led her, a mannequin, towards the bed.

Yvonne later reasoned that it was the matter-of-factness of Mortimer Jackson's actions that paralyzed her so. Had he been violent, she could have kicked him; had he been tender, she could have grown hysterical. But he treated her as though she was of little more consequence to him than a doll, and so, doll-like, she responded.

Placing his hands on her shoulders, he pushed her backwards so that from the hips upward she lay flat. He then picked up her legs and swung them gracelessly onto the bed.

"Are you all right?" he asked, his voice, high and tight, a surprise. She wanted to roll away, curl herself up into a ball, but was too afraid. Instead, her skin cold as ice, she lay with her legs locked together, arms clamped against her sides, a doll in a box. She was still fully clothed. Then Mortimer Jackson heaved all eighteen stones of himself on top of her. The bed listed. Yvonne felt her ribs crack, her stomach explode, her mother would find her suffocated, every ounce of breath squeezed from her lungs. His weight shifted as he leaned on one elbow and pulled up her skirt. With the pressure lifted from her bladder, a trickle of hot pee escaped, burning between her legs. Yvonne worried about the smell as she heard springs creak. Her mother settling into the sofa. Did the woman plan to sit in the living room and listen? take a drink and put up her feet while this indifferent freak did his worst? Something stirred inside Yvonne, a deep rumble, the switch of a long black tail.

With soft, fat hands Mortimer Jackson now pried Yvonne's legs apart, ripping her cotton stockings. She half believed then that he might stop, hearing the cloth tear; she thought he might understand that this was her resistance, that she did not want any of this to happen. Instead his breathing quickened, he grew more excited. He pulled at her bloomers in the same way, tearing both them and Yvonne as the pee-soaked seam at her crotch refused, at first, to give and instead cut into her flesh. Because she gasped in pain, Yvonne did not hear the door to their rooms open and close and her mother slip quietly down the stairs to the pub, her fist full of cash, hoping a few gin toddies would wash away her guilt. While Mortimer Jackson pawed at Yvonne's boyish breasts, while he pushed himself inside her, grunting, Yvonne pictured her mother listening outside the door. The creature inside her flexed and twitched, grew fangs. Now Jackson began kissing her face. He was crying. "Are you all right?" he sobbed. "You all right?" Yvonne turned her head to try avoid the wetness of his lips, his tears, but the mountain of flesh was inescapable. His mouth still clamped on hers, he shifted his weight to one side again and with his free hand placed her hand on his back. She let it slip off, and the creature inside threw back its head and howled. Yvonne bit down on her tongue, imagining her teeth clamped around Nell's neck, the pull before the give as her mother's skin first stretched, then burst, and Yvonne, she-wolf, shook her head, fangs sinking into gin-soaked flesh, shaking and biting till she heard the snapping of bones, felt the give in the muscles, then sucked greedily at the life force in her mother's veins.

VII

Vancouver: June 1952

Acres of blue above his head. Anton, sitting on the steps by the front door, stares at the vapour trail left by a passing airplane, a chalk mark in the sky, until his eyes water, looks away, then stares heavenward again. Harold took him once to Sea Island to watch the airplanes taking off and landing, like giant silver birds in slow motion. The roar of the engines overhead had been deafening, no need for speech, for forced and awkward camaraderie. Harold had bought him a hot dog and a cream soda, both had tasted faintly of gasoline, like singed hair.

A lilting voice. "Hello again." Light on her feet; Anton had not heard her coming. He turns his face towards her, prepared to drop his gaze, but is dazzled by her smile, the soft crescent of bruise-red lips. Inside his chest a small bird opens its wings. He manages a smile in response, just as Jasmine turns her head and bounds up the stairs to the front door. Anton stares after the space she just occupied, the air still vibrating from her presence. He summons her smile again, a smile that was just for him. He brings his hands to his face, smoothes his fingers across the high ridge of his cheekbones, the angle of his chin. Is it this face, his face, that makes her smile, makes her eyes widen?

It's possible.

Despite himself, Anton has been sneaking glances at his reflection in the mirror lately. Between exercises, first making sure his mother and her students are looking elsewhere, he crouches low on the piano stool, turns his head a fraction and shifts his eyes to the far right. But the mirrored wall is a long way off, and, too self-conscious to face it directly, all he gleans from these furtive looks is an impression of shape and colour, more profile than three-quarter view.

He gets to his feet and goes inside. His mother is shopping at Woodwards, took the bus half an hour ago, has no students until four. He has time.

Rather than face the full-length mirror in the practice room, Anton chooses the one in the bathroom, which cuts him off at the waist. He closes the door behind him, bolts it and turns on the light, locking eyes with those in the mirror. Already he feels clammy; butterflies brush the inside of his skin. Everything but his eyes is, for now, in soft focus. It is a while before he can unclench his jaw, pull down his shoulders, relax the muscles in his face enough that he can truly look at himself.

He feels naked, uncomfortably exposed, vulnerable. His penis lifts as his testicles contract. The butterflies have now congregated in the pit of his stomach, making him queasy. He tries a smile, then quickly looks away, intimidated by the handsome, smoky face in the mirror. He looks again, not quite able to believe that the ash-eyed, dark-haired gypsy face is his own. And yet he's traced those pale eyes, the long straight nose and broad flat forehead for years in the sharp black and white photograph of his father that he keeps by his bedside. Every night he picks up the tarnished silver frame and stares at the image caught there, touches it, kisses it, shares his hopes and fears with it. And every time he combs the fine but strong features in painstaking detail, searching for the cowardice Harold always spoke of so bitterly.

Anton grows more daring, leans closer, inspects every mole,

every pore, every tiny hair on his face, the pink at the corners of his eyes, their long, dark lashes. Every cell in his body is alert and tingling; his skin registers every movement of air.

An almighty crash. Anton jumps so hard his knees rap against the cabinet doors beneath the sink. Panic rises in his chest, stops the air in his throat. A dull thud, the sounds of furniture scraping. His mother? He strains his ears but can hear nothing more, only the pounding of his own blood. His hands shake, the face in the mirror is sheet white, his features only dark smudges.

Anton collects himself. The sound came from the front of the house somewhere. He splashes water on his face, dabs at it with the towel and draws back the bolt on the door. Walks slowly through the silent apartment, braced for the worst.

"Mama?" he calls, but there is no reply. He opens the apartment door, steps into the hallway. "Hello?" he calls softly.

Silence.

He walks over to Clarice Hart's suite. Leans one ear towards the door, rests it there, hearing only his own too-loud heartbeat. Tick tock. Tick tock. No. A clock, nothing else. He raises his hand to knock, then stops. What will he say if Clarice Hart answers? What will he do if she opens the door holding a knife dripping with blood? What if she has blood on her? What if he sees the old man dead? What if Clarice Hart then feels obliged to kill him too?

A door closes on the second floor. Anton jumps again, his brain is pressing against his forehead, his teeth are tender. A key turns in a lock, footsteps sound down the hallway. He flies back to his apartment, opens the door as quickly and quietly as he can and carefully pushes it closed. The footsteps are moving down the stairs now. Slip, thump. Slip, thump. A light skipping sound. Maybe it is Jasmine. Perhaps she heard the crash too, is coming to investigate. Anton holds himself against the door, his eye straining at the peephole. Mr. Cunningham. How could he mistake Mr. Cunningham's heavy steps for Jasmine's light ones? Mr. Cunningham strides by purposefully on his long legs, hat on, raincoat buttoned and belted despite the heat, newspaper under his arm. What is he doing home in the middle of the day? Mr. Cunningham doesn't even falter as he passes Anton's apartment, Clarice Hart's.

Anton waits until the house is silent again before opening his door and tiptoeing back across the corridor. Perhaps he didn't hear anything fall after all. Perhaps he imagined it or misheard another noise outside, a car backfiring or clipping a garden wall in a too-tight turn or another car parked innocently against the curb. He holds his ear close to the door again and knocks softly. "Mr. Hart?" He has no idea if the old man is a Mr. Hart, but that he's Clarice Hart's husband is as good a guess as any. "Mr. Hart, are you all right?"

This time a low sound. Unmistakably a moan. The old man must be hurt. Anton lowers his hand, unsure of his next move, whether he should be here at all. The landlady should be home soon. Would anyone be the wiser if he simply slipped back inside his apartment and carried on as if nothing untoward had happened? Who would know? He takes a step backwards. It's none of his business. And, frankly, he's a little scared. There could be a lot of blood involved. The old man might be fading from shock. Anton pictures himself dressing a gaping wound, giving artificial respiration. He lowers his gaze demurely in the face of people's awe, their gratitude. His neighbours. The police. The mayor.

Jasmine.

He swallows. Faint heart never won fair maiden.

Stepping forward, he grasps the door handle. Locked. Now what? Another rise of panic. He runs outside, but the bay windows out front are all shut tight. Around the side of the house he's in luck but needs something to stand on, something fairly tall, he isn't strong enough to pull himself up any distance. A ladder would be best but a stack of empty flowerpots would do, an old gate, anything. He's frantic, adrenaline like cool spring water threading through his veins. Whipping his head this way and that, racking his brain, he blames Mr. Cunningham for keeping the garden too tidy until he spots the handles of the wheelbarrow sticking out from behind a flowering bush. He has no choice but to wheel it over Clarice Hart's plants, squash some of the flowers. Snap. Snap. The heads fall brokenly at angles. He'll fix them later.

Tipping the barrow so that the wheel guard sits on the ground and the arms rest against the siding, Anton leans his weight into the wall and climbs the metal frame so that he's standing on the barrow's sloped back rise. Hooking his hands over the window frame, he flexes his fingers, grasps the sill and pulls himself up an inch or so. His toes jab against the wall, seeking footholds. The wooden siding strains and cracks under his feet. He pulls again, a few more inches, his toes repeating their scrappy dance. The strong afternoon sun beating down on his back makes him sweat, the muscles in his forearms tremble. A fly dives at his face. He wills himself a little further, but now his hands are numb, and the strain has moved into his neck, the muscles in his jaw. Another inch or so and his chest is level with the sill. In order to reposition his hands he grips harder with his feet, his calves hardening into spasm. Twisted in its shoe, his right foot begins a scream of its own, shooting pain up his leg and into his groin. The fly is back, or its brother, buzzing around his face. Flies like sweat. They drink it. They bite you when they do this. Anton screws his eyes up tightly, blows at the insect to get it out of his face. One more pull and he's able to rest his ribcage on the ledge. He

pauses to catch his breath, steady his heartbeat. A welcome
breeze cools the sweat across his chest and under his arms, in
the waistband of his pants. He leans forward into the window
and with his head he nudges aside the blind.

The smell of the room hits him first, musty, a dried-up
old-people smell, dirty underwear and stale sweat. It is so
dim that Anton, entering from the bright sunshine, has to let
his eyes adjust before he can make out the silhouette of an
armchair in the right-hand corner, a sofa against the wall to
his left. A large wall cabinet faces him from across the room,
its contents in shadow. There is no sign of the old man. Did
Anton only imagine the crash, the moan?

"Hello?" he calls, his voice strained with the pressure on his
chest.

A sound from immediately below him. Anton peers down
at a crumpled form on the floor, a frail old man half in and
half out of a turned-over wheelchair. He lies directly in front
of the window. Anton cannot think how he's going to get in
without landing on the man, crushing him. He must weigh
less than a hundred pounds. And he is so very still and pale
— increasingly things become clearer, the haze in the air thinning — his eyes closed.

Anton could perhaps slide in like a snake, let his arms take
his weight. He leans his face closer, then recoils as if slapped.
The old man smells strongly, the kind of cloying, stale, insti-
tutionalized odour that clings to people who have been indoors
an unnatural length of time, the stench, Anton knows, that
separates those who can leave from those who cannot. Squeezing his mind shut, he wriggles in further, breathing through
his mouth, his face within inches of the old man's body.
Reaches his hands to the floor, feels grit beneath his palms,
dust, some kind of hair. Forearms resting on the floor, elbows,
the backs of his upper arms graze the old man's back. How

thin he is, his ribs sharp even through the wool of his cardigan. Now Anton must hurl himself through, propel his legs over his head.

It's a basic somersault. He's done them in gym class. But not with a semi-conscious old man in the way. Feet balanced on the sill, he bends his knees, then pushes. Head tucked, legs sailing over, he rounds his back and curls downward. He coughs, dust in his mouth, wipes his dusty hands down his pants. Now he's inside he feels absurdly proud of himself, a hero come to rescue the fallen. He lifts his chin a little; already he's stronger, bigger than the boy standing on the wheelbarrow.

Rolling onto his knees, he shuffles to the prostrate form on the floor. "Sir. Are you okay?" Anton shakes him gently by the shoulder, then places his hand on the old man's. He feels cold. Old people feel the cold more so they have to be careful, make sure they are wrapped up well. As do people in wheelchairs. If Anton was silent or withdrawn, Nurse Wendy would regale him with the details of her work as she turned him this way and that to bathe him or get his circulation moving. On less vexing days he watched her, asked questions.

First he frees the old man's blanket, all twisted around his feet, then draws it up over him. Water. They always gave water to the patients who fainted or threw a fit or otherwise lost consciousness. The glasses are not where he thinks they should be. He has to open nearly every cupboard door before he finds them, a lengthy task, as this kitchen is much larger than his mother's, is probably, judging by the size and style of everything in it, the original kitchen to the house. The countertop is clear but for a tall china teapot, tannin stains around the spout and lid. It sits on an iron trivet by the sink, though, unlike the rest of the dishes, it obviously never gets washed. Anton runs the water till it's cold, rinses the glass and fills it. Before returning to the room, he quickly lifts the lid on a pot sitting on the stove. Cold soup of some description, the surface skinned with congealed fat. He makes a face and replaces the lid.

Back in the front room he kneels, cradling the old man's head, and holds the glass to his lips. Such wispy hair; his skull appears almost exposed, the skin stretched over it so thin. Water dribbles down his chin and into the wrinkled depression at the base of his throat. Anton wonders if he should wipe this up. If the old man sits up, it'll surprise him, a trickle of cold running down inside his shirt. He sticks his fingers in the glass to soak them, then sprays water drops on the old man's face. The old man stirs, tries to move his arms.

Anton stands and rights the wheelchair first, no mean feat; it's a heavy, clumsy contraption. It's hard to believe such a frail person could upset such a sturdy machine. Whatever could he have been doing? Reaching for something, no doubt. The blind, perhaps. Maybe the sun was in his eyes. Anton bends and hooks his hands under the old man's arms. It is like picking up a large doll; there is nothing of a child's robustness, solidity. As he manoeuvres him into the chair, it occurs to Anton that the old man may have broken some bones in his fall. His back even. But if such were the case, wouldn't he have cried out in pain when Anton moved him? He backs away, afraid now he may have done more harm than good. Should he leave or wait and see if the old man comes around? He doesn't want trouble, but he may have to telephone for an ambulance.

He steals a glance at the old man's slippered feet. They appear normal in size and shape, nothing twisted or shrunken. Must be his legs that are duds. Anton would take dud feet over dud legs any day, though if he were given a choice he'd take normal in both categories. He shifts his weight from foot to foot. It was definitely the old man's legs that were the problem. People with club feet didn't end their days in wheel-chairs, did they?

He looks away, wanting to wipe such thoughts from his mind. The apartment must be pretty much the same size as the one he shares with his mother, but it appears smaller. The walls, hung with heavy flocked wallpaper, seem to press inwards, pushing furniture that is dark and old and ornate towards the centre. Along a high shelf that runs all around the room sit dolls, faded and dusty. Some are tall, some small, their faces blank and unprepossessing, some shiny, others dull, vacant eyes with rosebud lips and mouths, some with hair tumbling out of elaborate hairdos. They put him in mind of the doll hospital on Seymour Street. Glass eyes. Plastic eyes. Painted-on eyes. Anton glances from wall to wall, convinced now that the dolls are watching him. A doll in a kimono. A black face atop a thicket of flowers and leaves. A pale-faced blond doll trussed up in a milkmaid outfit, complete with bonnet and bucket. A nurse next to a girl in a grass skirt. Obviously they belong to Clarice Hart. He shudders at the thought of mad Clarice ever cradling and comforting anything. Maybe the dolls all have faces of people she knows — the tenants, per-haps, storekeepers and bus drivers she's had run-ins with — and are stuck with pins.

There's an airplane sitting on top of the bureau. At least it's a photograph of an airplane, an old one, quite a flimsy contrap-tion, shadows in front, a group of men. Mr. Hart's old enough to have been in the First World War. He was probably around for the Battle of Waterloo, he's so shrivelled. Anton takes a step towards the bureau. Maybe he was a flyer. He could have been there when they brought down the Red Baron. The drawers could be filled with trophies from all the planes he's shot down. Anton reaches for the photograph.

"Gib me my peep."

Anton starts then spins around to face the old man in his wheelchair who shakes his head. The words are unintelligible. Harold. Anton's breathing comes fast and shallow.

"Shmow." A caved-in mouth in a crumpled face.

He squeezes his eyes shut then opens them again. Huh? Schmow? Now? "Now?" he says, his voice rising with exaggerated inflection. A barely perceptible motion, up and down. The old man is nodding his head.

"Now what?" Anton looks about him wildly. The old man is very slowly trying to look around the room.

"Does your head hurt?"

Again, another small nod. Now he points to his eyes, moves his fingers to indicate the room. Glasses. Of course, Anton thinks. He's lost his glasses, probably blind as a bat, wants to see his rescuer.

"I'll have a look," he shouts for no reason he can think of, enunciating each word carefully. It is then, his eyes fully adjusted to the subdued light, that Anton notices the teeth. A full set, uppers and lowers, their gums a hideous shade of pink, sit on the floor just an arm's reach away.

Mr. Hart expects Anton to pick up his teeth.

"Shoo haf puu weeve." Though weak and dazed, the old man is clearly upset. Anton casts about for something to grasp the teeth with. A poker and tongs at the fireplace, but neither is appropriate, the teeth might turn black, the old guy'll look like someone's punched him in the mouth. He can hardly use his feet, kick them over, not when they have to go back in the old man's mouth. Anton swallows impulsive laughter. He's going to have to touch them with his bare hands. He bends over, picks up the teeth between forefinger and thumb. At least they're dry, not covered in saliva or old food. Holding them far from his body as though they might be contagious, he hands them to the old gent, who gives them a quick rub on his cardigan before popping them back in his mouth.

Anton cannot decide if he's disgusted or merely surprised. But then what did he expect? "Are you going to be okay?" he repeats, then startles at the sound of a key turning the lock in the main door outside. It could be anyone. The old man speaks, his voice clouded with pain.

"If she catches you here . . ."

But Anton is already climbing back out the window. He has no desire to face the wrath of Clarice Hart. He doesn't have the courage.

VIII

London: December 1935

Alexei reached down to cup Yvonne's face in his hands. He rubbed his thumbs across her brow, her nose, her lips.

"You cannot stay here," he whispered. He leaned to kiss her nose, stroke her hair back from her face, rub her tiny ears. "You must go back to your mother. She will wonder where you are."

Yvonne frowned, then took his hands from her ears, laughing. "I didn't hear a word, you covering my ears like that."

"Shh." He put his fingers to her lips, then drew her to him. His breathing came fast and shallow. "*Odin, dwa, tri,*" he whispered into her hair. She pulled away to look up at him.

He stroked her face again, his long expressive fingers so tender Yvonne could almost feel the wooden places inside herself begin to soften and bend. She reached up to place her hands over his.

"Your mother," Alexei began, his voice cracked and hoarse, then pulled her to him again. It was as if he could not bear to have her look at him. "*Chetiri, piat, chešt.*" More whispering. "She will be worried, no?" A ragged sound as he breathed in. "*Sen, vosem.*" Yvonne felt a shudder run through him. "*Deviat, desiat.*" He let out his breath. "You should go back to her."

Yvonne stiffened. She felt older, greyer somehow.

"I want to stay here."

"But it is not safe here."

"Oh, but it is," she said, quietly, reaching behind her to touch the walls, take assurance from their solidity, their permanence. So much safer than out there. No snakes, no rats in here. She was thinking of the human kind.

"What if someone comes back? What if you get caught? They will call the police."

"I won't get caught, I promise. I can make myself disappear into nothing. Believe me."

"But this theatre is overrun with mice."

"Mice? Everything is so new. How can it be overrun?"

"Inside it is new, but this building is old. And the mice are everywhere. Every day you come into here, they are waiting. I think maybe they like to eat silk or maybe the glue in the pointe shoes. But always they are jumping out of your clothes, your locker, the baskets of costumes."

"A few mice are the least of my problems." She glanced at the small travel bag by her feet. Hand-tooled leather, her mother's favourite piece of luggage. She'd shredded the red dress, emptied her mother's purse. All bridges back to her mother mined and torched. Ahead lay Alexei and dancing and Ned Metcalf.

"Maybe you will change your mind when the lights go out." But Yvonne had waited two days and two sleepless nights to make her move. Lights or no lights, this was it. She felt light-headed with determination.

Footsteps down the corridor. Someone was coming. His finger to her lips, Alexei guided her gently backwards into racks of dusty costumes.

Yvonne heard only a muffled exchange. It would be so easy to hide in here. Warm, dry, safe from her mother. Lights were being turned off. The back door opened, a waft of icy air and a slam as it closed again, the pushbar clicked. A bevy of girls. Quick steps and giggles. Chatter, chatter.

"Coming," Alexei called to someone she could not see. A stab of jealousy. One of the girls. Would Alexei walk her to the tube station too? Pull her towards him and press soft warm kisses on her lips? She moved as if to leave her hiding place. Alexei pushed his head between the dresses.

"You are sure about this?" he whispered.

"It's just for tonight. I promise. I'll be gone at daybreak."

"Once the doors are locked you cannot leave. You will be here until classes tomorrow morning."

"Until classes tomorrow morning, then."

His footsteps retreated, joined others in the exodus towards the back door. Windows rattled, someone checking the locks, then the door heaved open and closed one final time.

At first Yvonne's ears rang with the silence, and then the thump thump thump of her quickened heartbeat. Now that Alexei and the others had gone and she was alone in this vast barn of a building, staying here didn't seem like such a good idea. A mouse skittered along the skirting board, followed by another. Then another. A pause. Now several more, a scurrying legion. One brushed by her foot, and she jumped, nerves on edge. She should have asked Alexei to stay, to wrap his magic and his charm and his words around her and keep her warm and safe. She rubbed her arms, the cold already seeping through her thin clothes. She'd even pictured herself saying the words, felt her mouth moving to form them, Stay with me, reaching to place her hand on his cheek. But had balked at the last instant. Better never to know than be told no.

Yvonne moved into a spill of moonlight coming through the windows by the backstage door. She undid the fastenings on the travel bag and dug out one of the candles and the matches she'd stolen from her mother's rooms. The theatre itself, windowless, would be pitch black.

A hiss, a flare, the smell of sulphur. Down the passageway, giant shadows from her small flame flickering on the walls. She remembered the layout from the night Kitty brought her here. A turn to her left, another passageway, a quick veer to the right, and she was standing in the wings. She backed up, hugged the wall, holding the candle aloft, looking for a bank of throw switches. Spotlight. Click. A pale orange glow lit up the stage, and Yvonne's eyes relaxed, no longer straining to read the grey scale of shadows.

Standing at the edge of light, she took off her boots. Despite her long woollen stockings the flesh of her legs felt cold. Alexei had told her of his days dancing in Leningrad, where the theatre was not heated and the school had barely enough money to feed the students bread. During performances, everyone had stood in the wings draped in cloaks and wearing felt boots, waiting their turn to go on.

Yvonne took a deep breath and ran across the stage on tiptoe, cape flying out behind her. Shh, shh, her feet whispered dryly. A film of light dust on the floor. Ssshh. She drew her left leg in a long arc before her, delighting in the sound. Shh. She drew it quickly towards her. Such a beautiful floor. So new, scarcely four years old, so unlike the tracked and worn stages of some of her mother's venues. Had her mother ever performed in any theatre so grand as this, she wondered? Not for a long time, if ever.

Throwing off her cape, she ran back through the centre of the spotlight and then around its edges, warming herself, shaking the cold from her bones, from her skin, from her heart. And always she kept her face turned from the cavernous black beyond the edge of the stage. Rising on tiptoe, she lifted one leg, a corresponding arm: arabesque — a step, a word Kitty had taught her. She pirouetted, a too-tight, graceless movement — her muscles were still cold — and lost her balance. She righted herself, face warm with embarrassment, then stared out into the darkness, the concentric rows of plush tip-up seats. Empty.

There was no one here. And it was this great emptiness that made Yvonne, raised with the cries and hollers of boisterous music hall audiences, feel awkward and self-conscious. Only the mice and ghosts from the theatre's former glory huddled in the shadows to watch her leap and turn, twist and sway. Stock still, facing the seats she could not see, Yvonne willed them filled: jewel-laden ladies in shimmery dresses, gents with snappy waistcoats and silk cravats, Alexei in the wings, his eyes filled with love.

She set her face into a mask, hair in inky waves down her back, and struck a dramatic pose: left knee bent, right leg ramrod straight out to the side, torso twisted left, arms and head angled towards the ceiling, palms facing upwards. The pose had something of the Egyptian about it, the early Greek, and more of Isadora Duncan.

Her audience, hushed, expectant, drew in a collective breath as the sound of a single oboe slowly filled the hall, pushing its rich, full tones at the high domed and chandeliered ceiling. Yvonne folded herself together, a ball, a pod, a chrysalis, before opening up. Then, swaying to the woodwind tremolo, a butterfly wakened in spring. She glided across the stage, her arms and legs, her whole body, all the muscles in her face, pulled together and pushed apart, knees up, arms and chest out, then head down, down so low she swept the stage with her hair. Effortless she moved, choreographer and conductor, dancer and mime. Drums began, and the audience, unable to contain themselves, rose to their feet, clapping and throwing crimson roses at her feet. She let out a shriek, her dance now exuberant and wild. Hair streaming out behind her, fingers, toes twitching, pulsing, wrists and ankles snapping, she built to a frenzy, heart pumping with the drumbeat, pumping hard enough to burst through her skin.

"Brava! Brava!" Hands clapping.

Yvonne stopped dead, her skin instantly cold, every hair, every cell taut. It was all she could do not to cry out. She slipped sideways into the darkness, whisper-light on her feet. Whoever was out there would never find her.

"Yvi. It's me. Alexei."

Alexei. Slowly Yvonne stepped out of the shadows. On watery legs, she crossed the stage towards his voice.

"I could not bear to think of you alone in here. So I un-fastened the catch on a window in the change room before I left." He held his arms wide and she stepped into them, slipping her hands inside his coat and around his back, pushing her face hard into his chest.

"I would not," he said, kissing her hair, "have slept anyway."

Yvonne pulled herself closer still, pressing the imprint of her body deep into his. If she could only climb inside his skin. Her head spun with this sudden and desperate need, pinpricks of coloured light swirling into darkness; it was as if her whole centre of gravity had shifted.

"Then we'll stay awake together," she said, holding him so tightly her arms ached and trembled.

But Alexander Nikolayevich will pay for his rashness tomorrow, for this lack of sleep, when, his concentration marred, his body fighting fatigue, his knees sore from jumping on a concrete practice floor, he will slip catching Peggy Hookham, a passionate and talented young dancer with the Vic-Wells Ballet company, who has chosen, at Ninette de Valois's request, to dance as Margot Fonteyn.

Part Two

IX

Vancouver: June 1952

"Demonstration. Fifth position, porte de bras." Yvonne looks over her shoulder at her son. "No music for now."

Anton slumps down on the stool, out of Miss Parker's line of sight. Miss Deborah Parker has come to his mother's school for a refresher course. She took ballet years ago and hopes to pick up where she left off. Poker-faced, she stares at Anton with her big bug eyes. Why do they all have to pull their hair back so tightly? In the course of the hour the room has filled with the acrid, metallic odour of Miss Deborah Parker's sweat. But her skin has no accompanying healthy glow. It is as when she came in, dull and waxy, its unevenness broken only by the band of tiny star-shaped scars across the top of her back. Pimples? Or chickenpox?

Anton stifles a yawn as rolls of thunder rumble overhead. Maybe the rain will stop soon. He flexes his hands, rubs them, flexes them again. It's as if he can still feel the old man's bony body, his tissue-thin skin, nearly translucent, the bluish veins at his temples. So fragile. These are not details Anton was aware of taking in at the time. But in his mind he has revisited that room so often he could reproduce its lines and shadows from memory. The photograph looms large in these recollections. A Sopwith Camel or a Nieuport? He hadn't been close enough to tell. Anton yawns just as his mother turns to ask him to resume playing.

"Keeping you up, are we?"

"Do not forsake me, oh my darling." Anton toffee-hammers the first few bars to a Frankie Laine number. He's been practising while his mother is out. For some reason she doesn't seem to like any of the popular music he listens to on Harold's radio.

"When you're quite ready."

Anton lowers his head as another yawn engulfs him, making his eyes water. "Da," he says, invoking the mute key, their agreed-upon signal to begin.

"And one two three, change two three, round two three, back two three."

This is the third lesson in a row he's sat through. The room is warm. No wonder he's sleepy. And distracted. He's anxious to check on the old man. It is the old man who is responsible for his lack of sleep. He'd lain awake half the night thinking about him. Was he all right? Was he awake too? What was he thinking? Did he even think anymore, or was his brain addled with age, with cabin fever? Anton doesn't need to talk to the old man to know he never leaves the apartment. How could he? How could he ever get down the front steps unless someone carried him? And the steps are wooden and badly canted, it would take a strong person to tip back his chair and wheel him down one step at a time. He could, of course, be carried. Anton doubts Clarice Hart ever does this. There is Mr. Cunningham, but . . . Anton had turned his pillow a thousand times, punched it, swivelled it, seeking a cool place for his throbbing head, lead-tipped fingers drumming at his temples. He'd fretted till his bed turned to concrete. Three forty-two, the luminous hands on his alarm clock read, and that was before he turned on the light to read. He considered getting up but doesn't yet fully trust himself in these surroundings. There are too many unfamiliar corners, furniture crouched and ready to pounce, and his mother sleeps like a cat, stirs at the faintest noise. She'd be cranky and difficult all day if he disturbed her.

The book he flicked through was *A Boy's Guide to World War II Combat Aircraft*. A childish book. Watercolour sketches instead of photographs, the Battle of Britain condensed into two paragraphs. He should make a trip to the library. Anton has lived through the Battle of Britain. Though he was not old enough at the time to be able to recall much now beyond the constant noise, like a never-ending chain of firecrackers. He remembers better the devastating impact of the buzz bombs and the V2 rockets towards the end of the war and the mounds of brick and concrete everywhere in the streets, the sandbagged walls and doorways, boarded up windows, signs that led to air-raid shelters, and of course the dumpy barrage balloon that bobbed and weaved in the wind at the end of their street. Still, two paragraphs hardly did such a grand aeronautic feat justice. And the book had nothing of what he was looking for, no history of flight, no pictures that looked anything like the plane in the photograph.

Anton knows the names of a few First World War aircraft and of the triplanes flown by the infamous Red Baron, but beyond that his knowledge is sketchy. The planes look so insubstantial. Had the old man been shot down in his? Maybe that was how he'd lost the use of his legs.

Miss Deborah Parker is wiping the sweat from her waxy skin with a small pink towel. Lesson over. Bravo, Deborah, he thinks. She smiles at him. Anton scowls in return, stays rooted to the piano seat. Miss Parker's skin colours. Finally. She excuses herself to get changed behind the screen in the corner, and Anton, seizing his chance, bolts for the door.

He stands in the hallway, hand raised to knock. He can't be sure Clarice Hart is out. If he knocks on the door and she answers, then what? Anton believes he heard her go out earlier, but he can't be certain. Even if she is out, he'll have to talk to the old man, say something so that he'll let him inside. If his mother hears him talking in the hallway, she'll come and pull him away. He decides to go outside and use the intercom.

A long wait, then a crackle. "Who's there?" Cautious, rusty. "Anton, sir."

A pause. "Anton who?" Querulous now.

"Anton . . ." He stalls. It's always the same Pavlovian response. Schools, hospitals, that other place, wherever he has to give his last name. Crouch. The word sticks like tar in his mouth. Crouch is ugly, a sneaky, slinking verb. Cowards crouch, people who live in fear. Anton throws his shoulders back and walks as straight and true as he can past the curled lips and cold, cruel eyes of those who line the corridors at school: *Anton Crouch Is a slouch, His leg is crook'd, His foot is bent, Poor old Anton Crouch.* Anton has always wanted his father's name. Kavanov. Such a strong, thrilling name. Anton plans to tell his mother this, but he's been holding off, waiting for the right moment. He stares at the row of buzzers, the names beneath them. Number three. Jasmine Daniels. Sweet, sweet Jasmine. He hasn't seen her for two whole days. He pictures her in the air, high above a sparkling ocean. A DC3 or a North Star? He'd like to talk to her about the airplanes but suspects girls know nothing of such things. He doesn't really know what girls know.

The front door opens and Miss Deborah Parker steps out. Anton pretends to be absorbed in the row of buzzers. Miss Parker clears her throat as she passes him. But Anton doesn't turn, he can't even breathe for the bird fluttering inside his chest. Yvonne Rose. Miss Parker pauses, then walks away. Her heels ring on the stone flags, making Anton cringe. Yvonne Rose? The name has been written very carefully in small capital letters, but it is unmistakably his mother's hand-writing — the long curled handle on the Y, the romantic loop on the R. Except Rose is not his mother's name. More importantly, thinks Anton, it is not his name. Rose was his grandmother's stage name. She was a singer. His mother never talks about her, so this is all Anton knows. This and the fact that she died long before Anton was born. Now Harold is dead, and his mother is a Rose again. Anton feels betrayed. She didn't ask him if he wanted to be a Rose too. She simply left him with Crouch.

"Who's there?" Crackle. "I said, who's there?"

The bird in Anton's chest grows large, ruffles its eagle feathers. He takes a deep breath. "Kavanov. Anton Kavanov. Sir." His voice grows bold with the hard edge of the syllables.

"Who?"

"From across the hall," explains the new Anton. "Apartment two. We, um, we met yesterday. I was the one who climbed in through your window. I heard you fall." There is no reply. Anton stares at the speaker. He can feel the old man hesitating on the other end. Perhaps he is ashamed. Anton is cross with himself. "Do you remember?"

"What do you want?" Short and irritable.

"I was wondering . . ." Anton has never been good on the spot. His tongue moves one way, his teeth another. He's practised this over and over in his mind. He clears his throat, begins again. "Sir, I was wondering what it's like to fly."

A long silence. Anton shifts from one foot to the other. A crow squawks from the plane tree in the front yard. He glances at the window where he first saw the old man sitting, but there is nothing but shadows, silhouettes of furniture. The old man wants to be left alone. Anton starts down the steps — he'll go for a walk. Anywhere. Maybe he'll even walk as far as Stanley Park.

"Well, I can't talk to you out there, can I?"

Anton approaches Clarice Hart's door at the same time as it swings slowly open. He holds out his hand towards the old man in his wheelchair. "Anton Kavanov. Pleased to meet you, sir."

The old man doesn't take his hand, though his eyes never leave Anton's face. "No. 104076. Lieutenant Thomas J. Hart. 66th Squadron. Royal Flying Corps." Pride burns in his eyes, eyes far brighter than they were the other day. And he's flushed, there's more blood running around his system. He turns the contraption he's sitting in around and wheels himself into the centre of the room. Anton follows.

The air darkens as the door clicks shut behind them. Anton freezes. The wheelchair squeaks as once again the old man turns around. Anton hears his breathing change with the effort. He squints, trying to accustom his vision to the gloom.

"It's like being with God."

The sun, passing from behind a spent thundercloud, fills the small window behind the old man with an otherworldly glow, framing his head. He looks like a shrivelled-up angel.

"With God?" God the curse word; God the avenger. *God will strike you dead, lad.*

"Are you a good boy?"

"Sir?"

"You have a look of the devil about you." He chuckles, a slow, mirthless sound. "It's those eyes of yours. Like a wolf's." Anton swallows. How can the old man even see his eyes? What with squinting so hard in the dark and the sudden brightness from the window shining like a flashlight in his eyes, his face hurts.

"Don't you have friends your own age, son?"

"Of course." Elliot. But Elliot's sick with polio.

"Then why aren't you with them, son? What do you want with an old man?"

Anton shuffles and stares at the blind covering the window to his right, the one he scrambled in through the other day. "I just wondered how you were doing. After you fell." It's true. He has wondered, but it's the photograph that pulled him back. He can't meet the old man's eyes, remembering his confusion, his teeth, and his humiliation then compared with his dignity now.

"Just a bit of a tumble, that's all." Voice gruff, dismissive. "Nothing to get all worked up about."

"But . . ." Words dry on Anton's lips as he shifts his gaze back to the old man. Though the window is filled with clouds again, he can just make out a bruise on Lieutenant Hart's forehead. But the old man has a stubborn set to his jaw. Harold used to look that way when he'd had a skinful. If you crossed him, you were liable to get a clip round the ear or worse. Anton turns his head towards the bureau against the wall behind him, straining to make out the photograph in the gloom, but all he can see is the shape of its frame. He wonders if the old man still has his helmet and flying goggles, his gauntlets, his long leather overcoat. Did the coat keep him warm up there in the open cockpit? What kind of plane was it? How many enemy aircraft did he shoot down? How did it feel? Dogfights? Medals? Heroes? There's a bottleneck of questions in Anton's throat. He takes a breath.

"Elliot's sick, sir."

"Who?"

"My friend Elliot, sir. He wasn't in school this week."

"What's the matter with him?"

"Polio." Polio is a terrible disease, much worse than having a club foot. You didn't recover from polio. Lots of kids had had polio. Elliot was the second student to disappear from Anton's class this year. And the summer promised to be hot, which, for reasons none of his teachers had ever properly explained, made it worse. There was talk of an epidemic. There'd be a run on iron lungs. But even if you were lucky enough to get an iron lung, it didn't mean you would survive. Anton knows that Elliot Nelson, with his congenitally weak chest, his chronic ailments, will not be back in September. "I have a congenitally weak chest," he told Anton the first day they spoke, the multi-syllabic word, much practised, tripping easily off his childish tongue. With Elliot gone, Anton will sit alone in class again, teased twice as hard by Craig Baxter and his bullying cronies because Elliot won't be there to share the ribbing.

"And is Elliot a good friend of yours?"

"Not really. I mean, I don't suppose we'd be friends if it wasn't for his always being ill." The words, with their awful ring of truth, give Anton a hollow feeling. "He's my project partner, if he's there." Anton thinks of when he lived in England, of all the time he spent away from school recovering from operations to correct his stubborn right foot, which, unlike the left, had not responded to treatment. Operations that gave him nothing but additional pain, months of boredom lying in a hospital bed listening to the whining of much younger or sicker children, all the while becoming more removed, more isolated from his classmates. When he returned, weeks, sometimes months later, his skin blanched an unhealthy white, his arms and legs thin and flaccid, the other boys turned their backs on him, shut him out of their games. Same story, every school year. Every school, if he counted the number he'd been registered in and pulled from since moving to Canada. All the work he'd expended in the beginning of term, trying to make friends, trying to make people not look down at his feet, come to nothing.

Lieutenant Hart is staring so intently that Anton feels again a compulsion to spill the truth. It's as if the old man can see right through him. Not that Anton is a deceitful boy, but before today he's been loath to admit, even to himself, the symbiotic nature of the bond between himself and Elliot: two weak links at the end of a chain of bullies. "We don't really have any common interests. Elliot enjoys collecting stamps, but I'd rather be outside, I'm more interested in cars. And planes."

Again he looks towards the bureau but can see only shadows. "Should I call you Mr. Hart or Lieutenant?"

"Mr. Hart will do, son." Anton wishes Mr. Hart would stop calling him son. He clears his throat. Is Mr. Hart ever going to talk about flying? Maybe he's shell-shocked. Maybe he doesn't remember anything. A terrible war, people say, the most terrible of all wars, though Anton can't understand what makes eleven million dead more terrible than thirty-five million, First World War shells any more destructive than Second World War shells. Anton awoke one morning in hospital next to a soldier. The wards were full, Nurse Helen said, there might be more. The soldier thrashed in his sleep, calling for his Colleen. At least that was what Anton thought he said. It was difficult to tell. The soldier was missing half his face, having, according to Nurse Helen, fallen onto an exploding shell. It was a face that for months afterwards gave Anton nightmares. Corporal Fine had no nose, and his right cheek had been completely blown away. He also had no right eye, only a shadow that deepened as the afternoons drew on. Every day Anton watched him fret and rustle as the nurses turned him and put salve on his ravaged face. At night he dreamed the soldier chased him through the hospital corridors, and he awoke bathed in sweat, for even in his dreams Anton could not run. One day a woman appeared at the soldier's bedside: his Colleen. She spoke with an unintelligible Irish accent. A thick rope of hair hung down the middle of her back and rippled like a muscle when she moved. Corporal Fine grasped her hand, but Colleen drew back. Anton read fear on her face, revulsion. This man had been her fiancé, now he was broken and hideous. Corporal Fine wept after she left. "There's none so cruel as a pretty woman," he said, catching Anton staring, the only words the corporal ever directly addressed to him. A week later he disappeared.

A tinny ring. Anton startles. It's an alarm clock hidden in the folds of the blanket across Mr. Hart's legs. He slips a hand out of sight and the noise stops. Taking a bottle of pills from the same hiding place, he unscrews the cap, swallows two and tucks the bottle away again.

"Want some tea?"

"No, thank you. But you go ahead and make some for yourself if you like."

"Can't stand the stuff. Reminds me too much of the damn war. Reheated and watered down, or stewed so long you could polish your boots with it. Give me coffee any day."

But he makes no motion towards the kitchen.

"Like a pop, son?" he asks eventually. "All boys like pop." It seems more of a statement than a question. Anton can hardly refuse the old guy twice.

"Sir."

The old man wheels himself through a doorway, leaving Anton alone in the front room. A minute passes. Two. Three. Cupboards open and close, drawers and their contents rattle. But it is not the precise, ordered rattling of a person getting something ready in the kitchen. The noises come in bursts, spasmodic, unpredictable, punctuated with little moans and larger sighs. Anton fidgets. Should he sit down? He could have picked up the photograph, looked it over and replaced it by now.

"Are you okay, Mr. Hart?" He's beginning to wish he hadn't come in. He stares up at the ghastly dolls again, their vacant unblinking eyes. He counts them. Twenty-three in all. There were twenty three dolls, sitting on a wall . . .

"Brought all those back myself."

Anton jumps again, surprised he didn't hear the wheelchair. Sales. All over the world, Mr. Hart's been, picking up those dolls. He makes it sound as though doll-buying has been his occupation. Spent a good deal of time in the Far East. Orient. Trading . . . something.

Were you ever in a battle with the Red Baron? Anton wants to ask.

The old man picks up the bottle of RC Cola he has in his lap, cookies on a plate. Anton can see he is pale and short of breath. It has been a monumental effort. He's grateful he refused the tea, otherwise he'd be here until tomorrow. Mr. Hart sets the cola on the table by the window, his arm trembling violently, then fishes an opener from his pants pocket.

It's frustrating to watch the old man struggle to lever off the bottle cap. Anton fights the urge to take over, he can see it's a matter of pride. Handed the open bottle, he sits down at the table and takes a sip. The cola is warm, which makes it somehow sweeter.

"Have you been here a long time?" He plays with the effervescence on his tongue.

"Longer than you've been around, son. This is my home."

"Longer than fifteen years?" Soda up his nose, bubbles behind his eyes. Anton coughs, and cola shoots out his nostrils. Quickly he wipes an arm across his face. "You haven't been outside in fifteen years?"

"What would I want with outside? Huh, son? Everything I need's inside here, and I can see everything I want to from the window."

Anton narrows his eyes at the old man. He's fooling himself. How can he not feel trapped? How can he not find it suffocating to stay inside all the time? "But the sky. You used to fly around up there."

"That little tent of blue up there. I can see all I want from here, son. All I want."

"Don't you miss being able to fly?" He stares out the window he climbed in through yesterday, at the old man's tent of blue, though today it's more shades of grey and white. It seems so much farther away from inside this room. "I'd give anything to be able to fly." The expanse of the skies, cutting the engine to glide and listen to the wind singing through the rigging wires and struts.

"But it's all up here, son." The ex-pilot taps his head and gives Anton a knowing smile. "It's all up here, son. I can go anywhere I want at a moment's notice. It's all tucked up and stored away in here, ready to be used whenever the fancy takes me."

"But don't you miss freedom? Being able to look up at the blue sky until your eyes water? Don't you miss the feel of the rain on your skin? The sound of the waves crashing against the shore in Stanley Park?"

The old man doesn't answer. Anton takes another sip of his cola, which is beginning to unsettle his stomach.

"Ever been to Salt Spring Island, son?"

"Salt Spring," Anton repeats.

"Ever heard of it, son?"

"No, sir."

"Flunked your geography, son? Salt Spring's one of the Gulf Islands, a little group that sits between here and Vancouver Island. You do know where Vancouver Island is, don't you, son?"

"Yes, sir."

"Always wanted to go back to Salt Spring Island, I have. Live out the rest of my days watching the tide come and go."

Anton fixes waves washing high against rocky cliffs. An island studded with twisted, saltwater-seeking arbutus, trunks flaky red. And in the centre a bubbling, steamy well, rising from the bowels of the earth. In the daytime people gather to wash themselves, feel the heat soaking into their aching bones, their poxy skin, their palsied muscles. People leave refreshed, cured. The blind can see, the sick are strong again, the lame can walk. And the animals go there at night, wading into the bubbles. It's like the baths at the hospital. Nurse Helen's cool fingers, so slender, her soft hands rubbing his tender skin, his wasted flesh. He twitches, clears his throat.

"You were a fighter pilot in the First World War."

"I was a pilot. Yes, son. I was a pilot."

The old man's voice is flat, his animation is leaving him. Embarrassed, Anton looks around the room. He begins nervously shaking his foot.

"All right there, sonny. Don't be going off on me now. No funny turns. Wouldn't know what to do with you. No funny turns now, see."

Anton looks down at his feet. Turns? He isn't likely to have any turns. Though the old man isn't the first person to make this kind of assumption. He feels awkward and angular. The light has gone from the visit. Mr. Hart is looking around the room as if he's never seen it before. He's making a sucking sound with his teeth. Sucking them off his palate. Maybe he's hungry. Maybe he's just a stupid old man whose mind has decomposed. Anton feels embarrassed. He badly wants to leave but doesn't wish to seem rude. He stands up.

"I have to get going now, sir," he says and gestures towards the door.

"No funny turns now, son," the old man mumbles, his face falling slack, his eyes clouded. "No funny turns." His face is vacant, expressionless, a drugged face, this much Anton knows, he's been on both sides of that face, knows the thick-tongued feeling inside, the sense of looking at the world through greasy lenses, struggling to see, to understand, face muscles throbbing with the effort, and then the surrender, the release, the thick fog that quickly takes over. He tiptoes to the door and lets himself out.

Hand on the door to his own apartment, he hears a key turn in the front door. Perfume fills the hallway.

"Good afternoon."

Jasmine. Her pretty red mouth, honey-coloured tresses cinched in a blue bow. In her uniform she reminds him of the WAAFs in England.

"Good afternoon," Anton stammers. "You're looking well." He flushes at the foolishness of his words, grateful for the afternoon's long shadows. She stops, turns to face him, miniature suitcase held in front, hands crossed on the handle. Should he offer to carry it?

"I hear you on the piano," Jasmine says. The colour leaves Anton's face, draining to his feet.

"I'm, well, I'm not really playing, I mean, it's just for my mother, her dance classes. She teaches ballet, you see. And I accompany her." A short laugh, too high, too loud. "I try, that is."

"Not that. I mean the Frankie Laine songs, Guy Mitchell, the songs they play on the radio."

Never again. He won't touch the piano ever again.

"I could give you a few pointers if you like. Some basic chords, short cuts. They're easier than learning to read music." She smiles. Anton's heart swells, clogging his throat.

"You don't have to." Words are like cardboard in his mouth.

She laughs. "You play by ear, don't you?"

"Uh huh." He nods. Language has left him.

"Thought so. I'll be away for a few days. Perhaps we could get together when I get back." Again her smile unravels him. She turns away, steps towards the staircase, then halts, head bent to rummage in her purse. Anton's eyes light on the nape of her neck, golden honey with the sun, the trail of wispy blond curls which have escaped her neat upsweep. If only he could . . . he brings his hand towards his mouth, the desire to touch her overwhelms, makes him dizzy. He can feel her peach-skin softness in his fingertips, the down grazing them, tickling.

"Here it is." She laughs, producing a key and breaking the spell. "Sometime next week, then?" she says and is gone, long, slim legs rushing up the stairs in a whisper of silk. Anton can barely feel the floor as he glides into his apartment and closes the door behind him.

X
___

London: July 1936

Yvonne was in mid-flight when the baby kicked, sending a white-hot flash of pain through her rib cage and knocking the air from her lungs. Bringing her hands to her stomach in reflex, she crouched as slowly as possible. Deep breaths. In through her nose, out through her mouth. She must find her centre of balance again. Lucky her dance was so free-form, the audience had probably not realized anything was amiss, though she was momentarily out of sync with the music. Like other dancers, she was used to covering up her mistakes, turning them into something else. Kitty had told her that only the most experienced balletomane ever spotted missed footwork, simple arabesques substituted for more difficult pirouettes.

Yvonne lifted her head, feeling ashen and shaken, and raised her trembling arms in an arc, pulling herself first to her full height and then up onto her toes. The baby kicked again, an excruciating jar to the base of her spine. Yvonne thought she might vomit, bitter saliva flooding her mouth. She swallowed, shuddered, then shuddered again, the second, intentional movement designed to suggest the same of the first. By the time the band had played out its version of Stravinsky's *Rites of Spring,* the pain had pushed its way into her face, tiny explosions of light in her eyes, and as she exited the stage she was trembling with more than exertion.

Interval. Yvonne had learned from her mother to covet the last spot before the interval, for the wings were then clear of people. But Harold had discovered this served his purpose too. Yvonne ducked sideways now to avoid brushing by him as she rushed off the stage. With Harold you always had to be on the lookout. He had a habit of placing himself — hands, arms, legs, sometimes his entire stocky six-foot body in the girls' way, particularly, or so it seemed to Yvonne, and also, disturbingly enough, to Alexei, in her way. He never made eye contact, never acknowledged that he had touched them, grazed their breasts, buttocks, thighs, the crease at the top of their legs. The girls could hardly complain, it did no good anyway. Harold would shrug his shoulders and start talking to someone else, or, if he'd had too much rum the night before, he might shout, hand some poor girl her cards. And with queues at the soup kitchens miles long, pit closures, shipyards sitting idle, steelworks running at half capacity, the city flooded with folk from up north — there were folk around who'd take your job for half the going rate.

Yvonne had been sidling past Harold for over six months.

It was Ned Metcalf who'd first pushed her Harold's way.

"So what can you do?" Metcalf had moved out from behind his desk to perch on the end of it. He was shorter than she realized, a disagreeable ferret of a man at such close quarters. He reached down and squeezed her knee. Yvonne shrank back in her chair.

"Dance." Her voice sounded small in the office, which seemed, if possible, more cluttered and untidy than before, the characters in the waiting room outside seedier.

"Stand and lift your skirt."

Yvonne turned to look at Alexei, but his jaw was clenched, his mouth, what she could see of it, grim. He wouldn't meet her eyes.

"Your gams, darling. I need to take a butchers. It's what the punters are paying to see."

"But . . ."

"Well, come on. I haven't got all day."

"Don't you want to see a few steps? I could dance a little."

"The skirt, sweetheart, just the skirt."

Yvonne stood and pulled her skirt up slowly, wishing she'd left Alexei with the clowns and freaks in the waiting room. But then he was there to protect her if necessary. A cold draught whipped across her stomach, a door opened some-where. Yvonne fixed her gaze on a pair of Bo Peep crooks resting against the corner, a stupid-looking toy sheep on wheels beside them, and tried to pretend she was elsewhere. Ned Metcalf's slit-like eyes left a trail of heat down her legs.

"Bit skinny, but they'll do. Give us a twirl or two, then."

Yvonne managed a few steps, but her knees were trembling and she lost her balance, had to grab the edge of the desk for support.

"I'm usually better than this," she said, close to tears, the muscles in her legs cold and beginning to spasm.

"You can still hold a bit of a tune, then?" Metcalf was writing something down on a piece of paper.

"Yes."

"Not that the punters'll care much what's coming out your mouth, darlin'." He laughed soundlessly, jumped off his desk and walked back around to sit behind it. He reached for his Woodbines and lit one, drawing the smoke deep into his lungs and closing his mole eyes, pleasure or grimace, she couldn't tell. The noisy clock ticked loudly while they waited.

"Twenty-five shillings a week. Tops. I'll wire the Empire, let 'em know you're on your way." Metcalf tapped ash into what looked like an old powder compact and handed her the piece of paper, then nodded towards Alexei, who was now standing at the window, his stiff shoulder hunched, staring at the soot-blackened brick of the building next door. "Dunno I can do much for your Ruskie friend." He smiled on the last word, mole eyes closed again. Did he ever look anyone in the face? "You'll have to talk to Crouch. Maybe you can come to some arrangement with him."

"Crouch?" Yvonne's skin was crawling. She desperately wanted to go home and take a bath. Ned Metcalf had filthied her with his insinuations, his ferret features, his grubby backstreet office. But where was home? She'd been kipped out on the plush but awkward tip-up seats in the Sadler's Wells theatre for nearly three weeks before finding the courage to come here. Her back and neck ached continuously. Her clothes were creased, her hair, washed with a bar of soap and cold water in a hand basin in the change room, was rough and dull. And now that Alexei was to lose his rooms at the end of the week on top of everything else, they stood every chance of being on the street.

"Harold Crouch. That'll be Mr. Crouch to you. Tell 'im I

sent you down and mention you're Nell Rose's little one. But that you're all growed up now."

When Yvonne walked into the Empire, Alexei trailing behind her, she saw Harold Crouch standing on stage, speaking to a small boy. As she moved closer, the child aged, his features grew thicker, coarser, his arms and legs appeared stubby and out of proportion. Crouch made a show of pulling a large watch from his vest pocket, glancing at it, and waving imperiously to Yvonne and Alexei to wait in the seats. It was clear that Crouch was angry with this strange child; his imposing frame bent towards the boy in an attitude of hostility, and though his words were muffled, they sounded sharp, annoyed. He straightened. One last flourish of his fist dismissed the boy. Though Yvonne had been growing more anxious by the minute, the boy appeared unperturbed throughout Crouch's ranting. The two parted company, and as the boy crossed the stage stiffly and drew closer, something in his face struck Yvonne as familiar. Before disappearing into the wings, he winked and stuck out his tongue, wiggling it. Yvonne blanched. It was the dwarf, minus his bright red beard, from Ned Metcalf's office.

Now Crouch turned to face them, and Yvonne saw that once he had been a handsome man. He was perhaps not so old, but Yvonne had seen the same dissolution scrawled across her mother's face: a slackness about the jaw, a network of red veins across the nose. Still, in his expensive coat, Harold Crouch cut an imposing figure. He nodded to a set of stairs at the edge of the stage, and as Yvonne and Alexei approached, he stretched out his arm and smiled, revealing three gold teeth in a row.

"Put your money where your mouth is, I always say." Up close, Harold Crouch's smile was more of a grin, a stretch in the mask; it never reached his eyes. Yvonne grinned in return and made a gurgling noise in her throat that she hoped passed for a laugh.

But for a busy man, a successful, busy man, and what with Christmas being only a few days away, Harold Crouch was appreciative and kind. He fetched a stool from the wings and sat to watch as she took a turn about the stage, a little stiffly, a little off balance — Metcalf had rattled her, and she was still upset over Alexei's dismissal yesterday from the Vic-Wells Ballet company — and in the end he agreed to let Yvonne dance her way on his stage.

"You a dancer too?" He was filling his pipe, not looking at Alexei, who had retreated to the wings during Yvonne's audition, but clearly addressing him.

"I was," Alexei replied, his eyes fixed somewhere Yvonne couldn't see, a place she was locked out of.

"You know those Russian high kicks?" Crouch paused to strike a match, suck air through his pipe. Clouds of smoke rose around his head, obscuring his expression but not his features. "The Cossack thing." He waved the pipe in Alexei's direction, dismissing him. "You can do those."

He turned to Yvonne, chucked her under the chin. "And you, sweet thing, you can flash your pretty arse and legs in this." He reached into an inside pocket and threw a pink gossamer scarf at her. Yvonne caught it as it floated through the air. It had seams. She turned it around. Armholes. Neckline. It was a flimsy gauze-like gown, no bigger in her hand than a handkerchief, no more substantial than a spider's web. She glanced up at Alexei, but he was still staring into space, his face bloodless. His shoulder acting up again, no doubt. Well, at least he'd be dancing again. Surely she deserved some credit for all her machinations, for enduring a creep like Metcalf. But her pout vanished as she held the airy garment up to her face, and anyway Alexei wasn't looking. As long as it covered the mark on her chest. She reached her hand into the top of her dress and ran her fingers across the nubby, cigar-shaped scar which was still red and angry-looking. The fabric was so fine, perhaps too fine, and silky, like the air she wished to emulate. A slow smile spread across her lips. Isadora, thought Yvonne, feeling excited, a warm glow stealing through her. I'll dance like Isadora Duncan.

In the dressing room, Yvonne now turned sideways to glance at her reflection. There was definitely a bump. She rubbed her hand slowly across her stomach. A baby. Hers and Alexei's. She was possibly harming the child, continuing to dance this late into her pregnancy. She'd kept pushing back the date she planned to give up working, convincing Alexei that the extra money would come in handy when there were three mouths to feed and only one wage. And she was so young, so well-trained — two performances six nights a week and practice every afternoon — and the muscles in her stomach so per-versely strong that she was still, at the end of her seventh month, carrying her child high up under her rib cage, tight as a ball.

The kicks were unusual. How they had laughed together over their indolent baby, hiding their private fears. "Perhaps he will be a painter or a musician," Alexei had said, his large, graceful hands cupped over her belly. "She will be the most beautiful girl in the world and will grow into the most beautiful woman," Yvonne dreamed aloud. "Wealthy suitors will throw themselves at her feet, and she will spurn them all, waiting for a prince." She leaned over to kiss his lips. "A Russian prince, of course." Alexei had laughed and rubbed her belly again, but the shadows were back in his eyes.

Yvonne sensed a movement. The dressing room door was ajar. She turned her head. There was Harold, his overcoat and scarf on, as usual, pipe in his hand. He was even wearing his hat. She wanted to knock it off his head.

"Gaining weight, I see." Harold nodded towards her stomach and pushed his way into the room. He closed the door behind him. Yvonne took a step backwards, bumped up against the costume rack. Dusty skirts tickled the backs of her legs, hangers poked her shoulder blades. Her eyes never left his face.

Harold laughed. "Not scared of me, are you, Yvonne?" He stuck his pipe in his mouth and began unbuttoning his overcoat. Yvonne was horrified. Harold always kept his coat on. It was the only thing anyone had ever seen him wear. That and his hat, a dusty Homburg, which he did take off. Winter, spring, and now summer, Harold wore that coat. It was a source of humour for the performers, the regulars and those who returned to the Empire after a season at the seaside or a tour of the Home Counties or up north. What, besides that big old ugly pocket watch to which he referred dramatically several times a day, did Harold wear under his coat? At first glance the coat seemed nice, camel-coloured, at least part cashmere. But on closer inspection — and Yvonne had been forced many times to stand too close to Harold at the side of the stage, awaiting her cue — one discerned cigar-ash smudges and tiny burn holes. The cuffs were threadbare and dirty.

Harold was barely two feet away. The coat fell open, and Yvonne spied a cardigan. Grandfatherly. Absurd. There were probably leather patches at the elbows. Nervous, she barked a short, harsh laugh, then bit down on the insides of her cheeks as Harold's face darkened. He took his pipe from his lips and peered into the bowl.

"I can't have you prancing about my stage in that condition. How's it going to look?" He stared down at her then, awaiting a response. Yvonne was too frightened to say anything. "And if you go, that sour-faced husband of yours goes too." *Hus-band.* He drew the word out, mocking her. Of course Harold knew the truth, he paid both their wages. He moved his mouth into a smile, the three gold teeth menacing in the changing room's cheap half-light.

"Is it too late to get rid of it? I know someone. And I could pay. If you . . ." He took another step closer. If Yvonne moved back any further, she would fall into the skirts and dresses on the hangers. Harold touched her arm, rubbed it.

"There's something special about you, princess." Yvonne caught the sour-sweet smell of last night's rum and orange on his breath but didn't dare turn away. "They come and go, all the girls, strutting their wares in front of old Harold. But you're not like them. You have something the others don't." He held his pipe, unlit, in the corner of his mouth and continued to speak. "Call it talent, call it class if you like. It just shines through everything you do out there. The punters know it too." He bent his face close to hers, and Yvonne thought he might want to kiss her. "You and me, princess, we could go places together." Stale tobacco now combined with the rum. Yvonne felt nausea rising. She wiped her hand across her mouth, the memory of Mortimer Jackson's wet kisses. "He can't look after you the way I can. He's too taken up with 'imself. He can't give you all the things you deserve."

His eyes flashed with desire and something else, something she could almost, if they were somewhere else, if Harold were someone else, have called love.

She pushed down the urge to knee him in the groin. She'd be on the street, as would Alexei. The baby pummelled at her bladder, then pushed at her ribs, anxious to be free. She could almost feel her stomach pushing outwards, towards Harold, the baby finally asserting its presence.

"Have the kid if you want. I'll still look after you," he said, stroking her cheek. And then Harold kissed her. It was a long, hard, passionate kiss. At least on his part. Yvonne held herself rigid. She felt one hand around the back of her head. Where was the other? Still holding onto the pipe? The kiss lasted an eternity. Yvonne's head filled with a prayer: *Please God, don't let him come in. Please God, don't let Alexei see me like this.* Finally, frustrated by her inertia, Harold pulled away. Sadness crossed his slack features, or perhaps it was just a trick of the light. Harold walked out of the dressing room without looking back. Yvonne covered her face with her hands and began to cry.

"Tell Harold I quit." The sun, already high in the sky, had turned the stale air in the room hot. Alexei opened the window, letting in a small breeze and the sickly sweet stench from the soap factory two streets over. They boiled up animal bones from the slaughterhouses, or so the woman from the room next door, her lazy eye flitting aimlessly, had told Yvonne. Yvonne's legs felt heavy and restless under the bedcovers, irritation rustled like a small animal up and down her chest. The baby had dropped in the night, and her stomach now ballooned. She prodded her new girth, surprisingly hard, as if someone had wedged a leather rugby ball beneath her skin. A bump off-centre, near her belly button, a tiny elbow — or was it a knee? — sticking out sideways. She stretched out stiff fingers. Her hands were swollen, her skin binding, her breathing shallow and rapid. Why didn't he turn around? She flung out her arms, thumping the bed with her balled up fists. Christ, it was hot in here. She picked up Alexei's pillow, still warm from his head.

"I'm not going in," she screamed through the threadbare ticking, the ancient dusty feathers. "Ever. Never, ever again." She pulled the pillow from her face to catch her breath, gauge his reaction. He had his back to her still, was filling the kettle, lighting the stove. Now her throat was sore, throbbing. What was wrong with him? Why didn't he say anything? Yell at her, throw things. Her mother would have cuffed her across the mouth, the stones in her rings cutting her lips. Anything would be better than this cold silence.

"Did you hear me?"

"Yvi," he began, back to her still, "it's okay. It's for the best anyway." He sounded worn out. Yvonne sensed he was keeping his temper in check. He never exploded at her, but the strain of preventing himself from doing so seemed to be slowly wearing him out. A fret of fine lines now splayed out from the corners of his eyes. In daylight his skin appeared dull and thinner, the flesh beneath it wasted. And he favoured his right shoulder, often wincing in pain when he thought Yvonne wasn't looking.

"But the money?"

"I said that it is okay. Do you not think I can provide for my family, for you and our son?"

"Daughter."

Alexei turned and smiled, as if at a wayward child. How old he looks, Yvonne thought, as she slipped further beneath the covers. "Our child, sweet Yvi. Boy or girl, it is our child." He handed her a mug of hot, sweet tea, poured some into a thermos for himself. He wrapped the remaining heel of bread with dripping in paper and stuffed the thermos and package inside the bag with his change of costume and towel. On Tuesdays and Thursdays he gave private lessons to the daughter of a cabinet minister. The man's wife had admired Alexei's dancing, had attended every Vic-Wells performance. It had taken her nearly four weeks to track him down after he'd left. She'd been waiting for him backstage after one of his Cossack routines. Her pity had been almost more, so Alexei had told Yvonne, than he could bear. Only by exercising immense self-control had he stopped himself from cursing her, walking away. Instead, he'd listened, head turned aside, while she offered him work. The money was sure to come in handy and — here she'd lain her hand on his — it would give him a chance to keep up with his ballet, draw something, at least, from all his years of training.

Yvonne took a sip of tea, put it down on the floor, sighed, and rolled over. It would be after midnight before he returned. What would she do with herself for the next twelve hours?

"I could come with you to your la-di-da lady's," she said to the window, the intense blue sky. The woman would be sure to serve tea and fancies. On real china. "I could just sit in the corner. I'd be ever so quiet."

"You know that is not possible, my sweet." He was leaning over her now. She would not turn her face towards him. "Bye, Yvi. Rest well." He planted a small kiss in her hair. Instantly Yvonne's chest ached, swelled with painful longing to pull him to her, cover his face with hot kisses, feel his hands, firm and warm, spread across the width of her belly. But instead she remained stubbornly put, face to the wall, with its water-stained wallpaper, its square of azure in the middle. The door opened and then the latch clicked shut. Slowly the room filled with the sounds of cars and people going about their work, newspaper vendors and delivery boys on bicycles.

When Yvonne opened her eyes again, the shadows in the room had lengthened and shifted. The air felt stiller, tasted staler than before. She licked her lips, her mouth dry and sticky. Outside the door, someone cleared his throat. Yvonne lifted her head from the pillow. Was someone outside? How long had he been there? Had he been rapping on the door? Is that what had woken her? As if in answer there came a sharp knock, insistent, as though the caller were losing patience. The landlady? Did they owe rent? Had Alexei left a black soap ring in the tub again? Sitting up proved difficult with her new girth, each breath a struggle, as if the child were bent on pushing the air from her lungs and jamming the entrance. She swung her legs over the side of the bed, stiff and slow from sleeping the day away, not limbering up. She hadn't even stretched after last night's performance, had quickly slurped a mug of cocoa, refusing Alexei's cooking, curled up in bed and prayed for sleep. She was, she realized now, quite hungry. Whoever was on the other side of the door rapped again.

"Coming," Yvonne called, her voice still snagged on the edges of sleep.

"Miss Hoyfield. Oh, Miss Hoyfield, open up, please." A man's voice, no one she knew. Young. Someone caught between boy and man. No time to change out of her nightdress. She reached for her cardigan, stumbled over a basket of Alexei's laundry, dusty tights and sweaty leotards, a pair of French flag red underpants.

"Miss Hoyfield, I know you're in there." How did he know? Yvonne yawned and rubbed her face with her hands. Had he been watching the front door?

"Who is it?"

"I have a message for Yvonne Hoyfield."

"Who from?"

"My name is Charles."

"I don't know any Charles."

"Oh, but you do." The voice sounded so near, yet so distant. She opened the door a crack, peered into the hallway. It was empty. The boy-man had vanished. Yvonne frowned. Had the voice been in her mind? She pinched herself. Not dreaming. She was about to push the door closed when some-one again cleared his throat. Yvonne looked down, then jumped back, alarmed. It was the red-haired dwarf who hung around Harold's office sometimes, slipping in and out of the building on his evil little feet. Immediately she grabbed at the latch and tried to throw her weight against the door. Too late. With a power far beyond his size, the dwarf pushed his way past Yvonne and into the room.

"Charles Randolph Fraser." He held out a miniature hand. Yvonne drew back, pulling her cardigan closed across herself, fingers brushing her scar. She'd never spoken to him, never really been this close before, but had often felt his eyes on her as she slipped to and fro between stage and dressing room. She fingered her scar like a talisman.

"What do you want?"

"I have something for you." No longer muffled by the wooden door, his voice seemed squashed and tinny, as if his head, too large, too adult for his stubby body, was trapped inside a metal box. She would have laughed had his glass-green eyes not transfixed and frightened her so.

He produced a grubby envelope. Grubby from his hands or Harold's? Yvonne clasped her arms tighter.

"I don't want his money." Was it payment, or was Harold trying to buy her silence? Either way, she wanted nothing to do with it.

"Not yet, maybe." The little man smirked. Close-up he looked about forty. "But later, when the bairn is born. Might come in useful then." He made no attempt to give it to her but moved towards the deal table on his stiff little legs, taking stiff little steps, and, first pushing aside last night's dirty dishes, he placed the envelope there.

Yvonne blanched as if chastised. She picked the envelope up

and held it out to him. "I want you to leave. And take his filthy money with you. I don't need it."

Charles Randolph Fraser raised one bushy eyebrow and glanced around the room. "My instructions are to leave the money, Miss Hoyfield. You must return it yourself if that's what you wish." He waddled back towards the door. "Oh." He turned to face her again, his mouth pulled back in a sour grin. "Mr. Crouch says you can have your old job back any time." He paused. "Your dancing job, that is." With surprising agility he then skipped out the door and quickly pulled it to behind him. The mug Yvonne had picked up to hurl at him hit the door instead, exploding. Hundreds of shards shot across the linoleum, dregs of tea ran down the scarred paintwork. The damn envelope, she realized, was still in her other hand.

"I hate you," she screamed, throwing it at the door, where it burst on impact, sending bank notes fluttering into the tea dregs and pottery shards. Yvonne stared, stupefied. It was an insane amount of money, money such as she'd never seen before in her life. It could not possibly all have come from honest sources.

God, how she wanted her mother. Wanted her here, now, holding her hand, stroking her head, whispering that things were going to be all right. When she wanted, Nell could be so kind, so gentle, so loving. And where was she now? Was she even still alive? Ned Metcalf could help find her. She'd go see him now. Her mother needed her, Yvonne was sure of it. She padded to the closet, wincing as splinters of the mug worked their way into her feet. A bloody pattern tracked across the floor as she gathered the fallen bills, stuffing them back inside the envelope. She'd give the money to her mother. Nell probably needed it more than she did.

For the bairn.

But when she pulled her nightdress over her head, a picture of Mortimer Jackson crowded her mind. And as Yvonne felt again the great weight of him pinning her down, constricting her chest, a fierce tattoo of pain began beating at her lower back.

What in God's name was happening? "Alexei," she whimpered in alarm as warm water rushed down her legs. Yvonne dressed slowly, terrified lest sudden movement release more water, maybe even blood. The baby wasn't due for another two months. She pulled her cloak around her shoulders and slipped out the door. She had to find Alexei. Something was horribly wrong.

XI

Vancouver: June 1952

A short, sharp pain stabs the back of his neck. Anton's been shot. He dives for cover as a barrage begins. Half a dozen rear shooters at least. Curling into a ball, he tries to stay hidden while a hail of tiny shells lands in a pitter-patter around him. Victims cry out or cuss, the shooters and their cronies laugh and jeer, egging each other on.

Crack, crack, crack.

Now someone is jumping on empty popcorn boxes, making them pop. Anton rubs at the back of his neck, which still stings. It was a good shot, hard and fast. Anton feels with his fingertips; a tiny welt now marks the spot.

The rain of peas has stopped. The shooters must be out of ammo. Anton waits for the raiders to switch weapons or tactics. Someone bangs the back of his seat, scuffles, raccoon in the undergrowth. He tenses, can almost feel himself rise and clamber over the back of his seat, the tip-up portion snapping closed on his legs as he leans over in a single moment of glory and grabs a fistful of guerrilla hair. But such a fleeting kingship would hardly be worth the reprisals. The noise behind him retreats, Anton lets out his breath as an empty popcorn box hits him in the shoulder. Again he grits his teeth. He should scoop the peas up, filch a straw from an empty pop bottle and fire back. After all, the darkness gives him anonymity.

Revenge.

Off the seat he slips, onto the floor, kneeling painfully on five or six rock-hard peas, and puts his hand on a wad of chewing gum, dirt from kids' shoes, a jawbreaker, sticky and covered in grit. He lobs it away in disgust, but it won't leave him, remains stubbornly stuck to his fingers. He wipes his hand on the vacant seat next to his own. The jawbreaker releases its hold and rolls away, but the sticky stuff left behind has now picked up a layer of cinema seat fuzz, like a second skin.

Anton sighs, closes his eyes. He should have known better, come in the evening. But evening performances cost more, and surrounded by couples smooching in the dark, he'd feel even more alone than he does right now. He peers at the screen through the crack between the seats. Is it worth trying to watch the rest of the movie? Gary Cooper's mouth is moving. He could be singing or screaming for all Anton can tell, the sound track lost in a theatre filled with shrieking kids. It's too slow for them. Forty minutes in and not a single shot fired. And it's in black and white.

Anton wants to wash his hands. The sticky one smells

faintly of aniseed and kid breath. How juvenile this whole matinee scene is. If he leaves by the bottom exit now, he can escape down the alley, walk back down Twelfth Avenue, cross Granville and pass the theatre on the other side of the road before the rest of the rabble leave.

He fishes around with the sticky hand — no point getting the other dirty — but can't feel his library books. They should be sitting beneath his seat. He sticks his head under for a look. Nothing. Had he accidentally kicked them away? Or has someone moved them? Worse, stolen them, ripped the covers off, flushed the pages down the toilet. He scans the floor to either side and under the rows behind him for telltale shadows. Nothing but candy wrappers, pop bottles and popcorn boxes. Please don't let them be stolen, he thinks. How will he ever pay for them? He sits back in his seat, sticky hand forgotten, and stares blankly at the screen. He'll have to wait until the lights come up. The library will be bound to send notice. Will it be in his name or his mother's? Will the library consider him old enough to accrue debt, or is it like voting, you have to reach eighteen first? There's nothing else for it, he'll have to intercept the mail, his first step toward a sock drawer full of unanswered letters, piled-up bills. And how exactly is he going to explain the loss of his borrowing privileges? His stomach gurgles and whines. All he can taste is stale popcorn.

A large clock fills the screen. There are a lot of clocks in this movie. And so far no fight scenes. No love scenes, either. From the look on Grace Kelly's face as she climbs the inn's stairs to visit the Spanish woman, Gary Cooper won't be getting kissed any time soon. Suddenly a black spot appears over the Rodriguez woman's head. It moves across the screen from her face to Grace's, a vacuum of space appears between them. Kids in the back rows — the shooters? — catcall, others join them, cheer, stomp their feet. Another black shadow hovers, then another. Now giant black wings.

Anton's chest fills with dread.

Butterfly ghosts. Nature's revenge.

He'd pinned them to the card the way Harold had told him to. *Straight through the 'eart, lad, they don't feel a thing.* And there they'd lain, perfectly still and brilliant, two monarchs and a swallowtail. He'd tucked them away in the cupboard, the card leaning against the back of a shelf. *Dry 'em in the dark. Keeps their colour.* And, caught up in the excitement of a boy's world, of Harold's erratic and short-lived attentions, he had forgotten all about them for two days. A mad flutter of iridescent wings when next he opened the door. Horrified, he slammed it shut. They were still alive. Harold had lied to him. Nearly two weeks passed before he dared open the door again, by which time the butterflies' wings were in tatters, pieces broken off where they'd struggled first against the pins that held them and then against the cupboard doors, battering themselves to death. For how long? Anton had taken his butterfly net and flung it into the field behind their apartment building. Harold had strapped him for being ungrateful.

The screen is almost obscured now. "Moths," an excited voice shouts. Some kid's science project, or had the moths been captured simply for this end — to be set loose in a movie theatre, where, following instinct, they would fly towards the projector light? What a waste of energy. Kids start to boo. Some shout, stand, throw things. The soundtrack garbles, the picture shudders, and the lights come up. Now, unless they pay again, no one will know if the townspeople come to Will Kane's aid, help him run Frank Miller and his cronies out of town. Though Anton supposes they must. Or they don't deserve him. He hunkers down in his seat to wait until the theatre empties. It was difficult to concentrate on the story anyway with so much on his mind. He wants badly to share Jasmine and the old pilot with somebody, with Elliot, perhaps. Briefly he wonders whether, if Elliot Nelson had been here watching *High Noon* with him instead of sick in hospital or at home or wherever he is with polio, they would together have joined in the ruckus.

The theatre is almost empty. Anton looks up to find the usher pointing at his watch. "It's time to leave. Matinee finished ten minutes ago." It didn't really finish, though, Anton thinks as he explains his plight. He waits in the foyer while the usher conducts a search. He uses the bathroom to wash his hands, check behind the toilets. The usher returns. Nothing. Could he leave his name and telephone number? If the books are found he'll be contacted. Could he write down the titles? Anton squirms, remembering the babyish pictures in the piano books he fingered and left behind. Thank God. *Good-bye to All That*, he scribbles down. A memoir by Robert Graves, he liked what he read of it. *A Short History of World War I*. Dry and factual, but it would give him a general overview. It's the George A. Drew book that he was really interested in. *Canada's Fighting Airmen*. If the old guy was a World War I flying ace, he'd surely be mentioned somewhere in there. But when he flicked through the introduction in the line-up by the circulation desk, figures had jumped out at him. By the end of the war, Canadian pilots had accounted for one-third of the more than thirty thousand officers in the Royal Air Force. An impressive percentage, considering the country's population. But unless Lieutenant Thomas J. Hart had distinguished himself in some way, finding out about him would be like looking for a needle in a haystack.

Anton peers out the glass doors at the front entrance to the Stanley. The stick lads and the kids with no summer jobs or organized activities to keep them occupied have, to his relief, cleared off. He squints as he leans into the door and the bright, hot sunlight hits him full in the face, making his eyes water, his nose prickle and smart. A bookless summer yawns before him. And who's to say, come September, that he won't be barred from the library at school? Libraries surely protect their own, close ranks, pass on information concerning tardy borrowers, those who underline passages, doodle in the margins, write cryptic messages on the fly-leaf. He could, he thinks, apply for a new card under Anton Kavanov. But he has as yet no identification with his new name; he has, in fact, no idea at all of how to go about legally changing his name.

The further Anton walks up Granville Street, the further from the Stanley and the library he is, the stronger he feels his loss, his exile from the land of books. Already he misses the library's comforting familiarity, the dusty shelves, the low-pitched hum of the overhead lights, the scowling librarian, the large sign reading SILENCE. Whole histories of the world on those shelves, of battles lost and won, the rise and fall of nations and generals, the heaving up of mountain ranges, the cleaving of continents, the marvel of the steam engine, the miracle of flight. And on the pages themselves, other, smaller histories, the collective scent of dozens of homes. A spill of juice? tea? bath water? Or something more ominous: sweat? blood? A scrape of mud. How did that get there? Pithy comments on the text, or smutty ones. Swear words tucked between longer, staider passages, passing comment, and once, an entire hand outlined in pen, the hand traceable by fingertips for several pages. That writer had wanted to leave his mark.

Of course it's a he, girls don't mark up books, have no desire to leave traces of themselves everywhere like spoor. Or do they? He climbs the wooden steps and turns the handle on the grand old door and steps into the cool, dark hallway. He sniffs the air, thinking of Jasmine and how her perfume leaves a trail through the building so her presence remains long after she's gone.

Anton opens his apartment door. The piano accompanist is here. Deft, keen notes, chop chop, full chords. He tiptoes past the dance practice room to his bedroom at the back of the house. If his mother hears him, she will rope him in to listen, learn a few things. She can afford to pay this woman to come only on Saturdays for the time being and wishes to extract as much from her as she can. But if he must learn anything on the piano, Anton would rather chase Jasmine's fingers up and down the keys.

He releases the handle on his bedroom door slowly, silencing the telltale click. She's been in here again, clothes have been folded and put away or whisked into the laundry hamper. His neck tenses. They've had words over this before. He's almost sixteen, other boys have bedrooms they can call their own. Always the same response. What can you possibly have to hide? Rubbing the fingers of her right hand with her left the way she does these days. What would you want to hide from me? At times, sensing his resistance, his pulling away from her, she's even shed tears. Why does he want to push her out, his own mother? After all she's done for him. It leaves him hollowed out, watching her cry. He never once saw her cry when Harold yelled at her, not even when he hit her, at least not at the time. Anton admired her mettle, her stoicism, understood her wish never to give Harold the satisfaction of seeing her crumble. The breakdown would come later, shrouded in the dark and silence of night, when she would crawl into Anton's bed, hold him so tightly he could hardly breathe and soak the back of his pyjama top with her tears.

He glances towards his desk. Clean. The flotsam from his end-of-term papers, his study notes, all jogged together at one end, books closed and neatly stacked. A clutch in his stomach. His love poem. The one he'd been writing for Jasmine. Please let me have hidden it, he prays, flicking through the papers, shaking the books for loose leaves. What if she's discovered it, pocketed it to pull it out as ammunition later? Aha! But I know what you've been up to, you lowlife, you scummy weasel, you filthy lech. He can see his mother in the corner of the kitchen, her mouth an ugly slash of red as she spits out these words, the cold emptiness in her eyes.

But Anton isn't any of those things. Or is he? Is it possible that he has, over the years, grown more like Harold than like his real father? After all, virtually all he can recall of the man is his long, graceful hands, the puzzling trail of shawl in his arms. How is it he can he see himself being held?

He steps over to his bed, slips his hand an arm's length under the top right corner of the mattress. His fingers touch the edge of paper, good. He sits on the floor and picks up the silver-framed photograph of his father, needing suddenly to find comfort there. Thoughts of Harold always chafe. He stares at the picture for a moment, trying to conjure a memory of the kind face that stares back at him. Unlike Harold, his father would never have hurt a gentle soul, would never have raised a hand to strike his mother, would never have put him in that place in the mountains. And Alexander Kavanov would never have deliberately hurt his family by stepping onto a chair, slipping his head through a noose, kicking the chair away. Never.

I found him swinging.

The cords on Harold's neck stand out in his mind vividly, the tiny black hairs in his nose, the greasy film on his skin, the biliously sweet rum and orange on his breath. Anton had taken a trembling step backwards. Half of Harold's face was grinning, the other half sad and slack, his three gold teeth now almost hidden behind a drooping half-mouth. Harold had, so he said, lisping, slurring his words, found Anton's father in the basement of the Flamingo Club, a grotty little revue theatre somewhere outside Doncaster. Harold's drunken lisp disguised the venom of his words, gave them more the feel of a shared confidence.

Anton pulls himself up onto the bed, straightens his spine, breathes in deeply. The air in his room is still and stuffy, it makes him dizzy, he can feel the pulse throbbing in his temple. *Stiff as the balls on a brass monkey. His neck was like this, lad.* Harold had made a vertical stretching motion with his hands. *Must've been a full sixteen inches.* Anton sets the photograph back on his bedside table. Lying bastard. How could a neck stretch so long? Sixteen inches. Two notches on his desk mark the distance, which is now the length of Anton's leg from the crease of his thigh to the top of his knee. It's the same sixteen inches from the bottom of his knee to the crease of his foot, his good foot, that is. Lying bastard, he thinks again.

Standing to straighten the covers on the bed, he notices a small buff-coloured envelope, invisible before in the bed-spread's busy pattern. "Son" scrawled across the front in shaky letters. Mr. Hart? No one else calls him son. But Mr. Hart can't have been in his room. He must have left the envelope with his mother. Here, something for your son. We've had quite the chat, he crawled in through the window the other day, picked me up from the floor, dusted off my teeth and handed them to me. Nice kid, missus. Anton cringes. His mother isn't the type to stand on anyone's stoop passing the time of day, likes to keep the neighbours at arm's length. You don't know who you can trust, she's always telling him.

He picks the envelope up, the shape and conspicuous weight of the object inside tells him it's no letter. He tears open the seal, pulls out an old-fashioned key, the long-barrelled type with hang-down teeth, the kind of key that opens only ancient doors down dark alleys, musty cellars or lean-to sheds, the loo in the corner of the yard back in the old country, though no one ever locked it anyway, at least not from the outside. There's no note, no explanation. But the key must fit a door somewhere, else why offer it up? His mother might know more, but Anton would rather avoid her until the accompanist leaves.

Back into the heat, the eye-swelling brightness outside. He pauses on the top step to peer in at the Harts' bay window. Someone's moving about in there. He leans closer, then jumps back at the sharp rap of knuckles on the window. Clarice Hart's face appears, mouth moving, there's no mistaking her anger, head bobbing, finger wagging. He smiles and sticks out his tongue. She disappears, and he rushes down the front steps and around the side of the house to the garden at the back, half laughing, half afraid.

The key does not fit the lock on the garden shed, and anyway the door is fastened with a thick chain and padlock. Anton steps towards the crack where the door meets the jamb and sniffs. Probably filled with past tenants, layers of them, tags on their toes: name, date of birth, apartment number, method of execution. He tosses the key in his hand, liking the solid weight of it. Now where? He looks back at the house. A lace curtain blows gently in and out of the window above the Harts' apartment. Jasmine. But she isn't due back until tomorrow. Strange she would leave her window wide open while she's away. He pockets his key. Now, why couldn't it lead to more interesting possibilities, such as Jasmine's place? He smiles, imagining himself opening her door, stepping inside, a trail of blossoms pulling him into a room filled with billowing lace. The intoxicating scent of lilacs. Jasmine, barefoot, in a dress as light as summer, weaves in and out of the ethereal fabric. Anton feels his skin prickle, a tug of desire between his legs.

He pulls his hand from his pocket, shuffles, clears his throat. Anyone watching? He squints at the Harts' bedroom windows, his own and his mother's, the railings between them, someone lurking down the basement steps perhaps? The steps, of course. They had to lead to a door of some sort. He crosses the garden quickly, grabs hold of the iron railing that runs down the wall on the side away from the house, and leans, craning his neck. Bingo. A wooden door with an old-fashioned keyhole.

As he descends the steps, he picks up the earthy smell of decay, the sharper sting of mould in the back of his throat. The key fits, but it won't turn. He shakes the door, but it's stuck fast, the wood swelled with the heat and moisture. He jiggles the key, but now that's stuck too; it won't turn, it won't release. Anton kicks the door in frustration. Then, both hands on the stubborn key, he throws his weight against it. A crack of old wood and the door suddenly gives, pitching him inside, the momentum hurling him to the floor. As he lies sprawled on the damp earth watching, the door swings back heavily and shuts with a scrape and a thud.

Darkness.

It's black as pitch. And cold, the floor feels almost wet. Tiny legs dance across his fingers, splayed to break his fall. He flings creatures from him in horror. Don't panic. It's only the dark, the dark can't hurt you, only what's in the dark. He jumps at a touch on his shoulders. Cold fingers? No one's here, no one's here, he tells himself. It's only a basement, there's no one here, only the rats. He stiffens, surprised by the cry of his own voice in the dark, how the walls throw it back and the damp concrete floor muffles it. He has no sense of the size of where he is, the space around him; he dare not reach behind for fear of finding walls, of finding nothing at all. Now the shape of a window emerges to the side of the door he can no longer see. Cloth has been tacked over it, and it is through this that the outside light now filters. Slowly he gets to his feet, steps towards the door, arms stretched out before him. He clutches at the air, groping for obstacles, for the door, the wall. A box, fingers scrabble, a switch, he flicks it upwards, and a light comes on above his head.

He squints, though the light is not bright, and turns. Now, slowly, as the fuzziness clears from his eyes, he can make out his dungeon. Boxes upon boxes line the right-hand wall, disappearing into shadows along the back. On the left a couple of large sea-chests, one stacked atop the other, then a monstrous, hulking shadow beyond them, the furnace, no doubt. He moves further in. A workbench with tools. And in the middle, furniture. Desks and tables and lamps, a chest of drawers, a man. Anton opens his mouth to scream, then giggles, giddy with terror, with relief. A dummy. It's a dressmaker's dummy wearing a hat. He's still shaking a little, laughing at his jumpiness, his overactive imagination, when, out of the corner of his eye he sees it, leaning up against the wall.

A bicycle.

This must be his reward, his medal for rescuing the old man. It's the bicycle. It has to be. There's nothing else here for him that makes much sense, and the bicycle, well, it's just something the old man would understand. Mobility. The key is for this bicycle. For the briefest moment his heart lifts but, as he draws closer to the bike, sinks back into his stomach. It's an ancient contraption. Where it isn't orange with rust, its paint is so grime-encrusted he cannot make out its colour. There's a tear in the seat, both tires are flat, and the chain, loosed from its sprockets, trails on the floor. In his bicycle dreams he has always seen shiny chrome mudguards flashing in the sun, black tires ringed with a sharp white band, a royal blue frame and a blue and white saddle, and nothing at all resembling this sad old rusted beast.

Grasping the handlebars, Anton pulls the bike away from the wall. In a series of soft clicks the chain comes off entirely to puddle in a small heap on the floor. Kneeling, he struggles to fit the links over the sprockets, front and rear. Not only is it old, but the bicycle obviously hasn't been used in years. The oil on the chain is so dry it flakes off in his hands. He gets to his feet and wipes his hands down his pants. Then, standing to the right of the bicycle, hands on the handlebars, he throws his left leg over the seat the way he's seen kids at school do. He isn't left handed, and it doesn't feel quite right, but he doesn't fully trust his right foot, isn't sure he can push off with it. And sure enough, the weight distribution is all wrong. The moment his right leg leaves the ground, he begins to keel over, bike and all.

Thwuump.

Again his hands break his fall, and this time they smart; he's grazed his knuckles. But no matter, his pride is hurt more than anything else. He stands, picks up the bike and tries again, this time throwing the right leg over and balancing on his left. Better. At least his bum is connected with the seat. But pushing off isn't so easy, either. His foot slips, the wheels wobble, and once again he hits the unforgiving floor, falling to the right and landing soundly on his hip, his feet hopelessly entangled in pedals and the chain, which has fallen off again.

Extricating his legs, Anton shuffles away from the fallen bike and pulls up his pant legs to check for bruises. The skin on the right leg is broken in a series of tiny crimson tracks, pricks of blood are swelling, and beneath them a welt, his second today, but this one angry, livid, and rising before his eyes across the tender inside edge of his shinbone.

He struggles to his feet and rights the bike against the wall, partway behind the furnace where he found it. He turns out the light, pulls the stiff door to and locks it. He can't even ride a bicycle. His leg is stinging and thumping, it hurts to put weight on that foot. And he's dangerously close to tears. He needs to bathe the wound away from his mother's prying eyes, her fluttering hands, the weight of her solicitude.

Leaning heavily on the iron railing, Anton pulls himself up the steps. Clouds are rolling in, and the wind has changed course and picked up. Jasmine's lace curtain blows in and out above his head, like a hand waving him in. If she were home now she'd look after him, tend his wounds, hold him in her arms. He looks up at the waving curtain again. What if it rains while she's gone? Her things could be ruined. He could go up there and close the window for her, tend to the wound on his leg in private. In and out. It wouldn't take more than a minute or so. Five at the most. And she'd never know he'd been there.

XII

London: April 1937

The front door opened. Yvonne heard the thump of her beloved's worn leather satchel as it dropped to the floor. More dusty, sweaty tights to rinse and wring out, more dirty practice clothes to launder, the room permanently damp from all the wet washing. As if her hands weren't already chafed raw from scrubbing and boiling Anton's nappies. She sat where she was on the bed, knees up under her chin, blanket over her legs because she'd had to let the fire go out again. He had to come to her. Why did she always have to rush to greet him? Why should the high point of her day involve flinging the door wide, arms open, face upturned for a kiss, dinner on the table? He'd changed since Anton had been born. He no longer scooped her into his arms when he came home; she couldn't remember the last time he'd taken her hand and kissed her fingertips; he had not called her his English rose in months. Lately, things had grown worse. When he returned from Harold's club at midnight, sometimes later — walking some chorus girl home? — he no longer climbed straight into bed to warm her still icy legs with his hot-blooded ones, cup her body so they lay like two spoons in a drawer. There were no more nights filled with tender kisses across the back of her neck, kisses that could coax her to abandon, lull her back to sleep.

Now he stayed by the window, watching for dawn, smoking cigarette after cigarette, the hollows in his cheeks growing deeper, his arms and legs ever more emaciated. Sometimes he'd sing what she could only suppose were Russian lullabies, rocking Anton while he slept in his bassinet.

It was one of the few things she'd bought with Harold's money. There was nothing else to spend it on except Anton's numerous hospital visits, the yards of bandages and sticking plaster he required. Alexei wouldn't hear of her spending any on herself or on him. She'd accused him of hypocrisy. But he'd fixed his eyes on her, there was a hunted look about him these days. "Poverty marks children, Yvi," he'd said. "As surely as the pox or club feet."

Yvonne cocked her head, listening jealously to the low murmur of father greeting son. Anton laughed, a rare sound, he was usually such a sullen child, though he followed his father adoringly with his eyes, lifted his arms to be picked up, swung around. A sigh, some muttered foreign curse. Alexei strode quickly over to the bed, he was holding Anton out before him, those absurd plaster of Paris boots dangling on the ends of the child's skinny blue-white legs. Yvonne grimaced.

"Did you take him to the hospital?" The vein in Alexei's temple was throbbing.

Hospital? She'd risen only once to feed Anton and once to bolt to the toilet down the hall, vomit up whatever was left in her stomach from yesterday. The hospital, with its antiseptic stink, was the last place she could bear, dizzy and weak as she was. Alexei set Anton down in the middle of the bed, then sat on the edge and began pulling off his boots, stripping off his practice tights.

"How many times have I asked you this one small thing? When can I take him? It is almost five o'clock. Private lessons, practice, work. I have no time. Now I must go and play filthy Cossack clown for your *Mister* Crouch with his band of drunken hecklers. Why could you not have gone today?"

Because she was tired, because her breasts ached, because she didn't feel like it, because she couldn't bear to look at his feet, stuck up in the air like tadpole tails, bloodless against the fleshy redness of the doctor's palms. How cold and distant she'd felt that first visit. Such a contrast to Alexei, who had volunteered to hold Anton in his lap while the manipulations were carried out and the straps applied. Yvonne had averted her eyes, fingers stuffed in her ears to block out his cries. When, later, manipulation and strapping failed to achieve the desired results and casting was required, she fixed her gaze on the doctor's hands and made believe he was battering fish in a chip shop, dipping the bandages into the plaster, waiting, hands poised in mid-air while the excess dripped off. Only when Anton's feet were covered could Yvonne relax a little.

"Why is it again so cold in here? What did you do all day?" Alexei continued, not waiting for answers. "Anton is cold. And he needs changing. He stinks, Yvi. He stinks like bad fish. Is that what you want for your son? That he stinks like some dirty fish stall?"

"The child is fine," she mumbled. "You fuss too much."

"No, Yvi. You don't fuss enough. This is your problem always. Today he was supposed to be at the hospital. These casts are not being changed enough. Every fortnight he must go. He is always growing, and these" — he reached over and grasped one tiny boot; Anton sucked in his breath — "they must grow with him. He will be crippled otherwise."

"He already is crippled. Can't you see that?"

Alexei got to his feet, walked over to the clothes horse by the fire and began feeling at the nappies drying there. "He has a problem, yes, I agree. But this problem, it can be fixed if you only take him as the doctor asks." He chose a pair of tights and sat back down on the bed to pull them on. "Sometimes, Yvi, I don't think you want him to get better."

"He'll never get better. So what's the point?"

Alexei twisted around to face her. "The *point* of all this is so he knows some freedom to walk, freedom to move about on his own. You want him staggering all the time around like a drunk person? Balancing all his weight on the smallest bones in his feet? You're a dancer, Yvi. You know that these bones cannot bear such a weight. And when he grows older? What then? You will be pushing him around in a barrow, my dear, sweet girl. Pushing your son because he cannot walk for himself because you were too selfish and stubborn for taking him to hospital."

"In case you haven't noticed, I'm not feeling well."

Alexei pulled on his boots in silence. He stood and began rummaging in the bread bin, the cupboard above the stove. He lifted the lid of the teapot, still on the table from this morning. "Is there anything to eat?"

"No."

Another Russian curse. He closed his eyes and leaned on the table for support. "No food, no washing, my son is dirty,

and you sit there like the Sheba Queen." He pinched the bridge
of his nose. "You could spend some of your precious time to
wash these dishes and to train him for the potty."

"The potty? He's nine months old."

Alexei banged his fist on the table. "It's old enough."

Yvonne held her breath as teaspoons scattered, teacups
bounced in their saucers. She braced herself for the dull poof as
they hit the floor. Panic knotted behind her breastbone. The
cups, with their hand-painted roses, an extravagance chosen
and paid for in the rosy afterglow of lovemaking one perfect
spring morning, were the only decent pieces of crockery they
owned.

"At least this way he will stay clean, and his little bottom
will not be so raw."

"You've broken all our cups," she said eventually, her voice
louder than she intended, higher, nearly hysterical.

Alexei's face darkened. "I am speaking about our child."

Yvonne glanced at him, then away, pulled the grubby blanket
further up under her chin. "I don't hear him complaining."

Alexei strode back to the bed, leaned his face close to hers.
"And you think this is something good?" He backed away. "He
doesn't complain about anything, Yvi. He is like a little soldier."

It was true. Unnatural, Yvonne thought, a little frightening
sometimes. Even when she hurt him, pinched him on the back
of the arm, twisting the skin. He would stiffen, but already he
had learned not to cry out. Just stared at her with his wolf's
eyes. Empty eyes. They reminded her of her mother.

Alexei was close to tears. "If I had known you were so lazy
I never would have — " He twisted away to face the window,
its grimy backstreet view.

Lazy? she wanted to scream at him. Lazy? She'd spent a
lifetime cleaning up after her mother. When was it ever going

to be her turn? And housework was nothing but thankless drudgery. It was nearly impossible to keep things clean. Alexei trailed practice gear all over the room. She would find his dance slippers at the foot of the bed when she stretched her toes out at night, on the table where they ate, in the communal bathroom down the hall. If he could be so slovenly, why should she have to be clean and tidy?

"Anyone would think you had been born to better things, the way you won't soil your hands with work."

Yvonne stared at her man gone mad. She hated it when Alexei got so angry. She wanted to hear only tender words of love and praise from him, wanted his body to wrap itself around hers, his lips, sweet lips to caress her neck, her breasts, her belly, her woman's secret. She wanted this noise to stop. But she didn't know how to begin to tell him so; sometimes she thought her mother had hold of her tongue.

"If his having a clean bottom is so important to you, I don't see why you don't change him yourself."

One small look — pity? disgust? Yvonne closed her eyes; some things weren't worth the pain of knowing — and Alexei was out the door, stomping down the stairs. Yvonne leapt out of bed, she was not going to be left alone with Anton again. But the sudden movement made her head spin, her legs were made of cloth; pulling on her boots, her hat and her cape proved more laborious than she had anticipated. When finally she had scooped up Anton and a nearly dry nappy and rushed out the door, she had to lunge first for the banister and then her neighbour's doorframe for balance. Righting herself, she knocked, and when Mrs. Mahoney answered, thrust Anton and the clean nappy into the surprised woman's arms. Mrs. Mahoney sniffed loudly.

"I'll mind 'im but I'll not mother 'im." She thrust out her hand, lazy eye roaming. "This'll cost yer extra."

"I'll pay you when I get back, Mrs. Mahoney," Yvonne called over her shoulder, rushing down the stairs after her man.

But Alexei had already disappeared. There was no sight of him in either direction. Yvonne accosted a man down the street walking his dog, but he hadn't seen a tall young man in tights and fur-trimmed boots, or maybe he didn't want to admit to having noticed.

Alexei had to be heading towards the theatre district. The afternoon was drawing to a close, where else could he go between now and curtain call? In the light drizzle, Yvonne began walking towards Holborn Street, the rain collecting like tiny jewels in her hair and eyelashes. It was all the brat's fault. Anton. *He will have the name of the finest playwright that ever lived.* He had done this. From the first moment they'd held him out to her, a pitiful, undersized, mewling whit, she had felt nothing. Why had anyone not told her babies were so self-centred, so needy? His cries had set her teeth on edge, filling the delivery room where they'd had to rush her after complications had set in and the midwife, a no-nonsense type, had simply wiped her hands on a towel and ordered, "Hospital." The nurses had wrapped him in swaddling bands. Too late. Did they think she had not seen the stubby feet, ankles bent like pale commas? And then feeding, the crowning insult, his mouth fastened on her breast, his greedy suckling that caused her breasts to engorge painfully and left her nipples so tender she couldn't bear to wear clothing. At times it had taken all her restraint not to hurl him against the wall. No spawn of hers, this freak, this cripple. It wasn't possible. Alexei was so lean and muscular, so graceful in limb and posture. So perfect. Someone had changed the babes in the hospital. Some evil witch had taken Yvonne's graceful infant with his lusty throat and apple-red cheeks and given her this limp, pale creature in its place. Her darling was now in the arms of some wealthy woman with bad blood who had demanded a healthy child she couldn't produce.

Yvonne took in a lungful of damp, smog-filled air, pea soup rolling in from the Thames, and wiped away tears the rain had flushed from her eyes. Already she was on the fringes of the theatre district, the one area of London that still knew how to be gay. The hawkers were wrapping up their wares, the flower sellers banding together the last of their spring stems. She fished out a coin from her change purse and pointed to a single daffodil. Breaking off the stem, she threaded it through her top buttonhole. Even in the grainy haze of twilight, the flower's bright yellow trumpet made a cheerful contrast with the drab charcoal grey of her cape.

"Suits you, darlin'," the flower seller said, and Yvonne, walking away, managed a smile at the effect.

If she could shake this lethargy and nausea for long enough, she would go back and dance for Harold. There was no other way out of the cycle. Anton could be left overnight with Mrs. Mahoney. A much better arrangement. If this was the only way she could hang on to her man, then it was what she had to do. But somehow she'd have to avoid ever being alone with Harold.

Yvonne was nearing the Drury Lane Theatre when she saw her, lying on a park bench. She had no desire to be recognized and so stood awhile at a distance, watching the sleeping figure. Her matted hair was a lifeless grey, and her clothes looked bulky, oddly angular, Yvonne guessed from newspapers stuffed between the layers for warmth. She stepped closer. At the sound of Yvonne's boots approaching, slowing down, the woman stirred, lifted her head a fraction, stared at her Samaritan with bleary eyes, their whites jaundiced. Not a flicker of recognition passed across her features. Instead she pulled her hand stiffly from her pocket and held it outstretched. Her swollen fingers curled up like a dried leaf, nails filthy and torn. She smelled strongly of alcohol and stale urine.

Nights she'd dreamed of this moment, speeches she'd rehearsed, and now that it was here Yvonne could think of nothing to say. Slowly, she undid the flower from her lapel, laid it in her mother's hand, and walked away.

XIII

Vancouver: July 1952

The middle section of the landing creaks as Anton shifts his weight to his extended foot. Eyes dart to Mr. Cunningham's door. He shifts back again. Another creak, lower in pitch. The sound of his heart fills his ears as he pauses, the rush of blood, swoosh, thump, swoosh, thump. The stairs were bad enough. It has taken him almost ten minutes to climb to the second floor, feeling his way across each tread, seeking the quietest parts, trying to memorize the places that squeak and groan. Memorize? This one time is all he plans, all he needs, a picture to place her in, though his primary mission is to tend to his leg, which throbs more painfully with each step, each heartbeat. He glances again at the tiny peephole beneath the number four on the door across from Jasmine's. Is Mr. Cunningham home? Anton never saw or heard him go out. But Mr. Cunningham could be light on his feet, like Anton's mother, who has often sneaked up behind him just to prove she can.

Number three. Anton pulls a sturdy hatpin from his pocket. The lock-picker's tool of choice, according to Harold. Jig it around a bit till you feel a click, he would say, then push and turn. Once you've engaged the mechanism, the lock should open. Anton never asked how or why he knew such things. The hatpin is his mother's, secured from a quick dash into the apartment — luckily a class was in progress — a rummage through her dressing table drawer, not nearly so nerve-wracking as what he's about to attempt. His pulse thumps in his throat, he can hardly breathe, his knees are liquid. Teasing the hatpin in the lock, he wiggles it up and down. It's insane what he's doing. Side to side, and now a circular movement. It isn't only insane, it's illegal. He could be arrested and charged with trespassing, maybe even breaking and entering, though strictly speaking he isn't breaking anything. But it's as if someone else has taken over, and the real Anton is standing in the corner of the landing, looking on as a bolder version of himself picks the lock that guards the inner sanctum.

Click. His breath catches as the door flies open, jerked from his grasp by an unseen force sucking the air from the room out through the window. Magazine pages rustle and flutter back and forth, and dead ahead the lace curtain snaps and cracks like an irate flag in the wind outside. Every muscle and tendon in his body buzzing with excitement, Anton steps inside the maelstrom. He closes the door, and at once the pages still, the curtain tames its mad dance, his heart leaves his throat to settle back behind his ribs.

Jasmine isn't so tidy, and this surprises him. In the kitchen, the sink and counter are filled with dirty dishes. He could not, before now, have imagined that any woman would go away for several days and leave this kind of mess behind. In the living room are blouses and camisoles, jackets and scarves — some bearing the airline crest and insignia — tossed carelessly across the backs of the sofa and chairs, some have even slipped to the floor. Magazines lie strewn about the couch, cups with lipstick stains sit herded together on the coffee table. This is no lace and satin fantasy but the living quarters of someone scattered, someone very much in a rush.

Anton crosses the room and kneels on the sofa to lower the window sash. Pewter clouds threaten rain, and the north mountains are no longer visible. Not wanting to arouse too much suspicion, he leaves the window open a touch, then hobbles to the bathroom.

More disorder. Towel on the floor, capless toothpaste tube between the taps, dried white trails in the sink, soap spatters on the mirror. He finds the plug and fills the basin with warm water. Balancing on his left leg, he heaves his right upwards. Balancing comes easy to Anton, the high arch of his left foot sees to that. On one leg he's like a stork, tall and graceful, still as a rock. It is walking that undoes him.

As he bends towards his shin, something hard digs into his hip. The key. He lowers his leg, removes it from his pocket, places it on the side of the sink next to the taps and swings his wet foot up again. The moment he rubs at the dried-on blood, the cuts begin to run again. The water turns pink. He opens the medicine cabinet above the sink, surprised by the order and neatness inside. A small box, a red cross taped on the front. The lid pops off with a burp of camphor. Inside, a roll of gauze, some adhesive tape, Band-Aids, a tube of antiseptic cream and tiny nail scissors. How can such order exist amid the chaos whirled through the rest of the apartment? It's as if two people live here. Anton dabs at his cut with a little of the ointment, cuts first a swatch from the roll of gauze, then pieces of tape to anchor it, and dresses his wound. He puts down his right leg, allows some weight on it, checks the dressing for spotting, then pulls the washbasin plug. Pink liquid gurgles down the drain. Anton rinses the bowl clean with fresh water. Leave no traces of yourself, Harold always said. Put everything back exactly as you found it. It delays the alarm process. Though it occurs to Anton that the sink is perhaps cleaner than before. At least the toothpaste streaks have all but disappeared.

He checks his face in the mirror. Pale, his eyes almost a light grey. He's still shaky from the fall. Or from trespassing? Still, he's here now. Why not do a little investigating? He steps from the bathroom, looks to the door on his left. The bedroom.

He enters this room slowly, with trepidation, the way one would a temple, a sacred place. The duvet has been pulled up haphazardly over the bed, leaving the pillows exposed. On one a small round indentation, the imprint of her head. Anton pictures a spray of golden hair, soft as spun silk, across the pillow's edges, and steps over to it, runs his fingers lightly across its cool surface. Then he turns to face the dark wooden dresser in the corner.

Bottles of promise and magic. Dozens of them, all shapes and sizes. Powders and lotions and creams, tiny pots of colour, lipsticks and brushes. Puffy, colourful atomizers, the rubber bulbs disguised in miniature crocheted bags. Anton bends and inhales. Perfume. Crushed roses. Honeysuckle. And his favourite, lilac. He closes his eyes, filling his head and lungs with flowers. The brushes are similar to ones his mother uses for putting on makeup. A giant powder puff sits in a shallow resting case of mother-of-pearl. Anton picks it up, powder on his hands, and bats his nose. A chalky cloud gathers in his throat, choking, slightly medicinal to taste. It floats into his eyes, which smart, then blur. He's going blind. He begins to cough, then sneezes. Once. Twice. Three times. Four. He curls his head into his shoulder to wipe his runny nose on the sleeve of his shirt, then sniffs loudly. He looks in the mirror. It's as though someone has sprinkled chalk dust over everything.

Leave no traces of yourself.

Anton grabs a discarded stocking from the floor and begins wiping, flicking his makeshift duster between the larger bottles, picking the smaller ones up to clean beneath. There. He gives the mirror a quick rub. Much better. She won't notice a thing.

Time to leave. As he grasps the bedroom door knob, his hand brushes across the robe hanging on the back of the door. The fabric, cool and slippery, feels almost wet. He flinches, draws his hand away quickly, but then reaches towards the garment again, rubs the back of his hand up and down its cool smoothness. He presses his face into the soft folds. Again flowers, and a trace of something a bit sour, more human.

Was that the latch? Anton's scalp prickles. His imagination, surely. But no. The unmistakable sound of a key being drawn from a lock. Someone is letting herself in. Jasmine? She isn't due back until tomorrow. Clarice Hart, then? He looks about wildly, must hide himself somewhere. Whoever opened the door is coming in. Anton drops to the floor, tries to slide beneath the bed. But the space is crammed with boxes. Scrambling to his feet, he hears the click of the latch as the apartment door closes. He holds his breath, prays the floorboards don't creak and tiptoes towards the closet. The door, thank God for untidiness, is slightly ajar, and so he steps inside, pulls it quietly to behind him, sinks to the floor and pulls his knees up under his chin.

Sounds fill the apartment. Heavy steps but the clicking of a woman's heels. The intruder, whoever she is, is not light on her feet, is not taking any care to hide her arrival. Doors open and close, he has no sense of where sounds are coming from. Running water. Kitchen or bathroom? There's a scrape of metal rings, a shower curtain being pulled back. Must be the bathroom. The intruder must be Jasmine returned early. Burglars don't bathe.

Radio static as she fiddles with the dial, looking for a station. Judy Garland. Through the slats of the closet's louvred doors, Anton can see the lower half of the room. He hears footsteps enter. Then the sound of rustling fabric. Jasmine is undressing. His Jasmine. Anton's heart beats faster. He can see nothing for the bed. The slats angle downwards, guiding his vision. If he stands he could . . . but she would hear him rustling about, and then what? Besides, Anton believes if he sees her naked, which, until now, has not comprised any concrete part of his daydreams, she would know it the next time they met. The knowledge would be inscribed on his skin, written in his eyes, his hair, his lips, even his clothes would scream *peeping Tom.*

Legs pass the closet. Anton shrinks further into the corner, pulls some of the longer dresses hanging behind him in front of his face. Now he's in utter darkness, and sound reaches him oddly muffled through the several layers of fabric. Jasmine, obviously still close by, begins humming along to the radio. Occasionally she sings snatches of the lyrics. Her voice is raw, throaty, not what he expected. He'd free his ears in order to listen closer if he wasn't so concerned with getting caught. She sounds a little off-key too. Surprising for someone who plays the piano as well as she claims to.

The singing drifts away, floats back into the room, drifts away again. If he could be certain she was sitting in the bath, door closed, he would attempt an escape.

Days pass.

Anton's legs are cramping and his feet have gone to sleep. Unlocking his knees with his hands he stretches his legs one by one out in front of him. His feet graze shoes and other items, boxes, bags maybe. He dares to pull the clothes away from his face and instantly feels sweat begin to cool on his skin. The clouds have broken, he can hear rain drumming on the roof. And a voice in the bedroom. Jasmine is talking to herself. Only she sounds nothing at all like Jasmine. Then who? A thief? Or Clarice Hart making herself at home? Anton shudders at this last thought. He cannot imagine anyone wanting to witness Clarice Hart peeling off her clothes. He kneads at his legs to get the blood flowing, leans towards the door. The voice does not sound like his landlady's, either. It's younger and fuller, with a charming lilt. Not a voice from anywhere around here, he thinks. American, perhaps. He rubs his legs, then bends them, pulls himself up slowly, hands creeping up the walls, into a squat, then squints through the slats.

Who is this woman, sitting so tall in the stool at the dresser, brushing her long, dark brown hair? Where did she come from? And, more pertinent to Anton's predicament, when is she leaving? In the mirror he has a clear view of her face. She's okay-looking, in a girl-next-door kind of way. Small nose, wide mouth, chubby cheeks. Well, not chubby, exactly. But she's definitely bigger than Jasmine. And plainer. Possibly a few years older too, though from this distance he really can't tell. She takes a drink of clear liquid from an odd-shaped glass, a long thin stem with a vee-shaped vessel. This, at least, explains her eyes, glassy even from Anton's obscure post.

And it explains, perhaps, her preening. She stares at herself a long time, brushes on some makeup, tilts her chin, turns this way and that, stares again, brushes on more makeup. Now she bends her head to fidget with something on the dresser. The smell of ether floats towards him, and Anton's back on a gurney, face towards bright light, masked surgeons with smiling eyes. The brunette is painting her nails, though for Anton the smell will forever be associated with hospitals and anaesthetics.

His legs rally by cramping again. Is she ever going to leave the room? He needs to stand, walk about, shake the kinks from his muscles. He also needs to go home, his mother must be wondering where on earth he is, though Anton has lost all sense of time trapped in here. The light coming through the slats isn't enough to illuminate the face of his watch. How long can someone stare at her own reflection? Her narcissism is embarrassing. But he must resign himself to his fate. No point getting himself all worked up and flustered. As his mother would say, he has made his bed, and, uncomfortable as it is, he must now lie in it. He lowers himself to the floor and stretches out, leaning back gratefully into the wall.

He dozes. At least this is what he thinks when he wakes with a start. Was he asleep? The closet is pitch black, and even the light showing between the slats of the door is dim. It must be dark outside. Nighttime. But how long has he been out? He can hear the brunette singing in the other room, a shuffle of heavy feet. Is she dancing with herself? An occasional giggle. Or has someone joined her? Anton is wide awake now. He could possibly slip by one person and out the door. Slipping by two would be next to impossible. He stretches and twists, shakes his feet, trying to regain feeling. His back, his bottom, his legs are all completely numb. Hands on the wall, he pulls himself slowly, stiffly, into standing position. Pins and needles rip and scratch up and down his legs. How can blood hurt so much? If suddenly given the chance to flee now, Anton thinks, he'd probably take too long to get the coordination back in his feet. He'd be caught hobbling across the room, an old man in a young boy's skin. But at this point it appears unlikely that the brunette will be leaving before morning. Anton's stomach rumbles. He's missed dinner.

A light switches on and she trips into the room. His view is now so clear and unobstructed he might as well be standing behind glass. The tempo of her dancing seems to have changed, there's something guarded about it, she seems almost self-conscious, as if she knows someone is watching her. But how? He has made no noise. He watches as she sits in front of the mirror regarding herself again. But this time she seems more demure, has lost her brashness. There's a flush about her cheeks, she seems to be less appraising herself critically than flirting with her image.

She's also wearing the gown from the back of the door, holding the front together above her breasts. Anton stares at her hands, sensing something about to happen. She moves, almost imperceptibly, and the robe slips from her shoulders. Her skin is surprisingly pale, the word alabaster comes to mind. She smiles coyly, then pulls the robe up over her shoulders again as if faintly embarrassed. Standing, she moves towards the door. The room goes dark. Anton can hear her rustling about. He holds his breath. Is this it? Is she going to bed? Can he finally leave? He hopes she sleeps soundly.

Click.

Another light, this time with a smaller, warmer glow, a light that casts shadows in the corners. It must be the lamp by the bed with the dusty rose shade and tasselled fringe. Does she plan now on reading awhile? Anton rubs the bridge of his nose between his thumb and forefinger. Patience. Now more than ever he must be patient. He breathes out slowly through his mouth, counts to ten and begins again. The brunette pulls back the duvet but then returns to the dresser and sits at it as before, watching herself shyly in the mirror. Anton's senses are instantly on full alert; his heart races in his mouth. Once again she lets the robe slip from her shoulders, and while one hand holds the silky edges together between her breasts, the other begins a journey of its own.

With her fingers she traces the contours of her face, nose,

lips, chin, the smooth line of her neck. Her hand disappears into her hair, which she then grasps, pulling it upwards and revealing to Anton briefly the tender nape, an alluring trail of wispy tendrils, before she lets it fall again. She runs her hand over her shoulder, rubbing and caressing, then draws a line to the depression at the base of her throat, where her fingers linger, stroking. As she closes her eyes, Anton can almost hear the intake of her breath, its shuddery release. Down the robe slips, exposing her upper arms, her elbows. Yet still she holds the edges between her breasts. Anton, legs pressed together, both wills her to let go and prays she won't. His eyes are burning at the rims, his nose so dry he's breathing through his mouth. And then she lowers her hand, revealing full, pendulous breasts, skin whiter than he ever thought possible. Lower still her hand travels, brushing her belly and disappearing briefly into her lap before reappearing again, this time to circle her nipples. She lifts her breasts, one in each hand, rubbing them, gently at first, then harder, with greater urgency.

Anton is roasting in his prison. His eyes and mouth have burned dry, the heat in his body has rushed to his groin. His penis is straining so hard against his pants that even through his underwear he can feel the shape and the individual teeth of the zipper. Heat licks up his spine, and, no longer able to control himself, he pushes the palm of his hand firm against his groin. Straining, pushing, straining, pushing, rubbing, rubbing, pushing, straining. The brunette drops one hand to her lap and begins moving her hips. Her breasts wobble and shake. Anton cannot breathe. His body quickens, every muscle, every cell strained to a pitch as he shudders in release. The cloying polleny smell fills his nose. He leans back against a wall of clothing, quivering as blood rushes tingling through his legs and into his toes, up into his chest, his arms, his fingers, neck, face, scalp. Convinced it must be standing on end, he runs a hand across

his hair. The feeling, the after-shocks of which are still winding
pleasurably through his body, has been unlike anything he ever
achieved before from a furtive grope beneath the bedsheets, a
slippery massage in the shower, his insides tensed, waiting for his
mother to hammer on the door, issue sharp quips about using
all the hot water.

But shame isn't far behind. As Anton's heart slows and his
skin cools, he begins to feel dirty. The brunette cries out once, a
gasp of surprise, of pleasure, and heat sweeps through his body
again like a wind. A moment of confusion, guilt, then he hears
the scrape of the stool across the wooden floor, the creak of
bedsprings.

The lamp clicks off.

Barely a minute passes before the room fills with the welcome sounds of gentle snoring.

It takes Anton a while to gather strength enough to move,
will iron back into his legs, adjust himself, now sticky and
uncomfortable, in front. Slowly, quietly, he pulls opens the
closet door and steps into the room, which is surprisingly light.
The brunette has not pulled the drapes across the window,
through which Anton can now see a full, bright moon.

While her head and hips are turned sideways, she is sleeping on her back, naked. Anton has always wanted to experience
the freedom of skin against sheets, but some habits are hard to
break, take different levels of courage. Between hospitals and
bedsits, his mother's fears and Harold's rages, he has known
little privacy. There is something both thrilling and diabolical
about what he's done tonight, what he's seen. But there is also
a sad and terrifying vulnerability now in the woman's careless
posture, and Anton can feel pity rising like bile in his throat.
Her breasts have slid to her sides, and their nipples, flattened
into dark circles, seem absurdly far apart, unnatural-looking.
Her mouth is open, and the rest of her face is collapsed towards

the pillow. Anton's eyes slip down her body, the rounded swell of her belly, the dimples in her thighs and the dark triangle between her legs. He turns away, loathing himself. Without so much as a drop of the man's blood in his veins, he was tonight, without a doubt, the incarnation of Harold.

As Anton reaches the door, the bedsprings creak. He tenses, waiting for the explosion, almost welcoming the reviling he knows he deserves, and then, unable to bear the suspense, he dares to turn his head and look. The brunette opens her eyes, looks right at Anton, and closes them again.

"G'night, sweet thing," she mumbles into the pillow and begins a soft snoring again.

XIV

London: September 1939

There were so many people crowded onto the station platform that Yvonne felt as if the whole of London were packed and leaving for the countryside. She had a tight grip on Anton's hand but could feel him being swept away with the surge of the crowd as the train pulled in.

"Pick him up, why don't you?" Alexei was holding Isobel, his face pinched and nervous. Next to the child's grey-white pallor and bright red cheeks, his skin was yellow. Perhaps he was jaundiced. That made people bad-tempered, didn't it?

"Change your mind and come with us, please, Alexei,

please?" She clamped her lips together in a smile and scooped Anton into her arms. The bucket and spade he was carrying banged against her. Anton was wearing his gas mask, a red and blue child's version with big black ears that were supposed to make the mask resemble Mickey Mouse. He happily played with it on for hours at a time; it was a task sometimes to get him to take it off. Yvonne craned her neck past the Mickey Mouse ears, willing Alexei to look at her.

"We'll all be able to eat well, these people are bound to be wealthy, opening up their homes to London folk the way they are. And the fresh air will do you good, do us all good." She jogged Anton in her arms, trying to release the pressure of his leg brace against her hip, all the while aware of the unfamiliar press of metal on her finger. Thin as a curtain ring, her mother would have said with a sniff. After less than one day, Yvonne's skin was already turning green. She reached out with her other hand to stroke her daughter's face. "By the time tomorrow morning comes around, even Isobel will be laughing as usual, clapping her hands and calling for Papa."

"I have to stay behind, help Harold with his show."

Yvonne closed her eyes for a moment, took a deep breath. Since when had he ever cared about Harold's show?

"But we're man and wife now, we're a proper family." Inside her new shoes, she flexed her pinched toes. She'd stood most of the day yesterday in line at the Registry Office with Alexei and dozens of uniformed soldiers and their weepy sweethearts. She had wanted to look her best.

"With your rich country family looking after you, I will be able to save some money, perhaps. It will not last, this war. You will be back before very long." He rubbed his fingers across his mouth. Yvonne tried to read his face. Was that resentment in the twist of his lips? Did he feel she'd badgered him into yesterday's ceremony? But with all the talk of war, she had believed it was the right and necessary thing to do. She still did, and suddenly she did not want to go to Clacton-on-Sea, no matter how green and pretty it was supposed to be, did not want to leave him behind. Something about it all felt terribly wrong. She shifted Anton onto her other hip.

"We're not going. Isobel has been burning up since last night, she needs to see a doctor."

"They have doctors in the countryside, Yvi. You must go. It is not safe for the children to be in the city, you know what the government says, the Germans could start dropping bombs any day."

"Then it isn't safe for you, either. Why should we go and you stay?"

"How many men do you see on this platform, Yvi? How many? What do you think that would be like for me? For people to say I am not man enough to stay behind in the city — that I must go to the countryside with all the women and children." He turned away from her. "You must go. Your government has said so." Your government. He always said your government, your country, your children, conveniently leaving himself out of the equation, underscoring his status as an outsider.

"Do you regret getting married?" Stones in her mouth. Her lips felt numb, unconnected to the rest of her. Isobel gasped for breath, and Alexei shuffled her so that she lay upright against his shoulder, his face cradling hers.

"Of course not." His words came out muffled through Isobel's hair.

It was difficult to speak then as the train pulled into the station, steam hissing, brakes screeching. Yvonne and Alexei stood still, holding onto the children as the crowd, mainly teachers with their classes — some of the children scarcely a year or so older than Anton — surged around them, pushing and shoving. There were men too, Yvonne noticed, but mainly they were older or frail-looking, wearing civil service suits and bowler hats.

"You should try and get a seat." Alexei nodded towards the carriage window through which passengers could be seen settling themselves, heaving twine-tied boxes and suitcases up into the overhead racks. "You cannot stand all the way, not with the children."

Like you care, she wanted to spit, but she swallowed instead, the words scraping down the back of her throat. But he was right, and so she made her way towards the carriage steps, her body and legs so heavy she might have been wading through glue. If only he would stop her. Put his hand on her arm and tell her he didn't want her to leave, that he needed her, that he needed his children with him. But when she turned, she could see in his face he was already someplace else.

"I'll write to you. You will write back, won't you?" She bent to place Anton down on the steps, and a pair of hands scooped him up and took him inside the carriage. Alexei handed Isobel to Yvonne and climbed the stairs after his son.

"Of course. I will write to you all." He kneeled to hug and kiss Anton goodbye, then jumped back down to the platform. "You will make sure Isobel gets to a doctor as soon as you get to where it is you are going."

"Clacton-on-Sea." Even the name of the place was beginning to grate.

He leaned forward to hug her, and it took every ounce of Yvonne's self-control not to cling and weep and beg. "The evacuation's voluntary. We don't have to go," was what she managed to say into his collar. Isobel, caught between them, fretted and gulped air. Alexei stiffened and pulled away.

"It is safer. I want my children out of harm's way."

The whistle blew, the conductor called *All aboard!* and

Yvonne stepped up onto the train. Alexei handed her the gas mask cases, the children's clothing and the hand-tooled leather bag she'd stolen from her mother the night she'd run away. Someone closed the door behind her, and the train began pulling away from the platform. By the time Yvonne had pushed her way to the window, the station was the size of a child's toy.

With so many bodies packed together, the carriage was sweltering. Her arms trembling with the weight of Isobel and their luggage and her legs with the effort of keeping her balance, Yvonne eventually found a seat. She squeezed Anton, now maskless, in beside her, Isobel on her lap. But with physical relief came the tears she had been fighting all morning. How was she expected to cope on her own with one child only three weeks out of hospital and the other sick? She should have stood her ground and stayed behind. Isobel needed a doctor. The heat from the child's body was scorching Yvonne's belly through her dress. And already she missed Alexei fiercely. She resolved they would stay one night only.

After a while the rhythmic clack and sway of the carriage felt comforting and soon lulled Yvonne and her children. Isobel's breathing changed, she was finally asleep. Yvonne closed her eyes.

As the train chugged along the last stretch of track before Clacton-on-Sea, children rushed to press their noses up against the windows. Yvonne, staring out over their heads, saw on one side fields of emerald in a landscape utterly flat but for the odd barn or farmhouse, a clutch of trees here and there. On the other, a gentle slide of land towards a grey-green sea. A thin band of silver marked the horizon, though it might have been the end of the world for all Yvonne knew. She collected her carry-all bag, the pillow slips with the children's clothes and the cumbersome gas mask cases.

There was no one waiting on the station platform like she had expected, no rush of open arms, no ruddy cheeks and simple shining eyes eager to take charge, lead them away. The station clock said five past five. Anton, his relapsed foot in a built-up boot, his leg in a brace, was not able to walk long distances comfortably, but Yvonne's hands were more than full with the lead weight of Isobel, awake again and irritable, and with their luggage. The station master pointed towards a large group of children who were being escorted, two-by-two, up the lane towards a nearby school. Anton sucked in his cheeks and put on a brave face. With every step they lagged further behind.

By the time they reached the school and found their way to the gymnasium where dozens upon dozens of children were being assembled for billeting, Yvonne was hiccupping with her own strangled sobs. But she could have thrown back her head in a full-throated wail for all anyone would have noticed. The noise inside the gym, magnified and hurled back by a cavernous ceiling, was already deafening. Exhausted from their long journeys, confused, travelsick and missing their mothers, many of the children were crying, others squabbled amongst themselves: the girls pinched and pulled hair, the boys kicked and punched.

The hosts milling about appeared to be a mixture of prune-faced spinsters, harried mothers and thick-limbed farmers looking for cheap labour. Some obviously thought that anyone from the city must be deaf or stupid or both. Many of the children probably were ill-mannered brats who'd been dragged up in squalor, but were these people with their harsh and unequivocal judgements any better? Didn't they at least know how to whisper? Yvonne tried closing her ears, but then it seemed the only word she heard as people passed her family by was *cripple*, piercing her to the core. Anton, she saw, was wearing his Mickey Mouse mask again and appeared oblivious.

Slowly the gymnasium emptied. Predictably the smallest, the homeliest, the dirtiest children were left till last. Also those very young who'd travelled to safety with their mothers. Yvonne laid Isobel on the pillow slips, asked Mickey Mouse to keep an eye on her and went to join the small queue that had formed in front of the billeting officer's desk.

The billeting officer — she had a badge pinned to her lapel with Mrs. Chilton written heavily in pencil on it — peered down at her much crossed-out and corrected list, then imperiously at Yvonne over half-glasses perched midway down her nose. "You'd have done better putting them on the train by themselves." She shook her head at Yvonne's short-sightedness. "No woman wants another woman in her kitchen, even a slip of a girl like yourself." Mrs. Chilton looked up at her again. "Would you?"

Yvonne crossed her arms in front of her chest. Two deep vertical lines between Mrs. Chilton's eyebrows mirrored similar lines beneath her bottom lip. They gave her face a mean and pinched look. "My daughter is only just gone eighteen months old. You'd put a child that young on a train by herself then, would you?" Without waiting for an answer she walked away, stopped, called over her shoulder, "Then obviously you've never had any children of your own, you dried-up old hag."

Yvonne sat back down for a long wait with her children; they were going to miss their tea. She divided the remaining hunk of cheese she'd packed this morning between Anton and herself, then picked up Isobel, now fractious and limp-limbed. The child had eaten nothing all day. Anton lifted his mask free of his mouth, popped in the piece of cheese, then lowered the mask again. It occurred to Yvonne he hadn't spoken in hours. She pulled Isobel's bottle from her bag and rubbed the nipple over her lips.

"Sugar water?"

Yvonne turned and looked up at the kind of face she'd envisioned at the start-up of the evacuation program, ruddy and round, hair clipped back under a navy hat with a tidy brown and white feather tucked along its side. She smiled in tired relief.

"It's all she'll take."

"My mother swore by it for colicky babies." She held out her hand. "I'm Ruby Mercer."

"Yvonne Hoy . . . um, Kavanov."

"And this is my husband, Fred." Ruby gestured towards a thin and dreary-looking fellow who stood some distance behind her. "Is she very sick?"

"A bit of a fever. But most likely it was the train ride did it. It was very hot." Yvonne smiled again, not wanting to jeopardize what was beginning to look like her only chance. Unmatched evacuees, another mother had whispered to her earlier, went home with the billeting officer.

"Don't see why we have to take the kids' mother, too," Fred Mercer mumbled loudly enough for Yvonne to hear. His wife delicately ignored him.

"And your little boy's foot? It's going to be okay, isn't it? I mean it isn't infected or anything?"

Yvonne followed Ruby Mercer's eyes to Anton's brace and the grubby bandage still wrapped around his right leg. "The stitches are already out," she said. "As long as he keeps up his exercises," and here she leaned to tip Mickey Mouse's chin with her forefinger, make him look at her, "he'll be fine."

The Mercers didn't actually live in Clacton but in a smaller village a short distance up the coast. When she learned they were to walk there, Yvonne pinched herself fiercely to stem tears that had begun burning behind her eyes.

"We never had children of our own," Ruby Mercer confided

on the way. Yvonne's arms were so numb and weary from carrying Isobel that she would have given her two away without a second glance, crumpled onto the grassy verge and slept. Besides, she was uncomfortable with Ruby's admission. Why was it people who craved children couldn't have them, while the beggars seem to pop out like champagne corks for those who didn't much care one way or the other? She stumbled in the gloaming, bumping into the back of Fred Mercer with her shoulder.

"Sorry," she said. But she wasn't. If Fred Mercer was half a man he'd have picked Anton up by now and put the kid on his shoulders. Yvonne's legs were trembling with fatigue. Ruby seemed oblivious.

"And although it isn't very nice what Mr. Hitler's up to over there, well, I look on this as a chance for us to have a ready-made family. It's a bit of a blessing, really." She looked awkward for a moment. "And having you is, well" — she reached out to pat Yvonne's arm — "I wouldn't know what to do with a toddler. She is going to be okay, isn't she?"

"She just needs a tuck up in bed and a good night's rest." The road heaved and swayed. "We all do," she said, stopping in her tracks. Unable to go on or witness Anton's stoic half-march a moment longer, Yvonne stepped from the road and sank against the stone wall that separated a farmer's field from the public road. "I'm sorry, but you're going to have to go on without us. I'm so shattered I don't care if you send back the neighbour's pig truck or leave us to sleep in this ditch. I'm not taking another step." Anton stumbled towards her, and she put her hand on his shoulder, shooting a look of hatred at Fred Mercer's retreating back. "I'm sure only the cruellest person would expect a boy his age and in his condition to walk all this way." She was addressing Ruby Mercer now but couldn't bring herself to look the woman in the eye.

Fred Mercer neither broke his stride nor looked back. His wife ran back and forth between him and Yvonne, rubbing her hands together and muttering, "Oh dear, oh dear." Yvonne sat in the grass and weeds and pulled Anton down beside her. Ruby Mercer finally chose to accompany her husband, and as the two disappeared into the twilight, Anton pulled off his mask and asked if he could hold Isobel for a while. She laid the burning child in her brother's arms — Isobel would keep Anton warm if nothing else — leaned back against the wall and closed her stinging eyes. Her arms and legs throbbed with fatigue.

She must have slept; suddenly there were lights in her eyes and men's voices. The silhouette of someone stepping from the cab of a small grocer's van. It was Fred Mercer in, if possible, an even blacker mood than before. It took Yvonne some moments to coax the blood back into her legs so that she could first stand and then arrange herself and the children in the passenger seat. To his credit, Fred Mercer rode in the back, but his ill humour must have been contagious, for the driver, a burly man with rounded shoulders and fingers as thick as sausages, could not bring himself to either look at Yvonne or address her.

But Yvonne, staring out the window in dismay at the humble offerings of the Mercers' village — a corner shop that doubled as a post office, a greengrocer's and a butcher's with tight-fastened shutters on the windows — was hardly in the mood for small talk. There was no cinema, no theatre, no Woolworth's. One pub. What did people do here? There wasn't even a fish and chip shop.

But there was one surprise waiting for Yvonne when she followed Ruby Mercer up the stairs of her rambling stone farmhouse and into one of the many bedrooms that led off the upstairs landing. A crib. Neither Anton nor Isobel had ever slept in a crib.

"I thought you said you didn't have any children."

Ruby Mercer looked embarrassed. "Stillborn."

"I'm sorry."

"It was years ago, lovey." She reached out a hand to stroke Yvonne's cheek. "Don't you fret. My heart's been mended a long time. Save your strength for that wee one," she said, turning down the cover on the crib. "I've another bedroom made up. The boy can sleep in there. Unless you'd rather."

"No. I'll stay with Isobel."

"Have you had your tea?" Ruby Mercer smiled. "I thought not. You get her to bed and I'll put a bit of something together for you." She winked at Anton. "The two of you look famished."

A bit of something turned out to be half a pork pie, two thick slices of bread and butter and an open jar of pickled onions. Two whole large red tomatoes sat like exotic fruit on a plate in the middle of the table. Anton picked one up, turned it over in his small hands.

"What's this, Mama?"

"Try it and see."

He bit into it like an apple, scowl lines forming on his forehead when the skin resisted the advance of his blunt milk teeth. Suddenly seeds and juice squirted out the sides of his mouth. Yvonne burst out laughing at the surprised expression on his face. Anton wiped a hand across his mouth, then ventured a small laugh himself. Shyly, he placed the offending fruit on his mother's plate.

The Mercers, when Yvonne and Anton passed through the living room on their way up the stairs to bed, were busy fitting sheets of black paper to the windows. Fred Mercer was balanced atop a stepladder.

"G'night," Yvonne said.

Fred Mercer never so much as turned around. "We'll not do the ones upstairs, so soon as blackout regulations begin you'll be taking a candle to bed with you." Yvonne shrugged at his wife, who smiled back in sympathy.

"How's the foot, Anton?" Yvonne asked, hoping to make the man feel small or guilty. The van ride had done little to alter her opinion of him. "As his father says, he's a regular little soldier. Never complains about anything," she said to the man's back. Hope you fall off your ladder, she thought.

Up in her bedroom Yvonne leaned her elbows on the windowsill. Such darkness she had never seen. She could make out neither the moon nor the stars. How strange it was to see nothing at all. Isobel fidgeted and fussed, her breathing fast and hollow sounding. But Yvonne was too numb with tiredness to lift her out of the crib and hold her. Isobel was asleep. Better she stay that way. The thought of asking Fred Mercer to bring the local doctor around now, after all the trouble they'd already caused, was enough to give her heartburn. When Yvonne eventually lay down, she could only drift in and out of sleep, thoughts of Alexei tumbling through her head along with worry for her sick child and a smouldering anger at Fred Mercer.

In the morning Isobel was calmer, the fever leaving her body. She was even a little hungry. Already Yvonne was restless, edgy. She wondered where Alexei was. If he was missing her. If he'd slept in their bed last night. Alone.

She stood in the back doorway looking out over the Mercers' vegetable garden, the chicken run and beyond. The farm the house had originally belonged to was long gone, but the land that had once been tied to it still stretched out until forever, fields that rolled all the way to the horizon, touched there by an even larger expanse of blue. Yvonne failed to understand the charm she knew such a view held for many people. It was too open, too startlingly green, too devoid of people; she was used to the city, having bookends on her view.

Even as a child, on train rides to and from cities on tour, Yvonne had spent most of her time playing draughts and cards with the other turns, not staring out at countryside that meant nothing to her. At the back of the Mercers' vegetable patch sat the corrugated arc of an Anderson shelter — evidence that the threat of war had touched this part of England also. Yvonne had seen dozens of them delivered on lorries to the better houses around her own neighbourhood — rooming house tenants were expected to use the underground. And she'd watched as the men of such streets had first pulled the stacked semicircles of corrugated iron apart and then dug up their precious lawns to submerge the ends in the earth.

Ruby Mercer came out and stood beside her. "She seems a bit better today."

"Yes."

"You'll be relieved."

"Very."

"Why don't you go down to the beach, take the boy with you?" She nodded towards Anton who was watching the chickens pad back and forth in the chicken run. "I'll keep an eye."

Yvonne stood on the beach, looking out to sea. A gentle wind blew her dress around her legs. She was wearing a headscarf Ruby Mercer had loaned her. Anton was standing by the water's edge, throwing pebbles. She thought of teaching him to skim, to pick only the flattest stones, hold his arm out to the side, bend at the waist and flick the stone sharply, so that it skipped across the surface several times before disappearing to the sea bed below. She even pictured herself doing it, felt her hands on Anton's tiny arm, placing it correctly. But he was too young, he didn't have the necessary coordination yet. She turned and began walking towards a group of children playing further up the beach. A young woman was with them, their mother or possibly their host mother — the kids would probably call her auntie — and Yvonne was starved for conversation. Out of the corner of her eye she saw arms waving, heard a tiny, distant voice crying out. She didn't turn, however, until Ruby Mercer was almost upon her.

"Your little girl," she gasped. "Your little girl's stopped breathing."

Yvonne tore back to the farmhouse and raced up the stairs, Ruby Mercer on her heels. When she reached the landing, she was confronted with a row of bedroom doors.

"Which one?" She turned to the red-faced woman and grabbed her sleeve. "Which one?" she screamed, inches from her face.

"There, there." A bewildered Mrs. Mercer, perspiring heavily, chest heaving, pointed, and Yvonne ran. But already Isobel was beginning to feel cold, her skin tinged blue. Yvonne picked her up and folded her inside her coat so that the child's head lay just beneath her chin. She sat on the bed rocking, Isobel in her arms, singing *rock-a-bye baby* over and over, scarcely conscious of the words and their morbid message.

A while later Yvonne heard voices downstairs, heavy footsteps, a tap on her door.

"May I come in?"

The reply in her head never made it to her lips, but the door opened anyway and a man, a doctor, obviously, with his black bag, stepped inside. He had silver-white hair and pale blue eyes that put her in mind of someone she knew. He reached out his hands, large and beginning to gnarl, took Isobel from her and placed her back in the crib. Yvonne watched him as if from behind a transparent wall, her arms so weighted with loss she couldn't have moved to stop him if she'd tried. The doctor then handed her some white pills and a glass of water to drink. He said something about meningitis, and then he helped her to lie down, covered her with a blanket. Yvonne stared at the crib by the window until her eyes grew heavy. She slept.

When she awoke, Isobel was gone. Alarmed, Yvonne stumbled from her bed and rushed downstairs. When he saw her, Fred Mercer finished his mug of tea in one long swallow, pushed back his chair and left out the kitchen door.

"Gone to check on the garden," his wife said. "It rained in the night."

"Where's Isobel?" How could she have slept a whole day?

"Through here, dear." She led Yvonne into the parlour at the front, then backed out, closing the door. The tiny coffin, sitting dead centre on a drop-leaf table, was cheap and stuffed with what looked like an old sheet, but Isobel was wearing a pretty pink and white dress Yvonne had never seen. Her skin had a china-white translucency, her features still and pretty as a doll's. She'd been washed, and her fine, dark fly-away hair had been combed so that gentle curls now framed her face. Mrs. Mercer knocked softly on the door and brought Yvonne a cup of tea. A neighbour had made a gift of the frock; she was a kind soul, her little girl nearly eight years old now. There was a buttered teacake in the kitchen for her. She thought it might have been sacrilegious to bring food into the room, but then that's what they did at wakes, wasn't it, ate with the coffin right there. Yvonne took the tea from Ruby's outstretched hands and sipped at it, scalding her tongue. Anton had eaten his breakfast with them, and they were all going to a neighbour's house to listen to the wireless. Mr. Chamberlain was going to address the nation at quarter past eleven. Mrs.

Mercer started to leave, then looked back into the room as if having second thoughts.

"If you don't like the dress, I can always wash through the clothes she came in. If you'd rather."

Yvonne cut her off, her tone sharper than intended. "No. It's beautiful. Tell your friend thank you from me. Isobel would have loved it."

It was some time later when she heard the high-pitched whine of the air-raid sirens. So the Germans were coming after all to kill them in their homes. She thought of the shelter in the back yard and the dirt Fred Mercer had already piled on top of it. He planned to grow Brussels sprouts on the roof. She stayed exactly where she was.

The parson was busy all day, what with one thing and another, but he was a good friend of Mrs. Mercer's, and he had promised. He was distracted, both he and his curate were off to join up, so he told Yvonne when she arrived with Anton and Mrs. Mercer, and he was busy, someone was coming up tomorrow to take their place. The man and his wife would have their hands full. But it was all God's work, and God was needed on the battlefield as much as he was needed anyplace else.

"Most would agree he was needed more." He barked a laugh. Mrs. Mercer cleared her throat. Yvonne was hot in the hat and gloves Mrs. Mercer had pressed her to wear.

The parson led them through the graveyard to the edge of a small but deep hole. Yvonne stared into it, pulling country air into her lungs, filling her head with the sweet, damp smell of the earth. Someone, Fred Mercer perhaps, had nailed down the lid on Isobel's tiny white coffin. Yvonne saw herself ripping it off with her bare hands, felt the pain in her bleeding fingertips. The heels on her wedding shoes sank into the soft, grassy earth. A chorus of birds burst into raucous song. The parson committed Isobel to the earth in a few words that Yvonne heard only as mumbles and sighs on the wind. He instructed her to pick up a handful of dirt and toss it onto the coffin as the sexton lowered her daughter into the ground.

The small ceremony over, Mrs. Mercer, Yvonne and Anton walked back to the farmhouse. The weather, as if in recognition of the declaration of war, of the loss of Isobel, had begun to turn, dark storm clouds gathering on the horizon. It was understood that Yvonne and Anton would return to the city. She had brought death into these old people's lives. In time, Yvonne, needing to place blame, to find some measure of reason and order in the chaos of her life, would look back and come to believe that the restless soul of the Mercers' stillborn child had cursed Isobel. But for now it was the war that had already dealt its first blow and claimed its first victim.

She stayed in her room all evening, sitting by the window and watching the slow sweep of searchlights across the sky. No planes flew overhead, no bombs fell, but Yvonne might not have noticed anyway, for she was trying, in her mind, to find the right words to say to Alexei.

XV

Vancouver: July 1952

His mother might have grounded him in a fit of pique, at a loss to understand where he'd been for so long, why he'd missed his dinner, but she needs someone to run her errands. One small pack of Black Cats doesn't last long, though he knows she likes to limit her treats, six a day, spaced evenly, each a reward for so many hours on her feet. Anton releases the latch on the apartment door quietly; he's becoming quite the expert. Eye to the crack, then an ear. It's the brunette from upstairs he's afraid of, the one sleeping — at least he thought she was sleeping — in Jasmine's bed. Though with her heavy feet, her off-key singing, he'd surely hear her long before he saw her. And if she saw him, what then? Would she recognize him as the prowler from the closet? Or had she really known he was there all along? Harold sometimes mumbled in his drunken sleep. Harold is his blueprint for all things ugly and unaccountable.

The silence in the hallway is palpable, pulsating in time with Anton's heartbeat, but no sooner does he step across his threshold than the Harts' door creaks open. Giant steps — Anton lunges towards the front entrance, grabs at the heavy brass knob.

"Son, is that you?"

Nothing wrong with the old man's hearing. Anton freezes, holds his breath.

"Son?" Unsure. A pause. Then, "I know it's you."

How? He exhales slowly. But the old man reads minds.
"Your mother wears perfume."

And what does guilt smell like, Anton wonders. For his skin is surely thick with it. He's showered, last night and this morning; he's wearing fresh clothes, but still there's a layer of something — shame? — that cannot be removed. His leg throbs once, as though he needs reminding of that other humiliation. Reluctantly Anton lets go of the handle; he turns from the door but does not step forward. Though the Hart's door is ajar, the old man is still hidden in the shadows, not even his feet are visible, or the wheels of his chair. Tom Hart is afraid to leave his apartment. Anton knows this suddenly and as surely as he knows that the floor beneath his feet is tiled, that Harold is safely dead and buried. He can feel the old man's fear thickening the space between them. Fifteen years. What mountains of self-delusion must he have buried himself behind, what fortresses of dread, bottles of little white pills. He waits, silently daring Tom Hart to rise to the challenge.

The old man must have waited in much the same way for Anton's mother that day, opened his door as she left the apartment or entered it, cajoled her into stepping towards him, taking the envelope with its heavy key from his frail bird-hands. Anton pictures his mother's left hand flying to her throat in alarm at the sight of the old man in his wheelchair, fingering the edges of the jagged scar beneath her blouse (or hiding it?), rubbing the fingers of her right hand with her left. You don't know who you can trust, she always says.

Mr. Hart clears his throat, the language of adults. It signals impatience: I'm waiting. Anton walks towards him, staring at the floor in front of the old man's slippered feet. "How are you today, sir?"

"Fine, son, fine. Did you find the bike?" His voice has

ragged edges. Anton is wary. In his experience, an excitable person is a volatile person.

"Yes, sir, I did."

"And?"

"And . . ." Anton sniffs, rubs his sore shin against the curve of his left calf.

"Well, what do you think, son? All right, is it? Good enough to get you around, then?" The old man's eyes are bright again, he's animated, hands stretched over the ends of his arm rests, fingers twitching, drumming, not idle in his lap. Anton's leg throbs again. He glances first up the central staircase and then past Mr. Hart's head into the dimly lighted room behind. He doesn't want to stand about in this hallway any longer than necessary.

"I can't ride a bicycle, sir."

"Small problem, son. I'll teach you."

Anton looks sharply at the old man. Is he kidding? "You! Um, sir?"

The old pilot sits straighter in his chair, draws in a deep breath through his nose. "Nothing to it. Ha." He slaps the arms of the chair. "Taught myself when I was four years old. Bring the old contraption up into the garden along the side of the house there where I can see you, why don't you, son, and I'll give you a few pointers." Anton glances up at the stairs again.

Tom Hart clears his throat. "She's away, you know." Anton flushes; he can feel the heat all the way up and around his hairline. "Got some girlfriend from Arizona staying there. A stewardess too. But she's not as light on her feet as our Miss Daniels." He smiles knowingly, and instantly Anton's blood shrinks back from his skin. How could he have forgotten about the Harts living below Jasmine? Had they heard him up there yesterday? There's a long and awkward pause as he gropes for words to excuse himself, his naked emotions. Mr. Hart barks a short, harsh laugh. "So you have the key?"

The key. "The key. Of course." Anton pats his pants pockets, relieved by the shift in subject, the need to suddenly do something. But of course he changed, his other pair of trousers, torn, soiled, are presently crammed under his mattress with the rest of his contraband.

"The key." He's repeating himself, his voice loud in the empty hallway. "Let me go and get the key." Problem is, he can't remember taking the key from the pocket of those torn, soiled, nightmare pants. And surely he would have felt such a large, clunky object when he'd first taken them off? He'd rolled them up, planning to toss them in the garbage, but fearing his mother would find them, had flattened them out again and stuffed them under his mattress.

Then, a picture of a washbasin, toothpaste minus its cap. Anton's stomach crashes through his bowels, rushes down his legs to the floor. The key is upstairs in Jasmine's place, in her bathroom. Unless the brunette has found it, moved it elsewhere. He pulls at the neck of his shirt, suddenly hot again. How could she not have found it, perched where he left it, in full view on the lip of the sink next to the headless toothpaste, for Pete's sake?

"Well?" Tom Hart again slaps the arms of his chair heartily. "Are you going to go get it, or are you going to stand here all day with your mouth hanging open?" Anton takes a wobbly step backwards, reaches behind him for the door.

"It's in my room. I'll just go get it." Has he already said that? He turns the handle.

Old Man Hart nods. "I'll meet you," his eyes twinkle, "in the garden. In a manner of speaking. Ha," he laugh-barks again, wheeling himself backwards, then leans towards his door to push it closed. Anton is still swinging on his own door handle. If Mr. Hart would just hurry inside, he could dash to the store for his mother's cigarettes.

"Hop to it then, son." The old man's waiting. It's a game. Who's going to close his door first?

"Back so soon?" Hand on his shoulder. Anton leaps in surprise. His mother. Quickly he backs into the apartment and closes the door.

"I forgot something."

"You forgot something." A small sideways tug at her lips.

Anton stares at the sofa, groping for inspiration. "My library card." He glances quickly at his mother. "There's a book I want."

Her head tilts a fraction, she's toying with him. "Weren't you just there the other day?"

"It was checked out." It gets easier. You tell one and the next one grows from it, its own limb. "But the librarian said it was due back today, and that she'd hold it for me."

His mother presses her lips together, then smiles. "Well, you'd better hurry," she says. There's a smudge of pearly pink lipstick on her front tooth. "I need you to accompany my four o'clock."

He slips past her and makes for his room. The card, to wave in her face as he leaves, and the hatpin from under his mattress, he hasn't yet had a chance to return it to her dressing-table drawer. Back out the door. Standing in the hallway. Up first, or out? He needs to be sure the brunette is no longer in Jasmine's place. He steps outside and buzzes the intercom for number three, waits. Buzzes again. No reply. She might return any moment, but it's a chance he has to take. What's the worst that could happen? That she would come home again, that he'd be forced to take refuge in the closet, that she would . . . he closes his eyes briefly against the slow thump of shame in his chest, the flush of heat through his groin, then gropes for the banister, heads up the stairs again, trying to dodge the creaky ones, though he is too flustered to remember any of the painfully noted sequence from yesterday.

The same rapid dance of his heartbeat as he pauses on the landing. Ear to Jasmine's door, just to be on the safe side, a furtive glance at Mr. Cunningham's. He pulls out the hatpin. Jiggle, jiggle, click.

Anton has a firm hold of the door this time, but there's no need. The window is closed, the whirlwind has vanished along with its devastation. Everything is neat and tidy, magazines out of sight, clothes gone, presumably hung and folded where they should be, dishes washed and put away. There isn't a chance Tom Hart's key will be where he left it. Already Anton envisions himself having to kick in the door downstairs, lob a brick through the grimy window. There must be another way into the basement, but he cannot recall seeing another door anywhere. Most likely there's one in the Harts' place. He's about to turn towards the bathroom when he spots it sitting dead centre on the coffee table. Thank you, he mouths to the gods of indiscretion, scooping the key into his pocket.

Mission accomplished. Now the cigarettes. He turns to leave. Wait. There's the library, in case his mother checks. He can't afford to get caught out in another lie. But it's such a long walk, and there's Mr. Hart, waiting patiently downstairs for Anton to appear with the bike. He doesn't have time. Besides, he's a fugitive from the library; he can't return now, not with the scent of lost books dripping from him. It's illogical, of course, the books aren't yet overdue, how would they even know he'd lost them? But Anton cannot run the risk. He wears his feelings too close to the surface, there'll be a glowing sign on his forehead by the time he reaches the circulation desk. Besides — his eyes shift to Jasmine's bookcase — there are plenty of books here, almost five full shelves of them. She couldn't possibly miss just one. His fingers select a volume, there's no time to look at titles, no time to be choosy.

Halfway down the stairs he hears the latch on the front door click open. Lilacs float towards him. Anton stops, right leg suspended. It's Jasmine, home from Zanzibar, Constantinople, the British Virgin Islands. Or do the Virgins belong to America? Anton slips the book behind his back, leans against the wall to hold it in place, stuffs his hands in his pockets. Jasmine's heels click across the tiled hallway. At the foot of the stairs she halts, peering up at him, a trace of something on her face. Disappointment? Worry? Honesty, he decides, is the best policy.

"I was just up at your place, seeing if you were home." His voice is quite steady if a little high, he's getting a handle on lying. "I knocked, but there was no answer." She raises her eyebrows a fraction. "Obviously," he laughs, "because you're here, aren't you?" She laughs herself, a delightful tinkling, and relief floods through him. She pauses long enough for Anton to realize she is probably waiting for him to offer to carry her flight bag upstairs for her. Now he appears rude. He takes one step down, but the book scrapes along the wall behind him. He pauses again, decides to wait until she has passed him. He guesses from the set of her mouth that she's thinking he should have offered to take the bag. But, stuck in his knavish alliance with the wall, he can't even straighten from his slouch as she walks by. As soon as she passes, he slips the book to the stair tread and overtakes her.

"I'll take that if you like."

"I'm almost there."

"Please." He's holding onto the handle, tugging. "Let me. I'd like to." So she smiles and agrees, though they are but three stairs from the top and no more than half a dozen steps along the narrow corridor to her door. He sets her case down by her feet.

"I'll be seeing you soon, then?" he says, smiling quickly. He's astounded at the confidence his voice now exudes. A few days ago he could barely stammer out her name.

"I'll come by tomorrow. All I want to do at the moment is catch up on my sleep." Even in the dim landing light he can see what she says is true, faint violet shadows circle her eyes.

"After lunch, okay? The studio's free until two."

"I'll see you then." She slips her key in the lock, and Anton holds his breath. Could the hatpin have damaged the mechanism?

He waits until she's inside, retrieves the book, then hurries down the rest of the stairs towards the front door. He's almost free and clear, but suddenly his mother is standing there.

"I thought I heard your voice. Who were you talking to?"

"Jasmine."

"Jasmine?"

"Jasmine Daniels. She lives upstairs."

"The air hostess?" His mother smiles. "She's much too old for you."

"I was just talking to her. We just said hello."

"Then why are you all flushed?"

"I ran all the way."

"My cigarettes?"

"I forgot."

"You forgot?"

He glances at his feet, then at the Harts' door, praying it doesn't open.

"Is that your book? Let me see." She holds out her hand to take it. Anton hands it over, rocks in his stomach.

"*Sons and Lovers*. D.H. Lawrence." She's pulling his leg, but he blushes anyway, it could be true, he hasn't yet had chance to check the title of his stolen property. "That's an odd choice for you. No books on planes? On war?" She tucks the book under her arm, as if she means to keep it. "Or perhaps you're trying to get inside a woman's head." She leans on the word woman in a way that floods Anton with guilt. The smile leaves her face and her eyes darken. "Did she give you this book?"

"No."

"You'd be better off finding a girl your own age, some harmless little wallflower who doesn't mind — "

"I'll get your cigarettes," he says, his voice flat, eyes downcast. He turns and leaves, slamming the front door on his way out.

It is nearing three-thirty when he returns to hand over his mother's cigarettes and her change. Anton feels drained and ill. He hates disappointing people. Almost forty minutes have passed since he arranged to meet Mr. Hart out the back. Slipping quickly and quietly down the side of the house to the back garden, he decides to get out the bike, show Mr. Hart he's at least made the effort. He owes him that much.

Down the basement steps he clumps, struggles with the key, then groans aloud when he sees the bike leaning against the wall, its tires flat, chain strewn on the floor where he kicked it free of his legs yesterday. Tears prick at his eyes. The pump at least is attached to the bike's crossbar. But still, by the time he has reattached the chain, screwed the valve into the correct end of the pump and reinflated the tires, stiff from age and lack of use, another twenty minutes have passed. His rib cage feels tight where a scream is building inside him, the basement air is fusty and close, stopping up his lungs.

The bicycle is a heavy and awkward contraption to be pushing up stairs. And dirty. Rust from the frame stains his hands and clothes orange, and ancient dust, unsettled in the bumpy uphill ride, catches in his throat, making his eyes smart. In the light of day, the bicycle is even more sad and decrepit-looking, and Anton is half-inclined to simply let go, let it tumble back down the stairs, put the poor thing out of its misery.

He wheels the bicycle along the flagstone path towards the window he crawled through the other day. He cups his hands towards the opening.

"Mr. Hart?"

Silence.

"Mr. Hart," he calls louder. "It's me, Anton." He swallows some dust, wipes grit from one eye. "Sorry I took so long." But the apology sticks in his throat. It wasn't his fault, just a chain of circumstances beyond his control. He wishes he were far away from here, up in the sky somewhere, surrounded by blue. He is about to turn away, the old man must be angry with him or having a nap, perhaps, when he hears him clear his throat.

"Where've you been?" Anton's skin prickles as he recognizes the thick-tongued slur of barbiturate use. The old man appears in the window, head and shoulders lit by the afternoon sun.

"My mother had me run an errand for her." That much was true. "I'm sorry," he says again, gritting his teeth. He can feel anger knotting his shoulders, a thin taste of metal in his mouth. God, how he loathes trying to hold a conversation with people strung out on drugs or alcohol.

"You have the bike?" Such slow, heavy speech. Anton squeezes the handlebars tighter.

"Right here, sir."

"Then push it out to where I can see it, boy. What's the good of my helping you if I can't even see you?"

Anton pushes the bicycle onto the lawn. His bruised and

cut leg throbs in anticipation. "Won't it mess up your grass, sir?"

"Let me worry about the lawn, son, you just line yourself up alongside that bike." There's a long pause. Has he passed out? Anton flicks the brakes in irritation. Left. Right. Left. Right. "Now . . ." At last! "Throw your leg over, place your right foot on the pedal and tilt the bike to your left." His voice still sounds muffled but the words are coming a little stronger, a little faster. Anton does as instructed. "You're right-handed, son, aren't you?"

"Yes, sir." He isn't sure he can trust his right foot to behave. "What do I do next?" Giggles from around the front of the house, heels on the pathway. Students. Four o'clock is fast approaching. His mother will be calling for him any minute.

"Bend your left knee and use it as a springboard to push yourself up onto the seat." Anton bends then waits, his leg beginning to tremble with the effort. "As you take your left foot off the ground use your arms to straighten the handle-bars, and as soon as you make contact with the seat, you should be pushing your right foot down on the pedals with all your strength."

Anton tries, but there are just too many things to coordinate at once. As soon as his left leg leaves the ground the bike topples over, taking him with it. He gets to his feet and tries again but with the same distressing result.

"I can't do it." Pulling the bicycle from the grass he drags it towards the open window, shoves it angrily into the flower bed.

"What's the matter with you, boy?" There's an edge to the voice now. Anton stares sullenly at the mess of broken greenery. "I never took you for a quitter. Stand back where I can see you."

"I'm not a quitter. There's just some things I can't do." He's almost shouting. He takes a step backwards but can't bring himself to look up.

"Learning to ride a bicycle takes practice. Everything takes practice. Do you think I could fly a plane the first time I climbed in the cockpit? Hell, no. Hadn't the first clue. Scared bloody stiff, too. But I didn't give up. My first take-off I was no better than a damn turkey trying to get off the ground, bump, bump, bump, bump all the way down the runway. Damn near brought up my breakfast, the ride was so choppy. All the chaps laughing at me — I was the best piece of entertainment they'd had in weeks. Never got more than three feet off the ground, ran the damn aircraft into the hangar at the end, smashed the propeller off the front. Took a long time to live that one down, I can tell you. But you know what I did? Next day I got right back in that machine and tried again."

Anton turns his head away and stares into sun. He squints, his eyes beginning to stream.

"Even though the propeller was broken?"he says, his voice small again, cracked with tears.

"When you quit feeling sorry for yourself, son, I can help you. Until then you're on your own."

When he turns to face the window the old man is no longer there. Stubborn, bad-tempered old mule. Anton gives the bike a swift kick and goes back inside.

London: March 1940

Yvonne trudged up the stairs to the flat, the aromatic newspaper bundle tucked under her arm. Her feet throbbed as they did every day after the nine, ten, and lately twelve hours straight she spent standing on the trams and buses, running up and down the stairs from lower deck to upper deck and back, her voice hoarse from calling out, "Fares, please." The delicious heat from the package warmed her hands, savagely chapped from months of tugging on the bell cord, the snappish springs on her ticket machine. And the weather. Winter had been heartless, enervating, the coldest this century, and on those long, dark mornings when the joints in her fingers had swelled stiff with cold and she had almost believed the sun could never pierce the shroud of blackout nights, she'd even envied those tucked inside warm and well-lighted factories, though they never saw the light of day all week.

Alexei was sitting in his usual spot at the window, shoulders hunched, chin on his chest. From the street he looked like some ghastly hooded ornament, a brooding presentiment of the times. But from the doorway he appeared merely broken. She pulled the hot bundle from inside her coat. Anton, playing with a toy train his father had fashioned from empty matchboxes, milk-bottle tops and string, turned his head as he caught the fish and vinegar scent, tiny nostrils quivering.

"Did you look for work today?" Yvonne shrugged off her cape and unbuttoned the jacket of her uniform. She told herself every day as she made her way home that she no longer cared whether he answered her or not. It wasn't true. Though she'd suffered more than six months of his silence — silence at times so loud her ears had throbbed — Yvonne still found herself after each question holding her breath in hope. "Your Prime Minister declared war on Germany today," he'd said when she returned from Clacton-on-Sea, as if she'd only been to the shop and back. It was the last direct statement in English she could recall him making.

Alexei moved only to draw on his cigarette, exhale bitter smoke in a sigh. She placed the fish and chips on the deal table. The table, a mess of sticky tea rings and bread crumbs, needed wiping down. Anton limped over to investigate. She unwrapped the newspaper and handed him a bag of chips, malt vinegar leaking from the bottom, then rolled up the rest to keep them warm. Anton pulled out a chair and sat down, arms and chip bag in the crumbs, uncaring, and began to eat.

Yvonne toed off her shoes and slipped her feet into a comfortable pair of old practice slippers, all the while tracing the long lean line of Alexei's back with her eyes. Ridges of bone now stood outlined through his thin clothes, and his hair curled limply into his shoulders. For hours at a stretch he perched at the same window, smoking his skinny hand-rolled cigarettes, drinking sweet black tea and watching the trams pass by, the paper boys, hawkers and vendors plying their trades. Yvonne walked over to the window and placed a hand on Alexei's shoulder.

"I brought your favourite. Fish and chips," she said, though it was unnecessary, the room now pungent with them. "Thought we could do with a treat." Alexei, all knobbly bone and stringy flesh beneath her hand, continued staring out the window. Yvonne glanced down the twilit street. Workers from the soap factory were making their way home. There were rumours that the factory was going to be converted. Ordnance — bombs, bullets, a factory of death within spitting distance. Jack Blunt, who lived downstairs, said it wasn't true. Said no fool would build an ammo factory in the middle of the city, not even a damn fool government like this one. It didn't make sense, what with it a likely target for bombs and all these people living around. No government could be that stupid. But it seemed to Yvonne that the government had already been stupid, and it was too late to start splitting hairs. Already it seemed that the government didn't care much about people's lives, tearing them apart as they did, pushing folk off to the countryside, putting the men at deadly risk by sending them to face machine guns and tanks on foreign soil.

"Come sit with us." She squeezed his shoulder. "Anton misses you." He hadn't said as much, but he didn't have to, the child had shadows under his pale blue eyes and had begun sucking his thumb.

Alexei continued staring. Yvonne watched passengers alight from a tram; soon it would be too dark to make out anything on the street. Alexei would either come into the room and sit on the bed or pull the blackout sheet down and around his shoulders and continue his silent vigil until morning. Yvonne was no longer sure when he slept. If he slept. Suddenly he cleared his throat, startling her.

"I'm not fit for service," he said. His voice, rusty and unused, sounded harsh as broken glass. He blew cigarette smoke fiercely at the windowpane. Yvonne's heart fluttered. Service? She brought her hand to her throat. Beyond the coldly practical, beyond muttered foreign curses, they were the first words he had addressed to her since she'd returned from Clacton-on-Sea and the Mercers, bowed beneath the weight of her soul-crushing news and carrying the pillowslip with Isobel's clothes.

Service in what?

Mrs. Mercer had washed Isobel's dress and socks, so Yvonne couldn't even bring her daughter back by smell. And she had no photograph, no way to hold her image fresh. Every night Yvonne lay awake, clutching the picture of her daughter in her mind, and every night the picture grew dimmer. Six months had passed, almost a third of Isobel's lifetime, and already her rosy apple cheeks and infectious giggles were fading. Anton had stopped asking after his sister. Perhaps he had already forgotten her. Time was a callous thief. Soon all that would be left would be the white shawl in which they had once carried her, and a feeling, the memory of her hot weight in the train carriage, the way she had jerked and twitched in Ruby Mercer's fancy crib — reaching up and out for her mother? — and the guilt of having been too tired, too absorbed with her own discomfort, with placating Alexei, with not vexing Fred Mercer any further, to put her daughter's needs first.

Alexei ground his cigarette end into an old tobacco tin he used as an ashtray and began rolling another. Yvonne's hand slipped from his shoulder, he might have shrugged it off. She wanted to respond, make the pain in his voice go away. She wanted to find the right words to soften his eyes, make him turn towards her, open his arms. But what to say that wouldn't send him screaming from the room, muttering his Russian curses? She fingered the scar on her chest. "I don't understand," she said eventually, quietly.

Still he didn't turn around. "What is there to not understand, Yvi?" Yvonne's heart split open at the sound of her name on his tongue, the way he almost swallowed the hard vee, spat it out again as a softer eff. She clasped her hand to her mouth, tears smarting in her eyes. "Not fit for service. Finished. Washed up, as you English say. Not good enough for my ballet company, and now not good enough even for your army."

The army. Yvonne clutched at the window frame for support. "You went to the army." Of course, on some level she knew this, but still the words came to her muffled by the confusion of noises inside her head. "To sign up."

"Of course to sign up." He struck a match on the sole of his dance slipper, lit his freshly rolled cigarette. "But your doctors in their long white jackets declare me not fit enough to serve." Now he spun to face her, and she saw that his eyes were wet. "I am not fit enough. Me! You hear that, Yvi? I am not fit enough. Not as fit as the duraks who hang on the corners of the streets with their sour breath and skin like uncooked dough. I who come from a country where winter shatters steel and freezes rivers in twenty feet of ice, I who have the true Siberian hunters' blood in my veins, I who have been training my muscles since I was able to walk. Now I am not even good enough for your pathetic little army."

So many words pouring from his lips. She wanted to hold out her arms and catch them before they rolled away, vanished through the cracks between the floorboards. She blinked furiously, gathering sympathy into her voice. "It's your shoulder," she said, and sent silent thanks to the doctor in the long white jacket who was keeping her Alexei safe from the path of bullets and bombs and all other manner of slaughter. Anton had left his seat, was walking unevenly towards them.

"Of course, my shoulder. What else could it be?" A cruel smile distorted his face. Anton was now standing beside his father, arms raised in the air.

"Lift me up, Papa," he said, a smile on his plump lips, shiny with chip grease. Alexei glanced at his son, absentmindedly ruffled his hair and then folded his arms, fixing Yvonne with a cold stare.

"You know what you need your shoulder for in the army, Yvi?"

"No."

Anton lowered his arms, his eyes widened in pain at the rebuff. Pity twisted behind Yvonne's chest. She bent to pick him up.

"To take the recoil from your rifle. Imagine this. I am not strong enough to kill another human being." He flinched then at his own words, his mouth crumpled, grief etched in the lines there as starkly as it had been the night she had returned without Isobel. Anton stiffened in Yvonne's arms, unused to displays of affection from his mother, or expecting punishment. Instantly she felt irritated with him, walked quickly to the table and sat him roughly in his chair. "Finish your tea," she snapped, as if this were the sole reason she had picked him up. Then softening, a wave of weariness overtaking her, added, "and wash your hands. Papa doesn't want to pick up a boy with greasy hands."

Now Yvonne turned back to Alexei, but the moment was lost. Already he had his back to them, staring out the window again. She pictured herself, in that moment before, flinging herself at his feet. "She looked so beautiful," she wanted to say, she had always wanted to say. "So peaceful." But now the words sat on her lips like rancid fat. "I loved her too, you know." The words pulsed in her head, pushing behind her eyes. She wanted to beat them into his back but held herself in check. Of course she had loved her, still loved her. She was Isobel's mother, and mothers loved their children, didn't they? Even dead ones. She frowned, pushing with the furrows in her brow at all the other voices running through her head, then she stared at Alexei's back. "What about me?" she wanted to scream, and suddenly saw herself pushing him violently from his perch, heard the crash and tinkle of shattered glass. She sucked in a mouthful of air, wiped her mouth with the back of her trembling hand. Why, of all the moments that had presented themselves over the past six months, of all the times she had tried to draw him out, had he chosen this minute to begin speaking to her again? And why was it war he was speaking of, armies and murder, when for six months she'd carried all her pain inside like a rock in her heart? Alone.

Because she had been alone. Where was Alexei's grief? His tears, where were they? All cried in private, on some street or in some park he'd wandered to during the day, shed away from her as if she didn't exist, wasn't important, as if together they didn't make up a family. But just as Isobel's death had scarred his heart, those first dark days of the war had scored his pride. Within hours of declaring war, the government had closed all theatres and cinemas. Instantly Alexei was thrown out of work. In addition, the minister's wife had pressed a week's wages into his hand, they wouldn't be needing him anymore, they were leaving for the countryside. And so Alexei had taken to the window and wrapped himself in silence.

"I'll butter some bread," Yvonne offered. She unwrapped the newspaper, globs of white fat congealing on the now-cold fish and chips. Alexei stubbed out his cigarette, stood up and reached for his coat.

"Nothing for me." How gaunt he looked, standing, only a thin layer of skin stretched across his bones. She could see the tendons moving in his neck as he spoke. "I have to go out."

"Remember how dark it is out there." Stupid words. He spent long hours staring into it, of course he knew. Time and again, sitting in the window after dark, Alexei had brought air raid wardens knocking irately at the door, waking Anton and the neighbours, citing blackout infringements with their sharp tongues, waving rule books at her, issuing ultimatums. At first she had suspected her neighbours of tattling on her, then

Harold. She would not have put it past him to stand outside and submit reports on them, true or false. Once, on her way home from work, she even thought she'd seen Harold's henchman, the red-haired dwarf, loitering in a doorway across the street. But it was more likely to have been a child. As the weeks became months, Alexei continued to mope at the window, coming alive only to inveigh — more and more often in Russian, which further isolated her — against those he believed sought to run him, in their eyes shiftless and filthy, from their midst. Yvonne began to suspect that Alexei was inviting the censure of those around him, that some perverse part of him was even revelling in it.

Alexei stayed away all evening. While air-raid sirens blistered the air outside, Yvonne, refusing to take herself and her child to safety, lay curled up tightly in bed listening to Anton singing nursery rhymes to the wall. She pictured Alexei sitting in the corner of a bunk in a public bomb shelter or on a platform in the tube somewhere, knees up under his chin, chain-smoking. When she left for work the next morning, Anton was holding her hand, dressed for a day on the buses.

When they returned that evening, Alexei was standing by the window with his coat on. The leather satchel by his feet was stuffed with his few clothes, his tattered book of Chekhov's works in Russian sticking from a side pocket. Yvonne felt herself dissolving around the edges.

"You're going somewhere?"

He turned to face her. "I went to see your Harold today."

Yvonne's hand fluttered to her throat. "He's not my Harold."

"About that, I would not be too sure." But the harshness of his words was muted, Alexei had turned away from her and was walking back towards the window. "He has put together a bill of turns" — he snorted — "rejects from your army, and is leaving on a tour."

"A tour." The light in the flat seemed suddenly greyer, flattened, the noises from outside the window unbearably harsh and grating.

"The usual. I believe you are familiar with all these counties and small towns."

"And you're going to dance?" A small smile quivered on her lips; she would force herself to be happy for him.

Alexei was quiet for a few moments. When he spoke there was a finality to his words that knocked Yvonne off balance. "We are leaving on the four-thirty train." He stooped to pick up his bag. "The tour runs for eight weeks." Now he looked at her. "If it is possible I will try to visit you before then."

Eight weeks. However would she survive? She folded her arms. "And what about your son?"

"Our son. You'll have to leave him with the charming and delightful Mrs. Mahoney. At least with your little job you will have money for to pay her with." He began walking towards the door, but Yvonne grabbed his sleeve.

"Wait. You never told me. Why won't you be dancing? If you're not going to dance, what are you going to be doing?"

"We Russians are not at the moment very popular with your countrymen, on account of Stalin's foolish pact with that German madman. It will be the ruin of Russia. So no one cares to see Cossack dancing."

"Ballet, then?" But Yvonne didn't believe this even as the words were coming out of her mouth.

He smiled at her, an ironic grimace. "You English have the very colourful term for this." He tapped at his forehead. "Ah, yes," he said, eyes glittering. "Dogsbody." And he strode out the door, leaving Yvonne speechless.

But life, however loath Yvonne was to admit it, was easier without Alexei. She no longer had to tiptoe around his sullen moods. And as she relaxed, so did Anton. And she knew exactly how much money they had to live on. A little more now that there was one less mouth to feed, though she despised herself for even having such a thought. After all, how much did Alexei eat, anyway? In these past few months surely not enough to keep a bird alive.

But there was that other money too. With Alexei gone, she dared to spend what was left from the bundle Harold had sent with the dwarf. She bought herself some household luxuries, not that new goods were easy to come by, what with factories and production increasingly being turned over to the war effort, but she managed to put her hands on a few things that made their lives a little more comfortable: a second-hand settee and a proper bed for Anton. Now the room looked cluttered instead of bare, and Yvonne even considered moving. She put aside a portion of the money for another and more complicated operation for Anton's foot, which had relapsed yet again, and began making inquiries about hospitals. Many, it turned out, had been evacuated, and Yvonne wondered whether it was wise to send him to the country by himself.

At the beginning of April, Alexei wrote a letter so filled with spirit and hope that Yvonne dared to believe they could be the happy family she imagined in her daydreams. The black cloud that had been dogging him was finally gone; he was reading again; he'd even gained a little weight.

She was not prepared, then, for the visitor who knocked at her door three weeks later.

It was her day off. A policeman filled the doorway, his large frame blocking the spring sunshine that filtered up to the second storey from the transom window above the front door. Another blackout violation? Had Anton been playing with the curtains again? Yvonne had just finished a cigarette, a habit acquired since Alexei's departure. The room was filled with a low-slung haze, the air redolent with the foreign stink of Pashas. She leaned on the door handle, the cigarette had made her dizzy.

"Mrs. Alexander Kavanov?" The policeman's voice was loud. Yvonne glanced at Mrs. Mahoney's door. No doubt she'd already have her ear to it, lazy eye spinning in excitement. "The name's Constable Green." He removed his peaked helmet. "I'm afraid I have some bad news. May I come in?" As she stood aside to let him pass, cigarette smoke wound its way into the hallway and over the staircase, where it dispersed, mixing with the other tenant smells, the damp wool, the mothballs, the boiled cabbage and pig bones.

XVII

Vancouver: July 1952

Anton's fingers are useless, not stiff exactly, but sluggish, as if he's had a fever. He can't manipulate them, his synapses aren't firing. He's made many mistakes already this morning, but he must force himself to concentrate; he'd rather be playing for his mother than moping in his room waiting for the clock to drag its hands around to lunch time.

His insides have felt weightless since he awoke a little after six this morning. He stared at the ceiling and daydreamed for an hour or so, fantasizing every moment of his lesson with Jasmine, over and again, trying to get everything just so: the exact pitch of her laughter, the way his eyes would seek hers and hold them, the measure of electricity in her touch. Then, the hour still too early for him to be up and pottering about, making his mother crotchety, he pulled out the poem to add a few finishing touches. He wants to give it to her, perhaps when the lesson is over, so she may read it in private, read and reread it, memorize the words and lines as he has. But a part of him also wants to present it to her at the beginning, so he can watch her eyes running over the lines, the slow shy smile form on her lips as she realizes his love for her, understands it, reaches out to touch him in reciprocation. She is, he has decided, his perfect woman. Strong and independent, a world traveller, a reader, an accomplished musician.

Once up, he showered, brushed his teeth until his gums bled, then tidied his room. Not that he thinks she'll be coming into his room, not that he wants her to, he can hardly bear to think of her feet stepping over his threshold, her heart beating within his four walls, her fingers running over the cover on his bed, her eyes glancing, head tilted, at the titles of his books — he must try to find hers, he hasn't seen it since he brought it into the apartment — and her long nylon-sheathed legs, crossing with a swish as she sits in his chair, slips off her shoes with a giggle, a flick of her long blond hair.

Slam.

His mother brings the cane pointer down on top of the piano. Anton leaps from the stool, hands crashing discords from the keys.

"A few missed notes I can forgive, we can all forgive." She extends her hand to include the girls, three nine- and ten-year-olds who have turned as white as Anton feels inside. "But when you simply stop playing, then I have to wonder, we all have to wonder" — again her arm sweeps across the breadth of the room, two of the girls have turned to face the window, their shoulders shake with giggles, ballet mistresses harangue their students and not their pianists, the third stares at her feet, uncomfortable with being included in this assault — "why you have troubled yourself to join us this morning." She tilts her head a fraction, raises her eyebrows with that bossy, questioning look. "Do you have other things on your mind?" She seems to be waiting for an answer. Anton shakes his head. "Do you, perhaps, have other things you would rather be doing this morning?"

Of course I do, he wants to yell in her face, picturing first Jasmine, then the movie theatre, the cool, dusty library, and finally the bicycle where he left it yesterday, tipped into the flower bed around the side of the house. He has bruises up and down his legs, and his elbow is still sore from landing on it, but suddenly any pain is preferable to this humiliation. He stands up, feels the shuddering scrape of the stool as he pushes it with the backs of his knees, watches his mother's face as it drains pale, as she bites her lower lip. She never bargained for this, never expected an outright mutiny. But suddenly there he is, rising from his seat, closing the piano lid and turning to leave the room. His shoulders and back are stiff, his muscles taut, though his legs feel like jelly and his back burns where his mother's eyes bore into him. He half expects something to hit him in the back of the head, the small of his back. The room grows bigger and longer, a Brobdingnagian nightmare, as each step brings him no closer to the door. He is hot and cold at the same time. At last he reaches the other side of the room and pulls at the glass knob, cool to his touch, feeling as if he has crossed the Antarctic. He cannot, however, fully let down his guard until he is out of the apartment, and even then his ears are pricked for every tiny noise, any hint that she has followed him with her cat-steps and is about to lay a heavy hand on his shoulder, turn him about.

And do what? Hit him?

But at this point any noise his mother might make would have to be loud to be heard over the racket from next door. He could hear Clarice Hart venting her murderous temper halfway across the living room, and the air in the hallway when he opens the door is blue with it. Most of the words are muffled, but the anger that fuels them is plain as day. *You stupid old man. How many times do I have to . . .* and the rest is un-intelligible. Pacing. Up and down. Into one room and out again, down the hallway, through the kitchen. Harold's rages charted similar labyrinths.

Thud. Thud. Thud. Doors bang, words scream, a grammar of frustration. Anton listens for Mr. Hart, flinching at the cruelty of the words he can hear, the bristling tone of the ones he can't. *If it wasn't for you I'd have a life of my own, a family of my own. But no, here I am, at your beck and call like some unpaid servant. It isn't fair. It just isn't fair.* There's no response from Mr. Hart. He should tell her she doesn't have a family because she's such a battleaxe. Does she ever listen to herself? Another spate of shouts. Again Anton strains his ears for a response. Doesn't Tom ever give back? Or does he just take what she dishes out, day after day, week after week, without so much as a murmur?

Anton moves towards the front door, filled with shame for listening, witness to his friend's humiliation, and at the same time ashamed of him for being gutless. Where is his self respect? He should stand his ground, fight back. A familiar pressure constricts Anton's throat. He would. He'd fight back. Light-headed now, he draws a deep breath, can't seem to pull in enough air. Or would he? His knees haven't stopped trembling since the scene with his mother. Perhaps he's still sore with the old man for barking at him yesterday, calling him a quitter. Had he and his mother ever stood up to Harold, really?

Anton had tried. Once. Life had been blissfully peaceful with Harold away in hospital, but once he returned, convalescing in Anton's room, Anton had stayed away as much as possible. And the longer he stayed away, the more terror accumulated around his bedroom. Harold was in there. He knew because of the snorts, the farts, the thumping on the floor. And Harold shrivelled up in bed was no less powerful and frightening than Harold on two feet with quick hands, eyes burning from the rum he'd consumed throughout the day. His evil seeped out under the bedroom door.

Yvonne was snappish and irritable, and her eyes were shadowed again. So one day Anton took a deep breath and, before he could change his mind, opened the door to his bedroom and strode inside. The room was filled with a sickly sweet smell overlaid with the tang of carbolic soap. Like a hospital. Anton's insides squeezed together. The monster was lying in his bed, sleeping. But Harold was only half the man he'd been before; he'd shed his extra weight as if it had been merely clothing, extra sweaters and jackets layered under his grubby cashmere coat. The cover lay across him, smooth and tight, fastening his body to the bed. Clearly, he never moved. But to Anton it was all an elaborate farce. Leopards, as his mother was always saying, even slimmed-down leopards, didn't change their spots. Harold, he felt certain, had been up and out of bed only moments before, prowling around, licking floors, rubbing himself across the furniture.

He stepped up to the bed, a pillow hidden behind his back. Up close, far from looking wasted and thin, Harold appeared lean and fit. The sheets were clean. Harold was clean, and clean-shaven. His hair was combed, his skin pink. Anton tried to picture his mother washing and shaving the beast, running Harold's cut-throat razor over the hard knob of his Adam's apple, up and under his neck. Was she ever tempted? Anton licked his cracked lips. Harold's eyes were closed. Taking one step nearer to the bed, Anton stubbed his toe on the bedside cabinet. A glass of water rapped against the ashtray, and Harold stirred, opened his eyes. Anton, momentarily thrown by the noise, the presence of an ashtray in his room — Harold could light his own cigarettes? — could only stare as his enemy turned his head slowly to face him. While Harold's grey hair appeared colourless against the white of the pillow slip, he looked alert instead of fogged by the slack-faced stupor Anton had grown up with. He couldn't call out, though. The stroke had taken away his sharp tongue, his quick hands. Anton held this thought hard. Harold could not utter a sound. He wouldn't be able to cry out *cripple boy* or *Frankenfoot* or any of the other hundred and one insults he'd hurled at Anton over the years. He wouldn't be able to call for help. He was mute. Anton raised the pillow as Harold's eyes locked onto his. He braced himself, set his teeth. A flash of fear. He tried to look away, but the pull was irresistible.

So Harold was a coward.

Pity and disgust filled Anton, and then everything changed. The eyes that stared back at him were limp, soft. Anton lowered the pillow. A ghost of a smile passed across Harold's face.

Anton steps outside and walks around the side of the house to where the bicycle has lain in the flower bed since yesterday's tantrum. It won't do to be leaving it outside all the time, he can see where last night's rain has pocked the frame and wheel rims with fresh orange discs of rust. He pulls a handkerchief from his pocket and gives the seat a wipe. If only he can keep straight in his head all the rules Mr. Hart barked at him yesterday. But staying balanced on the seat is the hardest part: try as he might, he can't keep the bike from toppling. He climbs off and looks hard at it. If the seat were lower, his feet would sit flat on the ground, and he could get accustomed to it better that way.

Into the basement for tools, an oil can to loosen the nuts. In twenty minutes, he is seated as visualised. Now he can walk the bike about, using his feet to propel himself. Over the less-than-even terrain of the lawns along the side and at the back of the house, this technique proves ideal. When he reaches the flagstone path, he dares first one and then the other foot on the pedals. It is all a question of finding your centre of balance. Before reaching the front garden, he circles around, walks himself seated on the bike along the side lawn, makes another circle around the back, and he's onto the path again. One foot, two feet, again and again. Tire marks snake across the grass like a frayed cable. The sun climbs higher in the sky. Anton loses his self-consciousness, all that matters is the bicycle and his gaining his balance. Another few turns around the garden, down the path, feet off the ground, one second, two seconds, and then, suddenly, it's there, he's in motion, riding, sailing down the path. He stops at the front garden, feet down, turns around, and this time he rides back along the flagstones and onto the bumpy lawn at the back.

Clapping. "Bravo, son. Bravo. Well done."

Anton stops and turns around. It's Mr. Hart at the squirrel-feeding window. Anton can see his hands, the rest of him is in shadow.

"Thank you," he beams, flushed with pride and exertion. He stands, panting, exhilarated. Then he remembers. Mr. Hart must have been banished to his bedroom. Are you all right? he wants to ask, but bites his tongue. The old man would be mortified if he knew Anton had been standing outside the door, listening.

"I knew you could do it, son. It just takes patience. Everything takes time and patience."

Jasmine trails lilacs into the apartment after her. Anton cannot still his hands. He is excited and still riding high on the triumph of conquering the bike. He fusses and frets and stands in the doorway so long without moving that eventually Jasmine clears her throat, then laughs.

"Sorry," he mumbles and steps backwards. They stand facing each other awkwardly.

"So," she says, gesturing with the stack of papers in her hands, "where's the piano?"

"First door on the right down the hallway." She turns and begins making her way there. "Would you like something to drink?" he calls after her.

"No, thanks." She smiles over her shoulder. He watches the back of her, how her hair, pulled loosely off her shoulders in a chiffon scarf, swings as she walks. His eyes drop to her skirt, the colour of pale sky. The skirt swings to the same rhythm, brushing her calves. Swish, swish, the skirt says, rubbing her legs. Anton's heart beats louder as his gaze travels upwards. He swallows, the skin on his face afire.

Just as he has to tear himself away, something on the sofa catches Jasmine's eye. She turns her head to see better, then pauses mid-stride before resuming her walk, now a trifle hesitant, into the dance room. Anton runs himself a glass of water in the kitchen, his mouth is already dry, lips sticking to his teeth. As he passes the end of the sofa, he sees what had arrested Jasmine. His book, her book, in fact, *Sons and Lovers* — even the title has the power to arouse, to stir — is lying open, face down on the arm of the sofa, in plain view of all who walk past. It wasn't there this morning. It hadn't even been there an hour ago. He knows, he straightened the cushions himself.

The moment Anton steps into the dance room, he can sense that what had hardly begun is already over. Jasmine is sitting at the piano, sheet music stacked in the stand, but her eyes are heavy with disappointment, suspicion has pinched her mouth. Each laboured step Anton takes towards her magnifies his limp, water slops from his glass with each lurch. He's perspiring, the glass threatens to slip from his hand. He is trying so hard to read the look on her face that he is staring. The book could just be coincidence, or is the cover marked, scored in such a way that there's no doubt it's hers? He wants to rush back and look, but he must keep on. Oh, why did he have to step foot in her apartment in the first place? What could have possessed him?

Jasmine gathers her music together from the piano, she must have set it out there intending to stay, but now she's read his face, his naked shame, and changed her mind: she knows he's guilty. She shuffles the sheets, and they slip from her fingers and scatter on the floor. She stoops to retrieve them. Anton places his water glass, now only two-thirds full, on the lid of the piano cabinet and crouches to help her.

"I can manage." He continues scurrying after the runaway sheets. She puts her hand on his arm. "Really, I can."

Anton colours and stands, Jasmine straightens, brushes imaginary hair from her face. "I don't think . . ." A fringe of cool around her voice. "You're very young, aren't you?"

"Sixteen."

"Sixteen."

"On Friday. On Friday I'll be sixteen." It sounds so juvenile.

"You're so tall, I thought you might be . . . look, never mind. This really wasn't such a great idea. I'm not that good anyway. And I'm sure you can do just fine without any help from me." A quick, embarrassed tug of her facial muscles. "I'll be going, then." She looks away, then back at him. "I'm meeting a friend."

Anton watches her leave. It seems as if all the light is leaving his life too, and all the air. He shivers. The room without her is colder, the paint on the walls shabbier. Dust has collected in the piano's scrollwork. He turns to the window and stares out at the laurel hedge that separates the Harts' garden from the neighbour's. A black squirrel runs across the lawn, then a larger grey one, chasing it. Anton feels his mother's hand on his arm.

"Don't," he says, his voice so cold, so unlike anything either of them has ever heard from him before that she withdraws it as if burned.

"She was too old for you."

"You don't understand."

"I was only trying to help."

He turns, looks directly in her eyes. "I don't need your kind of help." And then, almost as an afterthought, "I never have."

XVIII

Blackpool: July 1943

The wind whipped up the sand, which stung her legs, blew the ends of her hair, which she had tied back in a scarf, into her face. Yvonne squinted in the direction of Blackpool Tower, then cupped her hands around her eyes, shielding them from the sun, and turned to face downwind. Barbed wire corralled the beach, at least half of it was lost to the R.A.F. Yvonne dropped her arms and began walking towards the dirty brown sea, waves slapping onto the beach, and Anton with his bucket and spade, digging by the water's edge. A criminal four shillings and sixpence a day the bucket and spade were costing her in rental, though two and six was deposit, she'd get that back.

An inexpensive break from it all, he'd promised. It'll be quiet and relaxing. She pulled a face at the barbed wire. No air raids. Which wasn't true either. And she could hear their own planes roaring overhead at night, on their way out for night bombing over Germany. Lancaster bombers, Anton had said from his cot, one ear cocked to their drone. They formed up over the English Channel. You couldn't have three hundred planes all taking off from the same air base. It would take too long and be too noisy. Yvonne had pulled her covers and pillow over her head and tried to get to sleep.

She turned and squinted up the beach again. No sign of him as yet. Yvonne walked towards the water and Anton, who was engrossed in building an elaborate sandcastle, complete with moat and bridge. He'd decorated the ramparts with broken bits of shell and twigs, pods of dry seaweed. Occasionally a wave made it far enough up the beach to fill the moat, then the water would disappear slowly, sucked into the thirsty sand. He was good with his hands, she should be grateful for that much, it made up somewhat for the shortcomings with his feet. She glanced towards the stubborn one, his right, tucked underneath his skinny bottom. More surgery, the doctor had said. A new doctor. The foot was rigid. It wasn't responding the way the left had. The new doctor blamed the old doctor, his piecemeal methods, his ineffectual casting, which should have encased Anton's legs, not just his feet and ankles. The new doctor said it was now necessary to cut through the bone, the tibia, in order to correct its internal rotation. Anton was old enough, he said, she shouldn't wait too long. If it was done after the foot was fully grown, his joints might have to be fused, he would always have some stiffness there. Yvonne didn't fully understand the procedure, the long words the new doctor bandied about, but, he assured her, it would enable the foot to bear weight better. Yvonne's real concern was how Anton would react when she told him he was going back into hospital again.

The boy looked up as his mother approached, her stubby shadow not quite reaching the walls of his fortress. "It's the last line of defence," he said solemnly. "Here are the Jerries." He pointed to a formation of tiny pebbles. "They're trying to in-filtrate the castle, but they can't because of these cannons" — here he gestured at some twists of seaweed thrusting from narrow slits, windows probably. "Our soldiers are here." An orderly group of pearly shell fragments. Yvonne wasn't sure how shell could be seen as stronger or more formidable than stone, but she said nothing. Two larger pieces of shell stood on end in front.

"And these?" she asked.

"This is Papa," he said, fingering the larger of the two. "And this is me." Of course Papa. Papa would be there. Yvonne's heart snagged in her throat; she saw herself suddenly crushing Anton's sandcastle underfoot, but she knelt to contain herself instead. It wasn't enough that Anton grew daily to look more like his father, so much so that at times — when he made a characteristic motion with his hands, stared at her in a certain way — she could barely stand to be around him. He also had such a dogged grip on the past. But what could he possibly remember? He no longer had any recollection of having had a sister. It was probably more the idea of having a father that he was holding onto than concrete memories of the living, breathing Alexei. Sometimes Anton came home from school with tales of other children's fathers missing in action, killed in the line of duty or else wounded or maimed. These were more noble deaths, though surely no less painful, a loss was still a loss — Isobel a grey space that would never be filled in — and always would be. She wondered what Anton told his class-mates, if he told them anything at all. He walked with a girl called Abigail to a temporary school that had been set up in a neighbourhood church on account of the large numbers of returned evacuees, but Yvonne suspected he had few friends besides, if any. Still, you could say, My dad was killed at Dun-kirk, Sebastopol, a dozen other romantic-sounding names she heard on *War Report* and *Into Battle*, which Anton was always listening to on the radio, and hold your head high. My father died of pneumonia, which was the story she'd made up, lacked, in these dramatic times, the gilt edges of heroism.

"We've been keeping them at bay for days." He'd misin-terpreted the look on her face as interest in his miniature battle in the sand. His voice took on a quality of the war corres-pondents who sent back despatches from the battle zones. "Soon they will run out of food and ammunition. Already they are demoralized." Yvonne frowned. His vocabulary astounded her at times. Demoralized. Whoever had taught him to say demoralized? It was the kind of word she could only attach a feeling to; if she was asked to define it she would scarcely know where to begin. Ask Anton, she supposed.

A familiar silhouette appeared on the beach. Yvonne scrambled to her feet. "You play here for a while. And remember, you stay on this beach, you don't go wandering off. If the bombers come, you follow those people to the shelter." She gestured towards a group of older people seated further back from the water, only the knotted handkerchiefs on the tops of their heads visible over the striped windbreaks they'd set up around them. "You wait until the all clear sounds, and then wait for me outside the shelter, you hear? Tell me what I just said."

Anton repeated the instructions while shoring up a crumbling wall of his castle. The tide was moving in. "Watch your socks and shoes don't go floating out to sea. I can't afford to be replacing them." Anton's footwear — clubfoot shoes as well as boots with an extra piece of leather on the inside for reinforcement — was expensive. "You have sense enough to move back as the water comes in, I hope. And if you go paddling, you carry your socks and shoes with you, you hear me?" She glanced round at the few other holidaymakers on the beach. "You don't know who you can trust. Those socks are brand new. And don't go in the water past your knees. There's things in there'll grab your ankles and pull you under if you're not careful." Anton looked up at her sharply then. "I'll be back in an hour or so." And she turned away, first walking over to the group inside the windbreaks, exchanging a few words and extracting a promise to take him with them if the planes came, then hurrying up the beach to where Harold was pacing back and forth.

"You took your time," he said. "Who were you talking to down there?"

"I was warning the kid, that's all." She smiled a tight smile and linked her arm through his. "Yesterday he wandered off. I found him playing near that barbed wire section. Said he wanted to watch the soldiers."

"You should leave him at the hotel."

"Have a heart. There's nothing for him to do in there, no one for him to talk to. At least here he gets the benefit of fresh air."

Harold pulled out his gold pocket watch on its heavy chain, flipped the lid open and scowled at the face. "Let's go," he said, putting the watch away and walking towards the steps that led up to the promenade. "I don't have much time today. Sarge and Sally's poodles have come down with some mysterious ailment, so the bill's one act short. I've sent telegrams up and down the country looking for a replacement act, but it looks like I'll have to ask the others to stretch theirs out a bit." Yvonne paused at the base of the steps to take off her shoes and shake the sand from them.

"Trouble is, there's always more than a few punters reckon they can count. Think you're gypping them 'cos the bill says eight acts and they only counted seven." Yvonne climbed the steps after him in her bare feet. "They're a mingy lot, these northerners." He gave her a quick sideways glance. "You wouldn't consider doing a turn, would you?"

She stared down at her feet with their long toes, their high arches, alarmed at the sudden and rapid hammering of her heart. Her ankles were still slim and attractive. "I'm rusty," she said evasively. The stage, she thought, already feeling its gritty coolness beneath her feet. "Well out of practice."

Harold shrugged. "Just a thought."

It wasn't strictly true. She danced Friday dinnertimes in the talent competitions at the factory and at night by herself to the radio he'd bought her, the first of many gifts Charlie, the red-haired dwarf, was to show up with, along with a couple of packets of Pall Malls, a quarter-pound of sausage meat and a tin of American jelly candies she and Anton had made themselves sick on that evening. The gifts, often unavailable items — Harold, though she never asked, didn't want to know, was surely involved in the black market — made their living a little easier, a little more tolerable. In many ways, though, they ate better than they had before the war, many people did, rationing, in its quest for fairness and a balanced diet, saw to that. And the hardships of the home front, the restrictions on the use of bathwater, for instance, and the frequent difficulty in obtaining the most simple but necessary items, like matches and hairgrips, cups, glasses, spoons, toothbrushes and cleaning supplies, imposed an order on Yvonne's life that had previously been missing. She discovered she was good at eking out the ration coupons, found it a matter of pride to be able to make all her supplies last until the next set arrived in the mail. It was order, and order was easier than, and by far preferable to, the uncertainty of struggling with her mother, never knowing when her next meal was coming, how long they'd be staying in any set of rooms, whether there'd be a strange man pulling on his socks and shoes by the fireplace in the morning. Her life had been ruled by only one dictator then — gin. And the struggles hadn't ended after she left to live with Alexei, either. Oh, there was no doubt the war had brought hardships and death to people's doorsteps, but to Yvonne's mind there was also an intensity and gaiety to life that the pre-war years lacked. And she knew others felt it too. Her neighbours, some of whom had never exchanged a word in all the years they'd been living by each other, were suddenly swapping recipes or offering to share the warmth of their coal, their firewood.

Neighbourhood pageants and festivals had been revived with a fervour, and Make Do and Mend meetings were held regularly in church halls. In these Yvonne excelled, giving demonstrations and patient one-on-one coaching. Having sewn her mother's costumes from the time she was old enough to thread a needle by herself, cutting up old clothes to make new was as natural to her as breathing. And the security money could bring! A steady weekly wage from the munitions factory, to which she'd transferred when working the buses and trams at night had become too tiring and when in the dark hours of winter, she'd had to slap away too many roaming male hands. Yvonne loved the order of the factory, the piped music, the camaraderie, laughing and joking with the girls and men she worked with, and, not least, the Friday dinnertime talent competitions. Oh no, her dancing wasn't so rusty, not really.

"Something for you and the kid." Harold handed her a bag containing a couple of oranges, a chunk of cheese and a bar of chocolate. Dancing for the moment forgotten, she laughed in delight, taking his arm as they walked quickly towards his hotel. Yvonne hadn't seen an orange in months, and now she had two! Harold was the source of all things colourful and special. How could she not put up with him?

The tide had moved in several yards, and Anton was nowhere in sight. Yvonne hurried along the beach towards the windbreaks. Hadn't she asked these people to keep an eye? You really couldn't trust anyone. But as she drew closer, she picked him out, sitting higher up on the beach, almost directly below the promenade. Someone was with him. A soldier, possibly. Someone in uniform, at least. She'd expressly forbidden Anton to speak to strangers. He was so wilfully disobedient at times.

The soldier stood as she approached, tipped his hat. "G'day, ma'am."

His eyes seemed to laugh as he smiled, a flash of beautiful white teeth, deep lines around his mouth. "Your little brother here was showing me how to build sandcastles."

Yvonne folded her arms. "So I see."

Anton had graduated to the feudal system. There was an entire village in the sand, scores of smaller structures surrounding, as if bowing to it, the grand turreted and ramparted structure in the middle.

"He has quite the imagination," the soldier said.

"You're an American."

"Canadian, ma'am." And he laughed. "We're not as noisy as our big cousins."

Yvonne laughed with him, despite her misgivings.

He removed his hat and held out his hand. Yvonne noticed the flash of a ring. "Corporal Gerry Earle, Canadian Expeditionary Forces, ma'am."

"Yvonne Hoyfield. And this is my son, Anton."

"Son? But you're very young to have —"

"I may be young, but that doesn't mean I don't know what I'm doing."

"I never meant to imply such a thing, ma'am." He brushed a hand through his dirty blond hair. "I'm sorry I offended you. He's a nice boy. Reminds me of my own. David's his name." He smiled apologetically. "Here," he said, and, fishing a slim wallet from an inside pocket, slipped out a photograph of a smiling curly-haired boy sitting on his mother's knee. It was her curly hair the boy had inherited. But though he was about the same age, the boy looked nothing at all like Anton. Corporal Gerry Earle was obviously lonely for his family.

Yvonne handed the photograph back. "Your wife's very pretty. What's her name?"

"Dorothy. Dot to her friends." Yvonne bent to help Anton with his socks and shoes. Corporal Gerry Earle might have a family he loved waiting for him back home, but it was still disconcerting to feel his intense green eyes sparkling on her.

"Say, would you let me take you for dinner?"

"Pardon?" She turned her face to look up at him.

"Dinner. The three of us. My treat?" Those eyes. They could undo a thousand resolutions. "We may be off any day now."

"Off where?"

"Can't say, I'm afraid." He ran his hand through his hair again before replacing his hat. "Please say yes. You'll make my day."

She stood and pulled Anton to his feet, tried to put a little indignation in her voice. "How do you know my husband isn't up there on the promenade waiting for us?" She was thinking of Harold. Yvonne liked to pretend to herself that she was using him, but increasingly Harold was staking his claim on her, he had spies and informants everywhere. He might not like to hear about her chatting on the beach with a good-looking Canadian soldier.

Corporal Gerry Earle had the grace to look embarrassed. "I'm sorry. Anton told me about —"

"I can't."

"Can't or won't?" He smiled again. God, he was a handsome devil, she could scarcely find her tongue in her mouth.

"Can't. I'm dancing at the Palace tonight." She was? She'd have to send a telegram, let Harold know she'd changed her mind.

"I'll come and see you then, maybe Anton can sit with me in the gallery."

The child's face lit up. "Please, Mama." It was tempting. And she wouldn't have to worry about leaving him alone in the room for the evening. But then there was Harold's jealousy to consider, to minister to.

"Well, I suppose it won't do any harm." She was fingering the scar on her chest. "Meet us outside the Crown and Anchor at seven o'clock, and you can take Anton into the theatre. Then give me half an hour after the show's over and I'll meet back up with you both there." Why was her heart fluttering so? He was simply lonely, and it was Anton's company he wanted as much as hers. No cause to wax coy and schoolgirlish. She tried to push him out of her mind all the way back to their hotel.

Yvonne practised her routine in the hotel room a few times, bumping into the bed, Anton's cot, the dresser, before abandoning any pretence of seriousness and instead taking mincing ballet steps between and around the furniture, pulling outrageous faces and making Anton laugh. It was much the kind of dancing Kitty had done on stage while her husband Karl had sawed, poker-faced, on his cello, but those days had long ago faded into Yvonne's subconscious. Now, she thought, it was the attentions of the attractive young soldier that had made her giddy. She could feel the brightness in her eyes, the flush that tinged her skin pink.

When she stepped out onto the stage that evening and lifted her arms, raising herself on tiptoe, Yvonne felt the charge of the audience thrilling through her. A few steps forward with the music, then a sweep downwards. Arms, torso, her thick band of hair uncoiled, shaken free. Steps again towards the coloured floats at the edge of the stage, then a leap, a turn, a twist and a sway. How easily it all came back, how lithe her body was still, how limber, a body born to dance, to soak up the stares of a spellbound audience. Around and around she spun and whirled, leaped and shook, until, the music over, her body spent, she bowed gratefully to the audience, raising her head as the lights came up. Row upon row of servicemen cheering and clapping, hands above their heads. Corporal Gerry Earle was sitting out there with Anton, but she had no way of picking him out from the dozens of other uniforms in the crowd.

Catching her breath and euphoric from the applause, Yvonne watched the following two acts from the wings, drinking in the atmosphere. Her stage life might have happened in another age, another lifetime, it all seemed so long ago. But standing there feeling the thunder of applause, Yvonne knew that a part of her would always belong, not only to dance, but to the atmosphere of the hopelessly outdated and seamy music halls. It was, she supposed, in her blood.

But Harold was never far from her mind, and she slipped away before the final curtain. On the staircase she bumped into Madelaine, one of the bawdy singers. Madelaine had known her mother. Yvonne pulled the hood of her cape over her head, not wanting to be recognized. Madelaine giggled. Assailed by the old and too-familiar smell of gin, Yvonne recoiled.

"Oh, the King is in his counting house, counting all his money," Madelaine sang tipsily, miming an exaggerated version of Harold taking out his precious watch and reading the time. Then she laughed a great belly laugh. Yvonne scuttled down the rest of the stairs and flew out the rear exit and down the alley to the pub.

The corporal and Anton were leaning against the wall. "Bravo, bravo," they called out together, clapping. Anton was flushed and bright-eyed.

"Now you have to come for dinner with me," the good-looking Canadian said. "You must be ravenous after that wonderful dance." She beamed and curtsied, then looked nervously behind her for Harold or one of his flunkies.

"Quickly, then," she said, and the three of them swept down the alley out to the main road.

Anton, with the instant trust this tall, gentle soldier had engendered in him, bolted his food, then leaned across the bench seat, resting his head on the young corporal's arm.

"He misses his father," Yvonne said, as if to excuse her son's forwardness.

"Boys need fathers," Gerry said, then added, "but there's a lot of kids missing theirs because of this war, and they'll be a lot more before we're through."

They were quiet awhile. But Yvonne didn't want to talk about the war.

"Tell me about Canada," she said. "Is it all covered in ice and snow like they say?"

"Yep. We carve blocks from the ice and build igloos to live in, and all the kids ski to school."

Anton looked up adoringly. "What if they can't ski?"

Gerry blushed, realizing that Anton was probably comparing himself to such kids. "Then they use snowshoes. They're like tennis racquets that you strap to your feet."

"Like the Eskimos use?"

"Just like the Eskimos."

"Do you know any?"

"Eskimos?"

"I think Corporal Earle is only teasing."

"Gerry, please." He smiled his heart-stopping smile.

"I think Gerry is only teasing," Yvonne repeated. She was flirting with him.

"I've never seen an Eskimo in my life, and your mum's right, I'm teasing you. Sure, we get lots of snow and ice in winter, but in summer it gets hot, real hot."

"Hotter than here?"

"Much hotter than here. So hot the roads get soft.

"So hot your shoes melt?"

"So hot your socks melt."

"So hot your feet melt?"

"So hot you have to take your feet off and put them in the icebox." Anton, excited and overtired, giggled until he got the hiccups.

Yvonne took the cigarette Gerry offered and waited while he lit it for her. "If it's so hot and so cold, why do people live there?"

"Ah, well, that's because it's beautiful."

"Really?"

"Really."

"And in what way is it beautiful?"

"It's the size of the place. It's so vast. Some places, there's trees as far as the eye can see, trees as tall as Blackpool Tower, and in others, the land goes on forever, acres of green corn, and in the prairies miles upon miles of golden wheat. And lakes. Lakes everywhere. You like swimming?" he asked Anton.

"Don't know how."

"Then I'll teach you."

"Really?"

"Not a problem, little buddy. Long as your mum don't mind."

"It's fine with me. Not that there's any lakes in London to practice in," she said, shooting Anton a warning glance.

"There's a half a million of them in Canada, some bigger than oceans." He leaned back, sure of having impressed his audience.

"And where is it you live, exactly?"

"Little place called Guelph. Dot and I have a dairy farm there."

"So this hot and cold Canada of yours is just a lot of land and trees and water, then? No towns, no cities, no theatre, no night life?"

"Well, sure there are cities. Guelph's a town, though it's small. But Toronto and Montreal are famous."

Yvonne narrowed her eyes, blew smoke in a stream towards him. "For what?"

"Ah, well, now," he said, shaking his lovely head. "There you have me."

"Charlie, is that you?" The little man stepped out from behind a parked car and walked towards her. "Charlie, were you following me?" He looked down at his scuffed and broken boots, and Yvonne followed his gaze. It occurred to her that he must have trouble getting coupons for children's clothing, but then she dismissed the thought. Surely Harold, with his black market contacts, would be able to come up with something. Some people liked worn-out shoes.

"Just seeing you're all right." He sniffed, stuffed his hands in his pockets "The gaffer wants to be sure —"

"I know what the gaffer wants to be sure of." Though the words sounded more bitter than she'd intended, she managed a smile at the end. Charlie glanced up at her, a mixture of pity and fear. For her? For himself? A little of both, she supposed, they did have this in common. They were both, in their own ways, Harold's property, both trapped by a series of circumstances, by a greedy man who sought out and preyed on the weaknesses of others. And they were both — and this was perhaps the hardest to face — trapped by their own natures. They exchanged tight smiles, then Charlie stepped away, blending back into the night, and Yvonne went inside the hotel and trod softly up the stairs.

He was walking slowly, stiffly, as if he had aged in the night. She would not have believed it was him, but Anton called out his name and he waved at them, and so she stayed where she was, waiting for him to approach.

From thirty feet she could see the bruises, the blood, now dried to a dark smudge, that he had tried unsuccessfully to wipe from his eyebrow, the makeshift sling that supported his right arm. He laughed as he saw her troubled face, ruffled Anton's hair. "Can't be too careful about the people you meet in dark alleys around here," he said, making light of his injuries. But to Yvonne this wasn't funny. It was tyranny, blackmail. It was Harold's ugly hand reaching out to touch every part of her life. He'd been sullen and withdrawn when she'd met him on the beach earlier and had been particularly brutal with her in his hotel room, silent and punishing. As she ran her eyes over Gerry's injuries, a knot of pure hate began to form in her stomach. Harold had something to do with this, she knew it in her bones. Oh, she had reason to be grateful to Harold: it was his money that had lent a little comfort to their lives, paid for Anton's doctors, and he'd given Alexei a respectable send-off and a nice white headstone, which was more than poor Isobel had. She'd always known he was mean and could be ruthless, but for the sake of an easy life she'd pretended not to notice. Now, in laying naked the extent of his claim over her, he'd gone too far.

Gerry began to turn grey, sweat lined his upper lip, and his eyes were dull. He lowered himself gingerly to sit on the wall beside her. "Just don't feel much like standing." He smiled, but Yvonne could see he was in pain and needed medical attention. She excused herself, left Anton with Gerry and went to find a public telephone. Twenty minutes later two military policemen arrived.

"We'll take care of him from here, ma'am. Thanks for calling." Gerry could barely raise his eyes to look at her as they held him between them and escorted him into a military ambulance that was waiting.

"I'll be back tomorrow, kid," he managed to mumble. "We'll go swimming then." The doors closed and the ambulance sped away. Yvonne knew she would never see Corporal Gerry Earle again. The knot of hate in her stomach expanded, pushing its way upwards to the base of her throat. Yvonne felt powerless, torn between wanting to hurt Harold and wanting to escape the chains that were binding her ever more tightly to him. She would not, could not, ever let him think that he'd won. She would sit still, ear to the wall, and bide her time.

Part Three

XIX

Vancouver: May 1952

Daily Anton grows braver. Tiring quickly of the sedate streets of Shaughnessy he has begun venturing farther out, riding down Arbutus Street and into the edges of Kitsilano. Today the weather is fine, and after an hour or so spent riding back and forth between Connaught and Granville parks he decides to go all the way to the bottom, to the road that hugs the water's edge. He wants to walk barefoot, sand between his toes, on Kitsilano Beach. Depending on the time, he may push on towards Jericho Beach to watch the sea planes at Jericho Air Station.

He winds his way back to Arbutus Street and turns north to head downhill. Approaching Eleventh Avenue, he lifts one hand gingerly from the handlebars to salute the Armouries, and then again a block or so further on as the giant gloved hand atop McGavin's bakery balancing its loaf of sliced bread — *Build their good health* — comes into view. At Broadway, he stops for a red light. Already there is a content, achy tightness in his legs, though these days he is stronger, not only from the riding, but from carrying the bicycle up and down the basement steps. He can feel the slow burn of colour in his skin, the brightness in his eyes, and, as he crosses the intersection and begins an even steeper descent, the wind tousling his dark hair.

English Bay lies waiting, a band of iron grey at the horizon. Squeezing both brakes, Anton tries to check his descent without skidding, exhilarated and terrified at the rate at which, on this now almost vertical hill, he is gaining speed. He's flying, silent as a glider, off to cross the water, venture to unknown lands, meet people with blue skin, bones through their noses, tails in their hair. Tears stream backwards across his temples as he laughs out loud and then, unmindful of the stares of passers-by, gives a great whoop. "Aiyee," he screams, bones rattling, hair whipping his eyes and face. Dismounting at the base, he crosses Cornwall Street, legs trembling, chest heaving, nose and eyes smarting. There it is. The sea.

There are many people about, strolling along the sea wall, singles, couples and families. He pushes himself amongst them, eager to merge, join ranks. He sidesteps those walking dogs, positioning his bike between himself and the animals, which he knows from experience can be unpredictable. A group of teenagers pass a football amongst themselves on the grassy verge to his left. Four boys not much older than himself hit a shuttlecock back and forth across an imaginary net. On the beach, the tide well out, a game of volleyball is in progress. And everywhere — his poor, worn-out heart — there is Jasmine: a swing of long blond hair, a tinkling laugh, a click-clicking of heels, and once the scent of lilacs.

Anton climbs back on the bicycle, he feels less self-conscious perched on the seat than shuffling beside it. Since the day he learned to ride, he's been raising the seat in manageable increments, so that now it sits at a normal level for his height. He takes in deep lungfuls of sea air, calling out "Excuse me" and "Behind you" to people strolling in his path, and makes a mental note to check the basement for a bicycle bell.

The wind is picking up, blowing his shirt out like a sail. He can feel the tension of his fragile peace with his mother discharging. Stepping quietly past the practice room on his way out this morning, he had, from the corner of his eye, spied Yvonne swaying gently back and forth in front of the mirror, arms raised like a flower. Yvonne Rose. He and his mother have scarcely exchanged a word all week. His sixteenth birthday passed by with little fanfare. A card on the table at breakfast. Some socks and a pair of underpants wrapped in green paper beside it. Anton tucked his disappointment behind his heart and spent the day on his bicycle. He finds staying away easier. Yet, standing by the mirror this morning, his mother looked so lithe and graceful, so young and vulnerable somehow that he wanted to stop awhile and watch her. But she would have misconstrued this as capitulation and expected life to slip back into its old, comfortable pattern: her snapping orders and him jumping to attention. This is no longer possible. Last Friday the centre of gravity shifted. Anton cannot bring himself to forgive his mother for spoiling his chances with Jasmine.

Of course, if he's honest with himself, Jasmine is the other reason he's been out of the house for hours at a stretch these past few days. It means he isn't in his room brooding, composing letters to her and tearing them up — the poem is already shredded, tiny pieces of confetti he flushed down the toilet — listening for her footsteps in the hallway.

Walking barefoot on the beach is out. Too many eyes fastened on his unfortunate limb, too many looks of pity. He rides up towards the pool and onwards, thinking he might reach Jericho, even Point Grey. Beyond the air station, well beyond, there's a beach at the end of the spit of land the university sits on, and he's heard that if you stand there long enough, often enough, you might see a whole pod of killer whales. He consults his watch. Three o'clock already. He should have come down earlier. He cycles back towards the pool, then, still seated on the bike, leans against the wall that separates the path from the beach. Lots of kids splashing about, fetching girls in tantalizing bathing suits, mothers with one anxious eye on their children, the other enviously on the girls. He looks away, not wishing to be caught ogling, then watches as one man sets himself apart from the others, cutting through the turquoise water with clean, efficient strokes. A soldier on the beach at Blackpool once promised to teach him to swim. But then he had some kind of accident. It hardly surprised him that the man never showed his face again. Adults so often disappointed, went back on their word, lied. It had hurt him, though, at the time, made his mother crotchety, jumpy, biting her nails to the quick on the train ride back to London, making them bleed. Anton feels uneasy remembering his own lies, the deceit he practised around Jasmine. And her friend. The brunette with the milky breasts.

"Hey, buddy. Wanna make up our team?" Anton turns towards the beach and finds himself looking down into a lean, tanned face.

"Volleyball. We're one short. You up for it?" Anton scans the beach, counts eight others besides the one squinting up at him. All are wearing black or navy bathing suits. Lean, muscular legs, feet that from Anton's vantage point appear perfect. He stares from one to the other, speech dried in his mouth. They're asking him to play with them. All his life he's been ignored on the playground, the games field, the ball court, has stood a lifetime at the perimeter, hoping, praying the team captains would choose him, call his name, wave him over to their side, instead of being left until last, chosen by default, or, if there was an odd number of students, being assigned by the teacher, sloping towards the groans and rolling eyes of the unfortunate team members. And now, when he is least expecting it, when it is the furthest thing from his mind, someone, no, not someone, nine boys are waiting on his reply.

He waits almost too long. The speaker's face begins to screw up in distrust, he takes a step back. Anton realizes that to the young man he is simply a boy on a bicycle, no limp, no mis-shapen foot. Something else is running through his mind, something darker.

"I can't," Anton blurts out, just in time. The young man's features relax. He nods and begins to turn away. "I have to be at work soon." Another lie, Anton sliding rapidly, inexorably, into adulthood.

"That's okay," the young man calls over his shoulder with a quick wave, already halfway back to his teammates. Anton's heart is still pounding.

The luxury of being able to say yes. To stride across the sand with confidence and take up his position. As well as the obvious problem, Anton hasn't the first clue how volleyball is played, has no experience of the dynamics of teamwork and little enough of simply spending time with people his own age. There is Elliot, of course. Maybe he should pay him a visit. But he isn't sure if Elliot is at home or in hospital, contagious or not. He can't imagine what he'd say to him anyway. What did you say to someone who might be dying? He's witnessed enough awkward and tongue-tied hospital visitors in his life, he ought to be some kind of expert. The sun gods begin their game, lean, hard bodies in top athletic form. Anton lifts an arm in farewell, pushes off from the wall and begins cycling away.

"See you," he hears from the beach. A thrill rushes through him. Elliot, he thinks, with his sickly pallor, his frail consti-tution, isn't really the kind of friend he's looking for anyway.

It is a long ride back, most of it no ride at all but rather a gruelling push up the Fairview slopes. Anton's calf muscles are burning and cramping as he finally wheels the bicycle around the side of the house. At the corner he stops. Peanuts are flying from the back window. Mr. Hart is feeding his squirrels. Anton considers leaving the bicycle against the wall, that way he won't have to pass the old man, acknowledge his presence, have any sort of conversation with him. *If it wasn't for you, I'd have a life of my own.* How can he look the old man in the face again? Without pity filming his eyes? Also he is still in part angry and irritated with him. He wheels the bicycle towards the wall, then stops. It would not do to provoke Clarice Hart's ire; she is Harold on a bad day, volatile and dangerous. And she would involve his mother. Anton chooses the lesser of the two evils and wheels the bicycle beneath Tom Hart's windows towards the basement steps. He hears shuffling and scraping, and before he can help himself he is looking up at the window. A pale, bony hand rests across the sill.

"There you are, son." Instantly Anton feels hot with guilt. It occurs to him that in his excursions he has been avoiding the old pilot as much as he's been avoiding Jasmine and his mother.

"How are you?" he calls into the dark mouth of a window, irritated with himself for being unable to ignore the man, simply walk away. Anton isn't made of the carefree, self-assured stuff that allows other teenagers to casually brush their elders off.

"Come on in, son," Tom calls in his slow, raspy voice, and Anton squeezes his fists around the bike's handlebars. He doesn't want to sit inside the old man's fusty apartment and watch him slip in and out of a drug-induced stupor. He has no more interest in being friends with a spineless old-timer, someone who doesn't know how to stand up for himself, than he does with a weakling like Elliot. How much thanks can a person squeeze out of a decrepit and rusted bicycle?

"Just be a minute," he replies, almost whimpering with frustration. How difficult can it be to say no? Take a deep breath, lift his chin and decline the invitation with conviction.

He knocks on the Harts' door and walks straight in, mouth set in a grim line. He sits in the corner armchair, hands pinned under his legs, ankles crossed. There's a china plate with cookies already sitting on the table. A bottle of RC Cola. Warm, no doubt. Anton feels ambushed.

"So," Tom begins, masticating slowly. Anton fidgets, seeks out the photograph, maybe he should ask him if he can take it down, have a proper look. "There's a workbench down there, son, you ever feel like using it for anything. Help yourself. All kinds of tools."

"Sir."

"Used to do a lot of projects myself. Bit of carpentry, small plumbing jobs here and there. Even if a man works with his mind, there's something very satisfying in admiring his own handiwork. You good with your hands, son?"

"I suppose so, sir." Anton stifles a yawn, sneaks a glance at his watch.

"If you're going to trust your life to any kind of a machine, son, even a bicycle, you should at least have an inkling of how the thing's put together."

Anton looks at the old man through a fringe of hair. "Things?"

"Mechanical things, son. Machines."

"Like planes?"

"Of course planes."

"So you're saying you know how the planes you flew were put together?"

The old pilot shrugs. "There's no great secret to the internal combustion engine. And everything else was mechanical. Straightforward enough. They were simple machines."

"Were they easier to fly, do you think?"

"Hell, no." He slaps the arm of his wheelchair, looks Anton in the face. "Less complicated, maybe. All you had to go by was the air speed indicator."

Anton relaxes, moves back in his chair. "So how did you know you were flying level?"

"A lateral bubble up by the stick was supposed to tell you if you were on an even keel." The old man's hands demonstrate. "But if you were in the clouds a long time, it was easy to panic. No horizon as reference, see. Without knowing it, you could stand the machine on its ear and go into a spin."

"I watched fighter pilots on the newsreels. They went into tailspins all the time. Then, just as you thought they were going to smash into something, they'd straighten up and fly off." Anton mimes the fall with his hands flattened, fingers together, thumbs linked.

Tom Hart shakes his head slowly. "Back in my time, son, you got into a tailspin it meant your number was up." He looks away. "They gave you a revolver. In case of fire."

"Fire?"

He focuses back on Anton again. "It was just a flimsy crate of wood and varnished cloth. Fire was your greatest fear." He touches a shaky finger to the corner of one eye. Then the other.

"So how come you couldn't get out of them?"

Tom Hart stares at the boy.

"Tailspins," says Anton.

"It was a new game," Tom replies. "We didn't know all the rules." He is silent a moment. "We also didn't have the control over our machines that flyers have today. All that wing surface, just one small flap on either side. Any wind that came up tossed you around like a leaf. Even without a wind, heat bumps could send you up to four, five thousand feet."

"What's the highest you could go?"

"At twelve thousand feet, you could see the coast of England, the cliffs of Dover. That was a comfort. To see the safe place. For a while it was safe, at least. I was there on sick leave in 1917 when the Huns began bombing London."

"Sick leave. You mean you were shot down?" This is it, he

thinks, the battle that left him paralyzed. He probably won a medal or two.

"Conjunctivitis."

"Huh?" Is the old man pulling his leg?

"Conjunctivitis. Pink eye. Flying that low over the trenches for long stretches was hard on the eyes."

Anton makes no attempt to hide his disappointment.

"It was the oil fumes from the engine. Fogged up your goggles. Your job was to identify men in trenches. So you leaned out the cockpit without the damn things, in windspeeds up to sixty miles an hour. All that smoke. Archies, groundfire. Men got sent home all the time."

Perhaps he's just being modest. He doesn't want to brag about the number of kills he made. What if he asks him outright?

"Know what one of the biggest thrills of being a flyer was, son? The women. You could have all the women you wanted, when you wanted." Anton feels his face growing unbearably warm. Maybe Tom knows what went on upstairs. "And I'm not talking whores or any other kind of street rubbish. These were classy dames."

A door closes somewhere outside. Anton's heart misses. He swivels towards the Harts' front door. He's been absent a long time. In the distance a key turns in a lock.

"Speaking of which."

"Huh?"

"Pretty Miss Daniels."

Footsteps tapping down the stairs, light and fast. She's skipping, their fiasco the other day forgotten already.

"That's Jasmine Daniels's door. She's quite the peach." The old man grins, teeth showing. "Heh, heh, you've seen her, haven't you son?"

"Anton."

"Quite ripe for plucking too, eh, son?" The old man wheels himself towards the window.

"Anton. Sir, my name is Anton, not son."

"Anton. Anton?" The old man almost shouts. "A Bolshie name, eh?"

"Yes, sir." Anton hears the front door opening and closing. "My father was a dancer with the Sadler's Wells ballet company," he says quickly, alarmed to hear the shaking in his voice. "They're famous, you know. He was born the year the First World..."

"Mmm, mmm. There she goes, son."

"Anton." Anton is surprised to hear himself shout.

Thomas Hart gives a long, low wolf whistle. He lifts his arm to wave. Has Jasmine with the full red lips, with the beautiful blond hair — up in a ponytail? or curled gently about her shoulders? — turned to wave at this dirty old man? Surely not.

"A fine pair of gams on that one." He sits attentive at the window, almost leaning out of his chair, apparently watching her until she's out of sight, then turns his wheelchair around to face Anton, who is now standing in the centre of the room next to the table, pale-faced and trembling. "I wouldn't mind legs like those wrapped around my ears, eh, boy?"

His ears. Wrapped around his ears. Though Anton has no idea what the old man is talking about, liquid heat pulses through him. He pushes away the image that rears in his head. It's Harold, sitting in the wheelchair across from him, a leer on his slack face.

Flustered, Anton nudges the plate with his hand, knocking it to the floor where it breaks, biscuits and china pieces scattering across the room. Blushing, he stammers and apologizes, then walks quickly, stiffly, to the door and leaves.

It is dinnertime before the shouting begins. Though the words are still incoherent, muffled, for Anton they carry more freight this time. In the silence between Clarice Hart's outbursts, the clatter of knives and forks on china sounds like hammers. He should have stayed, should have cleaned up or at least picked the pieces from the floor. His dinner sticks in his throat — vegetable pie with a peanut butter crust. This is his mother's third attempt at the recipe, one copied down during a weekly meeting with the Ladies Home Circle, a group of local housewives who meet Thursday afternoons to exchange recipes, housecleaning tips and do-it-yourself projects. She has been trying to ingratiate herself with the group for months, but Anton can tell from the droop of her mouth and the set of her lips on Thursday evenings that the meeting has been yet another humiliation. He imagines the other women, jealous of his mother's youth and beauty — *your son is how old?* — her slim and pretty ankles, trying to embarrass her, keep her in her place.

Are you listening? The words are thunderously, murderously clear. Yvonne drops her fork. Peas shoot off her plate and land on the floor. Pat pat pat. They both watch the rogue peas roll away from the table. She closes her eyes. Anton pushes his dinner to one side of his plate and crosses his knife and fork. He is never quite sure if it is the recipes that are bad or his mother's cooking.

"Mama . . ." Anton has to break off as a vitriolic spew of words fills the air, only the occasional one reaching them intact. *Every goddamn morning . . . I . . .* A long pause. Neither Anton nor his mother move. *Are you listening?* This last utterance so hysterical, so shrill that the words must surely have shredded her throat.

"That's her father."

Yvonne does not look up from her plate.

Anton clears his throat. "That's who she's shouting at all the time."

Yvonne will not meet his eyes. Another spate of shouts punctuates the air. Anton strains his ears in vain for the old man's response. He stares at his mother beneath a fringe which now sweeps down past his eyebrows. There are lines of strain about her mouth, and the fretwork by her eyes has grown deeper. She is rubbing the fingers of her right hand with her left.

"How can anyone yell at her own father like that?"

"They're just words, Anton. She can't hurt him with words, can she? Surely you of all people should have learned that by now."

His mother can't believe this. All the abuse Harold piled on her head, week in and week out, a thousand times a day.

"Stay away from that apartment. You hear me? I don't want any trouble." She stands and begins stacking the dishes. "Have you finished?"

"I'm not hungry."

"You're altogether much too involved with that old man already. He gives you keys and bikes and goodness knows what else. What for, Anton?"

What does she mean, what for?

"What is he giving you all these things for? How much does he know?"

About what? Anton desperately searches her face.

"What are you telling him about us, about our lives?" She brushes crumbs from the table with sharp, jerky movements, one hand sweeping them towards the other, cupped below the edge. She drops them onto a plate, picks it up, and strides into the kitchen.

"Nothing, Mama, honest," Anton calls after her retreating back. What is there to tell, to give away?

"You don't know what it took to get here, that's all," she says, her voice flat, her frustration evident in the muted clatter and thud of cutlery and dishes in the sink, throwing things carefully lest anything break. She is, above all things, practical. Still, Anton's shoulders are up around his neck.

"You stop seeing that man, you hear?" Now she's standing in the kitchen doorway, glaring at him. "You stop seeing him. I don't want any trouble."

XX

Portsmouth: April 1946

She was standing on the edge of England, briny air filling her head and lungs. France just across the gunmetal-grey divide of the English Channel, a different feel altogether than on the beach at Blackpool, with its Irish Sea and, beyond that, Ireland itself, a green obstacle between her and the new country. Freedom. Gulls circled and screeched. Yvonne stepped onto the gangplank, pressed the thin soles of her shoes hard upon its wooden slats, determined to feel every minute, every sensation of this trip. Anton, having run ahead in excitement, was waiting just inside the cavity of the ship, next to a sailor in a smart uniform who was collecting tickets from the embarking passengers. He danced and waved, egging her on, but Yvonne, every muscle taut, every cell quickened with elation at what she was doing, with fear at what she had done, would not, could not, be hurried. The enormous effort of will she had brought to bear upon this trip could not be dissipated so lightly. She could feel the press of women behind her. A ship of women. Young women, mainly, women wed or promised to Canadian servicemen, clutching the belongings they'd be needing for the trip, fretting over those consigned to the hold for the duration. Fat, thin, tall and short women, pregnant women, women carrying babies, women in tears and women, like Yvonne, with hope in their eyes, dreaming of their futures.

The ship's horn sounded. Yvonne, startled, grasped for the railing, the cold of its steel another shock. She stood a moment collecting herself, steadying herself.

"Move along there, now," called the sailor at the other end. Mechanically Yvonne placed one foot in front of the other, barely able to credit her fortune as, assisted by the sailor in the smart uniform, she stepped from the gangplank onto the *Queen Mary*. A small sigh of relief. A shaky smile. She reached for Anton's hand. She had brought them this far unscathed, unseen.

Still, fear is not so easily shaken. Hundreds of people swarmed the dock, disembarking from the trains pulling in at the station across the other end of the wharf, alighting from taxicabs and automobiles. There was little point in scanning faces, too far away, too many hat brims hiding the men's eyes. Anyway, how would she even know who she was looking for? It wasn't as if Harold ever did his own dirty work.

Up the steps and onto the promenade towards the rail, Anton parting the people like a small Moses.

"Mama, I want to see. I want to wave with all the people," he pleaded. Yvonne followed in his wake before catching the sweet stench of refuse lapping at the ship's sides. She backed away, pulling Anton with her.

"It smells. As soon as the ship moves away from the dock, you can watch," she promised. But as long as the gangplank was in place, as long as they were still connected, however tenuously, to British soil, Yvonne still felt the need to hide. Too much preparation had gone into this venture. She'd spent more than two years waiting for the war's end, biding her time, suffering untold humiliations in the dark — unheeded, unacknowledged, just a removal of herself for the duration, easy enough to do, a deadening of the senses. Then the salting away of money, threepence here, a halfpenny there, not so difficult when you put your mind to it. And stealing from Harold, who always had fistfuls of notes, pockets heavy with change: a silver threepenny bit, a shilling, a two-bob piece, and once, the coppery taste of blood in her mouth — how brave she'd grown, how deft her fingers, slipping the note from his wallet while he was pulling on his pants, combing his hair in the mirror — a ten-shilling note. But two fares to Canada, even the cheapest berths available, and train tickets from Waterloo to Portsmouth, and suitcases to buy — even after all that, she didn't have enough. And so she'd taken Harold's precious gold watch. Taken it and fled.

Only when Yvonne felt the pull of the ship leaving its mooring post, the swell beneath her feet that told her they were separated from England, did she begin to relax. And while the other passengers were turning away from the rail, making their way down to the cabins to unpack, orient themselves, have a nap or a snack, Yvonne picked Anton up and spun him around, laughing wildly. The women smiled with them. Weren't they all off to a new life in Canada, land of snow and ice, half a million lakes, and farms as wide as English towns, and broad-shouldered, gentle men who would teach their children how to swim?

For the first time in two days, she was free to walk without looking over her shoulder. She could feel the tension dissolving from her back, her neck, her face, she felt years younger, a girl on a voyage with her young brother. Back and forth she swung her hand, Anton's clasped in hers, laughing and squealing, Anton giddy with his mother's excitement.

"Good day to you, miss," said a sailor in an even smarter uniform than the first, tipping his hat. An officer, no doubt. Miss. She rewarded him with a broad smile. See, already it was working, she was shedding Harold like an old skin, no longer useful.

Clockwise around the circumference of the ship they strolled, the wind stinging their faces, the temperature already a good ten degrees colder than in port, before an enervating force descended on her. She was bone-tired, barely able, arms and legs trembling, head throbbing, to make it down to the cabin. Anton gave her his arm, then left her to undress in the narrow, windowless room, where she instantly fell into the bottom bunk and slept. She slept the whole of that day and night and the following day, emerging from her fog around dinnertime. Anton, as if he had a third eye watching over her, tiptoed through the door ten minutes later.

He had, so he told her, unpacked both their travel cases. He showed her the tiny wardrobe with their coats on hangers, plus the two dresses she'd set aside for the voyage. He'd made a friend. Michael Dooley. Together they had covered the entire ship. They knew every floor, every exit, every stairway; they'd been in every lounge and every dining room. They'd even been up in the captain's watchtower, looked at all his nautical maps, had their hands on the ship's steering wheel. Yvonne smiled at his bravery, laughed at his comic descriptions of some of the passengers. She sent him away while she washed and dressed for dinner, then together they climbed the stairs to their dining room. Yvonne asked Anton to introduce her to his friend; perhaps the two families could sit together. But now Anton was quiet and withdrawn. He mumbled something to the effect that they weren't such great friends after all. Yvonne wondered if he was suffering from a little seasickness.

Finding their cramped quarters much too stuffy and claustrophobic, Anton and Yvonne spent all their waking hours on the top decks. When they could bear the cold, and the wind wasn't too high, they walked around the promenade, his arm tucked in hers and sometimes, when the sea was rougher, hers tucked in his. Anton leaned naturally into the pitch and swell of the waves, saving himself and his mother from toppling over or knocking into things; at such times he even gained a type of grace. Yvonne laughed and called him her little boat boy. He stood at the lounge windows for hours scanning the northern horizon for icebergs. The captain had described their beauty for him and the fear they struck in the hearts of all who crossed the North Atlantic. Anton told his mother how he longed to witness one of these white giants, to listen for the shudder, to watch as great pieces sheared loose and, with a rush of air, thundered into the ocean.

But looking out at the ocean too much unnerved Yvonne. She preferred to keep her eyes on the slippery deck floors, the passengers in their dreary Make-Do-and-Mend coats and wraps that had been cut down from dated pre-war garments. In the beginning she sought out people's eyes, stared as they strolled past, looking for herself in their expressions, seeing if they could read anything telltale of herself, that she was a runaway, that she was on the lam. Was that the sort of thing you could tell just by looking at a person?

Mid-voyage. A bright, fine day with no wind, and the passengers, rugged up in their hats, coats and scarves, were all outside. The deck hands had set up deck chairs and tables alongside the portholes, and Anton and Yvonne sat at one of these, playing draughts. A sleight-of-hand artist by the name of Charlie Farlie, whom her mother had billed with years ago, had taught her to play when she was a child. It had always been a good way to while away the hours they spent travelling on trains from one place to another. Anton was a quick study. She'd shown him the game for the first time after breakfast, and already he had a pile of her white counters stacked up beside him, had kinged one of his own pieces and was now set to cross and recross the board without penalty. Though losing, Yvonne was secretly pleased with her new opponent. Anton's turn. He picked up his king and was about to wreak havoc when a shadow fell across their board, a gloved hand reached out and covered hers on the table. Yvonne looked up, squinting into the afternoon sun, but the figure had no face.

"Shove off, kid." Harold. Yvonne's world crashed through the splintered and salt-sprayed deck beneath her chair. Anton looked as pale as she felt. His eyes searched hers for guidance. Lips pinched together, Yvonne slowly nodded her head. Everything seemed to be happening in slow motion, and not to her but to some hollowed out version of herself. How on earth had he found her? After all the steps she had taken, all the lies, the subterfuge. She opened her mouth but nothing came out. Anton's eyes grew round and wild. She tried again, but her voice sounded like it was coming from somewhere outside her head.

"Go for a walk around the deck. I'll catch up with you."

"Like I've caught up with you, you mean, princess." Harold lowered himself into the chair Anton had just vacated. He was grinning, his three gold teeth glinting obscenely. Why had no one ever wrestled the man to the ground, set upon him in an alley and prised them from his mouth?

"You think I was running away from you?" A small quiver in her cheek made her look away. She fussed with her cigarette pack, took one out. Harold struck a match he plucked from the sky and lit it for her. She blew the smoke out in a choking rush. "You flatter yourself." What in God's name was he doing here? Tears burned at her temples. In her mind's eye she saw herself standing in the middle of a large empty room, screaming, tearing out her hair in bloody clumps.

"Business is over. War business, that is."

"Crooked business, you mean."

"Now, you're a little sharp-tongued, aren't you, princess?" He lit a cigar for himself, making a long and showy process out of unwrapping it, rubbing it between his fingers and smelling it. He even had a tiny pair of clippers to snip the end off with. He sucked in hard to light it. Blue smoke rose in a lazy spiral between their faces until the Atlantic wind whipped it away. He looked at Yvonne as if he would burn a hole right through her. Then his lips twisted in a smile. "Did you think we weren't good together, you and me?"

"You have no hold over me."

Now he laughed, those damn teeth again. She should have taken them herself. She held what was left of her cigarette in her left hand, burning down to the cork, and curled her right into a fist, imagined driving it into his mouth. With three gold teeth they could have been in first class. No one could have touched them there. She closed her eyes, breathed out slowly.

"You wouldn't know about crooked business, would you, Yvonne? Pure as the driven snow." He reached into his pocket and placed a piece of paper on the table in front of her. Yvonne opened her eyes but refused to be baited. Harold smoothed the paper out, turned it around so she could read it more easily. "Take a good look, princess," he said, his voice now hard, "and tell me what you see."

Yvonne lowered her gaze and glanced at the paper, pretended to read it, then snapped her head away. She'd guessed what it was the moment he'd drawn it from his pocket, but her body was numb with horror. How many grubby sharks did he know? The man was everywhere, like a noxious fog, a contagion that crept unseen through the air you breathed. How many arms had been broken for this? "It's a pawn shop ticket," she said, flatly.

"For what?" Harold asked. Her skin bristled.

"A man's gold watch."

"A gentleman's gold watch is what it says here."

"A gentleman?" Yvonne raised one eyebrow, driving another nail into her own coffin yet unable to stop herself. "If you say so."

"Can you guess what else it is?" He was a cat with a mouse, pawing at it, batting it into a corner, relishing its discomfort. Yvonne unbuttoned the neck of her coat.

"Absolutely no idea." Now her voice cracked mid-sentence. She'd be arrested the moment they docked in Halifax.

"A marriage license." He leaned back in his seat, well pleased with himself. Yvonne could only stare while the horror of what he had just said sunk in. He couldn't be serious. But then this was Harold. She had not forgotten Corporal Gerry Earle's battered face, his pallor, his collapse. No. She'd jump ship the moment they docked, outrun him. One thing was clear. It was Harold and her now. No flunkies or goons to do his dirty work for him. She'd lose herself in the wilds of Canada and he wouldn't have a hope in hell of finding her.

"The ship's captain can marry us. It's all arranged." Harold rose from his seat, extended an elbow for her to take, and for the second time on this so very long short voyage, Yvonne felt a great inertia descending upon her. "If you'll come with me, Miss Hoyfield," Harold said, erasing all she had left of Alexei, "I will make an honest woman out of you."

XXI

Vancouver: August 1952

He's been this window route before, standing the wheel-barrow against the wall, scrabbling up the siding — easier this time because his limbs have grown stronger, more supple. He peers into the gloom. Tom Hart is sitting at the table by the bay window, his back to Anton.

"Mr. Hart." The old man doesn't turn around. He's sitting too straight in his chair to be asleep, and besides, Anton heard Clarice Hart speaking sharply to him on her way out the door not five minutes since. Anton suspects Tom Hart is angry over the broken plate, the tongue-lashing it precipitated.

"Mr. Hart, sir. You didn't answer the door, so I just wanted to see if you were all right." His mother's admonitions are pure folly; she knows little of the goings on outside her own four walls and understands even less. "I heard — " But he doesn't finish his sentence. How tactless. *I heard your daughter yelling at you.* If Anton has learned anything about Lieutenant Thomas Hart, he's learned his war veteran is a proud man. "Mr. Hart."

Still no response. The window ledge is cutting into Anton's chest, making it difficult to breathe, let alone talk. "Could I come in and . . ."

"Go away." The voice is thin, strained. "Go away. Can't you just leave an old man in peace, son? Just go away. Go find some friends your own age."

Anton is sorry things have come to this. He hates it when people are sore with him. Pulling himself in a little further, if only to take the pressure off his chest, move it down to the lower portion of his belly, he tries again. "I'm really sorry about the plate." The silence in the room is almost menacing. Anton tightens his grip on the windowsill. "I'll pay for it," he says.

"Just go, son." The old man's voice is weary, beaten.

"No. Not" — Anton gasps and wriggles, the window ledge is bruising his insides — "not until you turn around and face me."

"So you're giving the orders now, are you, son?" Anton presses his lips together. He should think before he opens his mouth. Tom Hart already spends what life he has being ordered around.

"I'm sorry, sir. I just meant that if I could see your face, I'd know everything is, well, sort of okay between us." He pauses to get the breath back in his body. "That we're still friends."

Tom Hart snorts. "You're a young boy and I'm an old man. It's a damn fool notion, our being friends."

"You're not that old," Anton says lamely, now balanced on his hipbones, the ledge painfully close to his groin. His eyes are starting to water. He's going to have to climb all the way in or back out and jump down before the sill cuts him in two.

"I'm sixty-three."

"That's not so old." It is ancient. Harold at fifty had been old. Unable to bear the pain anymore, Anton makes a choice, begins slithering the rest of his torso across the window frame.

"Don't come in any further, son." There's a hint of nastiness Anton hasn't heard before, but it's too late. Though upside down, he's already in, his hands have reached the floor. "I'm here now," he says, his upside-down voice compressed by his chest, muffled by his shirt, which has slipped over his head.

"Turn right around and go back the way you came in." A voice wavy with tremors, breaking down. "I'm warning you."

"Can't," Anton croaks, then rolls forward in an awkward somersault. "Ouch." He rubs the back of his head, then looks over at the old man in his wheelchair. But what he sees pins him to the floor.

Ropes.

Thomas Hart is bound by his wrists to the arms of his chair. That explains his not answering the door, not being able to turn his wheelchair around when Anton called his name. He can't move! He's been parked in front of the table and left. To do what? Sit and rot? Let his mind chew on itself?

Ropes.

A cold sweat pricks the small of Anton's back. Ropes that bind. The way buckles and straps bind. Anton flinches, feeling them one by one being pulled tight, the increase in pressure around his shoulders, his arms. Those shadowy figures at the edges of his eyes have grown distinct. He takes a gulp of air, grabs blindly with his fingers as they too are quickly bound and wrapped, tucked away. Once a memory is loosed, others trail in its wake: the stench of excrement, a woman with bright red hair pulling a filthy robe behind, people with burn marks on their wrists from where they've tugged at their restraints, screams that fill his ears and rub his heart raw. A sound — a cry? — escapes his throat.

"Son, just turn around and go back out the way you came."

Anton staggers to his feet in slow motion. The air around him has been sucked clear of all noise, all movement.

And then he steps out of himself.

Stunned and immobile, Anton watches as his other self walks up to the table and leans towards Tom. His ghostly twin raises one arm, finger pointing. "She can't do this to you," he says.

The mirage disappears.

Anton is back inside himself, trembling and cold. Did he just say what he heard himself say? The ticking of the clock on the mantle is now maddeningly loud. Time swells and stretches, like when his mind is distorted by fever.

"Well, don't just stand there gawking," the old man barks, snapping the still-tight air. "Get these damn things off me."

Anton stumbles forward and begins untying the bonds. Old and thin and coarse, with prickly fibres extending from them, they are more twine than rope. His fingers fumble, fear clutches at his mind, still grappling with having stepped out of himself. Has it happened before? And if he tells someone, could he be sent away again? The ropes chafe at his fingers as he struggles with the knots, inexpert, childish knots, knots pulled tight in anger and impatience. He keeps his eyes down, unable to look Thomas Hart in the face. How long did she plan on leaving him bound to his chair, a helpless animal? The muscles in his neck tense as his jaw clenches.

The ropes unravel. Tom rubs at his arms, as if to erase the feel of his bonds.

Clarice Hart must pay for this somehow. Anton's eyes are watering. The floor beneath his feet shifts, and the room begins to spin. He swallows, pushing his anger back down. The room stills.

"You can't stay here," he says when at last he trusts his voice not to crack and betray him.

Tom flexes his spidery fingers across his lap. "Can't exactly leave either, can I son, eh?"

Anton steps forward. "I'd like to help."

"Help?" The old man lifts his chin to look at the boy. Anton can still see traces of shame about his tired and rheumy eyes. "I don't need your help, son." Then he glances away, rubbing at his forearms again. He clears his throat. "Anyway, what do you mean by help? What can you do to help me? I'm just an old man, an old man who wants to be left alone with his memories."

"I can help you escape from here." The idea occurs to Anton as the words are tumbling from his mouth, but the moment it's out he feels it taking root, anchoring him. Thomas Hart should not have to stay shut up in this house like a prisoner and tolerate his daughter's abuse. He, Anton Kavanov, can help the old pilot escape. Instantly, his head begins to clear.

"Escape from here," Tom Hart repeats. "Why on earth would I want to escape from here, son?"

"To get away from . . . um . . . to escape . . ." But it's easier to think than to say out loud.

"Clarice, you mean." Anton begins to nod, then looks away, embarrassed. "She can get a little carried away at times."

Carried away? "She has no right," Anton announces to the floor, then looks up. Tom Hart's face has taken on a faraway quality.

"Oh, I don't know about that, son," he says quietly, almost to himself. "Her mother . . . I don't think Clarry would quite see it that way."

"You're feeling sorry for her?" Why isn't the old man angrier? If it were Anton, he'd be tearing down the walls with his bare hands.

"Things aren't always what they seem, son. People don't always . . . she has her reasons."

The way Harold had his reasons? Anton and his mother have never discussed what Harold's reasons might have been, and she must surely have known what they were. But since his death, his mother has not even once mentioned Harold's name.

"So," he says, louder than he intended, "do you want me to help you or not?"

"Help me? Help me what?"

Anton sighs. Open your eyes, he wants to yell. "Help you get out of here."

Tom Hart is silent for so long Anton wonders if he's gone

to sleep. He's heard old people can sleep with their eyes open. Anton rocks on his feet, looks up at the shelf and its ghastly dolls, then stares at the photograph. But unless he can hold it in his hands, the plane and the figures standing in front of it will only ever in this light be grainy and indistinct. When Tom Hart finally speaks, his voice is soft, almost wistful. "And where would I go, son? An old man in a wheelchair. Where would I go? Who would want me?"

"We," Anton says emphatically, slapping his chest with his right hand. "We, Mr. Hart. You mean where would we go?"

"You?" He narrows his eyes at the young boy standing, so suddenly and utterly sure of himself, in his living room.

"Yes, me. We'd go together."

He lifts a shaggy eyebrow. "And why would you want to run away from home, son?"

"Anton."

"Anton. Anton Kavanov, right?"

"Right." Anton is pleased and a little surprised that the old man remembers.

"Your father's name."

Anton nods. "He died when I was very small."

"And so your mother raised you by herself?"

And Harold. "You could say that." Anton hides his hands in his pockets.

"Not easy, that."

"Yes, but I'm grown up now, and she still treats me like a little kid, she's still trying to run my life for me." Through the window, he sees that clouds have moved in from the ocean. It'll rain soon, and he'll miss being able to ride his bike today. "Only problem is, she doesn't understand what it is I want or need." Images of Jasmine flicker through his mind: bruise-red lips, a blond ringlet of escaped hair brushing her cheek, slim ankles in shimmery hose.

"Ha. Welcome to the world of women, son. Only thing they know is, what's good for you is what's good for them too."

"So, we're agreed, then?"

"Agreed? What've we agreed to?"

"To escape."

The old pilot eyes him shrewdly. "And just where would we escape to?"

"Well, we could go to —" Anton draws a blank. He hasn't thought this far ahead, the idea's still raw, undefined. "Salt Spring Island," he says suddenly, the words once more out of his mouth before he's had time to consider their import. But this is exciting. "We can go to your Salt Spring Island."

Anton cannot see Thomas Hart's face because he is staring at his hands in his lap, but when he eventually looks up, his eyes are shiny with unshed tears. "And how, Anton Kavanov, do you propose that we get to Salt Spring Island?"

Anton shrugs. Details. "By boat."

"Whose boat?"

"Isn't there a ferry that goes there?"

"You need money for ferries, son. You got any money?"

"No, sir."

"That makes two of us, then." Anton looks incredulous, then sceptical. I have no money. It's something adults always say to children. "Well." The old man shrugs his shoulders as if Anton has questioned him out loud. "What would I need money for?" They fall silent, minds turning over.

"Could you get some from your mother?"

"Steal it, you mean?"

The old man shrugs. "Take it when she isn't looking."

"Right. Steal it." Anton shakes his head. "I'm not a thief," he begins, but he is, isn't he? The hatpin. Jasmine's book. *Sons and Lovers*. Heat rushes to his face. "I could rent the bicycle out," he blusters, as if he can drown out his lie with volume.

"Let kids have rides for a nickel."

"You'll need a lot of nickels to make up two ferry tickets."

"I could sell some of my old books." The library. Another stab of guilt. Those books have to be overdue by now. Way overdue. More money he doesn't have.

"Books won't bring you much, either. What you need is something with a bit of value. What you need," he says, eyes brightening, "is a rummage through those old boxes in the basement. Bound to come up with something down there, something one of those pawnshop dealers down on Main and Hastings will give a decent buck or two for."

A buck or two? Anton scowls. How much exactly are we talking about here? The boxes he's looked in are mainly filled with old clothes. But the old man, face flushed and hands aflutter, is charged with excitement.

"My father had this house built almost fifty years ago. There's probably an Aladdin's cave of stuff down there. Only I wouldn't let Clarry catch you carting out boxes. Women can get mighty possessive over their things, even if they aren't their things. Not yet anyway," he adds more softly.

"What kinds of things?" Avoiding Clarice Hart is a given. If he were carting out his own belongings, Anton would still give her a wide berth.

"Son," Tom Hart begins, leaning back in his chair the way old people do when they're settling in to tell a story.

"Anton."

"Anton." He laughs, strokes his chin. "Call me Tom."

"Tom."

"Anton, when I was your age this house was quite grand. Not as large and stately as some of the Shaughnessy homes, but it was special in its own way. Of course, that was before it was divided up into these apartments in the thirties."

"Oh. Why was that?" Anton pulls out one of the dining room chairs and sits down.

"Money. Same reason most things change, for better or worse."

"So what did our apartment used to be?"

"Well, part of it was the front parlour, where my mother would receive guests in the daytime. There was also a sitting room at the back, where the ladies would retire after dinner while the gentlemen stayed here in the dining room and drank brandy and smoked cigars and talked politics."

"Politics." How boring.

"Politics. Money. Vancouver was booming, had been for years. The family was doing well. There was money everywhere, and for the taking. Money for the wealthy, that is. Money makes money, son, remember that. It was like that right up until the war."

"Then you sat around the dining table and talked about going off to fight in the war, right?"

Tom smiles ruefully. "God is on our side, boys," he whispers.

"What?"

Tom jumps. Meanwhile, his words have seeped through to Anton.

"God is on our side?"

"Something my father said, the night before we left."

"Were you worried about getting killed?"

"No, son. It was all about adventure. Never thought about getting killed." He pauses a moment, then resumes, his voice so low he could be talking to himself. "I was too busy worrying about losing my girl."

The clock chimes the hour, and suddenly the hallway outside the Harts' door fills with the giggles of young girls — Yvonne's ballet students, coming and going. Anton gets to his feet. "I have to go home."

"Anton." Tom looks suddenly small and ancient; he won't meet Anton's gaze but nods towards the bonds on the floor. "If you don't want Clarry to find out you've been here" — he pauses, sucks at his teeth — "then you're going to have to tie those back on."

XXII

Vancouver: April 1950

"It's a bigger house, you'll see."

"Why do we need bigger?" It was all too sudden. There'd been a flare-up with Anton on the weekend, followed by two days of silence. The argument was something she hadn't witnessed, but from the pained expression on Anton's face, the way he'd locked himself in his room that evening and the whole of the next day, it was obvious the exchange had been vicious. What had they argued about? Harold had spent most of yesterday huddled in the phone booth at the end of the street talking to God only knew who. And now the house was filled with boxes and they were moving again.

Their third move in four years. Maybe for Harold the urge came from having been part of the music hall circuit for so long; a restlessness settled in your bones, made you uneasy, always anxious to be on the move again. Yvonne felt it herself at times. But it usually came when things weren't going so well. She watched Harold from the corner of her eye, his movements large and loud. He'd left his sickbed only a few weeks ago, and with the exception of the damaged muscles on the right side of his face, it was as if he'd never been ill. In fact, he appeared driven by an energy and purpose she hadn't seen since the war days. So why uproot them all now? It was baffling. What was he running from this time?

"Everyone wants bigger." He was darting in and out of the kitchen, patting her on the bottom as he breezed by, grabbing her breast, nibbling at her neck with his half-mouth. She smiled, slapped at his hands playfully, marionette responses. Inside she felt unsure, wary of this new Harold. The old Harold had been easier to predict. Usually she could trace the course of his anger: a run-in with some crony over money or goods or some warped sense of honour disgraced. He'd have three or four drinks, then turn on her. "Do you love me, Yvonne? Still dreaming of your Russian prince, are you?" He'd grind himself into her, rage and drink, then break down and weep. "Someday, Yvi," he'd say, stroking her hair, snot and tears running down his reddened face, "someday it'll be me you love." But then her stiff limbs, her unresponsive body would enrage him afresh, and he'd drink some more. Around the new Harold she wasn't so sure of anything. Harold pleased with himself — he was humming now, humming as he worked! — was almost more frightening than Harold with a mean drunk on, snarling and vicious.

"It's the dream over here," he called from the hallway closet, where Yvonne could hear the rasp of hangers being dragged across the metal rod. At least he was helping. When they'd moved from the apartment in the West End to this one in New Westminster, he'd simply gone out for the day and left her to do everything.

"Everyone wants to drive a big fast car and live in a big house in the country filled with mod cons. And you and me, princess" — with his half-paralyzed face it came out prinshesh — "we got it all coming to us on a big, shiny silver platter."

Yvonne bit at her thumbnail. He wasn't buying it, surely? First the car and now this. Where was the money coming from? "Is there electricity in this house? Plumbing?" She tried to sound teasing. She pictured pioneer women rubbing their hands raw, beating wet bedsheets on rocks, the week's laundry piled in a daunting heap inside rusted tin baths behind them.

"Is it near the shops? You know I can't drive."

"Women can't drive, my schweet," he sang from the kitchen. "That's why they have men to do it for them."

"It sounds pretty far out." She'd never heard of White Rock. It had to be smaller than New Westminster. "I don't see why we have to live in the country anyway. What's so great about the country?"

"The country, prinshesh, is where all the posh folk live. Always has been, always will be."

"But there's nothing to do in the country." The country was East Anglia. The country had killed Isobel. Vancouver was already a world away from Montreal. Why did he want to take them further out again? The city was good. And it wasn't a very big city, if that was his concern, contained as it was by the ocean on one side and the mountains on the other. It could never get as crowded and congested as London.

"Stop worrying, woman," he said, laughing at her fretting, "and get a move on with those boxes, will you, I've got a couple of fellas'll be here in an hour with a van to haul this lot for us."

They'd moved west when everything turned to mud, mud that soaked their shoes, then dried, splitting the leather, mud that splashed up the backs of their legs, their coats. It had amazed Yvonne that snow could ever get so dirty, ice so stained and gritty. It was spring, and the piles that had grown to eight feet or more along the edges of the roads (which were pavement here; pavements were sidewalks) melted rapidly, forming filthy puddles that froze in the night, slicked the morning sidewalks with black ice.

But it wasn't the mud that unglued him, so Harold said, it was the cold that had preceded it, the snow, the wind that bit at your face and any other flesh you might foolishly expose. He couldn't, so he said, understand why people would put up with such ball-freezing temperatures, especially after having struggled through a summer so hot it made even breathing tiring. Yvonne suspected that the real reason was the language. Languages. Harold had trouble trusting people who flipped back and forth between two tongues, sometimes three. He would set up some shady deal and then, at the last minute, untrustworthy and untrusting, pull out. He'd come home shouting, shaking his head and waving his hands. It wasn't so much that he was out of his league as that he'd joined the wrong queue. The number and kinds of contacts he made were now limited, his circle of influence shrunk.

Once her feet found land again and the ground stopped heaving as if she was still on the ship, Yvonne didn't mind Montreal. Montreal was a city, it was big, and it had something, if not of England, then of Europe about it. Also, that Montreal was a city of immigrants, displaced people with swarthy skin and troubled eyes, helped her settle in, helped her feel not so isolated and different. The immigrants nearly always spoke in harsh, unintelligible harangues, angry, Yvonne thought at first. But then they would clasp each other in the street with a heartiness she found alarming, kiss each other loudly on both cheeks. Sometimes the men had tears in their eyes. Though Yvonne had rarely seen grown men cry before, she grew used to such displays of emotion, after a while even allowing herself to be clasped by some of the women she worked with.

For Yvonne found work easily enough, found once again that

the years of repairing and altering her mother's stage frocks served her well. The rag trade required invisible menders.

Yvonne liked the mending work, liked sitting in a room filled with women. They ranged widely in age, though even the young ones already had hard lines on their faces and assumed a motherly air towards her. Because of the language barrier, much was conveyed through hand signals and facial expressions. Did she have any little ones? Yvonne, craving adult companionship, was only too happy to pull out the snapshot of Anton and herself taken on the beach at Blackpool, the tower in the background. She pointed at Anton, then drew one arm above the floor. Bigger now. *Ah, bigger. Yes.* They nodded, smiled, baring mouthfuls of stained and broken teeth. They pulled out worn and crumpled photos of their own progeny, aped her hand signals. *Yes. Also bigger.*

When she showed up for work with bruises on her face or her arms, the women would simply open their bags of food and thrust on her an extra piece of chicken or pie or tooth-ache-sweet baklava. She could not have named many of the things she ate, but the food was always tasty, if sometimes a bit spicy or oddly textured. The women seemed to believe that fattening her up would somehow make her heal quicker or fill the other holes Harold's punches left.

Yvonne had no desire to move so far west, almost the same distance she had travelled to try escape Harold in the first place. She stared at the pictures in the brochures he brought home and wondered what was British about lakes of aqua-marine and where in Britain one might find vast tracts of fir trees, thick forests banked by craggy violet-coloured moun-tains, mountain after mountain capped with ice and snow. It was open and hemmed in at the same time, nature in conflict with itself.

Folding in the flaps of the cardboard box she'd been filling with newspaper-wrapped plates and bowls, Yvonne lifted another from the floor. In a way she didn't really mind the idea of moving. She had no special attachment to New Westminster, with its smelly pulp and paper mill, the hillside spill of shabby houses that ended at a sluggish and filthy river. What had Harold ever seen in the place? The name? Moving meant getting away from pitying neighbours, their eyes averted from the bruises on her face, though he usually punched her in the stomach, the breasts, places that didn't show, in public at least. She'd be glad of a new start. And who knew, in White Rock maybe Harold would find the kind of contacts he was looking for instead of the usual collection of Cockney has-beens who managed to find him, men with empty pockets and get-rich-quick schemes. Maybe there would be an extra room she could use to start giving dance lessons to local children, make some money herself, gain a little independence. Maybe Anton might enjoy a new school more.

"How many rooms?"

"Plenty of rooms." Harold laughed. "Rooms to do as much as you want with."

"A room to dance in?"

"Two rooms." Her heart lifted, she dared to hope a little. Of course the room wouldn't be just for herself, it was important that Anton keep up with his stretching, keep his muscles loose, his tendons limber. Operations alone would never heal his foot. It wouldn't do to let things slide.

"There's so many rooms," Harold continued, his voice fading as he disappeared into their bedroom, "you can have a room just to decide what you're going to do with all the other rooms." She hadn't seen him this light-hearted in a long time. If ever. It could be a side effect of his illness, like the marring of his face. And maybe Harold really was a new person, a gentler, kinder version of himself. She was being ridiculous. He was still drinking. And of course there was the fight with Anton. If he'd just learn to stay out of the way more. Still, anything was possible. Harold had raised neither his fist nor his voice to her since the stroke. She wiped her face with her hands, suddenly warm. She hadn't exactly been kind to him at the time.

Alarmed by a crash from the dining room, Yvonne had run in to investigate, terrified of catching a cuff around the ear. Harold would lash out no matter what the cause, even if in his drunken state he'd knocked the bowl or saucer or glass to the floor himself. At times she was convinced he did it on purpose.

He was sagging in his chair, his glass sideways on the table, its contents spilled, his dinner plate upside down on the carpet. His face had turned shades of black and purple. A strange gurgling noise came from his throat, arms waving about — he was trying to say something. Yvonne stood rooted to the spot, frightened by what she saw. Undignified was her first thought. How angry Harold would be, knowing she had stood and watched him twitch and drool, was the next. And then her mind changed tracks. How would she cope alone? Harold took care of so many aspects of their lives. She didn't even know who to pay the rent to. Or how much it was. How quickly could she find work herself? Who would she give Harold's old clothes to?

Though watching him struggle and listening to his laboured breathing set Yvonne's heart racing in panic, she could feel something else: a glimmer of relief, an easing of the sorrow that for years had clamped her heart in its cold, heavy fist. The twitching and gurgling lasted for what could only have been seconds before Harold slumped to the floor, but when Yvonne tried to move, her muscles felt as rigid as if she'd been standing in one spot for hours. She walked stiffly back to the kitchen, sat on a stool at the breakfast bar and lit a cigarette. Her mind was trying to run on ahead, but Yvonne had lived too long with the bitterness of disappointment. She smoked two more cigarettes in succession, trying to stay in neutral, staring at the spiral of smoke curling towards the ceiling. She pictured the mess of Harold's dinner seeping into the carpet, cooling, hardening, and blocked out everything else. After stubbing out her third cigarette, she called the ambulance.

But Harold wasn't dead. He had suffered a stroke that would leave him mute and bedridden for several weeks, the right half of his body temporarily numb and useless. His face would never recover, the muscles on the right side forever condemned to express droll stupidity. It served him right. He hardly knew where he was, but as he'd been moved into Anton's room to convalesce, some of his confusion was understandable. Yvonne tried hard in the beginning to hide her disappointment, but as the days passed into weeks, her fear began to dissolve. She fed and bathed him at her own convenience and sat in a chair at his bedside smoking, blowing the smoke so that it hovered over the bed; occasionally she held the cigarette to his lips. She began teasing him with tales about the people she'd seen and spoken to during the day, the places she and Anton had visited. She grew bolder, embroidering her stories with details she could see burned him like hot needles. She was safe. She was getting even. She was sleeping through the night.

And then, against all odds, Harold, his speech slurred and spittle drooling from the caved-in side of his mouth, sat up in bed one day and announced that he was feeling fine.

Yvonne had been treading on eggshells ever since. The men closed the van doors. The last bed, the last dresser tucked away inside. They climbed into the cab and drove away. Now that the neighbours had run their judging eyes over every scrap of furniture they owned, Yvonne wanted to see the back of this neighbourhood as badly as Harold. She didn't know that any of these women, her neighbours, could no better have identified herself and Harold than she could those living two streets away. But looking up and down the street, she'd seen their curtains twitching all afternoon. Drapes. Curtains, drapes. Apparently there was a difference, though no one had ever explained to her what it was; probably she'd never got close enough to anyone to ask. More than four years, and still she couldn't get the language quite right. Making their assessments, these cold women with their shrill tongues.

Yvonne opened the passenger-side door of Harold's shiny brand new astral blue metallic Packard. He'd bought it as a treat for himself after recovering from the stroke, said he was sick and tired of wrapping string and paper around the fender of the beat-up De Soto he'd run around in previously. He was proud of this new car, washing it and polishing the chrome himself every Saturday morning, looking almost ordinary, almost like a real husband. Except no one else around here had a flashy new car, and Harold, she felt, paraded his, honking the horn as he pulled into the driveway and as he left, announcing his arrival and departure ostensibly to Yvonne but really, she knew, to the rest of the neighbourhood.

Down the street, left at the lights, down three blocks. Blocks. She was learning to divide space the way they did over here. Everything was in blocks, every road straight across or up and down, some numbered for even greater convenience. Streets laid out in a perfect grid. After London, finding your way about was as easy as crawling. Harold often said that between the streets and the sun you never needed a map.

Anton's school came into view. A new building. Lots of glass, and built of sections that were made in a factory elsewhere and brought to this site on large flatbed trucks to be assembled on the spot, a child's building blocks. Yvonne breathed deeply and sank back into the car's forgiving upholstery, allowed herself a small, tight smile. She tilted her chin, imagined herself walking through those new prefabricated halls. Heard her heels clicking across the floor. She'd changed into pumps before jumping in the car — her ankles were still neat and pretty — and drawn pearly pink lipstick across her lips, tidied her hair. "You look nice, darling," Harold had said, patting her knee. She saw herself opening the door to the principal's office.

"I've come to collect my son," she would say. "We're moving to — " What? A better place? White Rock. She'd never heard of it. Had anyone? And did that make it good, or, as she feared deep down, bad? A larger home. "My husband has just received a promotion. We're moving up in the world."

It was a nice scene. But this was school. Not her school, but school nonetheless. She'd probably sit on one of the striped chairs in the waiting room outside the principal's office, if there were such a place, she couldn't remember, having spent no more than the absolute minimum amount of time necessary to register Anton these what, five months ago? Or was it six? And she'd smile sweetly at whoever passed by, hoping no one would start talking to her about school. How long would it take one of those clever know-it-all teachers to figure out she'd never been to school in her life? She'd silently hurry the monitor who went to fetch Anton from his class. She might even send Harold in instead. Certainly he'd know better what to say, wouldn't get so flustered.

They approached the school gates, and Harold began to slow down. Swarms of children spewed out, shouting, yelling, running for any one of a number of single-decker yellow buses that were lined up along the curb. As he pulled almost to a stop, Yvonne straightened in her seat, smoothing her skirt in preparation. Then Harold took his foot off the brake and began very slowly to speed up again. Past the gates, past the school grounds. Yvonne was suddenly cold, her body realizing before her mind that something was horribly wrong. She whipped her head around to face him, but as Harold was staring dead ahead, all she could see was his slack and expressionless right side.

"Anton," she cried, terrified. She grabbed at his sleeve. "We have to go back for Anton. We have to take him with us. He's my son." She was screaming, half aware of the kids walking by, staring and pointing, some laughing, others edging away from the crawling car and its odd occupants, one hysterical, the other with only half a face. Harold would not turn and look at her. Yvonne put her hand to her mouth as if to keep her heart from flying out. All she could see in her mind's eye was Anton walking home to find them gone, the house locked up and empty. She began pummelling his shoulder.

"Anton's fine."

Fine. That bloody Canadian word. "Fine. Fine. What do you mean he's fine? What kind of a stupid, pointless word is *fine*? Where is he?" She lunged for his jacket lapel again, but he shook her off, sending her into the door. "What have you done with my son?"

"As I said, Anton is going to be fine." Harold turned to her as he pulled up at a stoplight, the living side of his face cold and cruel. "He'll be well taken care of."

Well taken care of? The chill left her bones to settle over her heart. Where had Harold taken him?

"Don't worry so much," he purred. "It's just going to be me and you from now on."

The sun had already dipped below the horizon by the time they arrived at the new house. Yvonne, numb and dazed, walked inside and straight upstairs to the bedroom, where the removal men had left the bed. She lay down on one side, facing the window, and stared as the moon rose in the night sky. She heard voices inside and out as Harold directed the men with their furniture and boxes. When, much later, the truck pulled away, he stole into the room and sat down on the edge of the bed. He reached out to touch her, but she shrugged him off.

"It's for the best, you'll see, prinshesh." His hand was back on her waist. She lay like a rock, not swallowing, barely breathing. "He'll be looked after properly. Don't be fretting yourself about where he is." He stroked her arm. "There's doctors in this place, and nurses." He paused longer than a beat and Yvonne, sensing he had more to say, held her breath and waited. "He won't be such a danger to himself there. Or to anyone else. He'll be just fine."

Anton dangerous? Her mouth was suddenly dry. Since when had Anton been a danger to himself, much less anyone else? She pressed her lips between her teeth, wise to Harold's tactics. This was simply his way around her silent treatment, and she refused to be baited.

Harold swung his legs up onto the bed and spooned himself in behind her. "It's gonna be just you and me, prinshesh. We're gonna be fine and dandy, you and me." Already his fingers were slowing their trail up and down her arm. Harold, as always, slept the sleep of the innocent.

But Yvonne was wide awake. In her mind she spoke to Anton. She told him to stay safe, to be happy, and assured him that she would come for him, just as soon as she figured out which hospital Harold had taken him to. That the house was small and insubstantial, not at all what Harold had promised, slid off her like the other lies and hurts he'd filled her life with.

In the morning, the full horror of the place hit her. Acres and acres of fields, for as far as the eye could see. And above them nothing but miles of sky. Without changing out of her rumpled dress, Yvonne rushed downstairs and stepped outside. The house was on the crest of a hill, and judging by the mud and the stakes and the bulldozers, the first of a whole street of as yet unbuilt houses, unpaved streets. She and Harold were the only people living here. There were no shops, there was no neighbourhood, there was no one to even nod to. A solitary streetlight, the only sign of civilization, stood on the roadside as if guarding them; there was nothing else for miles. In the distance she could make out farmhouses dotted here and there, but the rest rolled wild and open.

Yvonne began to pace up and down the dirt path. The muscles around her chest squeezed and bound her. She couldn't breathe. She pulled at her hair, pinched at her arms. Her skin throbbed and burned, but it blocked the other pain, the one inside her, the hole where her heart used to be. Where in God's name was Anton? She banged on her chest with her fists, drew in a great breath, lifted her head to the skies and screamed, a shriek that filled up the cold blue air and made it tremble. A sky that went on forever. So much godforsaken blue. Where did it all come from?

XXIII

Vancouver: August 1952

Salt Spring Island keeps Anton awake. It's all he can think about: red mud banks, the twisted, flaking trunks of Arbutus trees, and waters that heal. Beneath the bedcovers, he rubs his right foot with his left. Maybe . . . quickly he dismisses the idea, banishing it from his mind. There's a lot to plan first, details to work out, schedules to obtain. He rolls onto his back, locks his fingers behind his head, the energy of this new purpose charging through him. The ferry terminal, so Anton has learned from Mr. Wine at the variety store, is in Tsaw-wassen — *to-wassen* — which is down towards the U.S. border. Anton has also learned that service to Salt Spring Island from Vancouver is irregular. Only three or four times a week, Mr. Wine seems to think. Also, though you get to travel in style, swanning around the *Princess Mary* with its full-service dining room and staterooms, the trip takes eight hours. The only daily service to Salt Spring is aboard the *Cy Peck* out of Swartz Bay on Vancouver Island. The problem with that route, according to Mr. Wine, is the *Cy Peck* is a small boat, and he's heard of long waits. But, thinks Anton, grinning in the dark, two ferry rides instead of one. It adds another layer of excite-ment to the adventure, makes their route seem that much more convoluted. They'll be that much more difficult to trace. Anton had been tempted to ask Mr. Wine about ticket prices and bus service to the Tsawwassen terminal, but common sense had intervened. He knew if his interest appeared more than casual Mr. Wine might have started asking awkward questions in return. Ever since their set-to over Jasmine, Anton has made himself largely unavailable to run his mother's errands. In all likelihood his mother has been in Mr. Wine's store sometime this past week, buying cigarettes or milk or any one of a dozen things she is forever running out of.

Two ferry rides will, of course, make the trip more expensive. On top of which there are the bus tickets to Tsawwassen. And whatever form of transport they might need on the other side. He wants to turn on his light, start writing things down, but his mother might hear the click of the lamp. He shifts onto his side, rests his head in the crook of his elbow. Anyway, it's probably better not to have incriminating evidence around. What if it falls into the wrong hands?

The Tsawwassen coach must leave from the downtown bus depot on Dunsmuir Street. How to get there? A taxicab is more money they don't have. But a city bus is out. The wheelchair is a solid, heavy object; he'd need the driver's help getting it on the bus, that is if it isn't too wide for the doors in the first place. Even the wider doors towards the rear have a central pole that would block the way. Walking is out of the question, too slow. Perhaps he could somehow pull the wheelchair behind the bike. Anton pictures the two of them tearing down Granville at breakneck speed, the heavier wheelchair quickly gaining on the bicycle, Mr. Hart first mowing him down, then dragging him and the crushed bike behind. He brings his knees up to his chin. No, that would never do.

Now he wants to pee. He pads quietly to the bathroom, urinates, then lowers the seat, presses the handle to flush. What if he uses something rigid to connect the bicycle to the wheelchair, something like the arms of a cart? Then the wheelchair can sit either in front or behind. Is it easier to pull or to push? Horses and donkeys pull, but they're strong. Suppose he is pulling and Mr. Hart falls asleep or leans over the side to look at the flowers or something, and somehow just rolls out of his wheelchair? Anton, unaware, would keep on pedalling, he might not look around until Mr. Hart, a bundle of rags at the side of the road, is well out of sight. It will be easier, he thinks, to push, and at the same time he'll be able to keep an eye on his charge. He'll have a look around for something in the morning.

He climbs back between the sheets and closes his eyes. But what are they going to do for money? Besides the tickets, there's food and shelter to consider. If he takes an axe along, he might be able to chop down long branches and saplings and build a hut, much the way Robinson Crusoe did. But an axe will take up too much room in his haversack, and anyway Robinson Crusoe lived on a sweltering tropical island, not in the middle of a temperate rain forest. Anton has no reason to think it rains less on Salt Spring than it does in Vancouver. But it's possible. After all, it rains here more than it does in England, but when he tells people this they assume he's joking and laugh. As far as shelter's concerned, it might be better if they simply place themselves at the mercy of the islanders and knock on people's doors, ask for a room for the night.

He turns over. But they can't depend on the generosity of the Salt Spring Island people forever. He throws back the covers again and sits up. If worrying about money is going to keep him awake all night, he may as well get up and do something about it. There's less chance of Clarice Hart surprising him rooting through the boxes in the basement if he does it in the middle of the night. So long as he's quiet.

Out of his pyjamas and into his clothes. He tiptoes from his room, shoes in his pockets, carefully opens the apartment door and slips out, closing it gently to behind him. Blackout. He slides along the hallway to the front door, fingertips across the walls to guide him, then steps outside into the cool midsummer night air. There's a mist swirling above his head, fog from the ocean rolled in for the night. He sits on the top step to put on his shoes, pulling the mist with him in slow-moving ten-drils. It winds about his arms and legs, as if to bind them. He brushes its clammy feel from his face, cobwebs in his eyes, dampness already settling in his nose, his lungs. London. He's half tensed in anticipation of an air raid siren. Around the side of the house to the back and down the basement steps. Midway he freezes as a dog begins to howl. The sound is both eerie and lonely as it floats disembodied across the foggy backyards. Anton pictures sharp pointed teeth, eyes yellow with fury, and almost stumbles in his hurry to negotiate the remainder of the steps, hurling himself with more noise than he intended against the stiff wooden door.

Light. He picks his way towards the boxes piled high and dusty along the right-hand wall. A stack of pictures with heavy gilt-edged frames, their details lost in the gloom. Fusty table linens spotted with age and mildew. He coughs once and moves them out of his way. The box below is heavy and resists his attempts to shift it. Scores of old books inside, and inside the books, line upon line of painstakingly handwritten entries. Ledgers for some sort of business. Whatever had once made the Harts wealthy, Anton supposes. His mother has purchased herself a similar ledger to record the transactions of her business. She leaves it open on the dining room table the evenings when she's working in it. The number of students and classes has increased over the summer, and Yvonne has been calling on the services of her accompanist more and more. Anton has noticed the accompanist's name, Sylvie Fischer, filling up the debit column. If she can afford to pay an accompanist, then why not him? He would charge her less than Sylvie Fischer does. But there's such a wall between them now, she'd probably turn his services down. He grasps the heavy box of ledgers with both arms and moves it to the floor.

But could he really work for her again anyway? About the Jasmine affair he's inconsolable. He's the wronged party here; she is the one who should be grovelling, begging him for forgiveness. Instead she's buried herself in her work. Her dance school is all she cares about these days. In fact, the more he thinks about it, the more he realizes how selfish she really is. She didn't want him to have Jasmine because that might take him away from her. It had nothing at all to do with his well-being. With Harold out of the way, he can see his mother clearer. Her motives are more conspicuous. Everything she's ever done has been really just for herself.

In those first two years after Harold's death, he saw little of her. She was gone evenings, so he had to warm up the supper she'd left him and eat alone. After finishing his homework and tinkering with Harold's radio or reading for a while, he would take himself to bed. But she was always there in the morning, her face grey and lined, a cigarette stuck between her lips — she smoked incessantly then — and would make him breakfast, wrap a sandwich for his lunch and give him just enough money to take the bus across the bridge to school and back. She must have planned on moving to this part of the city even then. But nothing was ever mentioned. Anton never knew where she worked and never asked, sensing with a lonely child's acuity that she didn't wish to talk about it.

She talked about very little then, not about the dance school she had obviously been squirrelling money away for, not about the ordeal Anton had just endured, and not about Harold, especially not Harold. That he was gone from their lives and they should be grateful was the sum of the explanation she had given him the day she arrived in the taxicab, a pale and trembling angel, to spirit him away. Anton had not even realized that by *gone* his mother had meant Harold was dead until almost three months later. He'd come home early from school and seen a letter and a white cardboard box sitting on the little card table they used for meals and where Anton sat to do his homework. Anton had picked up the unmarked box — it was surprisingly heavy — and shaken it. None the wiser, he had started to open it. Then he'd glanced at the envelope. It was from a crematorium in White Rock. Harold. Harold was in the box. Anton dropped it with a shout, rubbed his hands up and down the legs of his pants, trying to rid them of the imprint. Harold's ashes. They were probably poisonous. He looked at the box again. The flap was open. He tried delicately to tuck it back in, using only the thumb and forefinger of his right hand, but he fumbled. The box fell over and slid quickly towards him, threatening to spew its contents. Anton leaped backwards. Harold wasn't finished with him yet. Holding his breath to ward off contamination, he picked up the box again and hurriedly tucked in the flap. Then he rushed down the hall to the communal bathroom, washed his hands, splashed cold water on his face. When he came back, the box and the letter were gone.

Anton is sweating and shaking at the same time. Harold is never just a thought or a memory, he's a physical sensation: a wrenching of the gut, a trail of acid down the throat, broken glass behind the ribs. Anton takes a few deep breaths, then pushes a second box of ledgers aside to reveal an old brown pulley-drawn steamer trunk. Releasing the catches, he opens the lid, catching his breath as the harsh basement light falls upon the treasure inside: Lieutenant Thomas Hart's pilot's uniform, neatly folded, his leather cap, flying goggles and gauntlets resting on top. Beside it, also folded neatly, is a leather flying overcoat. Anton runs his fingers reverently over the cap and goggles before reaching into the trunk to carefully pull the uniform from its hiding place. Mothballs scatter like marbles across the basement floor, knocking against other boxes, the legs of discarded furniture before coming to rest. He shakes the uniform out and, holding the jacket by the shoulders, fits it against his own. The smell of naphthalene fills the dusty air, and Anton sneezes several times in a row. Eyes blurry, nose running, he stares down at himself. The sleeves are a little short, but width-wise, it appears the jacket might fit him. Mr. Hart must not only have lost weight over the years but also shrunk. Maybe that's what happened to people in wheelchairs, their legs shrank because they never used them. He makes a silent vow to resume the stretching exercises his mother used to make him do every day, then hurriedly pulls off his trousers and steps into the uniform pants.

They're wool and scratchy, and like the sleeves of the jacket, the legs are a little short. The shoulders of the jacket are somewhat wider than his own, the chest a fraction fuller, even over his sweater. But as Anton lowers the leather cap onto his head, a nice snug fit, and pulls the goggles over top, he fancies he cuts quite a fine figure. He fingers the chevrons on the shoulder. Lieutenant Kavanov. He pulls on the gauntlets, flexes his fingers, now the length and shape of the young Lieutenant Hart's. He strides from the boxes to the door to the furnace and back, chin up, gloved hands linked loosely behind his back; he nods to the men in his flight: Bates, with five kills, always the practical joker, never missing an opportunity to get a rise out of the new lads; Smith, a man with a cruel scar across his cheek that matches a cruel streak through his heart, eleven kills and counting; Bingham, a new lad, eager, only been out for a couple of weeks and yet to down his first Albatross; Stryder, five kills also and the man slated to take his place if anything should go wrong; and finally Dan-the-Man Daniels, the kind of daredevil, all-round good guy you needed out there on your side.

Carried away with the scenario unfolding in his head, Anton lengthens his stride, venturing deeper into the back of the basement, and suddenly finds himself at the foot of a wooden stairway. So there is another way into the basement. Funny he's never noticed the stairs before, though it's darker back here, the light by the boxes doesn't illuminate this far wall. They must lead to the door in the Hart's kitchen, the one he saw when he first climbed in the window to rescue Tom.

He takes them slowly, but halfway up something bumps against his forehead, causing him to yelp in alarm. Gingerly he reaches forward into the dark space, fingers splayed in front of his face, seeking the culprit. A light bulb dangling from the ceiling on an electric cord. Which means there must be a switch somewhere. He gropes the wall, searching, brushing cobwebs and loose, chalky paint with his fingers, then takes another step, searching again until he finds it close by the door, and flips it upwards. The light hums and flickers, a weak glow that scarcely pierces the gloom around him. He tries the doorknob, but the door is, of course, locked. He wonders what time it is. How long has he been down here? Will the Harts be getting up soon? He hasn't found what he came down here to look for — items of value to sell. He needs to know more specifically what Tom has in mind. He doubts the old man would want to get rid of his uniform. And if he did, Anton would gladly take it off his hands. He wonders if Tom even remembers it's down here. Perhaps he could sneak it into his room later.

He settles himself down on the steps to wait. From here he'll be able to hear all their conversations, will be better able to gauge when his landlady plans to go out. Bingo is one of her excursions. She doesn't go every day. Three or four afternoons a week, Tom said, but he never said which days, or whether there was a pattern to them. It might be as well to find out if there is, such information could be useful for their getaway.

His back begins to ache, and he shuffles himself across the stair so he can lean against the wall. Supposing Tom can point him to an object of value in the basement, the money won't last forever. They'll need to find some way of earning a living. At least Anton will. But he isn't trained for anything, and he has no experience. He stares at the shadowy shapes of the boxes, the workbench along the opposite wall, the tools sitting neatly in their brackets along the pegboard.

Tools.

Suddenly he's sitting bolt upright. He can repair a bicycle. Sort of. He's good with his hands and can find his way around a toolbox. A repair shop. He could set up a bicycle repair shop. But how many bicycles can there be on Salt Spring? And how many of those would, at any one time, be in need of repair? Businesses, he's seen for himself, don't grow overnight. Though his mother's dance school is busier every week, she still doesn't have a full roster of students. But he needn't limit himself to bicycles. Radios. He once took Harold's radio completely apart — after two years he can still only think of it as Harold's radio — and got it working again. He had to backtrack a couple of times, undo some mistakes, but eventually he got the hang of it. And there are lots of other small appliances he could have a shot at: vacuum cleaners, toasters, irons, kettles. There can't be much to them. Most are either a small motor with a fan or else a heating element with a spring-based timer. He can practice on his mother's and the Harts' before they leave. Motors he's vague on, but Tom can help him out there. As the old pilot said himself, it helped to know something about the aircraft you were trusting your life to. Between the two of them, they can build a fine business. *Kavanov and Hart: Repairs.* He'll hire someone to paint a big sign that will swing high in the air on a pole and bring everyone on the island, appliances in tow, to their door.

Anton is beginning to feel cold, so he fetches the long, heavy leather overcoat from the trunk and wraps it around himself like a blanket. Positioning himself again on the steps, head resting on his folded-up trousers, he pulls the coat over his shoulders and closes his eyes.

When he awakes, stiff and sore from where the stair treads have cut into his ribs, he realizes it is morning. Through the door he can hear voices, mainly the landlady's, and some deeper rumblings which are obviously Tom. For once Clarice Hart isn't shouting, and Anton finds it odd to listen to her chatting civilly to her father, disconcerting even; it doesn't quite fit the ogre-like picture he has formed of her. She isn't supposed to be nice. She's telling Tom a story about a clerk in the grocery store where she was shopping yesterday. It's something she finds funny, and so she laughs, a witch-like cackle that Tom echoes with deeper laughter of his own. Anton is surprised by a stab of jealousy. If she was at the grocery store yesterday, she probably won't need to go again today, though when they lived in England his mother went shopping every day. Sometimes she sent him, and he'd stand in the requisite queues listening to local gossip. Sometimes they'd talk about whose house had been levelled in last night's bombing raid but, more often than not, about some treasure — limes, apples, cheese, lard — one lucky or resourceful soul had managed to get her hands on. Often they'd be passing a shop with a queue, and his mother would cross the road to join it without even knowing what it was for. Occasionally even the people in front didn't know what they were queuing up for either, but yet they'd stand there because a queue had to mean that something, whatever it was, was briefly available. But then she began bringing home

treats there couldn't possibly have been any queue for anywhere in London. Tins of meat and American chocolate. Anton
stuffed his face and held his tongue. After all, did it really
matter where these things came from?

He's growing irritated. Clarice Hart never stops talking.
And about nothing in particular, nothing interesting, just long
reports of what so-and-so at the bingo said and did, or what
so-and-so's husband said or did. Every sentence begins with,
And so she said . . . And so then he said . . . Also he's hungry
and thirsty. He hopes his mother's classes have already begun.
He doesn't feel up to explaining how come he's been out all
night. He stands on shaky legs, feeling slightly ridiculous now,
all togged out in the pilot's uniform. What exactly was he
planning to do, anyway, stroll through Tom's kitchen door, a
ghost from the past, and frighten the old man to death? Tom
might never want to see the uniform again. It might bring back
painful memories of that last ill-fated battle, the one in which
he'd lost the use of his legs. Anton treads carefully back down
the stairs and removes the scratchy pants and too-big, too-short
jacket. He folds the uniform up and is about to place it back in
the trunk when he changes his mind. No one will be the wiser
if he borrows it for a few hours. He just wants to see what he
looks like in the mirror. He stuffs the helmet and goggles
down the front of his sweater and puts the rest back in the
trunk, closes the lid and piles the ledgers the linens and the
pictures back on top. *Leave no traces of yourself.* Later he'll
sneak it out and into his room. For the present, he wants his
breakfast.

XXIV

White Rock: May 1950

Yvonne jolted awake. *You don't have a hope in hell of finding out where he is. Not a hope.* Harold had laughed, a forced, mean laugh intended to belittle. She picked up the clock on her bedside table and squinted at the dial. Quarter to four. *Not a hope. Ha, ha, ha. There's no hope you'll ever find out.* Harold had slapped his knee, tears in his eyes. It was all very funny. It was too funny. Harold was not the joking kind. Yvonne stared at the bedroom ceiling, the pattern of amber cast there by the streetlight. The room grew lighter as her eyes adjusted. She turned on her side, faced the stack of boxes she still had left to unpack: Anton's things, oppressive shadows in the corner of the room, boxes and boxes of his clothes and books. But no Anton. She had refused to move his belongings into either the second bedroom or the basement — the basement? Was he never coming back? — though Harold had chided her about it countless times.

Yvonne blinked away the pricking in her eyes, everything suddenly crystal clear. It was Harold who was stupid. He'd been stupid with drink all evening and stupid for thinking she wouldn't get the reference. He must have repeated it half a dozen times or more. Hope. There was a place called Hope up in the mountains, she was sure of it, she'd seen the name on a road sign somewhere close to here, out with Harold in the Packard. And something else. One of Harold's cockney cronies, lying, shoes on, ankles crossed — thank God for small mercies

— on the sofa one night, a belly full of liquor, laughing about a place called Hope. Imagine calling a place Hope, a place called Hope leading to a place called Hell's Gate, didn't the fucker who'd named 'em have one hell of a sense of humour. The man had laughed so hard at his own wit he'd almost choked to death. Hard to forget a face that purple.

Yvonne's eyes were open wide now. Hope. That was it. She knew it, knew the truth of it with irrational and unshakeable clarity. Harold had taken Anton to a place called Hope. And just knowing this was enough. Holding her breath, she swung her legs gently over the side of the bed and slipped from between the covers. Hope. Harold had played his little joke at her expense, now she was going to get even.

She grabbed her slacks and sweater discarded the night before, tiptoed around to Harold's side of the bed, reached into the pocket of his pants, neatly folded on a wooden chair, and carefully retrieved his wallet. Downstairs in the kitchen by the light above the stove, she counted out the bills — thirty-seven dollars — returned the wallet to Harold's coat pocket, tucked the money into her purse, and dressed. She then reached into the back of the pots and pans cupboard, feeling with her fingertips for the hard coldness of a silver picture frame. The frame safely in her handbag, she pulled on her jacket, pushed her feet into the loafers on the mat, and turned the key in the back door.

Outside she walked softly around the front of the house, though there was little need for caution as the path and driveway were still mud, and approached the Packard, which was parked on the street directly under the bedroom window, its chrome fenders yellow in the streetlight. She opened the door on the driver's side and slid behind the wheel. She wiggled her feet; they were a good twelve inches from the pedals, more. Fumbling with the catch at the side of the seat, she pulled the whole thing forward. Still it was not enough. She had to point her toes to even touch the gas pedal. Unless she shifted her hips sideways, the brake pedal was out of reach, dangerous even for a seasoned driver.

A cushion would do, a pillow would be better, but it would mean taking the stairs again, every creak a potential giveaway, every wasted minute increasing the likelihood that Harold would wake up and find her gone. What else? What else? She riffled through the downstairs closet, settled on her winter coat. Rolled up, it would push her far enough forward in the seat, but it would also keep her warm in the mountains. After all, it was only May, it might still be winter where she was heading. Map? No. She'd get that from a gas station along the way, no point hunting for something else in the house, especially something Harold so often, so loudly and proudly professed not to need; that was only asking to get caught.

She let herself back into the driver's seat again, positioned the coat so it propped her forward, then placed her hands at the quarter-to-three position on the big white wheel as she'd seen Harold do. Most of the time, of course, Harold drove with only his right hand in the twelve o'clock position; the other would be drumming some variety stage tune on his knee or the outside of the door if the weather were fine and the window down. But quarter to three is where he always started, and two hands had to be safer than one. She looked down at the floor. Pivoting her right foot on its heel, she pointed her toes forward then left, forward then left again. Gas. Brake. Gas. Brake. This was important. She couldn't afford to get them confused. No margin for error on this first leg of the trip. If only the house was a few plots over, the car would be facing downhill instead of uphill. Then she could simply release the brake and coast until she was out of earshot. She considered rolling backwards, but only briefly. The task before her was hair-raising enough; there was no need to make it suicidal.

Pulling the handle to release the brake, she turned the key and the engine burst into life, startling her, her nerves badly frayed. Right foot pointing forward, she pressed down gently on the gas pedal. The engine raced, but the car didn't move. She pressed again, harder this time. The engine roared, but still the car didn't move. She glanced nervously up at the bedroom window, heart in her mouth. There was something else she wasn't doing. It had to do with the skinny stick on the neck of the steering wheel. Think. Quickly. What is it? Harold always moved it when he started the car. Why hadn't she paid more attention? She pulled and pushed at the stick, but it wouldn't budge. Though the early morning air was cool, Yvonne was beginning to perspire, her hands sweaty on the wheel. Why wouldn't the thing move? And then it did. She pulled it towards the steering wheel and felt a catch disengage. She let it go and felt it engage again. Once more she pulled the stick towards the steering wheel and, feeling the catch disengage, moved the stick down towards the floor. The engine clunked loudly, the car shook and began rolling backwards down the hill. Panicking, Yvonne stomped down and the car shot backwards. The tires squealed and spun out sideways. Finding the brake, she slammed down on it, propelling herself first sharply backwards then snapping her head forward onto the steering wheel. She was all nose and ribs, pain radiating across her face and chest, the back of her head, in slow fuzzy circles. She struggled to catch her breath. Her head throbbed and her vision blurred. Blood, thick and warm, trickled to her lips. She licked it away. The car was facing almost completely sideways across the road, and her foot, still clamped firmly on the brake, was beginning to tremble and cramp. She should give up. It was all so much more difficult than when she had played it out in her mind. Blood streamed from her nose. She leaned her head back and pinched it. The buzzing spread beneath her eyes. She swallowed, mouth filling with the taste of iron as blood ran down the back of her throat. Coughing, she straightened up. Dark stains down the front of her jacket. She wiped at her nose with her hand, then wiped her bloody hand on her jacket. It was ruined anyway. She'd trade coats at the gas station, wear the one that was now wedged behind her back. Perhaps when the sun came up she wouldn't need a coat anyway. She drew the length of her sleeve across the bottom of her nose, leaving behind another long dark streak that faded towards her wrist like a comet tail. With fingertips she felt at her face, checking for swelling. The bleeding had just about stopped.

Bright lights in her eyes — Yvonne raised her arms to cover them. Another car coming over the crest of the hill. Who on earth, at this time in the morning? No doubt that was what the other driver thought too, for she was blocking the way. She eased her cramping foot from the brake and the car slowly rolled backwards. This time she was ready, foot poised above the lefthand pedal to press it down again at a moment's notice. As the car rolled, Yvonne pulled sharply on the wheel so that the rear end began to turn back down the hill again. Slowly, slowly. It didn't have to be perfect, just enough so that the other car had room to get by, and not so slowly or badly that the driver became impatient or alarmed and started beeping his horn. The Packard was now straight, though she was on the wrong side of the road. The other car pulled past her, the driver giving a quick toot, a shadowy wave as he drove by. Yvonne cringed and twisted to stare up at her bedroom window again. She waited. Ten seconds. Fifteen. Twenty-five. Thirty-five. Harold, thank God for alcohol, was still sound asleep. She let out a breath and turned her attention back to the skinny stick.

Clearly she was now in reverse. What she needed was to go forward. Forward turned out to be the next clunk down from reverse. She took her foot off the brake, and the car chugged slowly up the hill, past her house and down the other side. She braked, practiced the order on the column stick. From where she was it was up to reverse and up again to stop. And from the top: stop, reverse, forward. The order was easy enough. She slipped the stick into forward and pressed down on the gas. The car felt like a tank rolling along beneath her. She'd sat in the pas-senger seat countless times, but the feeling was quite different on this side of the car, the pedals beneath her feet, all the power of the engine at her command. Inside the car and out, the night was black as pitch. Ahead, nothing but inky shadows. Even the dashboard was unreadable. She braked again, fiddled around for a light switch. The wiper blades swooshed on, the radio, the blinkers — turn signals, Harold had said they called them over here — left and right, she was glad to find them, but no lights. She eventually pulled at a knob that refused to turn, and the road ahead lit up with a tunnel of white light. Foot off the brake, she began a slow progression forward again. The steering wheel was easy. Sensitive. She practiced turning a little, first swinging all the way to one side of the road, then pulling the steering wheel the other way to swing all the way back.

Yvonne figured it was probably easier to learn to drive in the dark because there weren't so many distractions, things to look at, people on the sidewalks, houses and buildings, trees and mountains. Certainly as a passenger she could never take enough in with her eyes. Driving in the dark had definite advantages, though being able to see more of the road surface itself would be nice, for every pothole, every bump in the road made her nose throb afresh. Towards the bottom of the road she slowed down, finally bringing the car to a stop at the stop sign. She looked left then right, left then right again — it was like crossing the street — before turning the wheel to the right. Nothing to it. There was no one on the roads at this hour. Next to no one: she hadn't banked on that car coming over her hill. She pulled out slowly, adjusting the wheel as the car moved forward, then straightened out and pushed down on the gas.

There was a sign up ahead. Hope, eighty-three miles. She was going in the right direction. Perhaps she didn't need a map after all. Harold never used one and he never got lost. But she suspected this was one more benefit to night driving: the sign had glowed when her headlights picked it out. She would surely have missed it during the day. She stretched her neck a little side to side, easing out the kinks and tension; she raised and lowered her shoulders, feeling some of the pressure lift and evaporate.

Lights swung out behind her, bright orbs jumping and twitching in the rear-view mirror. It was fascinating, her eyes drawn there instead of the road. She felt herself slowing down and glanced at the dash; she was down to less than fifteen miles an hour. The lights brightened then dimmed, flashing up, down, up, down. The Packard's wheels seemed to slip out from under her. A crunching sound. The ground beneath the tires suddenly soft, unsure. Her eyes darted to the road, but the white lines had disappeared. The lights in her rear-view mirror flashed impatiently. Medicine ball in the pit of her stomach, she pulled over. With a screech of tires the car passed her, horn honking.

Yvonne was burning up.

She sat for a while, catching her breath, before pulling slowly back onto the road. She had to keep her wits about her.

No daydreaming. No worrying about the past. No chiding herself for not having done things differently. What was done was done. She was set on a new course now. Consequences be damned.

The miles passed. Before or behind her there were no cars. The odd sign let her know she was still travelling in the right direction. She began to relax a little. Nothing but white lines and road signs to follow all the way to Hope. What could possibly be easier?

What wasn't so easy, after a while, was staying awake. The nosebleed and the headache had worn her out, and she was stiff from holding herself rigid. What time was it, anyway? She hadn't brought a watch. The dark was beginning to lift, and though she couldn't yet see the sun coming up behind the mountains, the sky was now the colour of tarnished silver, and there were other cars on the road, the beginnings of morning traffic. A cup of coffee would keep her alert, move the chill from her sinews, but Chilliwack was behind her, and she hadn't seen signs of another town or even a gas station in quite some time.

Yvonne was beginning to feel so far away from Vancouver that she must be in a different country. Or speeding backwards on the train that had brought them out from Montreal to this wilderness, this place where people lived so far apart they hadn't yet developed the habit of neighbourliness, and dropping in on someone was treated as trespassing. She saw a sign for Hope, and then the highway split. She slowed and nudged the car onto the shoulder, unsure of which direction to take. In the slowly brightening dawn, she could see that both roads climbed further into the mountains. Which way? Hope, a clutch of shadows and pricks of light off to her left, was nothing but a village on the edge of a river, with mountains at its base. How insignificant it seemed, sitting darkly in its forest glade.

It was the indecision that unhinged her, made her careless.

She pulled out onto the fork one way, tires spinning in the loose gravel of the shoulder, and suddenly there was another car right in front of her. She felt it before she saw it, clipping the rear fender. A screech of tires as the car wiggled its rear end angrily at her. Brake lights popped on, the car inched onto the gravel. A man climbed out of the driver's side and waved her over. Yvonne's foot was pressed down so hard on the brake pedal that it took her a few moments to relax it enough to release the brake, find the gas. Easy now, steady. She swung the beast around to the right and tucked in behind the wounded car. There was a dent in the rear right side, and it looked dirty, some paint missing perhaps. She leaned forward in her seat, squinting to get a better look. But then another surge to the gas, not the brake. The man leaped backwards as if for his life, and Yvonne heard the dismaying tinkle of breaking glass. His left taillight. The man ran towards her to assess this second lot of damage, pushing his hat further back on his head to give himself a better view. Then he spun away from her and put his head in his hands, resting his elbows on the roof of his car. Such a theatrical display from such an ordinary-looking man. She heard him bellow something about women drivers, then a fist shot out, pounded the roof.

Yvonne could only sit, frozen in her seat, staring, as he began walking towards her again. Would he use this fist on her? But then, just as he reached the car and she believed he was going to rip the door off, drag her from her seat, he stopped, a look of terror on his face. What on earth? Oh my God. She put her hand to her cheek. The blood. She'd forgotten all about it, streaked across her face and now dried there, rough to the touch. She looked down in dismay at her jacket, the muddy-brown smears, the drops, the finger and handprints. She hadn't changed out of it as planned. Bang, she slammed the gearshift upwards into reverse and hit the gas pedal. The man again leapt backwards as the Packard did the same, its rear end swinging around until, mercifully, she was facing ahead on the road. Brake. Forward. Gas. She was off, a shower of tiny stones spraying behind her, a smell of burnt rubber in the air, seeping into the car. The decision was made for her; she was on the road that led north.

Tall, skinny trees packed together, dark and dense, on steep banks, at the bottom of which crashed the Fraser River. A road of hairpin curves, Yvonne's heart in her mouth until a sign, black paint on a background of luminous white: Hope Mental Asylum. Hope Mental Asylum. That was it, that was what she was looking for. It made sense. Harold had had Anton committed. Her head cleared, her blood thinned, warming her hands and feet again. Now she felt nothing at all. Not anger, not indignation, not pity for her son who'd been locked away in the mountains in a building filled with lunatics. Harold, it seemed, had finally lost his capacity to shock and wound. Nothing surprised her anymore. Hope Mental Asylum. She supposed it was better than calling it Hell's Gate. Suddenly the drunk's words seemed funnier than even he had known.

Yvonne pulled up to a gate set in the wire mesh fence and stared at the building and its grounds. Not the medieval-looking façade that had first leaped to mind, not at all like Bethlehem Hospital in London. Bedlam. Except that it was built of stone, unusual for what she'd seen of British Columbia, where wood ruled the day. It put her in mind of a grand mansion and was set on an impressive acreage of tidy lawns. Rhododendrons in full bloom lent splashes of pink, white and purple to the scene. The only disconcerting part of the view was the fence. Was it, she wondered, trying to imagine life inside those stone walls, to keep in the patients or the staff? Who was more likely to want to escape? And if it was the patients and they did escape, what then? Where would they go? What would they likely be escaping to? Stumbling through the bush towards Hope? How would they even know where Hope was? Even find their way? Unless they followed the road, and, Yvonne supposed, many of the people inside those cold high walls were there because they didn't, at one time or for some reason or another, follow the road.

The building had an impressive entrance of wide flagstone steps and rows of windows. She wondered which one was Anton's, for he had to be there, it was her only hope. She wondered if he was looking out now and had seen Harold's car. He wouldn't know it was his mother who was driving, his mother who had come to rescue him. He might think it was Harold. She stepped out of the car. It was only seven a.m., but if he was standing by his window, watching, she wanted him to know that it was she who had come. She tried to imagine the conversation between the two of them as Harold had driven the Packard inside the large iron gates and pulled up to the impressive entrance. What had gone through Anton's mind at that moment? And when exactly had he understood that Harold planned to leave him here? She took a cigarette from the pack in her handbag and lit it, sucked deeply, welcoming the giddy rush.

She waved at the building from time to time. Maybe someone would tell Anton there was a woman standing beside a metallic blue car outside the fence, and Anton would know it was she and would come to the window and wave back.

Eventually someone came out, a man who began walking up the driveway towards her and the gate. As he drew closer, she could hear the keys he jingled absent-mindedly on his belt. Or perhaps he was nervous. Anton's jailer: the keeper of the keys. Remembering the blood on her face, she spat on her sleeve and began wiping at her nose and upper lip. It was too late, however, to change out of her stained jacket. She folded her arms high across her chest, trying to cover up the worst of the marks, but the man had now reached the fence and was appraising her with cynical, practiced eyes.

"Are you all right, ma'am? Do you need any help?"

Yvonne frowned. She had not planned for this moment, had planned nothing beyond driving up here. "I — I've come to take my son home."

"Your son." It wasn't even a question, just a tired flat voice repeating her words.

"Yes, my son. He's in there." She nodded towards the stone building. "And I've come to take him home." She pushed a lock of stray hair behind her ear. "There's been a terrible mistake, you see. He shouldn't be here. My husband —"

"Do you have a consent to release form signed by your husband?"

"No. I —"

"Then, ma'am, I'm afraid you won't be taking your son anywhere."

Yvonne looked around her, suddenly lost. She had driven all this way without any real idea of where Anton was, without a plan, without even a driver's license. And now this man with the keys was telling her she couldn't take Anton home without Harold's permission. Something pushed painfully at her throat — a stone? A fist? With difficulty she swallowed, tears pricking her eyes. Harold wasn't even his father, but somehow he had more control over what happened to Anton than she did. She who had given birth to him. Raised him. It wasn't right. It certainly wasn't fair.

"Would you like me to call someone for you, ma'am? The police could maybe help you out."

The police? They'd throw the book at her: driving without a license, leaving the scene of an accident — the man at the fork in the road had surely reported her by now — driving with blood all over her face. And if they contacted Harold, he would probably tell them she'd stolen the car. He'd probably tell them about the watch too. She'd been through his drawers and pockets countless times over the years while he was out or asleep, searching for that cursed pawnshop ticket, but she had never been able to find it. Harold had it hidden away somewhere, no doubt, ammunition to pull out in case of an emergency. "No. That's all right." She sniffed. "I'll be all right. Can I see him? My son? His name's Anton. Anton Crouch."

"No, ma'am, I'm afraid not. You need a visitor's pass signed by the admitting physician." The man stepped back from the fence and made as if to turn away. Yvonne shivered, suddenly cold. "You might want to talk to a lawyer," he said, then began walking back towards the building. Watching his retreating back, Yvonne suddenly remembered her handbag.

"Sir. Oh, sir. Excuse me." He turned around. "I was wondering if you could give something to him for me."

The man shook his head, then seemed to have a change of heart. He approached the fence again. "What is it?" Yvonne reached into her handbag and pulled out the silver picture frame.

"It's a photograph of his papa."

The man sighed wearily. "And how am I supposed to get it through this fence?"

Yvonne glanced down at the picture frame, then at the wire mesh, then across at the gates. "You have keys. Can't you open them?"

"I think you know the answer to that question, ma'am."

"So what do I do?" She was beginning to sound hysterical. The guard watched her calmly.

"Take the photograph out of the frame."

Of course. She smiled at him, then began fumbling with the back of the frame. In her haste, the glass cracked, and she cut her finger pulling the photograph free. She rolled it up and pushed it through the mesh. "Thank you," she said. "Thank you very much." The man gave her a wan smile before he turned again in the direction of the Hope Mental Asylum. Yvonne stood at the fence and watched until he mounted the steps of the grand entrance and disappeared inside.

XXV

Vancouver: August 1952

It's the bear that draws him; reared up on its hind legs, its mouth open in a roar, it must be over seven feet tall. A caricature of ferociousness. Not just because of the battered straw hat on his head, the red and green striped tie around his neck, but because of his scruffiness. One of his paws is broken off, the wrist a jagged stump. Sawdust has flaked onto his fur, which is dull and worn away in places. Moths maybe. He's come down in stature, this bear, since his days as hunter and gatherer of the forest. Anton leans his bicycle against the store window and from the basket he's lashed to the front lifts out a pillowcase with his pieces of silver.

A bell clangs by his ear as he pushes open the shop door. A bear of a man lumbers through a doorway at the back and halts at the counter. The man is not so much fat as he is a mountain of flesh on a large frame. His neck must be the girth of Anton's thigh at least. A lumberjack from the mountains, he should be felling trees, not buying and selling people's heartaches and excess baggage in this narrow, harshly lit store.

"What've you got, kid?"

Anton swallows to find his voice. "A teapot. It's silver. Solid, I think. And there's a milk jug and —"

"Let's see 'em." He slams a hand down on the counter, a brain-jarring slam. No ordinary hand this, it's inert, made of metal, a pincher in place of fingers. Anton's eyes dart to the other hand. Nothing. Not even an arm. Amputated clean at the shoulder, the sleeve of his shirt pinned up in a neat fold. But surely not by him. Not with that. A loud buzzing begins in Anton's head; it spreads by vibration to the pit of his stomach. His grip around the neck of the pillowcase tightens, nails digging into his palm. The bear was a warning. He backs away. The man's eyes harden to something like hate, then disgust. In Anton's backwards stumbling he has seen his limp, his thick-soled shoe. Choked with heat, Anton turns and flees. There are plenty of other shops.

Quickly he wheels the bicycle past three or four more pawnbrokers, his peripheral vision a blur of jewellery, crockery, gramophones, before selecting another to enter, as if shops too close might be contaminated by the amputee's anger. This door he pushes open with a little more trepidation.

"Come. Come. Quickly." There's a figure seated behind the L-shaped counter, head bent like a question mark over an object in his hands that he's inspecting or trying to fix, it's hard to tell in the dim light. "I haven't got all day, you know. Got a business to run here. Customers other than you to see to." Anton looks around. Every inch of wall and floor is taken up with merchandise, the remnants of other people's lives, mostly dark, hulking objects that seem to swallow the shop's light, but there isn't another customer in sight.

"I know what you're thinking. But someone might come in any minute. Someone looking to buy. You're not looking to buy something, are you?" Such quick speech for someone so still. The man has not raised his head once to assess his customer. How can he know anything about him? Anton steps up to the counter and removes the teapot, sugar bowl and milk jug from the pillowcase. The man slips off his stool, and Anton sees his back is permanently rounded, condemning him to stare down at the floor. He takes up the pieces one by one, weighs them in his hands, turns them over and holds them comically close to his face, checking the stamp and manufacturer's inscription on the bottom.

"Twenty-seven dollars. I'll give you twenty-seven dollars." A marmoset. Eyes as wide around as the lenses of his bottle-bottom glasses. He reaches for a pad of numbered tickets and plucks a pen from behind his ear. "Name?"

Anton is still playing catch-up. Twenty-seven dollars sounds like a lot of money, but he's spent half a lifetime watching Harold wheel and deal.

"It's a set," he begins, then clears his throat. "There's not a mark or a dent on any of the pieces. It was used to serve tea to the China Empress." He frowns. "No. Um. To the Empress of China, I mean." The marmoset, the bear, the amputee have all unbalanced him. He can't get his story straight. His patter sounded better in the isolation of the basement. He appeared more poised in the bathroom mirror.

"Twenty-seven dollars. I'll give you twenty-seven dollars," the marmoset repeats, pen poised in mid-air. His voice sounds neither more nor less irritated than before. Maybe he knows the *Empress of China* is a ship docked in the harbour, though something about his face, his dated and dusty clothing, suggests he rarely leaves his cluttered den.

Twenty-seven dollars. Anton has no frame of reference, doesn't know whether he's being offered a good deal or he's being taken. Nor does he have any idea how long twenty-seven dollars will last him and Tom on Salt Spring. But he

283

cannot summon the energy or wits to face another pawnshop owner. Such a peculiar lot. "Kavanov," he says, carefully enunciating each syllable. "Anton Kavanov."

At the door, the bills carefully folded and buried safely in his pocket, he turns back. "There's a matching set of cutlery that goes with it, the tea service." The marmoset neither answers him nor looks up, engrossed again in the object he was studying when Anton walked in. "Would you be interested?"

"Bring it in, I'll take a look."

Anton reaches for the door handle. "Um, how much do you think it would be worth to you? It's for twelve places." And must weigh close to twenty pounds. It'd be comforting to know he only had to pedal down Granville Street with it; pushing his bike alone back up the steep hill is onerous enough.

"No goods, no price. Bring it in and I'll take a look."

Fastened tight at an awkward angle in the bottom of the tea chest marked *Dining room silver*, the case is heavier than Anton remembers and difficult to grasp. He should have left it out when he first discovered it, instead of trying to cover his tracks. *Leave no traces of yourself.* As he braces himself, one foot in front of the other, and bends to tug again, the tea chest suddenly releases its hold. Anton stumbles backwards, loses his footing, splays his arms to right himself. The elegant wooden box with its twelve-place silver lode drops like a stone. On impact the clasps fly open, scattering all one hundred and twenty pieces across the concrete floor. Anton freezes. A faraway clatter of steel, a creak of hinges. A light clicks on, followed by sharp, angry footsteps down the wooden stairs. As if he weren't already weak and drenched with sweat from pedalling and pushing all the way from Hastings Street; now there's a small lake in the hollow of his back. He turns to face her as she marches towards him. Clarice Hart, hands on her hips, sleeves of baggy flesh wobbling with vexation.

"And what are you doing down here, young man?" With a sweeping glance she takes in the spill of silverware. "Planning on stealing those, were you?"

Anton is cardboard-mouthed. She'll truss him up like she did Tom. Leave him down here. It'll be days before someone finds him. Weeks.

"Want me to tell your mother what you're up to?"

His mother? A horde of great-winged beasts rises up through his stomach into his chest. Is he supposed to answer? "No," he says, staring past her, not quite able to meet her eyes.

"Wonder what she'll have to say about all this?"

That he's a disappointing and wicked son because his actions reflect badly on her. Suggest, without actually mentioning his name, that he's turning into Harold. She might even bring his father into the equation, compare the son unfavourably. Anton clenches his jaw. So what? He's through with her one-sided view of the world. Rose-coloured. There've been too many betrayals already: the piano; his name; Jasmine. She can't hurt him anymore. He won't let her. And as for Clarice Hart — he stands straighter, drawing himself up to his full five feet ten and a half inches, looks directly into her eyes.

"I wasn't stealing them." Not technically. He has Tom's permission.

"So what, exactly, are you doing?"

Whatever he says he cannot implicate Tom, put him through another of her bloody-throated harangues. Tom doesn't stand up for himself. But would he squeal on them? Probably not. He's been a prisoner of war. He imagines the Germans holding out on treating his leg injuries for information. But Lieutenant Thomas J. Hart was silent, stoic, a war hero. Which makes him think that perhaps Tom's silence in the face of this screaming harridan of a daughter is nothing more than that same resistance. Still, Anton doesn't want to put his friend through an unnecessary ordeal, nor does he fancy listening through the walls to her shouting and carrying on half the evening.

"I'll ask you again, young man, what are you doing down here?" Anton glances at the workbench.

"I came to get tools — to repair my bicycle."

"And what were you doing with my dinnerware?" It isn't yours, Anton thinks.

"Nothing. It was an accident. I wasn't minding my feet and I tripped." A white lie. He shrugs, relishing her discomfort. By bringing up his feet he has disarmed her. With awareness comes a heady rush of power. He swallows a tiny smile. "I knocked over this box and all the knives and forks came tumbling out." Her eyes narrow and her mouth pinches together. She doesn't believe him. But what can she do? The silver is all over the floor, not in his pockets.

"Pick it up."

Anton bends to collect the strewn pieces. He takes his time, drawing out his task, chanting under his breath, "Twelve knives, twelve forks, twelve teaspoons, twelve dessert spoons," playing up his limp as he steps beyond the edge of light to recover the more wayward pieces: Fish knives. Salad forks. Serving spoons. He arranges them back in the box, deliberately and slowly, pushing each piece into place between the box's tiny velvet jaws. Clarice Hart stands with her arms folded until he's finished. Anton swears he can see the steam coming out her ears.

"Do you have the tools you need?"

"Tools?"

"To repair your bicycle."

Stepping over to the workbench, Anton scoops up a pair of pliers, a large screwdriver and a set of three wrenches.

"Now go out the way you came." He glances at her quickly, then looks away. She is still the keeper of this castle. Clarice Hart follows him to the door, steps outside behind him, watches while he pulls the door shut.

"Lock it." The deadbolt clangs home. "Now give me the key." Even the crisp light of a summer morning cannot bleach the lines about her mouth or warm the frost in her eyes. What has made her so mean?

"But I need somewhere to store the bicycle."

"Should've thought of that before you decided to go rummaging around in other people's property." She holds out her hand. "The key." With a sigh of frustration, Anton drops it into her outstretched palm. So much for access to the basement. The folded banknotes lie below his hipbone, tucked in the crease of his leg. Twenty-seven dollars. Unless he wants to wait until she goes out, try taking the cutlery service out through the Harts' apartment, twenty-seven dollars is the sum total of their escape money.

XXVI

White Rock: June 1950

When the doctor cut away the cast and removed the splints, Yvonne's fingers looked both young and old. The bones had knitted together well, that much she could see. There were no odd lumps and no sign of the freakish angles she'd shuffled in with six weeks before, eyes glassy with pain, declaring to the admitting nurse, "My husband did this." The swelling had gone and with it her flesh, melted away. Her skin was green and yellow, loose over bones. How knobbly her fingers were, nails black.

"Exercise." The doctor smiled at her. "You have to build all those tiny muscles back." Yvonne watched his clean, efficient movements around the room. With one sweep of his hand, he cleared the table of debris; fragments of plaster and wood clattered into the bin he kicked into place to catch them. Some things were easy to get rid of. Harold, it turned out, had only had to make a few phone calls, visit a doctor or two, and Anton vanished.

"Just simple stretching at first, then picking things up, clutching, grabbing, that sort of thing." It occurred to her that that was exactly what had got her into this state in the first place: clutching, grabbing. This time she would try a different route.

"How long?"

"Three months. Four, maybe. A lot depends on you."

And the law, she thought. And the justice system. And money. Four months. It might all take that long. Four months. But what was four months after more than ten years, eleven. Christ, no, it was more like thirteen since she'd first met him. Anton was thirteen. Unlucky thirteen. But when it came to bad luck, Yvonne's stretched further back than thirteen years. She could get a headache thinking about it.

"I'll walk back," she'd told Harold when he'd dropped her off. She'd walk into town first is what she meant, and she was surprised, relieved, when he'd agreed, laying rubber in the circular driveway as he sped away, spraying gravel over the bed of impatiens that graced the centre oval, accorded the hospital grounds a splash of colour; he'd dropped her off much the same way two months earlier, refusing to go inside and answer long bleeding lists of damn nosy-parker questions.

There was a sameness to all small towns in Canada. While violet snow-capped mountains in the distance placed her here in British Columbia, the high street could have been anywhere. She was looking for a brass nameplate. Two or three doors down from the tailor's, Doctor Green, Howie — "Call me Howie" — had said. Solicitors liked to see their names punched boldly into brass or some other shiny metal. It announced they were here for the duration, smacked of prestige, wealth, reliability perhaps, rock-solidness. What Yvonne discovered once she'd climbed the stairs to the second floor and stepped inside, however, was that the rock-solidness pertained to a man's world, was what a man's world was built upon and against which a woman threw herself in vain.

The lawyer, Edward C. Prentice, sucked in a breath and shook his head. "In these kinds of cases, the father always wins." Yvonne sat ramrod straight across from him and stared, her face expressionless, willing different words from his mouth. The mouth stretched into a mirthless smile, then disappeared behind a tent of hands. Another voluble intake of air. "Do you have any idea of the powers you'll be up against?"

"I'm his mother." Yvonne's mouth was so dry her lips were stuck to her teeth. She could taste blood when the skin came away. "Shouldn't that count for something?"

Edward C. Prentice reached across his desk and plucked a pencil from a cluster in a small black stand. He alternately rolled it between his fingers and tapped the blunt end on his desk blotter. Again the mirthless smile, this time his eyes disappearing into the folds of fat that were his cheeks. He reminded her of someone, though she couldn't think who.

"No lawyer in his right mind would take this case on." Hope

that had bloomed hard and bright in her chest on the walk down Main Street shrivelled and dried, leaving her feeling flat and empty. "And if he did" — it took her a moment to understand what the man was on about, to register that what, for her, had been the death knell of hope had, for him, been but a dramatic pause in a longer and much-rehearsed speech — "how would you ever pay for it?"

"I have money."

"It'll be expensive. Doctors, certificates, a trial, possibly an appeal."

She'd steal it from him, hawk everything in the house; she'd sell herself if she had to.

"And then there's the matter of your own history."

Yvonne narrowed her eyes.

"His lawyers will be all over you like bloodhounds. Cases like these can get very dirty." He paused, running his eyes over her face, looking for — what? Lies? Secrets? "Would you be willing to stick your neck out that far?"

Yvonne slipped the sling from her arm, gently massaged the fingers of her right hand with her left. Hadn't she already stuck her neck out and paid for it?

"It is important," he said, stretching his mouth wide again — she wanted to slap him — "that there is nothing in your past that would or could reflect badly on your case, nothing the defence could suddenly pull out of a hat, nothing that would make me look ridiculous." The pawnshop ticket. Harold's gold watch. But it wasn't just that. Anton had been born out of wedlock — she hadn't even been of legal age to marry at that time — and so had Isobel. Her dancing had been nothing but glorified striptease. Her mother had been a drunkard. Harold could take her whole life and make it ugly. Uglier. He'd find a way to blame her for Isobel's death, Alexei's suicide.

Yvonne's hand was throbbing so hard it might have had its

own heartbeat. Slipping it back through the sling, she pushed back her chair and stood to leave.

"You're a woman," he called after her, as if she herself might have overlooked the fact. "You have no power," she heard, picking her way down his stairs.

But sometimes all you needed was a chance.

Yvonne was sitting in the kitchen. Ten days had passed since the cast had come off, since her futile visit with the lawyer. Ten long days. She sniffed the air. A scorching smell, singed hair left to curl up and frizzle. It reminded her of being a girl, the times her mother had had too much to drink and let the curling iron heat up too long. Pzzz, her hair would go, curling back on itself, shrivelling, disappearing into smoke, filling the dressing room with a charred smell. Yvonne's eyes began to water. Unconsciously she slipped her left hand inside her shirt, ran fingertips over the cigar of mottled flesh on her chest.

The smell was coming from the living room. Yvonne opened the door. Harold was asleep in his wing chair, his cruel face slack and stupid. Some people utterly changed when asleep, other aspects of their personalities emerged. Alexei had always looked like Prince Charming from the Pantomimes, a cupid's bow mouth and large, pale lids covering his large blue eyes, a soft fringe of dark lashes. Harold still looked cruel but even more stupid and slow in sleep than he did awake.

She assessed him with what she believed to be a healthy indifference. If she'd ever had any feelings for this man, they'd long since hardened into hate, then petrified to stone, flint. Thankfully, she had less dealings with him these days. He was out more, and if he was home, drunk more. He left her alone now. It was as if in breaking her fingers he had at last broken something in himself, had at last accepted that he would never, could never steal her heart.

He'd been cold. He was often cold. Bad circulation or years of wearing the same wool coat, season in and season out. But most likely it was the stroke. His chair was pulled up to the fire, a blanket across his legs. Yvonne stepped closer. He reeked of the rum and orange he'd been knocking back earlier. His five o'clock shadow made his face look dirty. As drunk as Harold stayed, sometimes for days on end, he always shaved. Every morning, holding his jittery hand steady, and every evening, sometimes weaving dangerously, Harold boiled up water, sharpened his cut-throat on the leather strop that hung from the side of the bathroom sink, and shaved. Yvonne's legs began to feel hot. She stepped aside. The blanket that covered Harold's legs was scorched, Yvonne now saw. The wool had singed and curled, turning brown. Her heart began to beat a little faster. She nudged him in the chair. The loose skin around his jowls wobbled. He stirred, emitting one loud, pig-like snore. Sickly sweet rum fumes hit Yvonne in the face. She shook him a little harder. He stirred but carried on snoring. Her heart beat faster still. This was it, now or never. She crouched, her insides so twisted she gasped in pain, and, hand trembling, turned up the flame on the gas fire. She tiptoed out of the room, her heart-beat pounding in her head, her stomach, her toes, and clicked the door shut behind her. She picked her purse up from the kitchen counter, slipped on her coat and stepped out the door. She walked quickly down the street, her heels click-clacking on the recently laid concrete sidewalk. Faster and faster she moved, her heart now only residing in the space between her neck and the top of her chest. Don't run. Don't run, she chanted in time to her quickening feet. Whatever you do, don't run.

XXVII

Vancouver: August 1952

"What did you do with the rest of the tea service?"

His mother is standing at his elbow, arms folded. Anton stares at the remaining toast on his plate and pushes it away. Clarice Hart has been busy. It's taken her less than a day to tally what's missing from her basement inheritance and apprise his mother of all his so-called wrongdoings.

"I took it to a pawn shop on Hastings." He takes a long swallow of milk.

His mother's eyebrows shoot up. "A pawnshop. And who gave you the idea to go to a pawnshop?" Anton watches her from under his too-long fringe.

"Tom. I mean Mr. Hart."

"The ticket, please." She holds out her hand.

Anton pulls the folded-over stub from his back pocket and pushes it across the table at her.

"And the money." The taste of milk sours in his mouth. It was all they had, he and Tom. How will they ever get to Salt Spring now? He places the rolled-up bills on top of the ticket, where they uncurl, flexing paper muscles.

"I trust it's all here?"

"Yes."

She moves to a chair and sits down at the table, her dark grey eyes fastened on his. She's trying to read his mind. "I hope for your sake the tea service is still there," she says eventually.

"Because your first job this morning will be to go down there and get it back." She rubs her fingers absentmindedly over the bills, ironing them flat. "You do know it's going to cost you a lot more than you got for them. Maybe half again as much. What is there here?" She flicks through the bills. "Twenty-seven dollars." Then she pauses, something on the ticket has caught her eye.

"Kavanov."

"Yes."

"You call yourself Kavanov?"

Anton is about to explain himself but can see by her face he doesn't have to. She must understand. Finally. She opens her wallet, which Anton realizes has been in her hand the whole time, pulls out a five- and a ten-dollar bill and places them on top of the others. All her movements are slow, trance-like. When she finally comes back into the moment, it's as if she's flicked a switch.

"You're going to be pretty busy working to pay off the commission. The remainder of your summer holidays and then some." Anton slumps down in his chair. Piano. She's going to force him to play all day every day, knowing full well he's avoided the instrument ever since the Jasmine fiasco. He flexes his fingers, already imagining them cramped and sore.

"Your second job today will be to help out Clarice Hart next door. She has some things she needs moving." Baggy Clarry. Anton closes his eyes. He'll take the piano any day. He'll even sing if she wants him to. His mother clears her throat. She hasn't finished with him.

"Now, I'd like you to help me out here if you could, Anton." His eyes snap open. Her voice is silky smooth, she's found her rhythm again. "Because I've been trying to understand what on earth would possess you to take advantage of a senile old man's kindness and steal his property." Senile? The milk sitting in his stomach begins to curdle. Anton opens his mouth to respond. His mother waits.

"Tom Hart is not senile," he spells out slowly, fists clenched so tight his nails dig into his palms. "He is confined to a wheel-chair." Anton enunciates each word in a struggle to remain calm. "This does not mean —" He falters, takes a breath and starts again. "It does not mean that he has lost his mind. But it has made him a prisoner in this house." It takes a monumental effort of will to look his mother in the eye. When he speaks again, his voice is a hoarse whisper.

"Don't you think I know what that feels like?"

Yvonne's hand flutters to her throat. She bites her lips, tiny nostrils quivering. Anton knows, in the long minute that passes as he watches his mother pull herself together, that the moment is lost. She's had years of practice.

"Then perhaps you could explain to me exactly what you need this money for?"

It took so much for him to say what he did. She must know this. All he went through in that place means nothing to her. He steels himself against tears, pins and needles in his nose, prickly heat climbing over his scalp.

"It wouldn't have anything to do with that floozy upstairs, would it?"

Floozy? Now he glares at her. She quivers and blurs between his lashes. She's a fine one to judge. Picking Harold.

"Because she's told us all about you sneaking around inside her apartment."

Stomach acid rises up the back of his throat. The closet. Those enormous pale breasts. Please to God his mother doesn't know about that.

"She says she doesn't want the police involved. Which is good of her, don't you think?" Anton is so close to vomiting that in his mind he's already halfway to the bathroom.

"The thing is, Anton, you never know who you can trust.
You see a beautiful girl. She's much too old and mature for
you, but still, you think she's perfect, and that she has your
best interests at heart. But in the end, people only ever care
about themselves. I tried to tell you this, I tried to protect you,
but you would have it your way."

"Protect me!" Anton's had enough. He stands up, legs like
bags of marbles, and stares down at her. "Then how come —
how come you left me in that place?"

It's out there between them, finally. It's her he blames. Not
Harold. Stupid, cruel, worthless Harold. Anton is so shocked
his muscles won't move. He's forced to stand and watch the
colour drain from his mother's face, and with it her youth. He
cannot believe how old she suddenly looks. Haggard. It isn't
even her face. But he can't take the words back now. Yvonne
stands and grasps his hands. Her eyes are wet with tears.

"I tried. I tried to get you out sooner. I really tried. They
wouldn't let me. I couldn't —" Anton shrugs off her hands. He
can't bear to be touched. He picks up the money and the ticket
stub, folds them and puts them in his pocket. He has a splitting migraine. "I didn't know what else to do," Yvonne says,
her voice small and pleading, like a child's. She tries to reach
out to him again. "I even drove up there to get you." But Anton
is already stumbling away from her. She can't drive. He's heard
enough lies.

When Clarice Hart opens the door, Anton hands her a box,
rattling it first so she can hear the chink of metal on metal.
"It's all there." He's looking at her but not really seeing her.
She means nothing to him. "My mother says you need some
help."

His landlady opens the door wider, inviting him in. Tom is by the front window, looking out. It must be where he was sitting the first time Anton saw him, indistinct in the afternoon shadows. He doesn't turn around. In fact, he doesn't acknowledge even having heard Anton enter. Tom appears shrunken somehow, a small man lost in a big steel chair.

"Quickly, quickly, young man. I don't have all day." She beckons him and disappears down the hall.

Deciding it's probably better to approach Tom some other time, Anton leaves the room to follow baggy Clarry. He's never been down here. At the end she turns left, leads him to the far door. This must be Tom's room, the room from which he was throwing peanuts the day they first sort of met. She opens the door, and Anton is hit with a blast of that stale, institutional smell he first noted on his old friend's skin and clothing. Funny, that. In the weeks and months since, it has come not to bother him.

Then he sees the boxes. On the bed and on the floor. He steps into the room. A couple of suitcases stand side by side. The dresser drawers are open and mostly empty. The closet tells much the same story; a few sad and mismatched articles of clothing hang crookedly from bent wire hangers. As realization sinks in, Anton turns to face the dragon lady.

"You can't do this," he says. "He's your father."

"I wouldn't have had to do anything if you hadn't started sticking your nose in, messing things up." She points to the boxes. "You can start packing what's left into these. Then you'll label them and store them in the basement. I'm sure you know your way around down there better than any of us." She turns to leave, then calls back over her shoulder. "Not the suitcases, of course, they go with him." And she's gone, leaving Anton speechless.

And guilty.

She's absolutely right. It is his fault. And now Tom is being sent away all because of him. He leans against the wall. His eyes ache. This cannot be happening. The latch on the apartment clicks as Clarice Hart, washing her hands of her callousness, leaves the apartment. Anton waits without breathing for the second click of the outside door closing. He swallows, his mouth suddenly dry. He knows what he must do.

"Back in a minute," he calls out to Tom, slipping out of the Harts' apartment and into his own. His mother is in the middle of a lesson. He wants to burst into laughter. Someone up there is on his side. Finally. He reaches under his bed for his haversack — after all, he's been planning this awhile. He checks the contents. A change of clothes, the tools from the bench in the basement: pliers, a screwdriver and the set of three wrenches. They're heavy, but he needs them to construct the ingenious brace he has in mind for Tom's wheelchair. A length of his mother's washing line for the same, and a sharp knife to cut it with. The leather flying helmet and goggles. They're a mite difficult to justify, even to himself, but they take up little enough room. The photograph of his father. A talisman of sorts, to ward off evil. Anton is convinced that, because the picture was stored in the cargo hold of the ship when they travelled to Canada, someone evil like Harold was able to enter their lives. When they unpacked in Montreal, the photograph was gone, disappeared. And for the four years and almost four months that Harold had lived with them, it had remained missing. Anton interpreted its mysterious reappearance — an orderly had simply handed it to him, no note, no explanation — as a sign from his father, a measure of faith that helped make the remainder of his incarceration more bearable.

I even drove up there to get you.

Had she? It was possible. He takes the photo out. His father stares back at him. A proud face. Anton shoves it back inside the haversack. It's easier to stay angry with his mother for the moment, less confusing. He slips on his jacket and, haversack dangling from one hand, stands outside the door to the dance room. He can hear his mother barking orders inside. Little girls whose only dream is to dance on the world's stages are feeling the raw end of Yvonne Rose's temper today. He stares at the handle, then walks away.

Back inside the Harts' apartment, Anton is all business. He marches over to Tom by the window and begins pushing his wheelchair towards the bedroom. Instantly Tom sits up straight, his sulk vanished.

"What are you up to, son?"

"We're leaving."

"Leaving?" Tom sounds wary, but then his face lights up. "Salt Spring?"

"Salt Spring," Anton replies, laughing. He's dizzy with excitement. "Is there a jacket you can wear inside one of those cases?" he asks bending over to unlatch the first one. It's locked. Both are locked. And baggy Clarry has the keys. Surprise, surprise.

Never mind. To the closet he goes. A couple of suits that look sizes too big. A green, blue and white striped jacket that resembles something a cricket player would wear. "Is this okay?"

"It's warm. What do I care?" Anton tosses it to him and, chuckling, Tom pushes his arms through the sleeves and buttons up the front.

"This too?" He drapes one of the suit jackets over Tom's shoulders. "Better too warm than too cold." He strides over to the bed, scoops the boxes onto the floor, and with one quick sharp movement yanks the blanket free. "A little something for your legs, sir."

"Why, thank you." Tom pats it into place. But Anton isn't

watching. He's seen something in one of the boxes, something familiar. It's the photograph he's tried so many times to get a good look at. Almost reverently he picks it up. A group of men huddled in a semi-formal pose in front of — Anton squints, checking the fuselage for the telltale hump in front of the cockpit — a Sopwith Camel. Which one is Tom? He opens his haversack and slips the photograph in beside the one of his father; he'll ask him later.

Out the bedroom and to the door. Anton pulls it open, pushes Tom through and then halts at the second, outside door. Fifteen years. This has got to be a big moment for the old man.

"Ready?"

"As ready as I'll ever be."

"Then hold on tight. The stairs out there are not very friendly."

The sky has clouded over since Anton was at the pawnbroker's. It's grey and heavy looking, not exactly what he would have planned. He takes a deep breath, tips the wheelchair back so that it rests on its rear wheels, and rolls it and Tom off the edge of the first step. Thud. Was it his imagination, or did the whole house shake? But it's too late to check the chair's descent, too great a strain on the muscles in his arms, his aching back. Thud thud thud thud, the momentum literally drags him down the remaining steps. At the bottom he feels nauseous, his bones all shaken out of place.

"You okay?" Tom nods, but he doesn't look so good. He's blinking a lot, and his skin looks pale and yellowish.

"Okay, stay there. I won't be a minute," Anton says, and dashes off around the back of the house for the wheelbarrow. When he returns, Tom's face has hardened.

"I don't think this is such a good idea, son."

"What do you mean? Of course it is." Anton bends to his task. Wrenches to loosen the nuts that hold the barrow's arms in place, screwdriver to turn the long screws. Perfect. He pushes down the disappointment Tom's words have roused. Taking the length of washing line and the knife from his bag, he tethers one barrow handle to each side of the chair, fitting them under the padded armrests and out of Tom's way.

"We can't be going to Salt Spring Island, son."

"Um, one more minute, okay?" Again Anton dashes off around the side of the house. This time he returns pushing the bicycle.

But Tom is spitting mad. "This whole thing is just some damn fool notion you cooked up by yourself."

Anton busies himself positioning the bicycle behind the chair. "That's not true," he says, and wipes his face with his arm. The effort of lashing the wheelbarrow handles to the bicycle's front wheel shaft is making him sweat. "We talked about it. We planned it all out, you and me." He straightens to admire his handiwork. Not quite a work of art, but clever none-theless. He steps in front of Tom, pulls the suit jacket tight around his shoulders, fastens the top button, effectively pin-ning the old man's upper arms, and repositions the blanket, tucking it in at the sides of the chair so that it keeps his legs and feet warm. Tom's wearing slippers, but it's too late to do anything about that now.

"Have you any idea what's involved in taking care of someone in a wheelchair?"

Anton has clambered onto the bicycle and is now straining to get it in motion, breathing through clenched teeth. Standing up to better throw his weight over the pedals, he grunts once as the resistance finally gives and they're off. Brakes at the garden gate to make a right-hand turn. Busy Granville Street, with its stores and businesses, its trolley buses and cars, is out. Anton plans on taking residential Fir Street. Tom Hart is flap-ping his hands.

"You don't know what you're getting yourself into." He tries to turn around again. "This is not my idea," he shouts to the neighbourhood. "I had nothing to do with it."

Anton is concentrating on clearing the corner. He doesn't want to go over the curb here as the impact might break the barrows' arms or jolt his passenger out of his chair. He straightens the handlebars and bears down on the pedals again; he has no intention of stopping, not while they're still within shouting distance of the house.

"Where are you taking me?" Tom yells. "Stop this thing. You hear me? I said stop it."

Anton clamps his teeth together. It's just cold feet. People get cold feet all the time. It's only fear. The old man hasn't been outside his apartment in fifteen years — that had to do something to a person. "But you said yes," he says when they're two or three houses away and he's steered the bike and the chair onto the smoother surface of the road. "You agreed. You can't back out now."

"It's kidnapping. That's what this is, son. Kidnapping."

"Shall we dance, pom pom pom," Anton sings at the top of his lungs, banging on the handlebars in time. "On a clear la di da di shall we fly, pom pom pom," he bellows, drowning out the old man's protestations. Tom Hart has to realize soon enough that he's fussing over nothing. They'll manage. The money'll come from somewhere. People are always scared of changes in the beginning. But they soon got used to them. Tom's fear will evaporate when they board the bus. Or maybe the ferry — when he feels the sea air in his lungs and sees gulls circling above, when his beloved island comes into view. Then he'll be thanking Anton for giving him back his freedom, for making his dreams come true. Eventually Tom falls silent.

Anton brakes at Sixteenth Avenue where Cedar Crescent turns into Fir Street. Between Fifteenth and Fourteenth is

Granville Park. He'll stay on Fir Street till it meets West Fourth near the foot of the Granville Street bridge. Once he's in the downtown core he'll veer off to the right and take Seymour and then jag over to Richards Street and down to the bus station on Dunsmuir. They'll get the money for tickets somehow. Even if they have to panhandle.

Around Twelfth Avenue it starts to drizzle. Anton continues cycling, blinking the rain from his eyes. For himself, he'd keep on going, but he quickly realizes Tom must be getting cold; the old man's hair is plastered to his skull, and he's bent over, shrunken in his chair. Anton turns into the curb, dismounts, and sets the brake on the wheelchair. Shrugging his haversack from his back he pulls out the leather flying helmet and goggles and walks around to face Tom. The old man's skin is grey, and the tips of his ears appear to be turning blue. He turns his head away to stare at the house they're stopped in front of, refusing to meet Anton's eyes.

"Here, put this on. It'll keep you warm and dry." Anton places the leather helmet in Tom's lap. Tom looks at the helmet, his face expressionless, then unbuttons his outside jacket, untucks a corner of the blanket lying across his knees and gives his head and face a good rub first. Anton watches sheepishly, painfully aware of how badly he's failing his old war hero. But he's forced to smile when Tom pulls the helmet over his head, which must have shrunk along with the rest of him. The helmet sits low across the top of his eyebrows, moulding his craggy features into a hangdog expression. "And these." Anton passes him the goggles, his hand now over his mouth to prevent laughter escaping. "They'll keep the rain out of your eyes."

Once past Broadway and on the final slope towards the sea, the bicycle, pulled by the weight of Tom's wheelchair, picks up terrifying speed. A block later Tom's hands begin flap-ping madly at his sides again. But Anton, wild-eyed, stomach in his throat, has pressing concerns of his own. Every time he squeezes the brakes, the bicycle wheels lock and skid. Fortunately, the brace he's built keeps him stable and upright, and he and the bike together aren't nearly heavy enough to pull the wheelchair off course. But he's out of control. One pebble, one tiny crack in the pavement and they'll both be head over handlebars over wheelchair.

A car pulls out from a side street and begins to turn in front of them. Tom's hands stop their mad dance. Anton opens his mouth, but his scream is sucked out by the wind. The driver, spotting them at the last moment, slams on his brakes and begins skidding across the rain-slick intersection. Anton closes his eyes for the impact, which doesn't come.

West Fourth is approaching rapidly, too rapidly. And the light is red. He knows he can't stop, but he can't make the right hand turn he needs either. He pumps the brakes again, but at this speed, on this gradient, in this rain, they are useless. People stop and point. He can hear voices calling out as he whizzes by them. All he can do is pray there is a God and go straight through. Please change, please change, he begs of the light, but it remains stubbornly red. Please change, please change. A figure on the left-hand sidewalk, running down the hill, waving his arms, dashing into the intersection. Anton is through and on the other side before he realizes that the runner probably just saved his life. His and Tom's.

Tom.

The old man must be catatonic. He's probably had a heart attack. Is dead in his chair. The road is beginning to level out, the bicycle brakes are biting again. Still, Anton is almost at West Second before he manages to bring them to a complete stop. There's no sound from the chair. Anton stumbles off the bicycle and sets the wheelchair brake. He's almost too afraid to find out. Then Tom's left hand moves. Relieved, Anton steps around the front, only to find the old man's right hand clasped over his heart.

Ambulance. He needs an ambulance right away. Anton begins looking about him wildly. Nothing but the grey and brown of industry and warehouses; a railway track curves ahead of him. He glances back up the road towards West Fourth, hoping to see his traffic saviour running towards them. Then he hears chuckling. Low at first, but steadily growing in volume, building on itself, wave upon wave. Tom's shoulders are shaking with laughter, now his whole body convulses. He slaps his knees and whoops aloud, laughter braying from his shrunken mouth. He looks a sight: a too-big leather flying helmet and goggles which are beginning to steam up; a dated suit jacket pulled across but hardly covering up a blue, green and white striped cricketer's jacket; muddy blanket over his knees and slippers on his feet. He sticks his hand under the blanket and pulls out his teeth, pops them back in his mouth.

"Haven't had this much fun in years," he manages to spit out before losing himself to laughter again. Anton finds himself smiling. The laughter is infectious. And Tom looks like a clown, a soggy, badly-dressed, shrivelled clown. "Afraid of swallowing my teeth back there," he gasps. "Took them out so I could enjoy myself."

Anton snorts, then laughs out loud: at his snorting, at Tom, at their surroundings, at the absurd picture they must both make, and then, as his eyes travel back up Fir Street again, at the sheer impossibility of his pushing Tom and his chair and the bicycle back up to West Fourth Avenue and the Granville Street Bridge.

"Was it as good as flying?" he asks when he can finally speak again. Tom smiles, eyes glistening behind the goggles and their spreading condensation.

"It was better than flying, son, much better."

It's a long ride to Arbutus Street pushing a solid-steel wheel-chair. The gradient is deceptive. Anton's thighs burn all the way to Kitsilano Beach. At least it has stopped raining and the sky is brightening. He parks near the beach house. Tom's absurd wardrobe and the bicycle-chair contraption have attracted a small audience. Tight-lipped and shy of all the attention, Anton unlashes the barrow arms from the chair while Tom removes his aviator helmet and goggles. People giggle and whisper, some point, nothing Anton hasn't experienced before. But Tom? He's afraid to ask. The sand, thanks to the rain, has traction. Anxious to steer him away from prying eyes, Anton pushes Tom down the beach towards the tide line. He kneels beside the chair and they watch waves being sucked up by the sand, a dog retrieve a stick thrown into the water over and again by his master, a couple strolling hand in hand. A silence grows between them. Anton can't think of anything to say. Eventually he reaches into his haversack, pulls out the photograph from Tom's apartment, and holds it out to him.

"Remember this?"

At first Tom frowns, perhaps a little surprised to see his old Royal Flying Corps picture. After all, he's sitting on a beach he hasn't seen in fifteen years, sea air filling his lungs and ruffling his thinning hair. He stares at it a long time before taking it from Anton's outstretched hand. Turning it over, he fiddles with the frame. When the back pops out, Tom pulls the photograph free. "Look on the back, son, and tell me what you see."

Faint pencil script. Anton tilts the picture towards the light.

Dead. Wounded. Missing in action. Wounded. Dead. Paralyzed. Burned. Captured. Dead. Blinded. Dead. Missing in action. Accidentally killed. Dead. Alive. Dead. Missing in action. Dead.

Gulls screech overhead, children dart back and forth, screaming with laughter, calling to each other, yet Anton feels swallowed by silence. His eyes keep coming back to the word *Alive*. Tom. After a while he asks, "How come you didn't write down paralyzed for yourself?"

"Because I wasn't."

"But your legs?"

"I walked out of that war in one piece, absolutely nothing wrong with me. How d'you reckon that makes a man feel, Anton?"

"Lucky?" But he knows as soon as the answer is out of his mouth that it's wrong. Guilty, he thinks, but he can't say the word. Tom is silent, staring out across the water. The clouds are breaking up, the horizon shimmering into focus.

"So how . . . I mean . . . what happened to your legs?"

"I tripped getting on a street car, July 15, 1927. Got dragged under. Severed the main nerves."

"I thought you'd been shot down over enemy lines."

Tom begins to chuckle. "That's a good one, son."

"And that you'd been held by the enemy and tortured."

A great belly laugh. "Tortured. Did I crack?" he asks, wiping tears from his eyes.

Anton smiles. "No. You were a real hero."

"Hmm." Tom grows sober again. "Heroes don't always wear a uniform, Anton. They come in all guises. I was no hero."

Anton glances at the photograph in Tom's lap and thinks he probably was, his guilt was just getting in the way. Or modesty.

"Are you disappointed we're not going to Salt Spring?"

"No, son. I'm not disappointed at all."

Out of the corner of his eye, Anton spots a plane taxiing across the water. It's in-your-belly thrum reaches his ears moments later. A PBY Catalina, a flying boat, he can tell by its dark blue colour and its shape. Tom follows his gaze, and they watch it gain speed, white foam churning from its floats. The engine winds higher as the aircraft roars past them and towards the huddle of West End apartments and rooming houses. Anton catches his breath. Just when it seems the plane must surely crash into the city itself, it lifts into the sky and banks away from them, revealing an underbelly of soft duck's egg blue. In silence they watch it shrink to a small silver dot before it disappears into the blue horizon.

Acknowledgements

I would like to thank my agent, Hilary McMahon, for her dedication and her grace. Many thanks also to the team at Goose Lane Editions, especially to Laurel Boone, for her enthusiasm, her perception, and her expert editorial guidance. The Ontario Arts Council provided financial assistance, for which I am grateful.

For encouragement and support I would like to thank the Burlington Writers' Group, in particular Sylvia McNicoll and Gisela Sherman. Also Amanda Rogers, for helping to clear the underbrush, and Mary Vincenzetti, for locating the only library copy in Canada of Brockman's *Congenital Club Foot*. Many thanks to all my friends and family members who took the time to read various drafts and give their feedback and encouragement, and especially to Ian, for carrying my books. For the historical background I used a variety of sources but leaned most heavily on Norman Longmate's *How We Lived Then*.